Greed

A story

by

Philip Wharam

Introduction

Firstly, I am moved to thank you for opening the pages of this book. Perhaps you have even bought a copy! Thank you!

Life is all about perception and perception is everything. This book revolves primarily around the lives of an extended Essex family. Extended to include work colleagues, members of the 'gang' and others. Extended to include friends, both male and female. Aah! Friends. True friends, false friends, old friends, new friends, if there are such things. You may quickly realise that the prima famiglia, the Bolds, are criminals. And you would be right. Criminals, bank managers, doctors, accountants, even solicitors. Hold on, you say, what have criminals to do with bankie, the doc, the bean counter and the lowest of the low? *Everything*! For there is seldom such a thing as a 'criminal'. Dean Bold, for example, our anti-hero, is the owner of a haulage company. He lives with his wife and family in Canvey Island, as do lots of other people. He has a mortgage, school fees to pay and drives a car. Well, three cars to be precise. His wife, Gina, owns a beauty salon. Through which he launders a little money. Not much, but some. For most of Dean Anthony Bold's life, he just does stuff. Goes to the pub, goes to work, goes home.

This book contains episodes of what he does. He laughs, he cries, he loves, he drives, he snorts coke, he beats people half to death, he makes millions, he goes to bed. He sleeps, eats, breathes and does everything else that the average fellow does. Plus a little more. Because life, kind reader, is like that.

We are all dirtbags. Some of us are bigger dirtbags than others. Some of us conceal it better than others.

And we all die. Eventually. Take the journey of the Bold family, but don't get too close...

Copyright © 2010 by Philip Wharam

All rights reserved. No part of this publication may be reproduced, distributed, or transmitted in any form or by any means, including photocopying, recording, or other electronic or mechanical methods, without the prior written permission of the publisher, except in the case of brief quotations embodied in critical reviews and certain other non-commercial uses permitted by copyright law. For permission requests, write to the publisher, addressed "Attention: Permissions Coordinator," at the address below.

Lynfa Publishing
3 Eckersley Road Industrial Estate
Chelmsford
Essex CM1 1SL United Kingdom
www.philipwharam.com

ISBN (13) 978-1519470928

Chapter One

Basildon, Essex, UK, September 2006. A Saturday.

Mr Chan's. Canvey Island. Ten-thirty pm. *Ish*. Mr Dean and Mrs Gina Bold and Mr Dave and Mrs Shirley Hilton together with their friends and family are having a large party at the best Chinese along the estuary. "The bollocks", as Dean would say. The party is already in full swing. Dean likes to start early. He's given up West Ham for now and goes to the gym instead. Gina spends Saturdays with Shirley and her sister, Debra. During the week, for Gina and Debra, it's nails followed by *their* gym, the hairdresser, the beautician, the wine bar and for Gina, a dalliance with Dave when he can get away from Dean. For Shirley, it's the kids. The ubiquitous Debra is there, together with sundry also-rans. She's trolleyed already, her cleavage practically in her lychees.

"More champers, Mr Chan. Come and sit down." The grinning and very happy owner of Mr Chan's, proprietor one Mr J Chan, smiles warmly at Dean and reaches for more Möet. The restaurant's packed, full of some of the less salubrious locals all trying to outdo each other, all happy to pour their ill-gotten right into his lap. Elsewhere, you'd try and squeeze the tables twice, but this is Essex and people like to take their time before 'going on'. Family is, after all, family.

Dean sits back in his chair, just for a moment and surveys the scene. His wife sits opposite, laughing, shrieking in fact with Debra, who is telling her one of the 'special stories' she reserves for Saturday nights. Debra's single and is a woman on a mission. To shag every available man in South Essex. In fact, never mind the available ones; any man in South Essex will do just nicely. She's kind of the entertainment factor. Dean can't stand her and the more he moves up the estuary social scale, the more he wishes Gina would ditch her. The snag is that she's Gina's sister and you're looking straight into a minefield there. Now Dave's Shirl was a beauty when she was young, but the four kids have taken their toll and she's descended into some kind of track-suited, make-up free Hell. On the other side of Shirl is Dean's old mate, Mick The Teeth. Aptly named for one who hasn't a tooth in his head. The dentally challenged one is one of the nicest geezers you'll ever meet, just so long as a) you don't owe him any money and b) you don't ever look at his missus. Not that you'd actually want to look at Mick The Teeth's missus, but he thinks the sun shines out of her rapidly ballooning backside. God bless her. Naturally, next to Mick The Teeth is....Mrs Mick, aka Karen. She is always known as 'Mrs Mick' and some people who have been around the Teeth for years actually don't know her name. Mick loves this and plays up to it. The one other person at the table who warrants a mention at this stage is Ali The Coat. Now surprisingly, not everyone who knows Dean has a nickname with the word, 'The' in there somewhere, but Ali does, on account of the fact that he *never* takes the damned thing off. Ali comes originally from Cyprus, the wrong side if you're of the Greek persuasion, the right side if you're of the 'Turkish Delight' variety. Ali The Coat's family have all gone back to Kyrenia and he's like a bit of a lost soul now. Dean loves him to bits and won't hear a word against him. Ali, in turn, hangs around Dean and would do anything for him. He is always trying to get Dean and Gina to go to Cyprus, but they are wedded to Torrevieja and won't hear a word said against that. Now bearing in mind that Dean's daughter, the lovely Benissa is attending to the needs of the local boys in a very cold Basildon night club car park at one o'clock in the morning dressed in no more than a skimpy little top and skirt and Ali is in the middle of a packed Chinese restaurant full of very tanked up people, you can guess where the coat is positioned. The story goes that it originates from the time when he lived in Romford Road and the family were always on the move, one step ahead of the 'social'. They were never going to stay long. Still, and everyone's noticed this, he's actually unbuttoned the coat for once. However, he's looking extremely nervous and eyeing up the door. Several of the female variety of the 'Dean crowd' have had a crack at The Coat, but all have failed. There are rumours, but no-one's ever got to the bottom of those.

"Ali, what the fuck is up with you now?" Dean's in full flow now and Mr Chan is very grateful that the entire restaurant is now well oiled. It's kicked off in here more times than even he'll admit to. He looks around, but the rest of them appear to have become a little disconnected too.

"What do you mean, Mr Dean, innit?" Ali laughs at his little joke and Dean joins in.

"Whaddya mean, Mr Dean" he starts thumping the table and is only restrained by a friendly Mr Chan who hands him another glass of champagne and toasts this wonderful gathering.

"My favouwite people. You make Mr Chan very happy." He loves hamming it up for the crowd that gets in of a Saturday night, and they respond in kind.

"Here you are, Mr Chan. Big tip, ten dollaaah, love you long time, heh?"

The evening degenerates further.

"Where's your Benissa tonight, Dean?" asks The Teeth, glancing proudly at Karen.

"She's over her mate's in Rayleigh. Watchin' videos or something. Girls stuff, eh Gina?"

Mrs Dean Bold's gold Gina stilettos are playing footsie with Dave. They've got her name on and Dean regrets the day that The Coat's sister told her about this Turkish shoe designer making classy heels. Dave's mind is already under the table but he knows that nothing's going to be done with that tonight. Shirl will be revving up her headache.

"What's that, darlin'?" Gina turns to Dean, all smiles and boob job. Dean paid for them last year in the capital of boobs, known locally as Chelmsford. She's laughing and keeps everyone 'up', especially Dave.

"Our daughter, babes. She's over Rayleigh, ain't she?"

"S'right, darlin'. She's coming back tomorrow. Troy's round the neighbours, so we got the house all to ourselves!" She winks at Dean, shrieks with the most outrageous dirty laugh and turns to look at poor Dave who doesn't know whether he's coming or going. She's slipped her shoe off now and is rubbing her foot up and down his leg. He can no longer stand up, should the situation demand it and the sweat's pouring off him.

"You alright, Dave? You look like yer cummin' over all funny." The ever concerned Shirley is doing her Mum bit, having stopped being a proper Essex wife long ago. She scrubs up quite well on the weekend though and there's one or two in here who wouldn't mind, given the opportunity.

"Sweet, darlin'. Top notch." He smiles at Shirley, the kind of reassuring smile that you give when you're up to something. She looks away, happy to get back to her conversation about the kids again. Gina grabs Dave's hand whilst it's under the table and eases it between her legs. Gina's teasing is legendary, but Dean has no idea how far it goes. She tastes great and Dave's hard on is in danger of splitting his Armani jeans. Dean gets up and makes his way to the loos, time for another bit of the white stuff. Thank God his friend Town's coming back in a couple of days. Dean doesn't like new people, especially new dealers.

*

Over in Basildon, Benissa Bold, eldest child of Dean and Gina and her closest friends are partying in the full Essex tradition. Her besties, Lisa and Kelly have got hold of some lads from Vange Rugby Club, big lads who look like they could handle themselves, but these girls are borderline professionals and they've got the lads eating out of their hands. Lisa takes one of them, a big lump called Wayne off to the dance floor and she's grinding away at him like crazy. She starts flapping her wings, something she learnt at Faces on a night out with her mates from work. Flapping was once a black girl's thing and Lisa's well up for that when she's out of sight. She's waving her arms up and down and gyrating her derrière in Wayne's face and driving him wild. Benissa spots this and decides to have some. She weaves her way over to the packed dance floor and starts to imitate Lisa and her flapping. Benissa could lose a few stone and her arse is wobbling like a big, flabby arse in the finals of the national flabby arse championships on National Flabby Arse Day. However, each to their own and all of a sudden, a big, good looking black lad has come over and he's playing up to Bee like nobody's business. She's luvvin it, luvvin it, luvvin it. In no time, they're grinding away like two cats on heat. There's a break in the beat and she's got his hand to lead him outside, wearing just the biggest grin. Kelly and a new girl, Beccy are watching from the table.

"Did you see that? What the bleedin' hell's she got".

"A dirty mind, Beccs. And she ain't afraid of tellin', neither. He's gettin' a well good nosh!"

Outside, Benissa's round the back, not for the first time tonight.

This time she's up against the wall and the lad's getting down to some action. Her eyes drop to below his waist and she's over the bonnet of the nearest X5, legs akimbo.

"I am so havin' that. Come on then, do me proper."

So like Mummy.

*

"OK people. PARTY!" Dean's back from powdering his nose and he's flying again. Not bad when he's on form, still got signs of the old Bold. The trouble is, one never knows which Bold one is going to get these days.

"You're all comin' back to ours. We are goin' to partay ALL NIGHT LONNNGGG!" He's waving his arms in the air and doing some kind of crazy dance all round the table. Estuary villainy. Saturday night. Cushti.

*

It's getting late in the club now; Benissa's back in with the girls and the lad's gone back to his boys. The girls are comparing notes and making plans to go on. They're going to go till the morning light.

"Got any hooter, B?"

"No, but I know a man who does!" She gets up and goes over to a well dressed man at the bar. They slide off for a mo and then she's back.

"Sorted, ladies. We are the proud owners of plenty!" Lisa, Kelly and Beccy's eyes light up, they know what's coming. Beccy's looking at her, dying to ask her a question.

"Bee?"

"Yeah?"

"'Ave you ever done it with another girl?"

"No! What do you think I am, a fuckin' lesbo?"

"Don't be daft. It's just that I was talkin' ter Leese an' that Wayne she's with reckons he wants to watch her with another girl".

"I bet he bleedin' does. All men want that".

"Well, if they want it, we ought to give it to 'em, else they'll find some other mare who'll do it, innit?"

"You're just a bleedin' pushover, you are, Beccy Granger".

"Well what's the bleedin' difference, when you've dropped a few Es anyway. I mean, girls is nice an' soft, cuddly like".

"I reckon you're well up for it, bird. You dirty cow!" They all shriek with laughter, as the barman comes over to politely ask them to leave the establishment.

"Oi, mate, you ever seen two gells doin' it? Well watch this then". Beccy proceeds to slide her tongue between Lisa's bright pink lips and within seconds, the pair of them are snogging like it's going out of fashion. Benissa's laughing like a hyena and Kelly, well, Kelly doesn't know where to look.

"I never thought she'd do that, Bee. What is she like?"

The barman's just standing there, like he's never seen it before. Lying bastard, happens every Saturday night these days. He's luvvin' it!

*

The Chinese restaurant party are all back at Dean and Gina's now. Somehow, he's managed not to lose anyone along the way and they're now spreading throughout the house, getting up to all sorts. Debra wanders in to the kitchen, almost catching Dave with his tongue planted firmly in Gina's sensuous mouth. They hear her just in time and do that thing where you pretend like you're not doing anything when it's patently obvious that you a) have been, b) were about to or c) were thinking about it. Red faces all round, but Debra's pissed out of her brains and thinking about a swim.

"You got any cozzies, Gee?"

"Just get ya kit off, babes! No one gives a fuck. Wooo hoooo!"

"I don't need to be told that more than once".

Off she goes, in search of playmates for the heated pool.

"Anyone fancy it? I am goin' in the pool! Come on, I'm gettin' me puppies out!"

She gets hold of a random chap who no-one knows and drags him off, through the glass door and into the pool room. As the door slams behind her, she's out of her dress, out of her knickers and wandering across the tiles to the waiting ripples.

"What do you reckon? Proper job, ain't it?"

She turns round and gives him a real eyeful of her 38 F cups. She's just got back from a little 'holiday' in Cyprus where she has allowed the post-op trauma to ebb away. The scars have healed, but the swelling hasn't gone down, much to his delight.

"Blindin', darlin', fuckin' blindin'!"

He's already down to his boxers and soon he's out of those and diving in after her. Now things with Debra are pretty inevitable, what with her appetite and all that and soon she's snogging the geezer's face off. Next minute, they're out of the pool and in the jacuzzi and he's got a handful of prime Miss D. Her arms are round his neck and she's sucking the life out of him. Dean wanders in, wondering what all the fuss is about, just at the moment when the bloke's putting his manhood in between Debra's gaping lips.

"Fuckin' stroll on! Who the fuck are you?" Dean's mouth tightens vice like into a thin, red line.

The door opens again and Dave's hand grabs him by the shoulder, dragging him back through before there's an international incident.

"Bruv, you got any hooter?"

"Bit of Charlie? Why of course, dear boy!"

"Keep it stumm, bruv. Don't want Shirl getting' wise. You know what she's like".

"Listen, what the fuck am I gonna tell her for?

Through a glass porthole in the door, the sight of the geezer's arse going up and down as he pumps Debra is just too much for Dave and he grabs Dean's arm, pulling him away before slamming the inner kitchen door tightly shut. Ali the Coat is talking very quietly in the corner to Mick the Teeth, Mrs Mick and Shirl are talking about the children and their PlayStations and Gina's disappeared. Some other people from Mr Chan's are standing in there knocking back Dean's booze but he doesn't care, on account of the sheer entertainment value Debra's silicone enhanced boobs are giving his guests. The only time that he *will* happen is if he gets the old Colombian Marching Paranoia. When Dean gets that, you don't want to be hanging around. You just leg it.

*

So, that's the crowd at play. Tomorrow, is a grafting day.

Chapter Two

Monday Morning

"Dawn, for fuck's sake, answer the fucking 'phone will you?"

The delicious, delectable Dawn Murphy sits filing her nails and generally pissing about all day. She's got that kind of red hair they only get in Ireland, the most beautiful pale skin, crystal clear green eyes and legs that go on forever, which when her father's not looking are well out on show. Dawn invented the micro-mini. And then cut a bit more off.

Tuesday morning. Bold Transport, Pitsea, Essex.

"Mr Dean, I've only got one pair of hands"

"Dean, I have checked and can confirm that she only has one pair of hands!" Ron smiles at the assembled throng. Bit of a Pete and Dud man, is Ron. Comes from Dagenham.

"And only one brain cell, eh luv?"

"Bold Transport. And how can I help you?"

The customers love Dawn's lilt and despite not exactly being the brain of either Essex or Kildare, she is a real asset. And when they come into the office, you couldn't get the bastards out.

Dean's busy with Dave and Ron Langridge, known colloquially as 'One Language', on account of the fact that his name sounds like that and he can only speak one language. Broad Essex and proud of it. Lingo, as he is known to his mates, is leading off about some of the drivers who have taken to bringing 'extras' back from the continental runs which the firm specialises in. His raised voice reflects his growing anger.

The firm's grown a lot over the past few years with the boom in continental haulage, though even Dean's been thinking about moving the operation to Calais to take advantage of the cheaper tax, fuel and just about everything else. So far, Gina and Shirley have kept the boys at home and they are, after all, Essex boys at heart. Lingo's got a really good point about the drivers though and the boys repair to the boozer to continue the conversation in

Dave's Mercedes ML. Dean's on the mobile and Lingo's in the back. As they turn out of the yard, they are almost flattened by a returning artic, emblazoned with the 'Bold Transport' logo.

"Who the fuck was that, Ling?"

"It's the Monster, coming back from Spar. He's done Cardiff and back this morning with that vodka from Germany. It's a wonder we've still got that contract after what happened last month."

"What's occurring with cuntocks then?"

"He's been charged by the church and he's due up in Dover Mags next month."

"If we don't get the trailer back, I'm gonna fuckin' 'ave 'im. Cunt. Who the fuck does this Dougie Fuller think he is, treating me like some fucking mug?"

"We was lucky to get the unit back, guv. They wanted to keep it for forensics."

"Forensics. Fucking forensics. Your 'avin a laugh. What do they want with forensics? The cunt brings back two MCs of Blues and that's the answer they give? They're making this job a joke."

Two MCs of Blues. Superking Blues, one of the biggest smuggled cigarettes in the UK. 'Cuntocks', one of Dean's favourite words he's picked up from Town Hall, who picked it up when he spent a period of time at Her Majesty's pleasure. His nickname comes from living with all the Brummies, who have their own version of rhyming slang. At least now it's caught on, it stops Dean using the phrase 'fuck all' every two minutes. Town Hall has some very choice acquaintances.

The boys are soon pulling into the boozer, just off the Pitsea roundabout by the A13 flyover.

"Talking of cuntocks, how's Town, Dee?" Everyone knows Town for his favourite phrase and since Dean's got a new best friend, he's often seen around the depot.

"He's back from the villa tonight. Got some news for me. Maybe some Russian wants to buy me out, eh Dave?"

Dreamy Dave's still a little distracted by memories of yesterday's little tryst with the G-String of Gina and has to drag himself back to reality.

"You what, mate?"

"What is it with you today? S'like you've left your fucking brain indoors. Get your Shirl to fax it over laters, yeh?" He digs One Language in the ribs, grins like some grinning thing on national grinning day, teeth shining from the dental whitening Gina gave him as a birthday present and they walk into the pub.

"Three lagers, darlin' and 'ave one yourself".

The barmaid gets to work, smiling at Dean. They come in every day and he's always generous. Her earrings are big enough for a show dog to jump through and the Croydon facelift, courtesy of a scrunchie on acid is spectacular. She's quite pretty, in a chavvy sort of way. The standard issue chewing gum is working its masticatory magic and she is a picture of health.

"Thanks, Dean". Nice friendly pub, very sociable. The boys move down the bar, then Dean peels away and they find a table away from everyone else, with a good view of the door.

"This cunt could bring the 'ole thing on top. I cannot have my boys thinking they can just do what they fucking want. Fags, booze, what's next, Ling? We've 'ad a right result over the past few years and this could fuck it right up. I'm not 'avin it, not at all." Dean's voice is changing, *la paranoia coca* is kicking in. He starts sweating and makes his excuses. Whilst Dave and One Language sit at the table, Dean's off to the bog to powder his nose with a couple of lines. He stares at himself in the mirror and laughs at the old Eagles song, 'lines on the mirror, lines on her face, didn't seem to notice, she was caught up in the race....' That's right, mate. Life in the fucking fast lane. Population: 1. Dean Bold. He wipes the sweat from his face and returns to the bar.

"When's 'e comin' in?"

"Supposed to be tomorrow", says Dave, finally with us.

"Bell the cunt now and tell 'im I want to see 'im this afternoon. Cunt telling me when e's gonna see me."

Dean's beginning to believe his own bullshit and the others can see where this is going. Fancies himself as a bit of a gangster, seen too many Guy Ritchies for his own good.

"From now on, Lings, mate, I want you to tell them, in words of one syllable, that if they ever bring anything back in their little cabs they're not supposed to, not only will they lose their fucking jobs, they'll lose their fucking hands! I am trying to keep this firm straight and I am not having some fucking cunt making me look like a fucking mug." The veins are standing proud on Dean's forehead now and his anger is starting to boil over. He's spitting all over the table and with his raised voice, people are starting to look over and mutter.

"Right, that's settled then. We'll split, yeah?" Dave's attempt at diplomacy seems to do the trick and the three make their way out of the pub, Dave's looking back at the barmaid, mouthing, "Sorry, love" but she's oblivious, couldn't give a shit.

Dean's leading the charge and soon, they're all present and correct and on the way back to Thurrock. Lingo's driving, Dean's in the front, Dave in the back.

Suddenly, Dave yells out as he sees the impending danger from his position in the back and the next thing, a car pulls right across the bows and turns left at the lights.

"What the FUCK was that?" Dean's been playing with his mobile again, trying to calm down by speaking to the delightful offspring, Benissa. No luck there, it's just ringing out.

"Some cunt's turned left across the fucking bows of the motor!" Even One Language is discovering long lost words now and the air in the Range Rover is blue.

"Follow the cunt, Ron. I ain't having that. Who the FUCK does the cunt think he is?"

Lingo swerves round the bollards and takes off the wrong way down the road in pursuit of the errant Sierra. It's not long before the crossing outside the car wash and the prey starts to slow down. Lingo's on this one and speeds up till he's right up behind it. Lights are flashing, the veins in his hands are throbbing and the boys are going apeshit. The quarry has sussed this now and speeds up again, through the red light at the crossing and away. But he's no match for Lingo and soon the Range is right up there again, to the bumper. He's away down a side road now and trying to double back to the duel-carriageway. He takes a turn through an estate and almost disappears up his own arse trying to get out. Lingo handbrake turns the Range and now matey's blocked in. The madness has taken over and all three of them are thinking something different. While Ron and Dave are still in the thinking stage, Dean's out, he's grabbed the baseball bat from under Dave's seat and he's bearing down on the Sierra. The driver has decided to front it and he's out as well. Dean's still running as he raises the bat and 'crack', he's connected with his head. The driver's hands are up, trying to fend Dean off, but the lucky first blow was too good to be true and he's already weakened. He's trying to stay on his feet. Despite this, Dean's got a coke frenzy around him now and the bat's flailing like a Bannockburn claymore on the end of a big grudge. A very big grudge. The bat's connecting with his arms, then after a good sideswipe, there's a gap and Dean catches him right across the bridge of his nose, splitting it wide open, all over his face. The blood's flowing freely now.

"That's all we fucking need. There'll be no stopping him now he's seen red. We'll have to call a halt to the proceedings, Mr Langridge". Dave's gone all comedian now and Lingo's raising a smile, what with the blood splattering the road.

Dean's really wading in and his prey's down, trying to cover his face. He catches him a good one across the back and there's yelps of pain echoing out around the car park. He sees the approaching duo, hands Lingo the bat, then sets about the now broken man with his boots. The first one's straight in the bollocks, then it's back to his head. Cracking bones, splitting flesh, the face is a total mess. The bloke doesn't know where to put his broken arms and Dean's smelling total annihilation. Boots are raining in despite Dave and Ron holding him back. As they drag him away, he's still yelling and shouting, kicking his legs out and the thing's descended into a bloody farce. They drag him back into the car and they're away. The body doesn't move.

"You went in a bit hard, mate. A quick slap would have done."

Dean's muttering under his breath now and his face is contorted with rage.

Down on the floor, there's blood on his boots and there's blood on the bat, which Lingo has carefully placed on a mat in the boot. The whole proceedings have taken just one minute from start to finish.

"That's fucking learned 'im, the cunt. I want to go and finish the cunt off." Dean's gone all intro now and they won't get any more sense out of him. He's desperate for another line and Dave's getting them back to Thurrock the back way, just in case anybody's rung the police. Dave and Lingo are exchanging glances in the mirror and they know they've got to keep him away from anyone for the next half hour. It's half two now and they need to get back to the office. Dave mouths the word 'Warehouse' to Lingo and they take the back way in to the unit, stopping outside a roller shutter. Lingo hops out and opens a side door and in two shakes, the roller door comes up and he drives the ML straight in. Dave's pulled it down and that's that.

"Mate, we've gotta get your outta those strides. There's blood half way up the fuckin' legs. Give us the shoes an' all. Lingo, get rid of that bat."

This looks like a practised method. These boys have been here before. Dean's calming down and starting to take charge of the situation.

"Anyone see us, Dave? What about that estate? No-one nosing around?" Dean's right back in Vange now, back in his teens when they used to get up to all sorts, real cheeky chappies were Dean and Dave. Motors, trading estates, sheds, nowhere was safe from their two man crime wave. They've just kind of graduated to another league. Lingo's already belled his mate from Rainham, who's on his way to sort out this little mess.

"Can't tell, mate, but I reckon we're cushti". This is just for Dean's benefit. It was the middle of the day, for God's sake. Of course someone saw them. Just depends who and whether they got the registration number. At least it wasn't one of the private plates. That'd be them up the swanny. Dave's made the decision. The motor's history. Time to report it stolen. Dean's really coming on now and he's all for getting back to work. Dave's got him some more strides and he's had a wash. No fists used so not a mark on our man, just a few dents in a baseball bat that won't be hitting anything again and a pair of workboots that are beyond help, what with the blood and gore all over them.

"If I ain't going back in the gaff, then I'm off indoors. Ling, get us the keys to the Merc, mate."

Ron knows better than to question him and he looks OK now. Maybe Gina'll do him some good. Fuck his brains out, or something. If she's home.

He hands Dean the keys. Thank God it's not far back to Canvey. Once he's gone, Lings is on to his mate in the 'cleaning and recycling' business and the job's afoot. Soon, help is at the back door, complete with low loader and car cover, they've got the ML on the back and the tarpaulin is pulled tight over. It'll be taken to somewhere on Rainham marshes, cleaned within an inch of its life, have the alarm chipped, new windows and numbers, plates gone and on its way to Dubai. Sorted. Dave'll get the insurance and a drink out of it to boot. Matey's got his cut, Dean's off the hook and everybody's happy. Except of course the victim who's now on his way to hospital and he's touch and go.

Chapter Three

Monday Evening, 7.00pm

"How's my little princess, then?" Dean bowls into the kitchen from his precious garage and sees Benissa sitting at the table, filing her talons. She's been to the tan stand again and her belly is poking out from under her oh so tight top.

"Chantal's got a new car, Dad. It's well nice. Can I have a new car? A Z8? Please, Dad" She looks up at him and flutters her spidery eyelashes.

"Course, my little princess. You still goin' for that job? You'll need a nice motor for that."

"Oh, yeah, Dad. Yeah, the job." She returns to filing the nails and stares intently at them.

"Where's your brother?"

"Up in his room. Where he always is. Reading."

"Least I'm getting' something from that school. It's costing me a fortune."

Benissa's eyes are raised to heaven. Books. Books or magazines. No contest in her eyes.

"Listen, darlin', your Dad's got to go out for a while tonight. Tell your Mum I'll get something to eat with Town."

"OK, whatever". Benissa's head's back in the nail filing again and she's gone.

Dean leans over and kisses his little girl's head and she looks up, smiling like sugar wouldn't melt. Daddy's sweet, innocent little girl.

Gina wanders in and throws her arms around Dean.

"How's my lovely big hunky man, then? Making lots of money, honey?"

She's been at the beautician's, the hairdresser's, the Nail Place, which Dean bought for her and where she spends a lot of her day, and the gym. She looks good on it, but the only one who's going to see her with her kit off in the next few days is lover boy Dave. She's feeling as randy as hell, in fact she's always feeling as randy as hell, but that's our Gina-G.

Monday night at the Bolds.

*

Dover Eastern Docks, 7.40pm

The rain is coming down in sheets, creating a swirling over-lit fantasy. A thousand harbour lights illuminate the night gloom as an enormous blue and white bow door is lifted the last couple of feet until a satisfying *clunk* resounds across the forward deck. Below, on the vehicle levels, engines are started and soon there is a thick fog of diesel fumes from the twenty or so thirty-eight ton transcontinental trucks lined up on either side of the passenger lifts. Slowly, these giants ease their way up the ramp and into the fierce storm building outside. Rain lashes windscreens, prompting a stinging reality check for still sleepy drivers. The line forms and the trucks snake their way towards the Ro-Ro sheds and the battleground of the A20/M20. The dark green and red logo of Newry European reflects in the deep water pools forming on the dock as the cream curtain-sided truck swings round into the home straight. The queue is funereal and the impatience grows. A load of them get waved through and then it's Newry's turn. The yellow jacketed Customs Officer puts his hand up, requesting a stop. This is definitely not an AA man saluting. Inside the warm cab, the atmosphere's calm. Declan Byrne is as cool as the proverbial as he winds down the window.

"Good evening, sir". Very polite at this point, Her Majesty's Revenue and Customs. "Could I see your licence, please?"

Declan hands it over, but the geezer barely looks at it. "Where have you come from?"

"Troyes, so I did".

"What are you carrying?"

"It's a groupage; furniture, car-parts, all kinds of stuff, so it is".

"Your destination?"

"Back to the depot". A man of few words is Declan. He has good reason.

"OK, Mr.....Byrne. Could you pull into the shed over there, please and switch off your engine and remove the keys. Thank you". With this little speech, Declan's mood has changed. He has been told that there will be none of this. Maybe a cursory stop and check the papers, but no stop and search. His arse starts to go a bit and he's wondering what is going on. *He has no choice.*

*

Essex, A120 Stansted to Colchester dual carriageway 8.10pm

Town Hall's on his way back from the airport now, flicked on the mobile and there's a missed call from Dean. This is going to be a good one, thinks Town. This is going to be the big time. He presses green and soon the ringing tone's coming through on the speaker. Loud and clear. Town, as usual, is alone.

"Hello, mate. Where's it to be? Chelmo, yeah, usual place. Sweet. See ya." *Click.*

Nice, not only is this going to be good, it's also going to be nice. They're off to meet at The Waterfront, Chelmsford's canalside restaurant. Very nice. Civilised. Proper. He drops his Tracy off at home, then heads out into the driving rain once more.

*

Somewhere on top of the White Cliffs of Dover, 8.47pm

No amount of foul weather clothing could have protected Eamonn Kenneally from the torrential rain hammering down on his body. His infra-red binoculars are trained on the queue a mile below, eyes riveted on Newry 57, he's not even flinching as the rain pours down his neck and into his boots. He blinks as the yellow-jacket brings proceedings to a halt, trying to see who it is, but the deluge is far too much for that and his frustration begins to build. As the truck moves off, his relief is great, but it soon turns to dismay when instead of passing through the tunnel, the truck takes a detour into the search shed. He's wondering what is going on. Covering his face with the sou'wester, he removes a mobile from under the coat and dials a number.

"We've a problem. Don't know how serious. Call you back in five". *Click.*

*

Dover Eastern Docks, 8.58pm

Eamonn Kenneally is not the only interested party who's suddenly woken up. Inside the shed, a yellow-jacketed Customs officer has just come off the phone to his daughter, who's got lost on the way to a party. He's walked back in to what is about to become his worst nightmare. Opening the door from the restroom, he is faced with the sight of Newry 57 parked up, a driver standing by the side of the cab and three of his fellow officers surrounding the guy. It is as if his whole life was passing by before his eyes. He knows *exactly what's going on* and there isn't a damned thing he can do about it. The driver is looking half pissed off and half shitting himself. There is something Kafkaesque about the whole thing. Frustration combined with faceless manipulation. Neither of these two men were expecting this, and it's all down to the errant daughter. Or so Yellow Two is thinking. Fuck, fuck, fuck, FUCK! Just for a moment, the driver looks up and sees the expression on his face. It's too late, he sees it all and now he knows. Yellow Two turns away, walks out into the tempest, preferring it to the carnage which is about to take place. As he leaves the shed, watchful eyes from the gangway are also eyeing the proceedings with grave concern. Unnoticed, this figure sends a brief but telling text message to *the powers that be.*

*

Somewhere on top of the White Cliffs of Dover, 9.10pm

Click. The infra-red binoculars are snapped into the 'on' position again and Eamonn's viewpoint is once again live. Things are most certainly not good now. The queue's down to nothing, the boat's taking cars and trucks on again and there is absolutely no sign of Newry 57.

Click. "If he's not out in ten, he's not comin' out at all. I'll be makin' me way after the next car".

*

Custom House, Lower Thames Street, London, 9.22pm

At precisely the same time as Case Officer Graham Stubbins' mobile burst into life, an email from Dover Central arrived in the general IMPEX Inbox.

He pulled the mobile from its belt holster and examined the screen. So not good.

"Problem. East Docks. Newry 57".

His heart sank. This was so not supposed to happen. The watcher now needs to do something. His fingers worked frantically at the tiny keys.

"Truck must leave. Do whatever necessary". *Send.*

The watcher receives this message and goes into action.

*

Down in IMPEX, the Duty Officer drains the last of his coffee and glances at the screen. Another email has just arrived from Dover East. As always, the text displays on his screen and he casually reads its contents.

'Vehicle NIW 3749 Scania Newry European stopped Dover Eastern Docks 21.44.54 13/10/06. Driver Declan Byrne detained and identified. Search commences 23.00. Cargo suspect. Tachograph incorrect'.

He lifts his overweight frame out of the chair and crosses the office. The two little words *cargo suspect* have prompted his speedy reply. Narcotics. Pure and simple.

'Ref: NIW 3749. Detain and hold. Do not repeat do not permit driver to leave. Hold trailer. Dogs required.'

Declan Byrne's fate is sealed for now.

The watcher is back on his mobile, reporting in. A disaster is unfolding.

*

Canvey Island, Essex, 9.30pm

Dean's kissed Gina and Benissa goodbye, grabbed his coat and he's away, in the 911. Silver, 53 plate, fully loaded. He snaps the CD player on, Eminem givin' it large, switches off the satnav, fairly sure of the way to Chelmsford and puts the Bold foot forward, leaving a spray of stones all over the front lawn. Takes around half an hour the way he drives. Back at the ranch, Gina and Benissa are comparing nails. Upstairs, Troy has watched his father disappear up the road, all guns blazing and he's back to his computer games. The ones you play on the net. The ones his parents don't know about, or from his point of view, care. He's playing tonight with a boy in Russia. Dangerous thing to do, Russia, but he has inherited something of his father's chutzpah and doesn't really care about these things. It'll be a long night, but Troy knows that he's not going to be disturbed. His homework's been done hours ago, a piece of piss, as his embarrassing father would say.

*

Doolans Bar, Torrevieja, Spain. 10.30pm local time

The place is rammed. The early half-termers have arrived and they've been knocking it back since about 6pm. Guinness and pints of prawns are still being ferried out of the madhouse that passes for a kitchen and the tills are jingling. Upstairs, the restaurant is still motoring and the basement nightclub is filling up. Padraig's got the place taped and with the rooftop seafood place just about cashing up, it's shaping up to be a good night. He's on his rounds now, glad-handing, buying the odd drink and generally keeping an eye on things. He's got a drink at every table, and he's hardly touched a drop. The man is cool, a true professional.

As he is just about to leave the Rooftop Bar, a mobile vibrates in his capacious pocket. Returning to the privacy of an empty alcove, he takes the call.

"Yes?"

"What?" His face visibly pales. "That's feckin' impossible. Can't happen. Did our man see it? Yeah? I want the full feckin' picture, not some feckin' half baked feckin' bollocks. Get him to call me now". *Click*. He's up on his feet again, pacing. Thank God the roof restaurant's flying. Best no-one notices his rage. This is *not a pretty sight*.

*

Somewhere on top of the White Cliffs of Dover, 9.34pm

"I'm away. There's no sign of our man. He ain't comin' out tonight. You'll be wantin' to do the necessary". Eamonn's up and off, back to his waiting car some two hundred metres from the cliff. He throws the sodden coat and sou'wester in the back and moves off, relieved that at least for him, the night is over.

*

Doolans Bar, Torrevieja, Spain. 9.48pm

Padraig sits alone in a corner alcove, his huge hands drumming a beat on the wooden table. It seems like an eternity since the last call and the veins on his forehead are close to bursting. All around him, the punters are lapping it up, spending their Euros like there's no tomorrow. He loves this place, but it's all gone right out of the window for now. Eventually, the mobile vibrates again and the news is not good. The conversation is short, he is not about to break the habit of a lifetime.

"Pick that feckin' cont up when his feckin' shift's ended. I want the feckin' truth. If you don't like what he's saying, you'll be wanting to *clear up the shite*". *Click*.

The operation has been compromised now. He snaps another mobile on. A thousand miles away in South Armagh, a phone springs to life.

"You'll be knowing all about this. I don't know what the feck's gone on, but I feckin' will. For now, I'll be suspendin' operations. Make feckin' sure there's no comebacks. You're sure about the driver? 100%. I thought so". *Click*.

*

Dover Eastern Docks, 10.05pm

The drug dogs are all over the truck now, twelve of Customs' finest are in the cab, under the unit, in the back and delving into the cargo. There's furniture from France, specialist Renault car parts, a consignment of shoes from Alicante and a few bits of furniture for some geezer who's moving back to the UK 'cos he can't stand the heat. They're taking the whole thing apart and all the time, Declan Fergus Byrne is languishing in an eight by four holding room, awaiting his interrogators. He's not been charged but he's going nowhere.

*

Dean's flying up the new road, past the Rettendon turn-off. He can't pass this without thinking about the boys in the shovel. When is somebody going to do something about that little miscarriage of justice, he thinks, raises a metaphorical glass to them and then he's at the A12 roundabout, anchors down, straight past some dawdler in a green Zafira, then hares off up the dual-carriageway towards Chelmo town centre. He's down to the single lane bit in what seems like seconds, then it's past the County Cricket ground and the double back over the bridge. Down below, the café bars are rammed. He throws a glance down at the throng and then it's Navigation Road and the 'front. Now it's the different Dean and he glides the Porker into the gravelled car park and spots a nice space next to the canal. The evening sun's glinting on the calm water and there are some people sitting outside on the decking. Looks like an office party, lots of birds in short skirts. The champers is flowing. Old men in suits, pretty girls. Must be a law firm, thinks Dean. He knows a lot about law firms.

Town Hall's already there. He's bang on time, is Town and he's already got the Bolly open, two glasses, one full, one now being filled for our man, who he's spotted long before Deano's on the case. He's got a table in the window, near the back so he can see all the comings and goings. There'll be plenty of those here. Dean nods to the maître d and the barman who acknowledge him with a nice bit of bowing and scraping. He shifts a few quid here.

"Deano! 'How ya doin', bruv?"

"Blindin', mate, blindin'".

They embrace, kissing each other on both cheeks. It's a London thing.

"Business good?", asks Town.

"Yeah, fine. 'Ad a few hassles this week. Cuntocks decided he fancied a bit of direct importing and we're having some unnecessary grief with the church. Fuckin' liberty. Nothing we can't handle". He lets out a laugh and grins at Town, winking as he lifts the tall slim glass of Bollinger to his lips. It tastes so good.

"What about you, matey? Spain alright?"

"More than that, bruv. Tracy loved the villa. Well impressed. Didn't half make use of the old jacuzzi. I met a few lemons. [NB. Lemons is rhyming slang for geezers, i.e. lemon squeezers]. Right touch. Nice bit of work". Town pauses to take in Dean's reaction. He looks a bit interested, but you can never tell with Dean, especially when his mind's on other things.

"Work? You was on holiday. Thought that bird of yours didn't let you out of bed?"

"Even she has to get to the shops sometime. When she's not on the Es, or on me". Dean looks down, he doesn't like the way this is going, wishes he hadn't mentioned the lovely Tracy. The problem with Dean is that he really does love the bugle more than anyone in the whole world. Finds it very 'easy company'. Trouble is, everyone else runs for the hills when Dean and the Peruvian Marching Band team up. He's a nightmare when he's right on it.

"Where did you get to, then? Get out much, or stayed close to the villa? Did you get up to La Manga?" Dean loves playing golf up at the La Manga Club. He's not a bad golfer, but these days, he's more and more on the Charlie and he's running short of partners at his home club in Essex.

"That's what I wanted to talk to you about. We was down town, right on the front there and we heard all this music coming from a bar. Country & Western it was, sung by some Irish geezer. Anyway, we went in and there's this massive bloke in there, right Paddy he were. He's sitting at the bar with some locals, eating lobster and drinking shampoo. I'm thinking, this is the fuckin' gaff for us, she's got her mincers all over the place, eyein' up the talent. The place is well nice and we gets ourselves a table and orders a bottle of 'poo. We've only just eaten, ain't we? She's laughin', thinks I've lost the fuckin' plot, but the Town knows what he's doin'. Anyway, after a bit, Paddy comes over and introduces himself, asking if we're alright, do we like the place, the music and all that bollocks. He's got presence, I'm thinkin', fair play to the geezer. He shakes hands and fuck me, my hands ain't small and he fuckin' swallowed them. So he says, have we seen the roof? She's lookin' at me. What, is he goin' to chuck us off? I'm laughin' like a cunt". Dean starts laughing and he's getting interested. Town's not known for going over the top, that's how he stays out of the shovel. Keeps his counsel. Clever bloke, Town; don't underestimate him.

"So, he looks at me and starts laughin' an' all. Next thing, he's come over and we're getting' on proper. Takes us up the steps and we're on the roof of his gaff. It's on three floors, every one's packed, pub, sports bar and the roof's the fuckin' restaurant. I tell, ya, Dean, it was well classy. Could do with something like that in Canvey. The birds would love it. He sits us down at this table, overlooking the sea and then, his missus comes over and she sits darn. The bubbly's flowin' and we're looking down on all the fuckin' arseholes on the street. Nice! I tell ya, this place is a cut above, mate. Turns out the geezer's only been open for four months. Place used to be a flamenco bar, but no-one wants that no more, so he's bought it cheap from some Spanish bloke. Must have spent a fortune on it. Oh mate, I tell ya, you'd love it. So his missus is talkin' to my missus and we gets up to have a proper butchers at what is proceeding. Then, from nowhere, his mates from the bar downstairs comes up and sits down next to us, all on one big table, like. All proper chaps. Two of them are Paddies and the other one's a Scouser. They look like they're well minted an' all. Everyone's talking the same language, know what I mean?"

"So what's the story with the Paddy, the big geezer? Sounds like he's proper flush. What's his angle?"

"Turns out, he's a farmer from the North. I mean, e's a pucker Paddy an all that, not one your fuckin' Ian Paisleys, but he comes out of South Armagh. Bandit Country, they call it".

"Bandit Country? Sarnds like Vange, haha!"

"Oh, mate, you've got no idea. These are proper connected. He weren't gonna reveal nothing. That's why they ain't had no grief from the Old Bill or the church. He's got some serious mates down there. We had a blindin' night, all on the back of buyin' a bottle of poo at the right time. Anyway, it's Sunday the next day and he's off on his boat and wants us to tag along. So, that's it for the night and the next mornin' we're all there, present and correct at the marina. He's got a Princess 55, oh, mate, you should see it. Fuckin' awesome. The boys turn up with a couple a birds, right tasty, bikinis already on. The food and booze is being loaded on by two of his barmen, he's talkin' to some marina bloke and all the time, the sun's beating down on this place. Mental! You should have seen Trace's boat. She's never been so quiet. Fair play, she's turned up with all the white clobber on, legs all over the gaff, but she's well gobsmacked".

*

Dover, 11.00pm

Eighty miles away, a Yellow jacketed man comes off shift, worried to death. The colour drained from his face at 8.58pm and did not return throughout the final two hours of his late shift. As he walked to the staff car park through the driving rain towards his waiting Mondeo, he felt the mobile vibrate yet again.

'Pik me up if u cn. Prty is crp. Laters'.

Party crap. You should try mine, thought the Yellow jacket. He climbed into the driver's seat and pulled out, unaware of the headlights switching on a hundred yards away. A quick call to his daughter and he thanked God the address was only five minutes away. A few twists and turns through the rainswept streets of Dover and he was there, outside a small, terraced house north of the town. Dozens of teenagers were pouring out onto the street, oblivious to the ferocious weather. He spotted his daughter through the mêlée and waved. She was kissing a boy goodbye. Can't have been all that bad, then. She climbed into the front seat, waved goodbye to her friends and they pulled away. Down the street, the lights came on again and a dark green Land Rover eased away from the kerb. A mobile rang.

"He's picked up his daughter. What do you want me to do?"

"He wants full closure. Nothing less will do. We're not a feckin' charity". *Click.*

The Mondeo moved to the end of the street, turned right and down onto the front, towards the A20/M20. The procession moved along the sea-front, past the marina and up the hill, all the time, the Land Rover maintaining the perfect distance. There was a wretchedness about the conversation taking place inside the warm Mondeo. His daughter drunkenly unaware of her father's catastrophe, he desperate to disguise his hopelessness. They pass the last roundabout on the hill by the Shell and then it's onto the dual carriageway proper and up towards Folkestone on the A20. About a hundred yards behind, the Land Rover is on sidelights, preparing to move in. The job has been called on. Yellow Jacket's fate is sealed.

*

<u>The Waterfront Restaurant, Chelmsford 11.25pm</u>

Dean can smell the money and he's gone from vaguely bored punter waiting for some Charlie, to shampooed up Canvey man who's just struck gold. He's looking at Town now with new eyes. And Town is full of it. He's loving this kind of re-living the whole Sunday with the Irishman thing. By this time, the Bolly's got right down to the bottom, the maitre d's been over and located another, opened it, poured it and gone. They know what they're doing here. He's left two menus as well, these two are definitely going to need some mopping up at some point. Anyway, Town's blathering on about how brilliant Paddy is. Turns out he really is called Paddy. Apparently, he spells it Padraig, a proper Irishman, no less. The other two are well in his shadow and the Scouser is, well, a Scouser. He's got dough, though. Very very flash. His bird's paid for, a Russian dancer from the club round the corner. My, how Torrevieja's moved on. By the afternoon, everybody has relaxed a bit and the Charlie's come out. Everyone's straight on it, but Paddy's holding back, just a little to be sociable. He starts asking Town Hall about his life and where he's staying, how well he knows the area, is he buying property. The gentle interrogation goes on until he's got all he needs to know. He starts asking Town about Dean. Seems that Paddy and Dean live about half a click from each other. Dean's on one side of the storm river and Paddy's on the other. As soon as Paddy hears that Dean's in haulage, he's right on it. Then as soon as Town bites, he cools off. The combination of Town's approach to life, the Charlie, the shampoo and the sun, together with Tracy sprawled topless on the sun-deck of this amazing gin palace, her legs coiled around his body, writhing has him champing at the bit, but his brain's fried now and Paddy knows it. The following day, Town pops in to the bar to say his goodbyes and Paddy's asking him about the next time Dean is coming over to his villa. The rest, as they say, is history.

The bar is full now, the late eaters and drinkers have arrived and all the tables are taken. No-one's putting Dean and Town under pressure. A plate of snacks arrives. This is the sign of a proper gaff. They know their clientele and know that if they don't combat the two bottles of bubbly with some linings, the noise levels will grow and someone just might kick off. It's a thin line with your best Billy Bunters, to know when and how to control them without them even realising.

"He's bang at it out there. I just know he is. I think if you want the bitta work, it's yours. He's checked me out already, I know that. I mentioned a few faces and he's had a word, just checkin' like. Proper chap. I told him you'd be over soon. Reckon it'd be worth your while".

So, that's it then. Paddy wants something.

"Gina's dying for a bit of a break. Reckons she ain't seen the sun for months. Amount of time she spends in that fuckin' tan stand, she'll have me bankrupt!" He's still putty in Gina-G's hands really. Just forgotten what his cock's for, that's all. Through the haze, he's still quite on the ball and his mind is already on the meeting tomorrow in the office. Just that the other's aren't expecting one, but they'll be there. He's starting to think about Cuntocks again and that's not good. Not good at all. The veins on his forehead start to come out to play again. Even Town's spotted this and suggests that a couple of stone baked pizzas and garlic bread might be a good plan. The food arrives so quickly that you could be forgiven for thinking that the chef had been making these every ten minutes *just in case*. Things, which could so easily have kicked off, calm down again and a bottle of Barolo appears. They're in the maitre d's hands and he knows just what they want. He always does. The girls love coming here for lunch when they're shopping in Chelmsford, which is at least once a week. It's either here or Geraldo's on the Square, but this is the haunt of choice for the Canvey Coven. If matey maitre's not keeping Dean under control, he's got the handful that is Gina Bold complete with side-kicks. Not exactly a quiet life.

The manager wanders over, takes a turn at pouring the silky dark red Piedmontese nectar and all is calm on the Water-front.

"Gonna join us for one, Spin?" There are very few people who call him that, but somehow Dean gets away with it and as probably the best customer, it just kind of gets tolerated. He sits down. The soul of discretion. They clink glasses at Dean's behest.

"How is Mrs Dean?" The perfect opener. Dean and Town Hall are troughing in to the mouth-watering pizzas and the atmosphere has calmed right down now and everyone's smiling again.

"Blindin', mate. Spendin' all me money, haha!" Dean's moving around in his chair, looking like the cat that's got all the cream, self-satisfied. What, after all, could go wrong?

"I thought you might like to know that we're having another themed night next month. Just launching the tables tomorrow. I wondered if you might like first refusal?" This man is some operator, especially with a man as volatile as Dean. Strange, isn't it, even he manages to behave here. Maybe it's because he loves it so much.

"When is it, my friend?"

"Thirteenth of October. Seven-thirty for eight".

"Cushti. Book us in for about a dozen. Gina'll be in touch, you know she'll want to get involved".

"Thank you, Mr Bold. I thought I could rely on you to get the ball rolling".

Dean's pissed now but he still puffs his chest out like a pouter pigeon. The manager toasts them once more and makes a tactical withdrawal.

"Quick little foray into the Cave? There ain't enough time to get down to Katz. What do you reckon, mate?" Chelmsford's pole and lap dancing club is just yards away on foot. Town's up for it, and judging by the way that Dean drains the last of his shampoo, he's not far behind.

"Got some blindin' gear. Sort you tonight."

"Blatantly, bruv. Blatantly. It's tits time". Dean calls the waiter over and they get the bill, which he will pay from a nice tight wedge of nifties in his back pocket.

"Get us a taxi, please mate". The pizza's lying a bit heavy now and Dean wants some action. However, the four hundred yards through Chelmo town centre is a bit _too_ much, so it's cab time.

"There's one waiting for you, Mr Bold. Good night". The waiter holds the door open for them and they stagger out into the night air and the comfort of Arrivals Taxis. Three minutes and five squid later, they are falling out of the cab and into the arms of the doorman at the brick-arched Cave.

"Evening gentlemen. Please come this way". The door opens as if by magic and they are absorbed into the thumping, pumping, writhing atmosphere. The sensual lighting's superb and at the bar, there are half a dozen girls dressed in evening gowns, slit to the thigh. Others are wandering around in hot pants and wrap-around mini skirts, tiny jewelled brassieres and towering platform silver heels complete the picture.

A particularly attractive girl sidles up to them.

"Hello, boys, fancy a drink?" The standard opening gambit admittedly, but she did it so well and with such a nice smile that the boys go for it in a big way.

"Shampoo, bruv?"

"It would be rude not to, matey".

"Is Carole in tonight?" slurs Dean, propping himself up at the bar and ordering yet another bottle of the fizzy stuff.

"Carole? Am I not lovely enough for you?" The girl puts on a mock pout and then howls with laughter. This _is_ Essex, after all and the locals are friendly.

"She's doin' a dance at the mo. Want me to get when she's done?"

"You, my darlin' are a little angel. Have a drink with Deano. What's your name?" He's kind of slobbering a bit at the moment, but don't be too hard on him, he's just a boy on a night out. Another girl joins the threesome and Town pours her a glass of bubbly too.

"I'm Lorna. I'm very pleased to meet you. What's yours?"

"I'm Dean and this, my old mate, is Town. Short for Town Hall".

"Town Hall? Is that your real name?"

"No love, I'm just breakin' it in for a mate". He collapses with laughter, as eventually does Lorna.

"What sort of bleedin' name is that? I've heard some bollocks in here but that takes the biscuit. Aaaaarrrrggghhhh!" She squeals with laughter, which works like crazy on the boys.

"And what's your name, sexy?" Town's settling in now and flops down on a bar-stool, addressing the other girl. She's tall and he's right at tit level now. Perspiration from a recent spell at the pole is trickling down between her gorgeous mounds and Town is oh so hooked. The girl looks him right in the eyes and her lip-glossed mouth parts,

"I'm Natasha. I am from St Petersburg, yes?" She really is and she really is. That's the nice thing about the Russian girls. They couldn't give a fuck about hiding their identities. They're here already. She's got those Slavic cheekbones which seem to start up by the hairline somewhere and end close to the mouth. Her eyes are bright and sparkling, her make-up heavy but stylish.

"Of course you are". He smiles at this vision of loveliness, eyes her up and down and returns to those eyes.

"And how long have you been working in here, Natashaaaaa?" His accent is really showing but it's rather lost on lovely boobs. She just smiles and licks her lips, the champagne tastes so good. A third girl arrives, as if by magic and Dean turns towards her, realises it's Carole and lets out a cheer.

"Hello, *darlin'!*" He gives her a big kiss on her cheek and calls for more champagne.

Dean leans over to Town and whispers something in his ear. Town nods his head and Dean beckons the barman over, tucks a pinkie in his top pocket and gives him a little job to do. Town's back on the 'poo and the girls are getting restless.

"Do you want a table next to the stage, Dean?" Lorna opens her eyes wide and stares right into his soul. Quick off the mark, these girlies, they know exactly who's in charge. They always do. Carole checks out the other two and off they go. On the stage, a willowy redhead with a healthy injection of silicone is doing a marvellous job on the pole, alternating swinging her endless legs around with floor work, thighs open, her garter already stuffed with tenners. The boys are baying for bra off time and right at the end, the girl turns her back, unfastens the clasp with practised ease and slowly turns around. Her huge tits make the boys gasp, nipples fully erect and she leans over towards the nearest guy, drawing the straps of her glittery bra across his face before retreating behind the curtains to a racket of applause and catcalls. The girls are laughing and necking the champagne. Carole whispers something to Dean and they're off for a private dance, out of sight of the others. Town's loving Natasha and Lorna's attention and they touch his leg and face from time to time, just to keep him interested. Just working the system, like. Natasha's keen and wants a private dance too, but Town wants more and as soon as Dean and Carole return, the three of them disappear off to the VIP area for more. As Dean sits down, the barman saunters over and passes a message to him. A message which lights Dean's face up like Blackpool Tower. He whispers something to Carole, who reels back laughing. She returns the favour and they're off for another lap dance, this time taking Lorna with them. Things are really starting to hot up. Natasha's got her arms around Town's neck. He leans towards her.

"Babes, do you, well do you work with anyone in here? Know what I mean?" He leers at Natasha's tits, but she doesn't give a shit now. The nifties are coming thick and fast, the more she dances for him. She's not too keen on the sharing proposition, but she knows a good thing when she's onto it and these two boys are a *very good thing*. She whispers in his ear that she has a friend from Budapest called Orla who is small, dark and very sexy. He looks around, but Natasha puts her hand across the back of his head and guides him back to face her.

"She's not here, darlink. She is, shall we say, at home. She can meet us though, if you want? Yes?"

Oh yes, baby, yes, thinks Town. He's just caught on. Dean's on his way back from the latest fifty liberating exercise of Carole and Lorna's, smile on his face, trousers a bit skewed. Natasha disappears to make a discreet phone-call.

"Go and get us some more 'poo, ladies!" The girls take their cue and sling their hooks for a mo. Dean leans over to Town and over the thumping music, lets him in on the fact that they've just become the proud owners of the last room at the County Hotel, First Floor.

"It's party time. We've just got to get these lot on the same page. Do you know what I'm sayin'?"

Town knows alright. It's like Birthday, Christmas and Easter rolled into one. The girls come giggling back to the table, make-up freshly applied, lip gloss factory on overtime. Town grabs hold of Natasha and checks out the friend situation, tells her that the party's on. She looks at him in mock surprise and waves her index finger from side to side before bursting into hysterical laughter. She gives him a little chaste kiss on the cheek and wanders off to get her mobile. Dean, meanwhile, is having a bit of a battle with the other two. They don't seem too keen on taking it further with Dean, but he is having none of it and he's talking telephone numbers to get the girls to put out. Eventually, the nifties prove too much even for Carole's morals. The girls remind them that they can't get off for another half-hour and that's just a top way of getting the boys to spend another monkey on the lap. Babe after gorgeous babe sashay out onto the stage to rapturous applause. Dean and Town are onto a good thing now and the wallets are well and truly open. The girls keep a close eye on them; they don't want to miss out on moneybags and his mate. After a while, Natasha comes over to Town and whispers in his ear that her mate is all fired up and ready to go.

"Where would you like her to meet with us, darlink", she purrs, pouting, blowing him a kiss.

"Do you have room?"

"Oh, I got room for you and yer mate!"

"No, silly, room, you book room for us, yes?"

"We're over the road, in the County. Got the last room, an' all".

"You give me room number, my friend wait in room for us. I think she will have, maybe little surprise for you?"

"Fuckin' stroll on. 'Ere, Dean! Natasha's mate wants to get into the room in the County".

"Listen, tell the barman and he'll speak to his mate over the road. Just get her name and give it to him".

"Here, love, what's your friend's name?"

"Her name is Orla. She is very beautiful girl. She is coming from Hungary. All girls from there are very beautiful".

"We'd better go there, then! Here, bruv, she reckons we gotta go to Hungary. What do you reckon?"

"If we go now, we'll never get back for cuntocks tomorrow! Besides, I ain't goin' hungry for no cunt".

"Fuck off! Fuckin' lightweight!"

"Come on, matey, time we went for walk. I've got the fuckin' horn".

"You and me both, bruv. Get the birds sorted and we'll fuck off".

"Come on, ladies, time to go!"

"Look, Dean, you leave first. We'll have to go off shift and meet you there". Carole's looking him straight in the eye and smiling.

"Oh yeah? What do you take me for? Some mug?"

"Really. We will be there. If we leave with you now, we'll lose our jobs. Honest. We ain't supposed to do this".

"I suppose it'll be OK. Alright, girls. Don't be late!"

Dean settles up with the barman and they're away. The County Hotel is just up the road from the Cave and even these two are prepared to walk that. They're both well up for it and once they get into reception, Dean can't wait to get the rigmarole over with and get up to the room. The night guy spares them the usual checking in bollocks – he's seen it all before. Spares them the 'breakfast's between seven and ten and all that'. Thank God! He does, however give Dean a wink as he leaves, what with him having let the delightful Orla into the room not five minutes before. They get to the room in no time at all and as they open the door, they are greeted by the sight of a curvy, dark beauty, dressed in a black basque, fishnet seamed stockings and black stilettos. She is lying on the bed, her perfect slim legs crossed, well, intertwined. She is propped up on her elbows and wearing the most wicked smile you've ever seen.

"Good evenink, boys. My name is Orla. I am Hungarian girl from Budapest. You like?"

"Oh, yes, babe. We like!"

"You may also know that Orla is, how you say, anagram for oral! I give you demonstration of my talents, yes?"

"Fuck me, bruv, is she for real?"

"Of course I am real girl. Even my breasts are genuine!" She falls back on the bed, laughing, flashing those beautiful pearly whites. This girl is the business!

"Where is my friend, Natasha? You don't want fuck her? I get other girl when you want?"

Eastern girls. What did we do before eastern girls? She's already sorted a few lines on the dressing table, generous too, which she points out to the boys.

"You pay for this, OK?" she smiles at them, before drawing one full line, dabbing her nose gently before returning to the bed.

Dean and Town are standing stock still, looking at each other like they've just got birthday and Christmas rolled into one. Then the moment's gone and Town sits on the bed and introduces them. Dean gets the drinks from the mini bar, decides he's being a fuckin' cheapskate and rings down to the night porter for some champagne. Best they've got at this time of the night is the house, but bearing in mind that everyone's fuckin' trolleyed, does it matter? Does it fuck.

Within a couple of minutes, there's a tap, tap on the door and Dean goes over to open it, what with Town and Oral starting to get to know each other on the bed.

"Room Service", is the voice from the other side of the door and when Dean opens it, the geezer ain't joking.

Not only has the champagne arrived, so have Natasha, Carole and Lorna, changed out of their working gear and into a collection of leather minis, a long black skirt slit to the thigh and a pair of what could only be described as hot pants. There are legs and tits everywhere and they come walking in, laughing like idiots. Looks like the old Colombian's been given an outing and all. Dean gives the night porter a nifty and tells him to put everything else on the bill. He gives Dean another wink and legs it.

"Come in, *ladies*!" Town's eyes are out on stalks and just for once, Dean is more interested in Slavic legs than Colombian white. However, Orla is lining up again and the girls are straight into some more. Lots more.

They're straight into the champagne. Town's serving up some fresh lines now just in case anyone's up for more, which they all are. The lights are low and the party begins. Orla and Natasha brush against each other as they sit down and as if on cue, they begin to neck, their tongues teasing and tantalising Dean and Town like mad. Natasha's fingers stroke Orla's erect nipples through the thin basque which makes Town start jumping around the room like some demented frog.

Carole and Lorna have moved over to Dean and are kissing and touching him, their hands rubbing him through his trousers. Carole begins to undress and this is the cue for the other girls to do the same. Soon, they are all naked and in the half-light, the bodies begin to intertwine. Dean's lying on his back with Carole riding him. Lorna's sitting on his face, her cunt pressed hard against his mouth and is kissing Carole in full view of Town and the Natashas. He's doing Oral from behind and Natasha's licking her clit from underneath, whilst Orla has her tongue deep in Natasha.

Back in Canvey, Gina is fast asleep, dreaming of her wild plans.

Chapter Four

Tuesday Morning Costa Blanca Spain

As the sun rose over the wide, crystal sea, Padraig Diarmuid O'Riordan slipped quietly out of his bed, the sleeping Mary murmuring just once before turning over and dreaming on. A gap in the curtains told him that morning had indeed broken. Paddy O, as he is best known to his friends, enemies and those who wish to God they'd never met him, was a self-confessed early riser. Came really from his upbringing on the farm in Cullaville, South Armagh, which is better known to those who are familiar with it, as Bandit Country. The memories of those days in the 1970s were long and deep, Bloody Sunday on the telly; the kneecappings and shootings a daily occurrence. The Dundalk road ran right through the village; to the south, the Republic, to the north, a sectarian nightmare. Sometimes, you couldn't even get a body into the ditch on Concession Road without booking a space first. First place you come to from the south, so whenever a Dublin gang wanted to dump an undesirable who had 'slipped up', they'd do the business, then drive the body over the border at Cullaville, shoot it through the kneecaps, chuck it in the ditch and slip away into the night. It would take the authorities months to work out what was going on.

But South Armagh, to the clever and resourceful man, was an opportunity never to be repeated. The border, which was nearly altered by the successive British Governments of 1970s Labour and 1980s Conservative, runs in a rather random way through rolling countryside, criss-crossed with hedges and ditches. Perfect places for snipers and remote controlled bombs. Perfect for smuggling.

Paddy O cut quite a dash as he put on his crisp, white shirt, left out for him by the devoted Mary. His strong, huge hands struggled as always with the tiny buttons. He always wins in the end.

*

Morning had brought new developments. Justice had been swift and now a Mondeo lay sideways in a wide drainage ditch some thirty feet from the A20, its roof crushed. Two people dead inside, a young girl of about sixteen, a man in his forties, decapitated by the force of the impact. On the back seat, a Yellow Jacket casually tossed there has hardly moved. No skid marks on the carriageway to help the investigating officers of the Kent Police. The heavy gravel on which the car is perched will show nothing of the boot imprints of one Gerard Conlon, the last person to visit this scene some ten hours before. No-one saw the 'accident', no-one saw him pull over onto the hard-shoulder. No-one saw him walk over to the car and check the outcome. No-one saw him watch the girl die. There had been green paint on the offside front wing, indicating the contact which Conlon's Land Rover made, just before it careered off the highway at seventy-eight miles an hour, rolling five times before coming to rest in the drainage ditch. That's now been skilfully removed. There is now a huge patch of oil on the road, which the coroner will conclude, was the tragic reason for this upstanding member of Her Majesty's Revenue and Customs and his gifted, Roedean educated daughter meeting such an untimely end. What sacrifices he and his poor wife must have made to afford such advantageous schooling for her. No longer will the bags of cash be arriving at such convenient times. But that was yesterday for Padraig O'Riordan's boys and a now dead Customs Officer. Job done and time to move on.

*

Walking out onto the terrace, between villa and expansive pool, he paused just for a moment. Five o'clock on a summer morning in Torrevieja is a beautiful time. Not a soul stirs, trees in the park resound with morning birdsong, yet that is so distant even Padraig's footsteps echo around the walls. The gardens are stunning, thanks mainly to Mary's love of the outdoors and Pepe's skilful horticulture. He is spending more and more of his time out in Spain, since the CAB moved seriously into his affairs. Following the murder of the respected Independent journalist Veronica Guerin, the Irish government formed the Criminal Assets Bureau, gave it draconian powers and sent it on its way. The net results have been investigations of the most far-reaching kind, its tentacles have ignored borders, old-fashioned 'agreements' and paramilitary amnesties. It's Al Capone all over again and this time, the authorities mean business. You may not be aware, but business in Ireland tends to ignore borders too and there are many people who live in the North and work in the South and, of course, vice versa. Padraig's farm lies close to the border in

Cullaville with the land backing on to McAleavey's Bar. Perfect for a little Thai dinner after a hard day's graft.

From half a mile away, the O'Riordan villa stands out clearly with its established bougainvillea bedecked walls, turreted roof and a huge electric gate. More and more of these villas are springing up now, directly in proportion to the amount of money flowing out from Ireland and the United Kingdom. There's even a bloody Ann Summers, for God's sake!

Padraig allows himself a moment's reflection, a deeply spiritual man is he. More importantly, he is very, very serious. Once this moment with nature is over, he walks down the steps towards the black BMW, pressing the alarm release before climbing in. Still, no-one stirs.

The electric gate moves slowly across, leaving a wide arc for Paddy to attack and the Beamer sweeps majestically onto the road and away. The gate closes swiftly behind him. Half a mile away, a camera shutter *click, clicks* to its heart's content. The man behind it makes a brief note on his pad and turns to his seated colleague.

"Right on cue. You could set your watch by this one".

Their bleary eyes betray another long night.

"We have precisely two more days of this, then we are going to be called off. When is he going to *do something*?"

"This one's been under obo for years, off and on. Not so much as a fucking parking ticket. We know he can't sustain his lifestyle, we know that nothing adds up, but he's got the angles covered. There has to be something out here. His MO demands it."

"Well we're all back to HQ if nothing happens soon. Where's the other two, Rick? Back at the hotel?"

"Emily's all ready to give up the ghost and Andy's trying to keep body and soul together. How did we get those two muppets on an obs like this?"

"'Cos everyone thinks this is everyone else's job. Newry don't want to know, Dover are too busy and Maidstone IMPEX are having their budgets cut. Couldn't even leave the motors running overnight on the Oakwood job. Freezing it was. November and we had to sit there all night. They're the best of a bad job".

Kim Evans loyalty to the job was being tested to the limit and she was secretly hoping for a transfer to anywhere.

"Right. It's back to the hotel and we're going to step things up. It's shit or bust on this one now. If we get no more within the next two days, I am going to recommend we're called off. Let's go."

The cameras are put away and for the moment, observation is ceased at 5.45am.

*

Padraig's drive takes him down past the new villas and into town. Soon, he's driving along the front; sparkling Mediterranean sea on one side and dozens of sleeping restaurants and slowly waking bars on the other. Shutters are just beginning to raise, bleary eyed waiters putting out tables for the early rising Brits, and delivery men unloading fresh bread and the rest of the day's supplies. There is a freshness in the air, though the summer temperature is already rising, bringing exotic aromas to life. In the distance, a few stragglers who didn't make it home last night are rising from the sand, already regretting the decision to rough it on the beach. Mini-skirted girls and tee-shirted boys cling together, hoping to get back into front-line hotels before parents cotton on. A Policia Local car lies empty next to the Murcia bus stop, its driver already cadging an early coffee and brandy from a dutiful café owner, smoke from his cigarette drifting across the pavement. But Padraig notices little of this, so focused is he. At the lights, hanger left and he's there, stopping the BMW right outside a large, Irish pub. The door is already open and with the cutting of Padraig's engine comes a large, ham-handed Irishman, dressed in regulation white shirt and black jeans to open the door.

"Mornin' Mr O. Yer'll be wantin' a coffee." This combination of question and statement identifies the mystery man. Dead on South Armagh. Another local. He takes the keys from Padraig and calls the order inside, before climbing in to the Beamer and moving it round the corner. Inside is already a hive of activity. For this is Padraig's home from home. He bought it three years ago from a genial local who was moving back to Alicante, retiring from the hurly-burly that is the Costa. He's enlarged it, built upwards, outwards and downwards. Señor Juan Gomez, mayor of this town has sold several pieces of land to Padraig and in return, cash is nicely washed through the pub, no questions asked. Juan's brother, Raul, all round good guy, golfer, socialite. Oh, and did I forget, general manager of the Banco Litoral. When these three sit together, they are known in the pub as the three wise men. Or is it the three wise guys. A mutually beneficial, legitimate business relationship. Perfecto.

"Anything in yet?" A figure appears from behind the bar. It's Declan, Padraig's general manager. Lock, stock and barrel, Mr O's ownership of this place and if you work for him, you work to his hours. The man is hard working and expects nothing less of you. He's fair though and the rewards are good.

"Nothing so far, Mr O. I'll check again in a wee while."

"How was last night?"

"Dead on, the band was great. Place was packed, so it was."

"Hmmm". Man of few words, Mr O. He picks up the takings sheets left for him by Declan and studies them intently.

"How's the new menu downstairs? Are they liking the fresh stuff you've put on?"

"Slow start, but it's coming on, you know the sort of shite the Brits normally like to eat. We're slowly educating them!" Declan smiles at this little joke, a pop at 90% of the clientele that gets into Doolan's Irish Restaurant & Bar, as this place is known. Padraig actually picked a name out of the Newry phone-book for this purpose. Jerry Doolan, fishmonger to the good people of Newry was thankfully unaware of his new found Iberian fame.

"I don't want to educate them, just want their money." Padraig doesn't even lift his eyes from the takings sheet, tapping his pen and raising his eyes from time to time. After around five minutes, he gets out of his chair and wanders up onto the roof, mobile in hand.

"Hello. You'll be wanting to come over. I've something for yous".

Click.

A man of few words.

He returns to the bar level and carries on with the takings sheet. After a few minutes, a car draws up outside and a tall, wiry man walks in, jacket slung over his shoulders, Armani jeans, loafers, white shirt. Police sunglasses.

"Alright, mate?" No physical contact. The two men are, however at ease with each other, there is a chemistry of comfort which passes between them like a kind of radar bounce on a friendly plane. Identified and approved. You see a lot of guys like this. It comes from having done enormous transactions over a period of time, yet even after that, the slightest thing could mess it right up. Strange thing, trust. It's strange, because it doesn't really exist. It's like an umbrella from the bank, an overdraft. It exists *in theory*, but when you need it, surprise! It just melts away and the guy you thought you could trust is your new enemy. Whoever said keep your enemies closer was right on it. One slip up here and it's not going to end up in the divorce courts. It'll end in Concession Road, Cullaville, in a ditch, hands and feet bound, a bullet in the back of the head, or at least it would have done a few years ago. More likely, it'd be just off the coast here, just the torso would turn up. The rest of it would probably end up as burgers.

"What did you make of yer man?"

"Sound, sound. Great". The new man is Don Beevers, currently of Torrevieja, Spain, late of Liverpool 8. He takes a chair next to Paddy, yet maintains just the right amount of distance between them. At the same time as a multi-million pound bit of work is called on, he would not entertain beaking in on Paddy's daily takings. You just don't do things like that to Paddy. It just *doesn't happen*. Jesus, Paddy is a complex man. People from that part of the North usually are. Quiet, yet with immense presence, monosyllabic often, yet when they speak, everyone listens. They talk very quietly, so you have to listen just in case you need to know whether they're about to top you or not. Take Paddy. He looks as if he'd be totally comfortable living in a caravan. He's no traveller, but he's got that kind of formality which you often find in that community. How often do you see a middle-aged traveller without a tie? Almost never. The other thing you never do is ask him direct questions such as 'Where have you been?' Incredibly private man, Padraig.

"OK, but can we work with him? *Can we trust him*?" Aaah! The trust word. Used often in this world of discreet deals and sleight of hand.

"When will he let us down, Don? *That* is what I want to know. We are in a strange position, you and me. We sit here, in the middle of a beautiful land, owners of all we see before us, and a damned sight more and we are talking *new business*. When do we start the car for him? When do we load the gun for him? *When is his time*?"

Don is visibly shocked by this monologue from his business partner. Padraig is a man of few words, a man of action normally who will sit quiet and then destroy men's lives without even the blink of an eye.

"He seems well fuckin' sound to me. It's this fella from Essex I want to see. We know Hall's not a wrong 'un, let's see what the other one's like. He sounds a right greedy bastard". With this, Beevers permits himself a smile. You could almost see a flicker from O'Riordan too, but you were probably wrong. Padraig reserves that kind of behaviour for behind closed doors.

"We've seen them come and go, Don, but I am seriously questioning the wisdom of this one. When Kelly's finished his *enquiries* and gets here, we'll have more of an idea of what's been going on, but until then, I'm keepin' me options open. He's got a lot of eejits to have a *little chat with* and you know he's got to get the romper room ready first". *The Romper Room*. That takes him back to some of his darkest but most satisfying days. The Estate, Belfast 1980s. Too many things going down, too many RUC and army successes. Belfast was not South Armagh. Belfast was open season. UVF, UFF, IRA, INLA and the bloody Special Branch on top of that. Roadblocks, drive-bys, kneecappings, the SAS. Factions. That was the word. *Factions*. No longer did Padraig look over his shoulder for the SAS dagger or the sniper's bullet. Now it was the C.A.B., the Customs, the Gardai Siochana, the RUC. At least *they* stayed the same. The most dangerous faction now? His rivals. The same boys who had worked with him before were working against him now. Kelly would find out what had been going down last night in Dover. Padraig's mind had been working overtime since receiving the news, trying to narrow down the possibilities. Retribution against the Customs officer had been swift and absolute. It always had to be. *To encourage the others*. He had been paid well, yet it was he himself who had to pay the final price.

"It is the thrill of the chase, so it is, Don. It's the only thing that keeps me goin'. Well, that and the greed, of course. Where are we with our friends in the docks?"

Beevers worked tirelessly with his Spanish counterparts entrenched deep in Alicante container port. Always discreet, always on time. He had taught the locals a bit of British time-keeping and in return, they had taught him how to relax. The casualties along the way were too numerous to recall, yet there still existed some humour, some savoir-faire of the bulk cocaine business which they so jealously guarded. Padraig's money was like the sunrise. You waited for it and each morning, there it was. In full, on time, guaranteed. He paid the same price each time, no negotiation, no fucking around. Don Beevers was a different breed from so many. He never mixed business with pleasure, preferring his R n' R in the bars and nightclubs of Oporto and Split. He had his regular girls there, Isabel the blondie in Club 69 in the back streets of Port Wine's capital, Roxanna the redhead in Q-Girls in that beautiful Croatian city. Both knew what Don Beevers was there for. Fucking and snorting. Top and bottom of it. Oh, and the champagne. Lots of it. Pink and ice cold. Laurent Perrier. Every time, referee. If they'd made red champagne, that would have been Don. His greatest weakness was Liverpool FC. He always tells you that it will be his downfall. Not the Charlie, not the tarts, but *the club*. When he takes himself back home, these days an altogether riskier business since the demise of certain Liverpool born individuals from the honourable trade in Colombian Marching Powder, you will still find him in the middle of the Kop, scarf aloft, singing his heart out. After that, it's a Chinese down Stanley Road, then a couple of brasses and Cream. A local boy, at heart.

"I've got a meet with Paco and Sandwich tonight". *Sandwich*. Now there's a case. *Un typ, un mec* as the French would call him, so named because whenever you go out for a night with him, and you'd better have your wits about you, he'll always have two tall blond Natashas with him, one on each side. Hence the name; Sandwich. Easy, really, when you know how. His partner, Paco is as sound as the proverbial pound. A street kid from Alicante, no parents, no school, no family. He prefers to see it as *no ties*. He it completely without morals, but if you pay him the money, you will get the merchandise, whatever it is. He will beg, borrow and steal to do it. If it's necessary, he'll top some bastard to get his way. He is small, wiry and very tanned. Always wears a silk shirt and a pair of black trousers. He would never come to Doolans. Being mistaken for a waiter might not be such a good idea for whoever suggests it. His contacts in North Africa are secret and plentiful, from the dealers, to the police, the port officials in Algiers, the girls, the pimps, the slavers, the terrorists. For some reason, they all do business with Paco. His yang is Sandwich. Tall, with long, curly hair tied back in a knot, he never takes off his shades. He comes from one of the wealthiest local families who own about half the remaining first line land along the coast northwards towards Benidorm. His father detests him, his mother loves him. University educated in Madrid, he speaks five languages fluently and collects art and wine for fun. Just has a thing for hundred euro hookers, that's all. Oh, and the Charlie. Swans around the province in either the 911 or the Lamborghini. Not a care in the world. Beevers, Paco and Sandwich make one hell of a team when they're on the razz. Which is going to be tonight.

"We're going to have to tighten up, Don, so we are. We've had a good run recently, but I think it's time to reign in the feckin' horses. We're gettin' careless. Might be time to call it a day".

"You serious, Paddy?"

"I met a man a long time ago. He said to me, when you're goin' out to do a bit of work, picture yourself in the dock and work backwards. If you don't like what you see, then you don't want the work. All I'm sayin' is that we need to be feckin' right on it, if we're gonna stay ahead o' the game".

"Sound. Fockin' sound. What happened to the man?"

"Went to Magilligan for twenty years!" Padraig let out a gale of laughter you could hear a block away, only to be joined by Beevers' cackle a couple of seconds later.

"Yer a fockin' maniac!"

"Just get what you can from the boys. We've gotta meeting very soon, an' I want to know that everything's right".

The two men embrace and then Beevers is gone. Padraig is left alone with just the sun for company. His thoughts are far, far away.

Chapter Five

Canvey, Tuesday morning

As Dean comes in through the front door, his daughter runs out of the kitchen and throws her arms around him.

"How's my favourite Dad?" Benissa's really cosying it up for Dean this morning and he picks her up, swinging the poor girl round, which for the pair of them is no mean feat. He is dressed for business today, blue suit, open necked Armani shirt and favourite Gucci loafers.

"Blinding mate. Bit hammered last night. Stayed over with Town. Proper good night".

"Decided I'm going to get that job. I know you don't want me sittin' on me arse, so I'm gonna make ya happy".

"Sweetheart, you've made my day". He gives her a kiss and walks into the kitchen, his daughter follows.

"That is, unless you want me to come and work with ya". Benissa looks doe-eyed at her dad, but this is a step too far.

"You don't wanna work in haulage, princess". He turns away and that's that. His daughter looks rather downcast, but all she's really doing is trying to blag her way out of proper graft. Lazy mare.

Gina comes in and sits down. "Good night, babes?" she asks, settling down to fruit yoghurt and muesli, her pink tracksuit open sufficiently to display magnificent cleavage.

"Top night, darlin'. Give old Spin at the 'Front a bell today will ya? He's got a Blues Brothers night on the thirteenth. Said we'd take a table. Leave it up to you, sweets. Town and Tracy wanna come, plus all the usuals. Oh, and I'll see if Jimmy Jag fancies some. He ain't bin out for fuckin' ages, know what I mean". He leans over and kisses both Gina and Benissa. "Where's the bleedin' professor, then?"

"He's over next door's".

"Is he ever here any more? I want him to come down the

Hammers with me on the weekend. See if he's got a window in his diary will ya? Oh, and pick up the Porsche from the 'Front car park when you're there, babes".

"Yeah, laters, darlin'".

With that, Dean's off, picks up the keys to the Jeep and away, leaving Gina and Benissa to do battle over her job. However, they are more interested in each other's antics. Bee tells her mum everything. More of that anon.

For today is the day when he deals with Cuntocks.

*

As he turns onto the A13, he's straight onto the mobile. First it's Jimmy Jag, then it's Ali and then finally it's Shotgun Kev. The A team. The punishment squad. This is not going to be pretty.

Dave's waiting at the office in Thurrock, taking care of business. Dean sees today as a turning point for him, a watershed where he is going to move into the big league. Last night is weighing heavy on his mind. It's the first time he's had a shag in weeks and it wasn't Gina. He's half scared, half proud and half nutter today.

Click. "Dave. All sweet? Cushti. Jag, Shotgun and the Coat are cummin ta the meet. Is Cuntocks still in the dark? Sweet, mate. Laters". *Click.*

His mobile emits the little *Beep, beep.*

'*Mmmm! L O bigboy fancy a lik? X*'. It's from a number he doesn't recognise. *Who the fuck is this*?

It's all coming back to him now. Last night. He's only gone and given the bird his mobile number. So what. He's on a roll now. Turning the CD up, scratching his bollocks, flying down the '13. As he passes the Vange turn, he's suddenly a little boy again, playing in the street, waiting for the old man to come home from the docks in Tilbury. He's kicking a ball against the metal garages. Billy Bonds, Brooking, McAvenny, Taylor. They're all there. Dave's in goal, Ronnie Clapton's playing Billy, Dean's Alan Taylor, recreating the winner against Fulham in the Cup Final. Ronnie's elder brother Jimmy turns up and starts dribbling around them all,

Charlie Big Potatoes him. Big, lanky streak of piss was Jimmy. The old gang. Dean's prized possession, his old man's programme from the '75 Final. Still got it too, on the wall in his little study on the Island. Two-nil, two-nil, two-nil, two-nil. TWO-NIL! Fucking Fool 'em. Hah! Poor old Ronnie. Still goes and puts flowers on his grave, does Dean. Got stabbed up at Millwall. New Cross Gate Tube 1984. He got separated and some fucking pikey done 'im. They found him up an alley, seventeen deep wounds. Never stood a chance. Them were the days.

His mood's changed and he stops the Jeep in a lay-by just by the tea stand. Thank God for tinted windows, as he's reached under the driver's seat and brought out a little bag of hooter. Good old Town, never lets you down, does Town. Dean laughs at his little joke. It's got to be the quick version, back of the hand, so he tips a little of the old powder out, retrieves the outer case of a Biro and bob's your uncle. Well, Charlie's your uncle, but you see what I mean. Mmmm! That's better! Minute later and he's off again. All the melancholy of earlier is gone and he's ready for action.

In no time at all, he's at the unit. As he pulls in, the sign over the roller door greets him. 'Bold Transport'. Too fuckin' right. As he climbs out of the Jeep, he feels ten feet tall. He's been lap-danced, fucked, sucked and now bugled up.

Dave's in the office, as is the lovely Dawn. One Language has just drawn up in the Shogun and is getting something out of the boot as Dean walks over.

"Awright, guv?" Lingo's usual greeting is met with more feeling than Dean's been giving it for a long time.

"Blindin' mate, blindin'. I could right fuckin' blend in anywhere today, know what I'm sayin'?" He has a real spring in his step. "You got Cuntocks sorted for this mornin'? The boys are all comin'. Gonna be a right tune up".

"Told the cunt to be over Essex T around ten."

"Who's over there today, besides the bird?"

"Jus' Daz the Door. E's only there lookin' at her threepennys".

"And she's got plenty of that, bruv".

They walk into the reception of Bold Transport and straight through into Dean's office. He's had it done out with all his Hammers stuff. All pale blue walls and maroon leather sofas. Claret and blue. His pictures of the '66 boys are up there, signed shirts, Moore, Peters, Hurst, Brooking, Bonds, Dicks. Dean photographed with just about every bloke who's ever worn a West Ham shirt. It's all leather and chrome, thick carpets and models of Scania trucks.

"We'll get Cuntocks sorted then we've gotta meet in Ilford. Some Indian's gotta bitta work for us. Turns out they've got the new paperwork sorted and are happy to pay top dollar for the transport. Just outside Antwerp straight into Barking. We're mee'in at that Chinese just off the roundabout. Funny that, Indians in a Chinese. Nice touch".

"Must be some fuckin' outfit if they've got that sorted".

"Well, you and I know there's only one firm in Ilford capable of that, eh bruv?"

"They couldn't give a fuck, them geezers".

"Still reckons he's got to make up a bit of ground, know what I mean?"

Dean calls through, "'Ere, Dawn, get us some coffee in 'ere will you. And get us some of them Penguins an' all".

Dave wanders in and sits down on the other sofa, opposite Lingo. He's just sitting there, all quiet.

"How're we playin' this mornin', bruv?"

"I wanna frighten 'im. Really frighten 'im. Bit of an Ali special. You know no-one expects the Coat to be the fuckin' danger man. We'll take 'im round the back, into the unit. Send the bird off for an hour. Give her a score and send her over Pitsea market, tell her to buy a new dress or something. We don't want her listening to the cunt screaming."

"Usual set-up then. Chair, wire. D'ya want the golf clubs an all?"

"No. Forget the rope, we'll use cable ties. More effective. And get a nice big car battery. Is he familiar with the Bosch drill routine?"

"Dunno if he heard the story. Even the Brummie press kept a tight lid on that one".

"That'll do. Don't want any further machine tools. Place'll look like fuckin' B&Q".

Dave slopes off, he's got a reception to organise. Special treatment for the gentleman.

Dawn comes in with the executive refreshments, right on cue. Flaming red hair is tied up right on top with the ponytail falling down over her bare shoulders. She's wearing a tight corset and jeans with knee-length black boots. She looks the absolute business on National Looking the Absolute Business Day. As she bends down over the table with the tray, she gives Dean a right eyeful of her arse and he's back in the Cave last night, only then it was Carole's arse and there were no jeans between him and her. As she stands up, she gives him the full tit treatment on top. That's torn it.

"Dawn, love, give us a break will you. We're trying to work in here. You'll have someone's eye out with them". He looks up at her grinning face.

"Well, Mr Dean, you shouldn't really be lookin' now should you. Are you sayin' that a good Catholic girl like me's got to cover up in this place?" She winks at him. Saucy's the word. It's the only one that will do, in the circumstances. A kind of Barbara Windsor moment, you might say.

Dean grins, but that little scenario's run its course and she goes back to reception.

The coffee is drunk, Dean tucks into his Penguins and it's time to go.

"Mind the shop, there's a good chap", Dave nods at Ron.

"Thanks, Dave. Appreciate that".

*

Ali, Shotgun Kev and Jimmy Jag are already there. Ali's got his coat done right up to the neck and stands there looking like butter wouldn't melt. Apart from the baseball bat that's swinging from his right hand. Kev's playing with a brass knuckle duster and Jimmy's got a starting handle. Old habits die hard.

They've gone round the back, keeping well clear of Sandra in the office, who's being chatted up by Dazza. A car draws up out front and a burly figure climbs out, dressed in Adidas trackies, Hi-Tec trainers and a West Ham replica shirt, beer gut swinging freely underneath. As he approaches the door, Dazza raps on the wall. The signal.

Mickey Rainsford comes swaggering in. *Mickey Fuckin' Rainsford.*

"Awright, my darlin'? How's the most beautiful gell in Essex, then?"

Sandra looks up at him and raises her eyes to heaven, but his braggadocio is too much to even register her displeasure.

"'He's in the warehouse. Go on through." Serious nail filing recommences. Dazza bungs her the twenty which has been left and off she goes. Doesn't need to be asked twice to piss off down the market for a couple of hours. Once she's gone, Dazza puts on the answerphone and files out the front. Just keeping dog.

*

The door opens into a large, breeze-block lined warehouse. In the corner, a Scania unit sits quiet and dusty. It's been nowhere in ages. Sundry pallets lie scattered across the floor; shredded shrink wrap, long since used litters the oil stained concrete.

"Dave? You here?" he shouts, his voice echoing around the high walls. The door slams behind him and he spins around but it is oh so too late. Jimmy turns the rusty key in the lock and stands four square, facing Mickey. From behind the redundant Scania come Dean, Dave, Kev and Ali.

"What....what's goin down here, then? The fuckin' cavalry?" Fair play, the cunt's got some bottle. From behind him, Jimmy's whacking the starting handle against his open hand. It's making a kind of nice slapping sound, sort of comforting. Unless you're Mickey, that is.

"Calm yourself, Mickey. We want to 'ave a little chat. Friendly like".

Rainsford is having none of this and sizes up the scenario, looking at his options. Back through the door looks the best of a bad job and he lunges at Jimmy, catching him slightly off guard. The punch wings his cheek, knocking him back against the steel door. Jimmy stumbles and Rainsford aims a kick at his bollocks. He knows he's got just a couple of seconds before the others make it across the warehouse floor and on him. He slips on a patch of oil and loses the initiative in one fell swoop. One of those delicious moments, as his other foot leaves the floor and momentarily, the whole lardy arsed body is in mid-air, belly wobbling like jelly. Jellybelly. Jimmy recovers himself and begins to laugh at his would-be assailant, lying in a heap at his feet. Mickey's just lying there now, as the other boys arrive, standing over him. As he looks up, they form a little circle of faces, staring down at their quarry.

"'As anyone hit him yet? Jimmy? Have you assaulted this gentleman in h'any way?" Dean asks, mocking the fallen Mickey with his moody accent. Kev removes and replaces the knuckleduster, smiling a wide, toothy grin at Cuntocks, who is now beginning to regret the rashness of his actions.

"Would you like to come and sit down, Michael? It really is so h'undignified, what with you down there and us up here, what?" Dean squints at him, laughing. Dave has produced the chair and cable ties. He beckons Mickey over, a single curled finger doing the job rather well. The rest of them back away. The initiative is now theirs, but no-one really wants another attempted clump from him. Not really *desired*.

Slowly, he gets to his feet and walks gingerly over to the chair, now placed directly in the middle of the floor. It is more than forty feet to the walls and there is nothing, save shrink-wrap between him and the concrete. He sits down.

"Your hands, Mickey. Give us your hands. Don't want any more excitement, now, do we? Just want a nice, cosy chat". His head is bowed now, his spirit is broken. He offers up his wrists and Jimmy quickly binds them behind his back, wrapping the black industrial cable ties around the metal chair legs, intertwining them around his ankles, just for good measure.

"Nice, Jimmy, nice work. You are a credit to your profession".

"Why thank you, governor". Jimmy replies, tugging at an imaginary forelock, bowing and retreating.

"David, how are we going to approach Mr Rainsford here? He has, after all, transgressed the moral code. We put our faith in him and how does he repay us? Why, with a little 'private enterprise' of his own. A little *smuggling*, I think they call it down Dover way. Why, Michael? Why did you feel the need to express yourself in this callous and selfish way? My partners and I, to be quite frank, feel somewhat cheated by your reckless behaviour. Not cricket, dear boy, not cricket at all".

"My feelings, Dean, I believe are shared with yours. I too, am experiencing sensations of hollowness. To be honest, I feel FUCKING LET FUCKING DOWN BY THIS FUCKING FAT FUCKING CUNT". Dave's fist smashes into the side of Mickey s face, splitting his cheek wide open, each expletive tearing a new gash. Blood and spittle spray through the dank air and down the claret and blue.

"David. I say, that was somewhat rash". Dean is absolutely in charge now and looks around at his boys, revelling in the hunt.

"What you want'?" Rainsford splutters through his broken mouth, tasting free-flowing blood oozing from the split cheek. "Please, it was a mistake".

"A mistake? Mistake, eh? Well whadda mistaka da maka! I don t *whack* like *whack* mistakes". Jimmy's moved in and crashed the starting handle down onto his thighs, timing the blows perfectly with Dave's monologue. Screams of pain are coming from Mickey's bloody mouth now and the others are watching eagerly as he starts the slow downhill progress. Kev is busy with the car battery, wiring it up in full view of Mickey. Ali produces a tool box from the Scania's cab and removes a large commercial Bosch drill, fully charged. He walks back to Mickey and right in front of his eyes, inserts a quarter inch drill bit and tests the power.

"These Bosch drills really do exactly what they say on the box don't you know?" Dean laughs. Kev places the knuckle-duster on the ground and slowly connects the two wires, one to positive, one to negative. He then takes the dirty red wire and winds it round the now bloodied sleeve, placing the exposed copper strands underneath Rainsford's watch. He waves the black wire in front of his maniacal eyes, taunting, mocking. His gloved hands undo Rainsford's belt and pull down his boxers, exposing his tiny, podgy cock. Muted laughter echoes around the warehouse.

"Do I have your undivided attention, Michael? Just nod, if you can? Yes, there's a good boy. Excellent. Now that I *do* have your attention, we just need to clarify a few things, just so that we understand each other fully, if you get my drift. Shortly, I will go to work on you with these tools. As you can see, we have thought of everything, no expense spared. However, before we do that, we need to be sure that you will make recompense for what you have stolen. You see, we are still minus one….new….thirty-eight ton truck and curtain sided trailer. We are also short of a client who is missing his eighteen thousand bottles of brandy and has been put to considerable inconvenience. All for two Mastercartons of fags. Very, very bad move, wasn't it? Now, you have a chance to redeem yourself, Michael. What would you say, if I was to give you a chance to *make good your transgression*? You could, perhaps avoid the considerable inconvenience which I am about to administer to your bollocks. Perhaps you would like to avoid the additional holes which Mr Kev is planning to drill through your knees? I thought so. You see, Michael, we are very concerned that you may feel cheated by us. After all, from the message which you seem to be sending, *loud and clear*, we are not paying you enough. You didn't even know who was paying you, yet you chose to take the unilateral decision to steal from them. From us, Mickey. From your employers. It really is an entirely unacceptable set of circumstances, now isn't it? Now I am reliably informed that whilst you may not be a man of means, you have some rather interesting acquaintances who are, shall we say, minted, to use the vernacular. Now, I and these other gentlemen present, don't give a fuck how you get it, but you, my friend, owe us, big time".

"Anything….anything you want", Mickey spits and splutters, the blood starting to coagulate on his face now. He has his head down and is talking to the floor, anxious to avoid any eye contact with the assembled throng.

"Honest, I didn't know it was your team what owned the firm. I never would've done you. Never would've fucked you over".

"So you would have been happy to have 'fucked someone else over'. Is that what you are saying, Mickey?"

"Yes…no…I..don't know what I mean. I mean…" SMASH. Following the nod from Dean, Kev's knuckle-dustered fist knocks his head right back, almost breaking his neck, splattering nose all over fat, podgy mug. The claret's flying everywhere, a vile concoction of blood and snot. He screams with anguish as Kev goes in again and again, same place but harder. His face is now totally red, his eye sockets filling with tears. Through this surreal, watery vision, he sees Kev intently wiping his blood from the knuckle-duster.

"Look what you've done, you cunt. Made a right fuckin' mess." He looks Mickey straight in the eye, walks around to the other side, then in comes the fist once more, splitting his other cheek wide open, causing a new rivulet of blood to flow freely down his face and onto the now blood soaked Hammers shirt, the soft flesh no match for Kev's beautiful, shiny brass KD. He is crying like a child now, begging for mercy. Kev checks with Dean who gives him the 'one more' signal. He takes a step back, swings his fist around and drives it right into Mickey's open mouth, scattering teeth everywhere. There is a sickening thud as brass meets gums, a sweet echo reverberates around the warehouse as his mouth is split, lips open up like filleted beef and his head slumps forward, oblivion the only release from the thudding pain which fills his battered head. Broken teeth fall from his gaping mouth, mixed with blood and vomit.

"Leave him for a bit, Kev. Looks like he's had enough for now". Dave's gone a bit pale.

Dean walks over to the Scania, leans inside the cab and has a quick toot of the white stuff, which he takes from his jacket pocket. He walks back slowly, licking the back of his hand ostentatiously. He goes right up to Mickey, right close to his face and examines The Gun's handiwork.

"Nice. Very nice, Kev. Blindin'!" He collapses into hysterical laughter as he looks at Mickey's blood soaked eye sockets.

"Can you hear me? Yes? Just nod if you can. Fully understand if you don't want to talk, what with your Hampsteads missin'. Yeah?"

He looks around at the boys. Smiles and laughter greet this little aside. Jimmy's still playing with the starting handle and Kev's cleaning the KD. Ali just looks, licking his lips at the purity of the situation. Sweet, untrammelled violence. He puts on some gloves and wipes the thick blood from Mickey's eyes.

"Hello, again, Michael. Feeling better?" He beckons with his other hand and Dave hands him a jug of cold water, which he throws straight into the broken face. He reels backwards, the icy liquid finding sockets where teeth once were. His screams become a baying howl, desperate for relief from the blinding, thumping, searing pain. Ali is tapping the baseball bat against his gloved hand, making a rather satisfying slapping sound.

"Now, Michael. It's time for some straight talking from you. I get the impression that you understand the gravity of your situation. *The situation*. You owe fifty grand, give or take. Now, as you've seen today, we're reasonable people. Very reasonable. You were lucky that Mr Bold was in a good mood. Just try and imagine if he had got out of bed on the wrong side! Doesn't really bear thinking about now does it?" Mickey's head is moving from side to side, he is frantically trying to ease the pain. It isn't working.

"Now, we're going to drop you off somewhere familiar. You are going to get yourself cleaned up and then you are going to use that big brain of yours to work out how you're going to pay us back the money you've stolen. Hard earned money, Michael. Grafted money. Someone else's money. When you've worked out how you're going to do it and as I said, we don't give a fuck how you get it, or who you get it from, you go and get it. In a week, we'd like a little update, an all points bulletin as to how you're getting on. If we like what we're hearing, then it'll be all well for you. I don't need to cover the alternatives really, do I?"

His face is right up against Mickey's. Despite Ali's immaculate appearance, the loser is having the full benefit of last night's chilli kebab from the close proximity of his mouth. However, that is the least of his worries right now. As he pulls back from Rainsford, he takes a huge swing and the baseball bat meets the seated man's knee on the downward, followed by the sickening thud of breaking bone.

"Cut him free, please Kevin. I think we'll take him in the van. If you would be so kind as to bring his motor-car, James? So kind". Ali backs away, removing the blood soaked gloves and admiring his work.

A terrified face looks up, unrecognisable now.

"You ought to get that looked at, mate", says The Gun as he walks past.

*

There's a rusty old skip at the back of the Grapes in Basildon and that's where Mickey finds himself as he wakes up. In his mouth, he finds his car keys which Jimmy Jag has kindly left for him. Last night's slops and scraps from the pub accompany him in his temporary abode as he awakens. As he removes the bunch of keys which have been crudely inserted from his torn mouth, he raises his head off the piles of foetid waste and rotting food and brings his other hand up to touch his contorted, bruised face. Thankfully, he cannot sense anything of his cut cheeks and broken teeth, but soon the feelings will return and the agony will really begin. He climbs out of the abandoned skip and slowly crawls across to his Mondeo, opens the door and collapses onto the driver's seat. A glance in the mirror confirms his worst fears and he cries like a baby, big, fat tears well up in his puffy eyes and he wails until there is nothing left. Finally, he starts the car and tries to leave the car park, but the pain is too much and he stalls the car, trying to change gear. He fumbles for his mobile and eventually removes it from his bloody trousers.

"Uh, it's Mickey. Fuckin' help me, man. I'm at the Graaa…". He can barely get the words out and tries to send a text, but his fingers are shaking so much that it's just not happening. He slumps over the steering wheel and passes into oblivion. His nose begins to bleed again.

*

"That was fuckin' Mickey's phone. Couldn't tell what the fuck he was on about, but he reckons he's at what I reckon was the Grapes. Sounds like he was on fuckin' drugs or something. Get over there and have a fuckin' butchers, bruv".

*

By the time they get over to the pub, Mickey's passed out, come to and passed out again. The pain is killing him, it's so bad. There is nothing like a good professional hiding and this one's taken a proper one. A lot of the blood has congealed, exposing the true damage which his face and body have endured. He's taken a lot of stick. His nose and one cheekbone have gone, there's a hairline fracture to one eye socket, so the eye's part hanging out and needs some surgery big time. One femur's gone and the other leg's pretty knackered, on account of Ali's knee work. They lift him out and get him slowly into the van.

"Who's done this to you, mate?" The absence of a reply doesn't surprise them one bit and soon they're trying to revive him once more, now fearful for the geezer's life.

"He's well beyond old Struck Off. We're going to have to get him to the hospital, chavvy. Else he won't last the night. We'll have to take our chance with the Old Bill".

See no evil, hear no evil, speak no evil. They get the van going and they're off to A & E.

"When I find out who's done this to him, they're gonna be fuckin' toast. The cunt's only a fuckin' nobody. I don't get it, just don't fuckin' get it".

"Well, this ain't no playground business. This is a proper message. But who's it for?"

"We'll know sooner or later, bruv. Yer mush'll make it. Gonna take him a while, but he'll talk within a couple of days. Meantime, some cunt'll bubble it up. Just keep your fuckin' lugs open".

They're heading down the A13 now, not far to go. Rainsford's moaning like crazy in the back, the pain is kicking him in and out of consciousness and fresh blood is coming from his nose.

"Check him, bruv. He don't look like he's taken a kickin' to the body, but I ain't happy with that claret what's coming out of 'is hooter. He looks proper fucked".

"How can I fuckin' tell? What am I, a fuckin' doctor? Give us a break, bruv. We'll be at the hospital in a mo".

Sure enough, the hospital A&E lights fill the windscreen and they turn in, up to the entrance and straight to the ambulance bay. As soon as they stop, a hospital lackey comes steaming out and tries to stop them.

"Listen, you cunt! We've gotta geezer in 'ere who don't give a monkey's which fuckin' entrance he goes in. He's dyin' an' your coming at me with all the 'you can't stop here' bollocks. Now be a good boy, go and get someone who knows what the fuck's goin' on. With a fuckin' trolley an' all. This fella ain't up for walkin'. Know what I mean? Chop, chop!"

The bloke gets the message, runs off through the glass doors and within a few seconds, out come the team. Fair play, they've got Rainsford out of the van and onto the trolley in no time and off they go, straight to the duty doctor. He's moaning, still switching in and out of reality. The harsh hospital lights really show up the state he's in. They've seen some sights in here, but even the experienced staff look away as the full facial injuries become apparent. They soon ascertain that he's lost all his front teeth, both his cheekbones have gone, the eye sockets have been fucked up by Kev's efficient use of the KDs and both femurs are broken in his legs, plus the knee. The starting handle has really worked its magic and the flesh is split, revealing the smashed bone beneath. As they get him into the A & E cubicle, they are already cutting off his trackie bottoms, one nurse is working on trying to remove some of the caked on claret which covers his face, head and neck. He looks like a one-man war zone. They've already called down a senior surgeon to check him out and it does not look good. The blood is still flowing from his nose, oozing slowly out, indicating far more serious injuries than they can see. The staff look at each other from time to time, their expressions say it all.

"Blood pressure, heart rate dropping. Diamorphine, please nurse. We need to stabilise him before he can go into theatre. He's lost a lot of blood from the thigh injuries. My feeling is that he's got a ruptured vessel in the head which is causing the nasal bleeding. He's going to need a cranial CT scan. Good. The morphine seems to be doing the trick".

The boys have already gone, legged it before the Bill arrive. In the van, they're already on the case.

"It's Freddie. Yeah. Listen, Mickey R's been done. Proper job. He's in the hospital now, in emergency. He don't look too clever, bruv. I've seen some fuckin' sights but this one's been proper sorted. Get Ricky Razors an' Kermit to meet us at the pub. We'll be there in about twenty. An' tell the Guvnor. Cheers".

"Whatcha thinkin'? We ain't going to find nothing now, are we?"

"I ain't havin' it when one of our own takes one. Just ain't happenin'. I'm gettin' straight onto this".

"Do you want me to get the other boys onto this? Someone's gonna bubble something up sooner or later".

"Just fuckin' do it. Double quick, bruv. This needs sorting".

*

Morning brings better news for Rainsford. The nose bleed was caused by a weak vessel in the nasal cavity and by the time he gets a visit from Kermit, he's sitting up in bed and eating his breakfast through a straw. He looks like he's been in a war. Which he has.

Through a series of grunts and hand signals, pen and paper and eye movements, he gets it right across to Kermit who's given him the pasting. He in turn is straight on the horn to Razors and he gets the news to Freddie the Fixer. He calls a mid-day meeting down at the caravan site club in Canvey. It's more of the same, bit of a council of war.

By the time he turns up, his boys are already there.

"What's the latest, Kerm? Is the cunt gonna live?"

"Yeah, sweet. It ain't as bad as we thought. He ain't lookin' too pretty just now, but he'll recover. He weren't no oil painting before this happened so don't reckon his missus'll notice much difference! He ain't happy though. Reckons Bold and his mates have gone soft. Said if it'd been him, he'd have finished the bleedin' work good and proper".

"Any truth in that? I always had Bold down as a proper geezer. He's always got a nice little firm round him. Bit of a flash cunt, but ain't we all?"

The place is starting to fill up and there's a few of the usual faces plotted up around the bar. Major respect all round and the atmosphere's cool.

"Listen, I've got a meet down Woolwich. You boys alright gettin' to the bottom of this little fuckin' scenario? I'll take Kerm with me".

Freddie and Kermit get up to leave and the situation relaxes down a bit. More drinks and the conversation turns to the state of Rainsford and what they would have done under the circumstances.

Behind the bar, Kiera Fletcher listens intently. When it goes quiet, she's on the text to Dawn Murphy. She calls back and Kiera treats her to the reported conversation from the bar.

"They is well disrespecting your boss, Dee. It ain't right. Best tell him". *Click.*

Dawn's Irish blood is close to boiling point as she calls The Lingo man.

"Hello! Ron? It's Dawn here. Dawn from the office. Listen, I don't know what this is all about, but me mate says there's some geezers over Canvey talkin' about Mr Bold. She knows who they are, but she ain't sayin' over the phone. They're in the social club. Yeah, that's the one, by the caravans. Okay, Mister L. I just thought I should tell you. See yous later". *Click.*

*

"Who we meetin', Freddie?"

"Just some geezers from Ilford way. They're connected to the Indian brothers. The pub's theirs but the old man can't put 'is name to it proper 'cos the Church are still beakin' in on him. Reckon they've got a bit of work for us. Trouble is, I've gotta feelin' that's not all they want. I heard from matey that they've got a security problem and our favourite *gangsta* is on the case. Don't be surprised if he turns up on the Harley in his leathers!"

"Just what we fuckin' need today".

"He's on the fuckin' skids an' all. That's why he wants a bit of action there. I heard the cunt's potless".

"Naaaa! He's always got some angle workin'. Tells some blindin' stories an' all".

"An' that's all they are. I was two'd up in Belmarsh last year with some geezer out of Watford way. Reckons the cunt's all front".

"You 'ear some stuff in the shovel, eh?"

"Ninety percent bollocks and the rest of it is total shit!"

As the motor disappears over the QEII bridge, back in Canvey, the boys are getting a bit loose lipped. Kiera is all ears. In the meantime, Ron Language has sent his boy over to earwig the chat. What he hears back, he doesn't like. He's straight on the horn to Dave, full report. Now Dave's suspected Rainsford's connections all along and this is the perfect opportunity for him to raise his profile, put him further up the troughing order with Dean. What passes for a plan, chez the brain of Hilton, begins to take shape.

Chapter Six

Wednesday Morning

Custom House, Lower Thames Street, London. Special Ops Section, Room 315.

Stephen Carmichael stared over his horn-rimmed glasses.

"This operation, Graham, is nothing more than a fucking joke. I told you at the time and I am telling you now, whatever we think about Patrick O'Riordan privately cannot justify the creation of a bottomless pit from which we take huge expenses and achieve precisely nothing. I am not, repeat not, putting my career on the line because of some half-baked suspicions and a highly dubious report from the Newry office. The Good Friday agreement has been hammered out by greater men than you, and the powers that be on both sides of the Irish Pond will want blood if this gets out. I want those people pulled out now, before the shit really hits the fan. I mean, what exactly do you expect to accomplish from this, beyond some wildly egotistical wanking, Graham?"

"The reports we have are substantiated by the C.A.B. in Dublin. Our sources inside say that their own coverts have identified O'Riordan's activities as renewed and re-activated. He is back at it again, and they want to clean up this time. I say we take him ourselves, Stephen. He is, after all, a UK citizen, a dual citizen. We have to have some pay-back for all the piss taking of the past ten years. Surely you can see that. Or are we just going to let him walk all over us, waving his bloody flag and preaching peace and reconciliation. He may have declared peace in South Armagh, but his bloody war against uzz has never stopped". Graham Stubbins' broad Yorkshire had not deserted him in all the years at Dover, Maidstone and Lower Thames Street, nor had his hatred of all things O'Riordan.

"Then let them bloody well get on with it. He's bloody Irish when all's said and done, for God's sake. Let them deal with it and suffer the bloody consequences. You are turning into a one-trick pony, Graham and I can't defend you forever".

"What am I going to do wit' team in Spain then? Just pull them out without a by your leave? Is that what you want? They could be onto something right now and we will just throw it all away". Voices were becoming raised now and in the neighbouring reception office, all conversation had ceased, ears were open and faces were horrified at this unexpected tirade.

"Graham, you're a good officer and I've supported you through thick and thin. You got some good results, granted, but this is 2006, for God's sake. New brooms *are sweeping clean*. Since Broadbent went, we have to be seen to be doing the bloody job properly. I mean, I don't like it any more than you do, but the fact is that the Attorney General just won't support us blind like before. We have to follow procedures".

"Well I say fuck procedures. You know that. I've always been a field man and always will be. I didn't help wit Disruption Protocol just to see it shot out of the sky. If we think they're up to summat, then we should finish 'em off, we're not the bloody police and the CPS".

"But we soon will be. It's not just the name that's changed, Graham. The right to prosecute has gone and it will not come back. There is a burden of proof which we now have to adhere to. It's no good just bringing these prosecutions to court and watching them fall apart. Tony wants results. The press has been very bad since London City Bond and the Allington business. I know we kept a cap on it and the Operation Stockade thing came to nothing, but there is a wind of change blowing through our organisation and we are going to have to present ourselves to the courts differently from now on".

"I still feel we should be doing more to nail the likes of O'Riordan. We bloody *know* he's as guilty as hell".

"But knowing just isn't enough, Graham. Where is the proof? Show me the proof. The cold hard evidence".

"We have been on him for eleven weeks now and I know we're getting close".

"Close. If. Maybe. For God's sake, Graham. If your aunty had bollocks she'd be your uncle".

This momentary lapse into humour deflated the atmosphere, but there was no giving way.

"You pull them out now, Graham. I am no longer going to sign off this Op".

"If that's your final word, then OK. I'll get onto it in the morning. Thanks for your time."

Stubbins filed out of Stephen Carmichael's mahogany panelled office and down the corridor, past the liaison office and down the stairs. As he returned to his own, more modest abode, the mobile rang.

"Graham. Where are you?"

"In my office, Jan. This is an unexpected pleasure".

"That it may be. Could you come up? Alone?"

"Of course. I'm on my way".

"Excellent". *Click*.

He placed the tired, grey Nokia back onto the desk and sat for a moment, the disappointment of the meeting weighing heavy on his mind.

Slowly, he rose to his feet and made his way to the sixth floor.

Janet Weatherall's office lay at the back of Lower Thames Street, with an uninterrupted view of the Thames, Tower Bridge and the South Bank. Below, the comings and goings through the barrier and car park, were clearly visible. It was through here that returning undercover officers would make their way back, to file reports and to be de-briefed. Lunchtime drinkers sat outside the vast Horniman pub by HMS Belfast, carrying on with their idle conversations, blissfully unaware of what was about to take place hidden from view in the dark halls of this very British Lubianka.

Stubbins knocked on the door.

"Come", was the response from within. A deep, but distinctly female voice spoke authority and confidence. As he opened the door, he was met by a seated woman, facing him, the morning sun streaming through a closed window, casting its shadow across the plush carpet. He blinked for a moment, adjusting to the bright light.

"Graham, please forgive the secret squirrel. Coffee?" In the corner, a percolator bubbled away, filling the room with its deliciously dark aroma.

"Thank you. This really *is* an unexpected pleasure".

"Aren't they just the best ones?" She smiled, yet Stubbins could detect a hidden agenda. This was no social intercourse.

"OK. Let's get straight to it", she directs her stare right behind his eyes as she hands him a china cup of steaming Java.

"Your G3 team has been working on the O'Riordan matters. No luck or indeed anything else, I understand. Operationally, as you know, the floor just isn't permitted the resources any longer. However, from our point of view, the time for Mr O'Riordan and his acolytes has come. We have long felt that he has overstayed his welcome in the free world and it's time to swap the Mercedes for a cell. An overview has told us that he has moles in the Newry office, of that we can be certain. One particular Grade 9 was of considerable interest to us and we had been monitoring him for some time. Sadly, Birmingham had him for one of their MTIC operations and he's now doing some time on the mainland. That operation has seriously undermined coverts in the whole of Northern Ireland. Good result though it may have been for disruption, it has put us back a long way".

Stubbins' attention span has just gone up about a million percent. He never gets to hear of such things and cannot believe his good fortune.

"This is precisely the sort of problem we have been experiencing for too long. Small, local operations crashing into each other, petty jealousies and empire building, resulting in the square root of fuck all. Communications are still being conducted using so-called internal email and how secure are they? O'Riordan can afford to pay a high price for his information and he is *always ahead of the game*. From today, I am personally taking over this operation. Officially, what you have just been told stands and you are to pull out your team. I am correct that you have been informed of the department's decision regarding 'Watchtower'?"

"That is correct, yes. I've just come straight from the Carmichael. I am to contact the team leader and get them out".

"So a little voice has just told me".

"Good God, you were quick!"

"Hmm. I would like your views on the individuals. Do you feel they have been compromised in any way? Are they experienced enough? Any weak links?"

"You'll know that I am very supportive of all my obs teams, ma'am. I don't like to undermine, but at the same time, I feel that an expansion of the team would be beneficial".

"Good answer, Graham, but who are the weak links?" She grinned at his discomfort.

"I feel that Loader and Meacher need a little more experience. The other two are coming on in leaps and bounds. They don't shirk the shitty bits and the reports I have received back from them suggest that they are doing their best despite everything. Long hours for little reward".

"So they're good journeymen, is that what you are telling me?"

"More than that, I feel. A lot more than that. They've had very little to go on and very little to play with. Years ago, we would have sent them into Newry to liaise, but the mere sight of UK based officers over there now and they're screaming interference. They're more interested in the value of their bloody houses these days".

"Nevertheless, we are still getting good intelligence on cross-border obs. However, as well you know, the old army watchtowers are coming down shortly and then we will lose a hugely valuable source of information. We will need to increase our ground-level activities if we are going to have any hope at all. This, Graham, is where you and your team come in. You see, what we are proposing is a formal end to Operation Watchtower. Disband the team, close the file. Your Torrevieja team will be transferred officially to other departments and that will be that. I will control the team from this office and you will commence the new day to day activities from downstairs. Your own office is to be re-decorated, which will keep the gossip to a minimum. We know there is a leak from within here but that is not the priority for the moment. Hand-picked personnel will be involved from now on. It's going to be a lot more hours, Graham".

"I honestly don't think I'll be missed at home. Since she discovered line-dancing, that's been it. Tried to get me to go once but it was half-hearted. She's never at home any more. To be quite honest, ma'am, it's time to move on".

"I need total commitment on this one. The meeting's scheduled for half-term week. That'll sort out the committed from the passengers".

Weatherall's unmarried status allowed her considerable leeway, though her partner's hours dictated that their time together was at best organised à la ships in the night. She liked it that way. Devotion to the job.

"What is going to happen with the boss? He's going to want to move me onto other projects now. Bound to be some paper that needs shuffling".

"It's not you who needs to be concerned. Greater men than you and I have decreed that there is to be new liaison with Europe, following the successes of early 2000. He is going to be heading up the Brussels liaison office, with immediate effect. Before you ask, yes, he does know. I expect he was going to let you know sometime". This open ended throwaway remark stung like fresh nettles. Eight years of trusted work and he found out the second hand way. Calm, Graham, calm. She deliberately looked down, allowing him a private interlude of reflection.

"I don't need personalities jockeying for position on this either. No room for egos any more in this service. We had that in London City Bond and look where it got us. It took me six years to even get noticed. Six years of reports and intelligence and I am overridden by some out of town hic who 'knows what he's doing'. That style is gone, Graham. The question is, can we leave it behind too? Can you leave it behind?"

"I really want to be in on this one, Jan. I have been waiting to see some heads roll for a long time. I cannot think of one area of the law that O'Riordan has not flouted. He laughs at us, waits for us to move, then his lawyers tie us up for years. Next thing, he returns to work and all the time, he's giving us the single fingered salute".

"I cannot deny, Graham, that it will be dangerous. The intelligence we have from the Armed Forces is good, but we have no real idea to what extent his empire extends. For the moment, your operatives are getting nowhere, because we are not close enough to him. We lack resources, so now we take the fight to him, instead of watching and waiting. The team will have twenty-four hour support from right here. The office next door is being turned into ops HQ and there will be two co-ordinators on at all times from the Maidstone office working three shifts a day, making a total of six. They have all been checked and identified as kosher. Your obs team will increase to thirty, based in Armagh, London, Alicante and Antwerp. We are maintaining the same name, Operation Watchtower. Officially, it will have been disbanded, but it will save the allocation of a new Op name, with all the extra attention that might bring. Back burner stuff. I am not having something as basic as that buggering everything up. As far as the rest of the service is concerned, No 10 has called off all obs on O'Riordan and the rest of the former boyos. Good Friday has won".

"When am I going to move?"

"For now, we will let the waters settle. Say nothing to the Boss. He will move tomorrow, which is why your meeting with him today was sadly a gimme. Keep your mobile on tonight". Weatherall looked down at her papers again, indicating that the meeting was at an end.

"Thank you, ma'am". As he got up to go, she stood, extending her strong hand toward his.

"And Graham, don't take it personally, yah?"

He filed out, quietly. His thoughts were very mixed as he left the room. *Mixed up*. He felt like he'd been given a ringside seat to the biggest match of the year. He was going to be involved, granted, but how much? Weatherall was the flavour of the moment. There was no doubt about that. The kind of money she was talking about for the Operation was like nothing he'd ever witnessed before in his entire career. He was used to running things on the back of a fag packet and this was, frankly, too much. He walked quickly down the steps and to the main lift. Seconds later, he was out in the open air, standing next to the fag-break brigade. Most of them young, girls and boys fresh out of some university that used to be a polytechnic in his day, equipped with degrees in underwater basket weaving, seduced by the excitement of a life in the church. Puffing away on the old Marlboro' Lights, dressed in black, getting paid less than twenty clap a year. Across the road, the successful graduates are already on around a hundred, working for brokers. Tomorrow's jealousy just brewing nicely. Just wait till you discover the whole system's against you, he mused. He looked at them, looked at himself. The tweed jacket, the faded trousers, the down at heel brogues. He was a dinosaur and he knew it. Knew his time was up. He looked up at the sky, could feel the melodrama washing over him, then even that was bored and moved on. Slowly, he walked back in through the main entrance, his head bowed, yet something made him return to his office, to keep going. Was it desperation?

*

The last few minutes of Graham Stubbins' life had not gone unnoticed. Convenient. All too convenient. The curtain fell back and the watcher watched no more. For now. He did not suspect a thing.

Chapter Seven

Canvey. Dean's boat "Benissa Costa" October 2006

Dean's called a meet. When Dean calls a meet, everyone turns up. He's been supporting the boys for a long time now and in their eyes, he walks on water. He never fails to remind them of this and lately, those reminders have become one hell of a lot more frequent.

The cars arrive in Canvey Marina, park up and the occupants walk the twenty or so yards to 'Benissa Costa', Dean's pride and joy. The Sunseeker cost him an arm and a leg. Bought it from some geezer who had it in St Katherine's Dock in the 1990s and got burned by his little spread-betting habits. The Dock was a bit too posh and a bit too far for Dean, so he had it shipped along the Essex coast to Canvey, bought the house and that was it. Sorted.

One Language, Dave, Jimmy Jag, Ali the Coat, Shotgun Kev, Mick the Teeth and bringing up the rear, Town Hall. With Dean, it's the full gallon. Time to formalise things. One by one, they walk the plank onto the rear deck and inside. This is strictly business. There's four cases of Stella in the fridge, two sleeves of Estonian Superking Blacks on the table, one notepad and one very determined Dean Reginald Bold.

"Besides this gentleman 'ere, you all know each other. For those of you who don't know who he is, I'd like you all to meet Stevie Hall". Dean makes a meal of pronouncing the 'H', laughing as he goes.

"Everyone calls 'im Town, as in Town Hall".

Some of the others eye him up and down with great suspicion. Dean's never done this before, bring a new geezer into a meet. A proper meet. There are rumblings.

"Now, Town's given me some ideas. Blindin' ones as it goes. Seems we got to get organised, gentlemen. It's all got very, very sloppy. You all know about the little problem we 'ad with Cuntocks in Dover. Well he's gonna be eatin' his Christmas dinner through a fuckin' straw and that goes for anyone else who's got any bleedin' clever ideas about private enterprise. You know what I'm sayin'?"

Dean pauses and looks around the room. Some heads are low, others staring him right in the eye. A smile plays around Ali's lips. Dave is shuffling about, not really knowing what the fuck to do just now.

From under the table, Dean produces a small, black Uzi sub-machine gun, looks at it for a moment and places it calmly and quietly on the desk, taking his time. He looks up, expressionless and with narrowed eyes.

Gasps of air are expelled, faces widen, eyes sparkle, throats run dry.

"For fuck's sake, Dean. What the fuck is that all about?" Dave's face is a study. Baseball bats, knuckle dusters, knives, fair enough, but shooters?

Dean remains silent, watching, waiting, *checking*.

On his left is Ali. Face isn't moving a muscle. A born soldier, a *capo*, the trusted one.

Town Hall. Sitting back, avoiding anyone's gaze. The interloper.

Mick. Hard man. The face that took a thousand punches. And still knocked the other cunt out. Ready for action.

Jimmy. Ditto. Swallowing hard, but the sharp suit was a skin, ready to be shed at any moment. Recovering already.

Dave. Reeling. Dave'll be alright. He always is. Dean's right hand man.

Language. A trickle of sweat runs down from temple to cheek. His eyes haven't left Dean's.

Shotgun. Curiosity. Hunger? Desire! That's it! *Desire.*

"I'm not much for words, mate. Give me a balaclava and a sawn off and I'm right at fucking home. When do we start?" Shotgun's smile lights up the room.

"Like your style, Kev. At least I know who's with me, bruv".

"Mate, we're all with ya. Just a bit of a shock, that's all."

"I think this is for protection, Mr Dean. Yes?" Ali looks directly at Dean, his face on one side, always the diplomat, always the politician.

"We've sent out a powerful message this week. Town's proposals, and I say *proposals*, involve something of a new direction for us. You might call it a diversification of core business activities. It is time we moved on from small time swerves, a few MCs here and there. We are talking big pay-days. The risks are the same, the rewards ten, twenty, a hundred times what we have had. We are moving up. Are you in? Are you with me?"

No-one wants to be the first to ask the obvious question. There is a murmuring at the table. Dave whispers to the nervous Language whilst the noise levels are up,

"He's been watchin' too many fuckin' Hollywood films. Lost the fuckin' plot". Lingo barely nods in agreement, but the sound of the pound has him right focussed. However, he makes a mental note of Dave's comment. Stores it for later.

"Right. Down to business, then. We are talking, gentlemen, something which we have been avoiding for too long. It appears some of our *competitors* have been getting a bit busy with the old powder game. We think the *swerve*'s had its day. The new rules are making it fuckin' impossible to make a crust. The boys moved in, the boys are movin' out. This time, we're movin' with them. Chance meetin' of Town's has resulted in a little 'opportunity' for Bold Inc. He reckons we can by-pass the usual routes and go straight in at the top. He's got the selling sorted 'ere. Over to you, mate".

"Thanks, Dean. I know this sounds a bit heavy, but these opportunities are rare".

Dave's looking hard at him.

"Listen, bruv, I'm not being funny or nothing but what do you need us for? If it's that fuckin' easy to get in, why don't you do it on your Jack Jones?"

"Good question. Thing is, I ain't got the haulage and I deffo don't have the experience. I can buy and I can sell, but not at these levels. I'm short on funding and short on quantity. This fella in

Spain has what we need to start".

"And what's the problem with his current scenarios, then?" Jimmy puts his five eggs in at this point.

"New plans, new players".

"Does he want to be robbed again?" Now it's the Coat's turn. Trust him. He's smiling that special smile. "Just kidding, innit. But we're not being set up, are we?" He laughs and claps his hands together.

"He's a big player. Pukka gaff an' all. His straight business is worth a fortune, never mind what else he's got. There's something about the geezer. Bit of a one off".

"Cheers, Town. Everyone clear? Any objections? Not that I'm gonna listen, you lot, but, as chairman of this meetin', I gotta ask; know what I'm sayin'?" Dean thumps the table with the flat of his hand, looks around and sits down.

"Get the Stellas movin' bruv," he looks at Dave and the group breaks up for a breather. Cigs light up and a couple of them go up on deck.

Town's left sitting at the dining table.

"Bit of suspicion there, bruv. Not so sure it was exactly a resounding success. Dean looks down at him, Stella in hand.

"Bollocks, mate. Blindin' job. They ain't all as quick off the bleedin' mark. Sometimes, you gotta spell it out. I'll lead, they'll fuckin' follow. If they don't want to, they know what they can fuckin' do an all". He thumps Town Hall on the back and grins.

Up on deck, Jimmy Jag and Ali the Coat are huddled together.

"It's a right fuckin' move up the ladder for us, no mistake, bruv. Is he sure? Ah mean, we're a small outfit, ain't we? We're talkin' fuckin' premier league business. We ain' got no room for passengers".

Kev joins them, roll-up dangling from his gnarled fingers.

"Your thoughts, Mr Shotgun?" Ali looks him right in the eye.

"I'm not much for all that talkin'. Now give me a balaclava and a sawn off and I'm right fuckin' at home...." Kev's voice trails off and is replaced with a wide, toothy grin.

"I'll take that as a yes then Kev. As usual". Ali's eyes are everywhere, watching, observing, *looking for clues*. A little gesture here, a nervous flicker there. He knows what he's looking for, done this for years, just can't see it yet. Mick the Teeth and One Language are at the other end of the boat, out of earshot. They are having an in depth toe-to-toe, but the noise of the other craft on the water is too much. Ali's focused and making mental notes by the score. The Lingo's making hand gestures and Mick's responding in kind. Dave's still down below and Jimmy's hanging over the side, taking deep drags off his Superking. Old habits. All dealing with the news in their own little ways.

Dean shouts from below and they file back into the main cabin.

"OK, chaps. Any thoughts? Or are they beyond you?" His welcome back is greeted with a torrent of abuse and a couple of empty Stella cans being banged together in his general direction. He's in a good mood, he's got his boys around him and it doesn't get much better than that.

"Who is guaranteeing the loads? Not us, Dean, please tell me it's not us". The fruits of Jimmy's thinking become obvious and everyone's eyes are on Dean now. It's getting serious.

"I am". You could have heard a fucking pin drop. This is the moment, thought Dean. Are they with me, or are they out on their own?

"I'm putting me own scratch into this. We've got tank and it's fuckin' time we used it. I've bin making fuckin' millions for likely cunts from 'ere to fuckin' Hackney and I've ad it up to here with their fuckin' whinging and whining. We've got the haulage, the customers", he nods at Town Hall, who is barely concealing his glee at Dean's impassioned delivery, "and now we've got the fuckin' product. Proper, Mother of Fucking Pearl 92% if we want go that far. We ain't gonna wholesale, neither. Oh, no. Town here's gonna see to that. We are talkin' seventeen grand a key in Spain, fuckin' thirty-two ere and a ton on the streets, via our good friend Mr Hall. We're startin' small, abart twenty keys, and build it up, nice and slow like. My intention, is to go right to the fuckin' top. You're all in, if you want. But if you do want in, it's today or never. I ain't waitin for no-one".

"But are you sure about this geezer in Spain?"

"I'm goin' over on the weekend, ain't I? See what he's all about. Town reckons his gear's blindin' and judgin' by the little tasters I've had, he ain't fuckin' jokin', know what I'm sayin'?" He sniffs a bit and laughs.

"In fact, it's about time you lot sampled his wares". He reaches into a holdall and brings out a bag the size of a house brick and dishes it up right in front of them on the table. There must be half-a-key there.

You could have cut the atmosphere with a knife. These boys have been around a bit, but what with Dean being new to the game and all that, this is a bit OTT.

"Fuckin' stroll on, bruv. You makin' some kinda statement?" Jimmy's eyes are like saucers, while Town just sits there, grinning like a bleeding Cheshire cat.

"I want it all, boys. The fuckin' whole shebang. I've had the calculator out and we are going large. Supersize. We've had a few results in the swerve game, but we ain't gonna make the big league on that no more. The smart dough's going back on the hooter game and this time, we're in an' all. Biggest fuckin' growth market this country's ever seen. They're all at it. Fuckin' city, West End and all points in between. Fuck me, there's guys makin' more money on the side serving bugle than dealin' on the fuckin' futures market. And we, gentlemen, are goin' to supply them. Ron, how's your brother getting on down the big house?" Ron's been very quiet so far, just listening and learning. Some of them are thinking he's up to something and are blanking him a tad.

"Bit quiet, like. Nothing' like it was, mate. It's mostly legit work now".

"Still doing his old job, yeah?"

"Yeah, he's doin' Docklands and Tilbury. Barking's gone dead".

"Might need a little word in his shell like, yeah?"

"Just say the word and I'll get him along to a meet. No worries. Listen, Dean, I need a word. Just heard something you might wanna listen to".

"Later, matey, later. Now is the time to fuckin' party!"

Ron's anxious face is lost amongst the raving madness which is growing throughout the group. He slips away unnoticed. He looks at Dave, any sign of recognition, but he's gone an' all. Planet Zanussi for Dave.

Dean's chopping up the charlie and makin' some monster lines. The boys are all in and taking turns at trying out the merchandise. Couple of lines each, like, just to get the party going. The volume level's gone right up and someone's put the sounds on. Dean loves his Bose and soon, a nice bit of R&B is filling the boat. Tasteful, like.

"Blindin' bit of gear, Town. Fair play to ya". Town Hall's credibility is going right up and the boys are already looking for more. Dean's straight back in the trough and their all lining up for *just a leedle beet more, señor*.

"This is the quality we're talkin' about, boys, none of your cut to fuckin' ribbons with your mum's fuckin' baking powder lark. This is PROPER!" Dean's striding round the boat now, waving his can of Stella in the air.

"It's time to move on. Onwards and fuckin' upwards. Are we on, boys?" Bedlam breaks out and they're all screaming and shouting, dancing like nutters. Dean looks at his little firm. The boys. Proper geezers. Even old Ron, Look at him, the silly old cunt, raving like some fuckin' teenager on a Saturday night, his slicked back hair shining in the setting sun.

"Jimmy! I say, James! JAMES!" Jimmy Jag's only dancing round the pole holding up the deck. He's giving it some, make no mistake and the boys are laughing and clapping as he fucks it with all his might. Dean's trying to get his attention but he's far gone, he's luvvin it, luvvin it, luvvin it. The music changes and then Mick's on the case, swinging round the thing, almost pulling it off the ceiling. Dean puts his arm around the Jag and shouts in his lug,

"Any er your limos around today?"

"Yes, mate, the ten seater's just come back from some race meetin' up north. Just got it cleaned up".

"Sorted. Get it over 'ere, soonest. Fill it up with some champers an' all. Ali, get on the fuckin' blower an' get some brasses over 'ere. The boys is goin' on tour".

Total mayhem now. More charlie appears and they're all off on planet fucking Large. Dean's gone into Top Cat mode and he's issuing orders all over the gaff. Ali's *other family business* is the provision of sophisticated young ladies for dinner and functions. Or is that *fucktions*, one might ask? He's getting the girls sorted and Jimmy's checking the Cristal is on board the limo. Somebody's definitely pulled Mick's chain – he's come right out of his shell and is trying to break-dance in the middle of the rear deck, hat still on.

*

An hour later and it's all happening in the stretch. Ali's had them picked up on the way to the marina so when the boys climb in, they're treated to the finest show in town, in the form of six half-naked girlies of all nationalities sipping champagne. They're giggling like fuck and by the time Dean's got the charlie out and about, the party's in full swing. Two of them go into entertainment mode, giving *very close* lap dancing to each of the boys in turn and one of the girls gets a bit excited and starts licking the other one's fanny right out. She responds by pulling her arse cheeks apart and then it's a free for all. One mass of drinking, snorting, licking, shagging, dancing bodies. And they haven't even got through Barking.

"Where we goin', darlin'?" asks a pretty redhead, her mouth pulled momentarily away from Town's bulging cock.

"Up West" was the reply. "We're on tour, love. Play your cards right and you're with us all fuckin' night! Big pay-day! Just keep your laughin' gear round that and you won't go far wrong!" He pushes her head back down onto his cock again and she's soon noshing away happily.

*

"Listen, love, I've left them to it. I ain't into all that no more. I'd sooner get down on me little boat. I'll be home soon. Just got a bit of business to take care of".

Ron's away and down towards Canvey town, into the pub and up to the bar, where Dawn and Keera are waiting for him.

"Alright, gells? Get yourselves a drink, have whatever you want and we'll sit down, all nice and quiet like, over in the corner. And you can tell Uncle Ron all about it".

Keera fills him in on the conversation which took place in the caravan site club. Ron, as always, the loyal Ron listens intently, nodding from time to time as he takes it all in. The girls chatter away the more involved he becomes and within a few minutes, he's got all he needs. He buys them another drink, just to be sociable, like and then he's away too, home to ponder his next move, knowing that the mayhem in the limo is not going to give up any semblance of order till the morning. In the meantime, he starts to draw up a plan of action. And when Ron L draws up a plan of action, you so, just so do not want to be on the end of it.

*

The boys are lying back, necking down the champagne as the car arrives at the Café de Paris. Dean's had Ali phone ahead to speak to his mates who own the place and as the stretch pulls right up into Leicester Square, the doors are opened by two massive, built like brick shithouse security guys with earpieces and Hollywood biceps. The girls spill out onto the pavement, all heels and tits and the whole lot of them, the whole shebang are escorted downstairs before there's a fuckin' riot. Inside, the place is jumping and Dean's straight into the Laurent Perrier Rosé, a dozen bottles thereof for the drinking. They're straight off to the VIP area once the nifties start flying. The manager says a quick hello and makes a quick withdrawal. Total professional. Knows when to play, knows when to quit. It's champagne all the way for an hour or so, then it's off to Fedenzi's and total fucking oblivion.

Chapter Eight

Canvey

"He's confusing me, Dave. I don't even recognise him no more". Dave and Gina-G are sitting in Corks Wine Bar in Canvey. She's wearing shades and a dark, uncharacteristically sober trouser suit, little corset underneath, her hair's up in a pineapple. Gina stilettos complete the picture. Dave is desperately nursing a *monster hangover.*

"Come off it, darlin'. You've known him long enough. It's why you love him. It's why we all love him. He's just Dean".

"Maybe for you, Dave. You're a bloke. You don't see what I see. He fuckin' scares me now. It's like I'm the only one who sees it in the house. Bee's the apple of his bleedin' eye and Troy's never there no more. Just spends his time with his posh mates from that school. She flutters her eyelashes at her old man and he gives her a new motor. What's that all about, Dave? We ain't had sex for months".

Dave's delight at this news is muted by the tears rolling down Gina's face, long rivulets of waterproof mascara forming black streaks as she pours out her heart to him.

"Steady on, babes. Yer'll be alright in a mo. Here, dry your eyes". He hands her a napkin from the rack on the table. Real gent is our Dave.

"I'm sorry. Really I am. I just don't know who to turn to. It's like everyone don't believe me. Sorry, Dave, I know you see him for what he is. I hope he's gonna be different when we go to Spain". It was as if she had become smaller, her shoulders hunched, her head bowed. He had never seen her like this before. He was shaken at the effect Dean's behaviour was having on a woman who had always known how to handle him.

"Let me talk to him, babes. Come on, don't let this get in the way". He takes Gina's hand in his and holds her tight.

"I'm sorry, Dave, but I just can't do this. Not with him like he is. It's just not right, darlin'. You will talk to him, won't ya?"

Dave has never had such an incentive to do anything. He's just about to lose his bit on the side and he is so cuntstruck by Gina and her 'little ways' that he is so going to sort this one.

"Course I will, babes, course I will. Let's have something to eat, then you'll be alright. Come on, chin up, gell".

Dave calls the waitress over and orders some pasta and wine. She gives them the once over and is privately horrified that people of 'their age' even get upset. What could they be doing with each other anyway?

Gina sips her Chardonnay and stares out of the window, over the Thames and out towards the estuary.

"What…what does this mean for us, babes?" Dave's gone all doe-eyed.

"Dave, are you on something? You ain't on that bleedin' charlie as well, are ya?"

"What do you mean, sweets?"

"I mean, you're askin' me about *us*. You stupid bastard, there ain't no us without him, is there? How long would you bleedin' last without him, eh?"

"You sayin' I'm thick or something?"

"I ain't sayin' that. The only thick thing about you is ya cock, lover!" She shrieks with laughter and the atmosphere changes. "We gotta keep him straight, keep him happy, or there ain't gonna be no future for no-one".

"That's what I'm sayin'." He's suddenly woken up to the fact and is now jumping firmly on Gina-G's bandwagon. How often do you have to hear that from some idiot who's just caught on? Congratulations, Dave.

"Between us, we're with him most of the bleedin' day. Somehow, we need to cut his little habit down. He's spendin' more time with that Hall fella these days and I'm sure he's dealin' him. He says it's just recreational, but I don't see no fuckin' roundabouts". Dave's grinning at her little jokes.

"You ought to be on the radio with that type of stuff".

"D'ya think so, Dave? Aaahhh! Yar a lovely man". She leans across and touches his hand, strokes it, then runs her long nails up and down his wrist. He's looking at her, enthralled and she returns the favour by running her tongue over her heavily glossed lips. So provocative. Poor Dave's got the horn big time now and he's squirming in his seat.

"Down boy. Eat your food". The timely arrival of the waitress, complete with more Chardonnay and two plates of carbonara, keeps Dave from losing it completely and he pours some more cool wine into Gina's nearly empty glass. As soon as the girl has gone, she's slipped her foot out of the Gina four inch heel and started massaging Dave's leg, working her way up and up until she is running it over his swollen crotch. He looks down at the perfectly pedicured red painted wiggling toes and he's desperate. Desperate for her now, but she's just playing with him. It turns her on to see him squirm. She wants his big, fat cock so badly, but he's going to have to wait. It's going to be a little different this afternoon. No more fumbling in the car. Today, it's the Holiday Inn on the A13 and fuck the consequences. Dean's back at the office and Ron? He's gone to a meet in Dartford, at the Stakis. Oh, yes, she loves it when a plan comes together. A stray trickle runs down over her chin and she gathers it up on a manicured finger, then licks the double cream slowly and deliberately. Dave is total putty now, there is one part of his body that is oh, so hard, the rest is like jelly. She can feel wetness emerging onto the tiny gusset of her La Perla thong. Dave's trying to eat, but his mind is totally dominated by thoughts of Gina's soaking panties. Slowly, she slips her fingers down inside the waistband and scoops a dollop of love-juice from deep within. She brings them out and slowly draws them up to her lips, gradually opening them so that he can see the stringy liquid between. Her tongue is out again and gently licking the musky juices. He is transfixed now, begging for some affirmation of later. He reaches across for her hand, takes it and brings it to his lips, the aromas wafting, driving him wild. He licks them, licks every drop, taking each finger in turn and lovingly cleaning as he goes. His cock is bursting against the tight suit.

"What are we having for dessert, Dave?" she looks him straight in the eyes.

"Oh, babes, it's got to be you, ain't it?" All the time, she is eating the creamy pasta sauce, tongue flicking, taking alternate sips from the ice-cold Chardonnay. She's quite pissed now and feeling very heady. All the worries of Dean are gone for both of them. Her libido has taken hold and she is desperate to feel Dave's cock pounding her cervix. Her heart is racing and her hands are shaking.

"Shall I get the bill, sexy gell?"

"I thought you'd never ask, big boy. Just leave 'em a nifty and let's fuck off".

He extracts a crisp new £50 from his wedge and chucks it into the ashtray. She slips her strappy Gina back on and they're up. The waitress, and indeed most of the staff have witnessed this seduction and they're amazed it's taken this long. Don't miss a fucking thing, waitresses. You think no-one's spotted you. Forget it. They all know. Trust me.

She's got her hot hand in his and in no time they are in the car. Dave reaches for her crotch, but she moves his hand back to the gear lever.

"I've gotta little surprise for you, big boy. Take me to the Holiday Inn, James and DON'T spare the horses". She shrieks at her attempt to *do posh*.

"Awright!" Dave's fumbling with the keys now and eventually gets the motor into gear and away. The journey to the hotel takes a lifetime, yet in reality, they are there in under ten minutes. Clever girl's already pre-paid the room on a credit card and in no time, they've dispensed with the 'Welcome to the Holiday Inn, Basildon' bollocks and they're in. Now, statistics will tell you that the average couple has sex within five minutes of closing the door behind them. She's got his flies undone and his fat cock in her mouth inside ten seconds. Go, Gina, go! The roles are reversed now and she's on her knees, going at it like a steamhammer. He collapses onto the bed and hits his head on the 'All Day Breakfast' menu, followed by the complimentary towels. He is so far gone, he could have hit it on a brick and would still be pushing against Gina-G's throat. He's getting her jacket off, then pulls down her corset, exposing magnificent tits, nipples erect. They stand for a moment, ripping clothes off and throwing them all over the room. Then they are naked, hot and rampant and back on the bed. The kids have made no impression on Gina's size ten figure and her belly ring looks as good now as it did when Dean paid for it all those years ago. Dave leans down and removes her tiny silk thong with his teeth which brings hilarious laughter from her. As the wispy gauze slides down her dark, tanned thighs, he gasps at the sight of her smooth, waxed crotch.

"Babes, when did you get that done?" His heart is racing, can't take his eyes off the exposed puffy pink labia in all their glory.

"Done it yesterday. All for you, darlin'. Be amazed if he sees it before the weekend". She opens her legs wide and pulls up her thighs, giving him a real eyeful. "See anything you like, Mister Henry Higgins?" She gives it a real Eliza Doolittle, dipping her middle finger right inside and wiping it across Dave's mouth, driving him wild.

"Fuck me, babes, I really need it". Dave goes to his jacket and removes a condom packet.

"Sod that. I want it all. I wanna be filled up. It's been so long". She's playing with herself, rubbing her clit fast and furious. Dave leans over her and puts his engorged cock against her and eases himself in. She is really wet and just sucks him in effortlessly as he starts to pump her. They are at each other like animals, her nails are tearing at his shoulders, his back and his arse. His mouth is over hers and their tongues are flicking in and out, licking each other. He moves to her tight breasts and rhythmically sucks her hard nipples, all the time ramming his cock deeper and deeper into her. A mobile is ringing somewhere, but they are too far gone. His desperation overtakes him and he pulls out, burying his head between her thighs and plunging his tongue deep between her soaking lips. He works her, lapping hungrily at her juices, covering his face with them. She is moaning with pleasure, desperate to cum. He alternates between clitoris and labia, his index finger is inserted in her anus, pressing hard on the prostate, driving her wild. He can feel her rising, her tanned, waxed thighs are pressing hard against his shoulders, her hands grasping the headboard.

"Hardaaah, hardaaah, HARDAAAH!" She's screaming at him now, her hands pulling at his hair, begging him to finish her off. From somewhere, he finds just a little more pressure and she's there. Her whole body shakes, racked with her earth-shattering orgasm, every downward flick of Dave's tongue gives her another and another. She is screaming out loud, "Lick me, fuck me". He keeps the pressure on and without warning, a gush of warm fluid covers his face, followed by another and another. The bed is soaked, and still the hot gush squirts out. He pulls back and watches with awe as she continues to ejaculate over the bed. Her screams turn into laughter, happy, fulfilled almost hysterical laughter. Dave is overcome with desire for her and plunges his engorged cock back into her gaping cunt. She just sucks him in easily and he fucks her hard, up to the hilt.

"You sure about this, gell?" Dave's exhilarated and frightened at the same time.

"Just fuck me, babes. Fill me up, pleeeeese!" Dave's going at it hard now and she can feel the pre-cum oozing from his bursting helmet. She digs her fingernails into him, drumming her feet on his calves as he unloads his spunk deep into her.

"Fuck me, FUCK ME!" He is pushing harder and harder, then he is done. He collapses on her, covering her body with his. Their arms are around each other, holding on tight. She begins to cry. He rolls off and takes her in his arms, protecting her. From her world.

After a while, her crying ceases and he passes her a tissue from the box at the bedside and she wipes her eyes.

"Oh, Dave. What the hell are we gonna do? I mean, what if he finds out? He'll bleedin' kill the both of us. I am so frightened".

"It's a bit late to be frightened, babes. Ah mean, we can call it a day, if you want but I don't think that's on the fuckin' agenda, is it?"

"Oh, Dave, it's bin lovely, but I'm not sure I can carry on. I mean, I've got me family, you and all. I've got to get me feet back on terra cotta firma, ain't I?"

"If that's what you want, babes, then that's what it'll have to be." They hold each other tight, cling together like two lost babes in the wood. Outside, the storm clouds are gathering. It's going to be a heavy one.

Eventually, and it would never be long enough, they have to rise from the bed and get back to reality.

"We'll have to cool it. Give it a brake for a bit. Maybe it'll all work out. I know you lot have got a lot of work on. I hear him on 'is mobile. Deal this, don't deal that. I ain't stupid, Dave, I know you're gettin' into some heavy shit, an' don't tell me you're not". She starts to cry again, for herself, for Dean, for Dave, for God knows who.

"It ain't what you think, princess. Nothing like you think. It's just Dean, you know how he likes to brag".

"Oh, please! I'm his bleedin' trouble, for fuck's sake. I've known him since we was kids, just like you, Dave Hilton. I know everything about the man".

Dave's sitting there with his head in his hands. *If only you did, gell, if only you did.*

"He worries about all of us, you know, G. I know he don't show it, but he's always talkin' about you. Drives the boys bleedin' mad, he does".

"Huh! The boys. You're like some bleedin' playground gang, the way you lot carry on. Who do you think you are anyway?" The tears are flowing down her cheeks now; she doesn't even know what she's saying.

"That's enough, love. He wouldn't want to hear you talk like that. He is the father of your kids and all. He just has his ways".

"What, like killing people I suppose?" Thank God Dave's looking at the window away from her as the stark realisation hits him. Where the *fuck* did that one come from? He digs his fingernails into the palms of his hands and turns around.

"Now where on earth did you hear that one? Someone been tellin' porky pies? Who's bin fuckin' bubblin' that fuckin' rubbish up?" His face has changed now, no longer the genial Dave. He's boiling mad.

"Tell me! TELL ME!"

"No-one, Dave. No-one at all. I...er...I...just heard him on the 'phone the other night. They was talkin' about some geezer what had it comin' to him. Something like that".

"Who was talkin'? Who, Gina?"

"I don't know. You'll have to ask him. I'm all confused now". Dave looks long and hard at the weeping Gina, she's sitting back on the bed now, all the bravado of earlier has gone. His relief is tangible, but he's not giving the game away.

"Just you mind you keep your trap shut. We don't want that kind of talk getting' about!"

She looks up at him, tear-stained but still pretty. There is begging in her eyes. Begging for forgiveness. She knows she's overstepped the mark.

"I won't, Dave, I promise. You know I'd never say nothing. I know the rules."

"So why are you offing him to me, you daft mare?"

"I...I...just thought, that's all".

"Well don't. Leave that to people who know what they're doing. Now come on, we got to get you back. Back to that bleedin' salon of yours. We don't want Shirl comin' in wonderin' what you've been up to, do we?"

Like *she*'d go to the salon. Only time she ever darkens the door is when she's picking Debra or someone up. Frumpy bitch.

"Yeah, best I get back. Will you follow us back to the main road, please Dave? I feel safe when you do that". The big eyes are back, she knows that flattery gets her everywhere with Dave, what with him getting meagre rations on that front from Shirley.

"Come on then, gell. Move your Harris". As she gets up, she reaches out for him to steady her and she plants a big tonguey smacker on his lips, her eyes narrowed, cat-like, staring into his.

"Thanks, darlin'". Balance restored. Gina-G? You've done it again, girl. "See you in the car park, lover!" She gives him another kiss and she's gone. He clears up the room a bit, then he's off to reception, gives the girl a knowing wink as he pays the bill and then straight out the front door, bold as brass. She's already in the Boxster S and waiting by the exit. Dave's in his M5, tints, fully loaded. The journey back to Canvey is thankfully uneventful and he sees her right to the car park opposite the flower shop. She gives him a wave as he roars away, narrowly missing Debra who's just arrived for her nail appointment. She sits in the car for a bit, just sorting herself out, repairing the damage and covering up the kiss-rash which still marks her otherwise tanned face. As she stalks towards the salon, she feels a distinct wetness between her thighs, bringing a wicked grin to her face. She's horny again.

"Hiya, babes!" The air-kissing thing has really caught on and she and Debra go through the ritual before giving way to a big Vange sisterly hug. "Late night was it? You look fucked!"

"Gawd, is it that bad? I was in a bit of a rush".

"Bit of a rash more like! What are you like, Gina Bold?" She's all excited and her spectacular boobs are jiggling under the burgundy satin corset she's almost wearing. "You should be ashamed of yourself! Who was he, anyone I know?"

"Oh, Debs, I couldn't say. He's sworn me to secrecy. Pleeeeese don't say nothing".

"What? Like always you mean? Sisters' secrets, Gina!" She taps the side of her nose and takes her sister by the hand. They walk together towards the salon, arm in arm.

Inside, it's busy, as always.

"Afternoon, Mrs Bold. Would you like some cappuccino?"

"Better have something a bit stronger, Trace. Hair of the dog an' all that!"

"We got some rosé from the shop? It's nice! Would you like a couple of glasses?"

"That would be lovely, thanks Tracy," pipes up Debra, licking her lips. She's been giving it large for ages now, ever since her sister bought into the salon. In fact, she's been generally larging it up big style since matters Bold took a turn for the better. She thinks she's got some kind of divine right to their money, their friends, their lives. Thing with Debra is that she's such good value, even if you have to pay for every last thing. She is the *ultimate party animal*. She's just as gorgeous as her sister, but with a kind of *magnetism* which works on men and women. She makes the Bolds' parties go with a bang. Literally.

"Come on, sis. Let's have the goss' then. You ain't getting away that easily".

"It's right close to home, gell."

"Blimey! NO! What have you got yourself into? Don't tell me you've got problems with this one? You always said fuck 'em and forget 'em. You've been shittin' on yer own doorstep, ain't you?"

Gina's head hung low now. Debra's harsh but incisive words cut straight into her and all the memories of earlier came flooding back. Slowly, the tears began to flow down her cheeks and she fell into her sister's arms. The place went silent as Debra took her out the back to sort herself out. And get the gossip.

Chapter Nine

Suite 237, Stakis Hotel, Dartford

"Ladies and gentlemen. Welcome to Operation Watchtower, Mark Two". Laughter all round on that one, more from a release of tension than anything else.

Janet Weatherall, Graham Stubbins, Emily Loader, Rick Gibbs, Kim Evans, Andy Meacher, Howard Leach, Martin Heath, Jo Kent, Claire Goater, Matt Harmer, Donald O'Neill, Peter Trench. One boardroom table, pads, pens, charts, laptops, videos. Silence.

"You all know why you're here. Firstly, I would like to clear the air. For Graham, Emily, Rick, Kim and Andy, some of this will be old ground. For the rest of you, particular attention is vital. This will all be about *attention to detail*". Weatherall was not going to take any prisoners today. She seriously expected casualties.

"Graham is responsible to me for the whole ops structure. Rick, you will be in charge of Alpha Team, Martin; Beta Team, Claire: Gamma, Scott: Delta. Your briefing packs contain your team-members names, together with contact names and backgrounds. The four locations will be; Torrevieja/Alicante, Dover, London and Newry. Antwerp and Croatia will be dealt with later. Donald, you will have overall authority for South Armagh. Your team has been picked mainly from 'Derry City and Belfast. In view of what's been happening in the Newry office, the compromised officers are too much to risk. It is our belief that there is more than one mole in there and as yet, despite exhaustive enquiries, we have hit a brick wall. It will be very difficult to maintain effective obs on O'Riordan in the current climate. The Good Friday agreement may be good for some, but it's bugger all use to continued operations. The latest news we have from Graham's original team is that things seem rather quiet on the Doolans Bar front. Thank you, all of you here, for that. The usual comings and goings, local villains, tourists. Trouble is, now the place has really taken off, it's becoming more and more arduous a task to monitor his associates. Every time we've sent on site obs in, the staff home in on them and it's outski time. It's like they can *smell* us. O'Riordan's staff are all from *the old country*. They have blagging in their blood there. Partition just honed their skills, that's all. It's time we started fighting them on equal terms. We have funding for six months on this. Six months, ladies and gentle*men* before I get my head chopped off and we all get put out to grass. As they say in Hollywood, the DA will be bustin' my ass". Further relieved laughter fills the room. Coffee and biscuits are passed round.

"Yes, people. Biscuits. *Proper funding*! Graham, screen please".

Stubbins gets smartly to his feet and switches on the interactive whiteboard screen. After a couple of seconds, an image of Padraig O'Riordan begins to appear, against a backdrop of a churchyard. In the foreground are hooded men, holding Kalashnikovs. Behind them, a priest reads at the graveside. O'Riordan is flanked by two men, one bearded, one round faced with curly hair. They are soberly dressed, black suits and ties. O'Riordan wears a trilby hat, pulled well down. The whole scene is shown in black and white.

"That, ladies and gentlemen, that thing there, is Padraig O'Riordan. From now on, better known as Zulu One. Memorise his face, get to know him, read your background packs, learn the history, most importantly, read the *failed operations log*. It won't make you very proud of the service, that's for certain. Smuggling, fuel fraud, cross-border scams, duty diversion, cigarette smuggling, evasion of VAT, the list goes on. That and whatever he was involved in prior to the GFA. Local intelligence on the street is telling us that there has been a vast increase in high quality cocaine. Not the usual twenty to thirty percent crap which washes around the clubs of Hoxton and Clerkenwell. We're talking the high grade, barely cut variety. The punters are screaming for it. It's just like the old days, before the dealers got greedy and cut down the already cut. Foreign intelligence is drawing a complete blank. As you know, we have put some of the biggest dealers comfortably behind bars recently, yet we *know* that someone, some big operator is playing hard-ball here and we don't have a thing to go on. We have nothing to link O'Riordan to any of this, any more than we can link anyone else, but someone with real clout is getting this in. Someone accustomed to bringing in large volumes, undetected. We're certain it's not coming in by air. The usual amounts will, of course, continue to filter through the normal channels at Heathrow and Gatwick, but without that *collateral damage,* we would lose all our PIs. We have no indicated increase in airside activity. It has to be coming in by truck or by sea. Dover Eastern has been reporting increased seizures, though a truck which may have had O'Riordan connections was found to be clean when searched last week. I say 'may' as so far we have nothing to connect Zulu One to Newry International. One strange occurrence to report did, however take place that night. An officer coming off night-shift who was in the customs shed at the time was taking his daughter home from a party in Dover and appears to have run off the road. No evidence of foul play, but it does strike us as odd, in view of the fact that he was a known teetotaller, that there was alcohol in his body at the post-mortem. No other vehicles involved. An inquest into the death of the officer in question has been opened and adjourned, but we are not expecting too much from that. I am proposing an internal investigation into his circumstances leading up to that fateful night, just in case we have missed something. As a precaution, the driver, who we had to let go, has been placed on the Zulu list".

"Are you saying that there may be a connection between O'Riordan, the lorry and the officer's death?"

"I am not saying anything at this stage, but until we have satisfied ourselves of the manner of this unfortunate accident, I am keeping an open mind. Now, before I run through known associates, shall we have a comfort break? Don't leave the suite. If you need a smoke, use the balcony".

The smokers reach for hidden packets of Marlboro Lights, everyone else reaches for more coffee. As soon as they get outside, Emily, Andy, Claire and Matt go straight into a huddle, smoking furiously and talking against the backdrop of the relentless traffic pouring off the Dart Bridge.

"Is she for real, Matt?" asks Claire, fumbling with her lighter. "I mean, this accident, it's all a bit sensational, isn't it?

"Dunno, mate. Can't work her out yet. She seems dedicated, can't deny that, but there's something about her which I find intriguing. She's like *enigmatic*". Matt exudes a sense of belonging, he's really happy to be there, feels part of something at last.

"She's certainly that. Why do I feel like I'm either in a movie, or Jeremy Beadle's going to burst out from behind that bloody whiteboard".

"Where the hell did that come from? Are you on something?"

"I just feel that this doesn't have much to do with the NIS. We're getting involved in police matters, Northern Irish terrorists, bloody.."

"Whoa! Steady on. No-one's actually said this guy's a terrorist. Not everyone in Armagh is in the IRA, you know".

"Really? That's not what I'd heard. Bloody bandit country, that's what they call it. Middle of nowhere and everyone's driving a Mercedes? What the hell is that all about? Come on, Matt, wake up and smell the coffee".

"Well, maybe it's what we should be getting involved in then. Where have all the Mercedes come from? They can't all be shipping arms and since the decommissioning, there's no market for guns, unless I'm missing something".

Emily takes a long drag on her Marlboro, stubs it out on the balcony floor and they walk back in. The traffic noise disappears as the doors are closed and once again, the room is in quiet anticipation.

"Welcome back, everyone. I trust we're all ready for more? Good. Now, as I said, the army watchtower system can't be relied on in the old border areas for much longer. As a result, intelligence sources are few and far between now. Sending officers directly into South Armagh would be futile, as the opposition has its own people on the ground and every newcomer is still treated with extreme suspicion. We *will* however be introducing limited local area support, just to keep tabs on certain individuals. The main thrust of the initial operations will be in Spain, Armagh, London, Dover, Antwerp and Croatia, where we are certain a large and sophisticated money-laundering operation is in progress. Banking laws are still in the process of being reformed in the old Yugoslavia, and Croatia in particular seems to be a friendly port for our friends in green. You will liaise with a team already established out there, part of Operation Cruella. We also believe that he may be enjoying the support of some of his old friends in return for favours granted. I have asked for and will be receiving from Army Intelligence a full list of known associates, together with members of those organisations released under the Good Friday Agreement. There will be, I am afraid to say, considerable man hours spent dealing with this and burning of the proverbial midnight oil will be necessary. I hope you have understanding families". She pauses for effect and reaction, both crucial to her future planning. The response thus far is favourable. They have been the forgotten for too long. They are desperate for action, of any kind.

"So; known associates. We have a list here of all sighted KAs at the bar, largely compiled by Graham's earlier, rather low-budget operation. Thank-you, Graham for doing your best in the face of all adversity. Where we are lacking, severely lacking, is with his importation routes, if indeed it is him. I am putting together a team for the Split, Croatia end of the equation, for future upgrading of our activities there. Any volunteers? It may be a rather arduous trip, I'm afraid. Nice place, shame about the co-operation levels. They're still very suspicious of anyone who might destabilise their fledgling economy. So whoever goes will need to tread very carefully if they are going to uncover anything on the money laundering front. We believe that it's going to be property orientated. High growth, low-interest. The Germans are moving out of Spain and into the old East, Hungary, Yugoslavia, Turkey, Greece. Won't be long before we're following the buggers to Bulgaria. Give it time, the villas are already being built. The problem we have, if we can actually bring matters to court, is proving ownership and origin of the funds in these countries. The problem O'Riordan and his acolytes have, is getting it there. You are all aware of the situation with the C.A.B. in Eire. We are now beginning to achieve great success in the retrieval and sequestration of funds in the UK. Even traditionally hostile countries such as Spain are starting to toe the line and are restricting cash credits to hitherto secret bank accounts. Life is becoming harder for them, but as you know, as fast as we close one loophole………….."

"Are you saying that we are going to be concentrating on proceeds of crime or detection and prevention? It seems to me that this is all about the former. Surely that is not our job?"

"I am afraid that it *is* our job. It's rather a case of the Al Capone scenario. Find the money and we can work backwards towards the crime. The likes of Padraig and his friends don't soil their hands with the dirty cash or the drugs. They have soldiers to do that for them. It is the route *to them* that interests the service. The purpose of extensive observation is to build up a picture that we have never been accorded prior to the creation of the Special Funding Executive. Welcome to the new world of Her Majesty's Revenue and Customs!"

Mention of this produced the usual catcalls and mutterings of derision from the floor. The jealousies of old die a slow death and meddling Inland Revenue were that last thing that old stonearse Customs officers wanted.

"Now, now children. This is not to say that our work at Dover is to be treated lightly. Quite the opposite. As I said, there *are* certainties. Naturally, it is being produced in Colombia. We are as sure as sure can be that it is not coming directly to the UK. The Royal Navy has made some significant breakthroughs in the Caribbean and the Canaries on that score, though of course, despite the wonderful coverage given this kind of work by the media and press, we all know that seizures such as these come directly from informants and not stop and search. I am afraid that will remain the stuff of fiction. We are now coming around to the idea that the old fashioned Spanish connection is being revived. Just because some of the old East End die-hards chose to eliminate each other in a gangland style shoot-out recently does not mean that trail has gone cold. So Torrevieja has to be a main priority. O'Riordan's cousin Ronan, page two of your packs please, works full time at Doolans. Does a good job, by all accounts. Thank you, Kim. There are a number of other men working there of Irish origin who we are currently checking on. Most of them are young, which precludes recent paramilitary involvement, but they may still have family, or other connections. The Irish 'question' has existed for hundreds of years. It does not go away as a result of political expediency by one ambitious Prime Minister and an equally ambitious Taioseoch. It is said that there are more millionaires in South Armagh than the rest of Northern Ireland put together. They did not all succeed by farming sheep, ladies and gentlemen". This produces riotous laughter from the floor. It's a Customs thing. You have to be there, *to be them*.

"I would like you to split into your groups now, to examine the Target Packs and to share any information you may have on any of these individuals. We will then reconvene when the Zulu list will be circulated and after that, we'll stop for today. Any questions? Good. Thank you".

She sits down and the group leaders gather their troops together. On the table in front of her is a green folder, marked Most Secret FYO. She picks this up and leaves the room. She walks downstairs and into the bar area. She sits down and after a few minutes, she is approached by two men, one overweight and with short blond hair, the other short and slight with greasy dark hair.

"Craig, Joe, how nice to see you. I have your report here, thank you so much for that and thanks for coming at such short notice. I am just a little concerned by the lack of information coming via Birmingham. You were always so good at that".

"Er, I won't lie to you, Janet, it was a bit of a hassle to get here. We're working on that for you. Just doesn't seem to be much happening up there. London's where all the action is at the moment. I think our partnership has been a bit too successful". He smiles and winks.

"Well, we can't be too careful with you two, now can we? I have arranged the usual sum for your information, in Euros. Keep an eye out for anything on the Irish front. I know drugs isn't your field, but they have crossed over into spirits many times and I need to have fast information. You two have never let me down yet".

"Thanks, Janet".

"Well, must go. Keep up the good work, gentlemen. Oh, and Joe, well done on the new job".

She leaves via the rear of the bar and the two men sit down, waiting for someone. They order coffee and make calls on their numerous mobiles.

Upstairs, Weatherall returns to the meeting and begins to work her way through the small Zulu list.

"It's a small start on this front. Most of the information gleaned is from Graham's work on Watchtower I. Watchtower II is, as you are aware, going to take in a much wider sphere of activity, both from our side and from the Zulus themselves. We have the O'Riordans for starters, Padraig and Therése. They are the prime focus of our attention and the main targets. Then there is the cousin Ronan O'Riordan. Our interest in him centres on the fact that he works with Zulu 1 and is a blood relative. Zulu 4 is Martin Keenan, a new addition and not on Graham's original list. He works as a driver and gofer for Zulus 1 and 2. He does not, at first sight, appear to work at Doolans. A number of the original Zulus from Graham's list have been removed, due partly to their dropping off the radar in some cases or because operational decisions have been taken at the highest level. At this stage, all our observational activities will be concentrated on Doolans Bar, O'Riordan's villa, his farm in South Armagh and the money-laundering connections in Croatia. We believe that a concerted effort in Spain will result in the list growing rapidly, both in numbers *and* in locations. Unfortunately, as I have stated previously, close up observations have proved largely fruitless, due to the nature of Doolans and its remarkable collective knack of spotting you lot!" The room dissolves into restrained mirth, brought about more by Weatherall's expression of resignation than anything else.

"However, from now on, the ball is in *our* court and we are taking the battle to *them* for a change. Your team leaders have been briefed on the initial upgrading and re-organisation of the operation. In front of you, you will find the briefing packs and the Zulu lists, which I know you are all dying to look at! We are moving fast on this one, people. Say your goodbyes quickly. You'll be flying out tomorrow. This meeting is now at a close. Good luck!"

A stunned silence is followed by low murmuring as the group breaks up. The atmosphere is heavily charged and they know they're now part of something big at last. Small groups form, the excitement overwhelms them. From a distance, Stubbins watches. A little part of him has just died.

Chapter Ten

Alicante Port, Spain

A dark figure moved slowly between the shadows. The cranes run along wide, deep rails at this point in the harbour and you'd better watch what the hell you're doing unless you want to lose a foot or worse. This is Paco Alvarez's domain. His manor. He knows every inch of this sweating, grimy, seething mass of activity, from the overloaded Algiers Ferry to container ships disgorging their exotic cargo from the four corners of the world, and small coastal freighters calling in from exotic North African ports. Spices, leather, pottery, icons from that continent. Garments from Indonesia and China, designer, fakes, designer fakes, you name it. Alicante is big business now and Paco moves within its confines like a scavenging fox. He IS Alicante port.

Sliding into the Bar Union facing the Customs House, he smokes a thin roll up. Old habits die hard. Coffee and brandy arrive unannounced. It is night, dark night and his fellow drinkers sip quietly at their Carlos Prims and San Migs, grateful for some respite from the wind coming in off the sea. The TV's on, it's Champions League and Valencia are playing a group three match against Monaco. Half the bar's for them, half against. It's 1-0 to Monaco and there's twenty minutes to go. Paco glances up at the TV, then at the table of uniformed Customs officers, intent on their game. He slopes off, into the night, leaving his coffee and Carlos Primera sitting alone. No money changes hands.

He walks down Quay Four, all the time treading carefully across huge steel chains and pulleys, avoiding the pools of diesel oil which shine mirage-like in the reflected glow of the harbour lights. The half moon gives him some aid, but it is native wit and local knowledge which are getting him to his destination. A lamp glows dim outside a tiny wooden hut, tatty lace curtain at the window. A careful recce up and down and he enters the hut, carefully closing the door behind him. Inside, a small wooden desk houses a grimy workstation and two telephones, equally used. A greasy haired, boiler-suited man sits with his back to the door.

"Buenos noches, mi amigo. Que tal?" His deliberate and precise Castellano belies the blue collar situation and Paco's reply takes them straight to the vernacular, the Valenciana dialect of the street, of the gutter.

"New routes, my friend, new routes. When will they leave us alone?"

"Aaah! They. And how are *they* tonight?"

"Sitting in the Union, necking Carlos, watching the Orange lose. Just where we like them, eh?" Paco's joke is lost on the old man. He couldn't give a flying fuck either way.

"The unloading will finish in the morning now. There is not time for the men to work now. They want to sleep and to fuck, yes?"

"Nice for them. I have to earn an honest living". Paco smiles and lights another roll-up, offering one to the man. He is deep in his papers, but stops to look up and accept this small gesture. His gnarled face betrays the years on board, long forgotten memories of Zanzibar, the Wide Sargasso Sea. There is a knackered picture of a spice island, ends curled up over the desk. Lists of men pinned up on a noticeboard, jobs allocated, plans made.

"Any interest from our friends?"

"Nothing so far. As you say, new routes. I have my man on the deck tomorrow, watching. He will see. He will miss nothing".

"I hope so, old man. My partners are very nervous people".

"I think you are confusing me with someone who gives a fuck". He returns to the papers, the signal for Paco to leave. He removes a wad of hundred Euro notes, leaves them on the worn table and pats the old man on the back, a symbol of a relationship which goes back to when he was a street urchin and the old man would give him a *bocadillo,* some shelter from the burning sun and send him on his way. Men of the street know this.

The walk back along the wharf takes him past the empty Danzas Shipping office, the giant sleeping cranes and across cold steel railway lines. Dim floodlights shine through steam emerging from concealed vents, barely showing the way and several times, he stumbles across discarded pallets and the assorted detritus of yesterday. This time, his mind is on other things. Eventually, he is back at the roadway and the comforting San Miguel sign indicating the Bar Union's open door. The place is abuzz with animated conversation. Glancing up at the screen, he can see why. The on-screen TV clock tells him that there is two minutes plus injury time to go. Somehow, John Carew has equalised for the Home Team and now they are peppering the Monaco penalty area with an aerial bombardment more akin to the Luftwaffe's efforts at Guernica. Everything's aimed at the towering figure of Carew, but so far, no cigar. Suddenly, Monaco break out and hoof it up the park. The noise reaches a crescendo, but it ends with the ball striking the Valencia crossbar, goalkeeper beaten all ends up. The boys are screaming at the TV now, baying for blood. The heavy tumblers of Carlos are being replenished as fast as the barman can go and the beers are getting slopped all over the floor. After a midfield tussle, Valencia break away and the right winger whips in a cross which Carew gets right on the end of and bang! In it goes. Top corner. The place goes fucking mental. The neutral wind-up merchants are dejectedly silent, the Valencianas are leaping around like demented chimps on speed and the barman's waving his cloth around like a shillelagh.

"Al final, al final" they scream. The customs officers are dancing a jig round the tables and waving their truncheons at each other. You have to be there………..

Paco finishes his now cold coffee and drains the last of the Carlos, shakes the barman by the available hand and slips away, whilst the madness continues unabated.

Across the way, his car lies waiting. A cursory glance around the wharf tells him that the Orange's victory has ensured silent and deserted streets. He is alone. *Click*. The car door opens, he climbs slowly in and guns the engine, driving away unobserved. The drive into Alicante town takes him along the front, past crowded bars and brightly lit cafes, full to the brim with celebrating Valencia fans, drunken tourists caught up in the wave and local girls looking for love. Swarms of people move from bar to bar in a never ending flow. He turns off the strip and up towards the centre, to his favourite nightclub. To his friend. The yin to his yang. He stops as two mini-skirted girls totter across the black and white and into the *Internacional*. It will be good tonight. He stops the battered old Seat and hands the keys to a car jockey. Straightening his trade mark black leather jacket, he enters the fray, nodding to the colossal doorman as he goes. Once inside, he is greeted by the cloakroom girl, the manager and the receptionist who respectfully takes his jacket and hands it over. The manager takes his arm and they walk through a heavy velvet black curtain and in.

The thumping bass-line of 'Don't call me baby' blares out from the huge wall mounted Bose speaker system as a half-caste girl dances naked on one of the podium stages close to the bar. Keeps the guys there which is just how the manager likes it. She's really giving it some, twisting around on gold platform heels, rolling onto her back and opening her legs wide to reveal the smoothest shaved pussy in town. The guys cheer and throw twenty Euro notes onto the mirrored stage floor as she writhes around, stroking already erect nipples, her thick, black curly hair falling tantalisingly across them, playing hide and seek with the lustful watchers.

"……*you know I don't belong to you…. So don't call me babeeee."*
Her cute behind is bouncing to the rhythm now, pelvic thrusts just driving the guys wild. Paco smiles at her as she turns to check out the newcomers to the bar area. She waves and blows him a kiss, then slips a finger into her pussy and licks the lovejuice from painted talons, all the time maintaining eye contact with the guys closest to the stage. There's almost a riot breaking out now, as the notes float onto the stage under the heels of her stilettos. Just as the plot is about to be lost, the MC's voice comes over the PA, thanking Marlayna for her wonderful dancing and she's picked up the Euros and gone, sashaying through a red and gold curtain at the back, wiggling her stunning arse as she goes. The music is lowered and the lights are up on the pole dancers, three ultra slim Russian girls who wind themselves expressionless around shining, glistening poles to the slow erotic thump of Donna Summer's 'Love to love you baby'. The girls straddle each pole, twisting and swirling, their impossibly long legs stretched out wide and far, oh so far apart.

Paco wanders to the bar, but there is already a girl on her way to him, a tall flute of champagne sits atop a glass tray, which she hands to him, accompanied by a wide smile. He slips a ten Euro note down her front and taps her on the bum as she returns to the counter. The champagne tastes like nectar. He takes out his mobile and checks for missed calls. Just as he is doing this, he feels a light tap on his shoulder and spins around. He is greeted by a wide smile. It is his oldest and most trusted friend, Felix, a.k.a. *Bocadillo* a.k.a. Sandwich, to the Irish boys. Never disappoints, does Felix. Two beautiful, heavily made up Russian girls flank him, wearing identical jewelled bikini tops and mini-skirts. Their towering heels bring them almost up to his height. Almost. Felix hates people being taller than him. *The Russian girls know this.*

"How are you, my friend. These are my two lovely *chicas* for tonight. I would like you to meet Anastasia and Ocsana. Say hello to my friend Paco, please ladies".

They respond; lips smile big for Paco, but eyes betray cold isolation. Their arms are interlinked with Felix's, warding off any girls who might even be contemplating the thought of poaching the richest man in the *Club Internacional*.

"*Encantado, señoritas.* Please, let me get you all some drinks, yes?" He looks around but the champagne is already on the way.

"The manager has your table ready, whenever you want it, Señor Alvarez. It is near to the stage, as always. Please allow me to pour you champagne from the house".

He leads the way to the best table in the club and they sit down. Paco is looking around, looking for something, *for someone.* His eyes are everywhere, then suddenly, they light up like a fairground. He stands and waves at a girl right on the other side of the club. For a moment, she can't see him, then for no reason at all, she turns around and spots his frantic, boyish gestures. Her face breaks into the biggest smile and she begins to walk across the crowded floor towards him. His impatience gets the better of him and he leaves Felix to his Natashas for a moment. Almost running towards him is a tiny, dark skinned girl with the thickest, blackest hair you have ever seen. She is dressed in a long, red evening dress slashed to the waist, towering gold platform sandals which just about bring her up to his chest and a red flower in her lustrous locks. Her brown eyes resemble dark pools of deep water, shining brilliant with reflected shafts of light searing into his soul, her glossy red lips begging to be kissed. She looks up at him and they smile, laugh like two teenagers. He takes her hand and shakes it, then raises it to his lips and kisses the back of it with great sensitivity.

"Buenas noches, Señorita Faria. Encantado!"

"Buenas noches a usted, Señor Alvarez."

They collapse into childish giggling. Just for an instant, they are back in the gutter from whence they both came, two tiny, unwanted waifs huddling together for warmth and protection. Then the moment is gone and he takes her arm, guides her back to the table where Felix has again become Sandwich with his two girls all over him. As they sit, the music levels increase and a double girl show begins on the stage. The three girls clap and cheer as the two dancers hit the podium, whipping up the crowd into a frenzy as the MC introduces them. Naturally, the three know each other, but this does not hold Paco back and he insists on formal introductions for all. It's just something that he does. Always.

Faria snuggles up to him and plants kisses on his cheek every few minutes, each time he opens his mouth to speak, in fact. Later, she will dance for him. But for now, he is captivated by his little scenario. Getting off on the whole *Club Internacional* thing. They are like children who've been used to a rubbish strewn alley and have just been magicked into Disneyworld. That's what the pole dancing clubs are all about, really. It works just the same for the girls as the clients. They all go there to escape. And for the money. And the power.

The girls are into their routine now, Robyn S's 'Show me love' is thumping out over the exquisite sound system. One is sliding erotically down the silver pole whilst the other is gyrating in time, her pelvis working the crowd so easily, the men cheering with each thrust, the money again flying onto the stage. She leans down towards one crowd of young suited guys and they put twenty Euro notes into her pink garter while she blows kisses towards them. They beg her to remove the gauzy bra which is just about restraining her perfect silicone mounds and she teases them mercilessly by lowering and raising the spaghetti thin straps crossing her exquisite shoulders. The temperature's rising now and she leans down once more, this time they get to put the notes down the side of her tiny thong. The two girls swap and then she's twirling and whirling around the pole, though miraculously the money stays where it is. She swings herself back, then opens her legs so wide, before wrapping them round the pole and thrusting herself against it. Once more they swap and now it's for real. She comes right to the front of the stage and eases off her bra, drawing it down between her legs before casting it to one side. Her boobs are jiggling to the music and the guys are going wild with desire. The money's flying onto the stage; they really want her to go all the way. A nod from the manager gives her the go-ahead. He's got a high spending crowd in tonight and wants to give them something to remember. As she spins around the pole, holding on with her left hand, her right begins to play with the thin elastic, all that is separating the guys from heaven. She runs her hand around her back, just for one second pulling the cheesewire away from her rounded bottom. The music changes to 'Eye of the Tiger' and the lights go lower. From somewhere, she is handed a hunting knife and begins to flash the blade around and around. The light catches it briefly and the reflection is almost dazzling. She is away at the front of the stage now and the blade is swishing to and fro. The men are totally captivated and she works them brilliantly. As the music reaches a crescendo, the lights go down and dry ice begins to swirl around the darkened stage. The place is in uproar, as she appears from *inside* the ice, the hunting knife slipped between thong and skin. As the song hits its peak and the musical gap takes the place to split second silence, the knife flashes and the tiny thin elastic is cut right through. The thong falls away to reveal her shaven *concha*, labia visible and proud. She arches herself backwards, leaning towards the pole, her hands reaching behind, knowing just when and where to steady her lithe body. As her hands meet the shining steel pole, she slides down, her legs opening synonymously. Her arse hits the stage, her hands quickly move to between her legs, she parts her labia just for one moment and the lights go out to rapturous applause and a hail of Euros. Pandemonium reigns supreme and the men are clapping and cheering long after she is back in her dressing room. This is the moment when the lap dancers move in and the punters just fall at their feet. They will pay anything just for a glimpse of more pussy.

Paco and Sandwich, together with their girls are clapping too. The champagne's flowing in rivers now. Over on the *Club Internacional* dance floor, some of the girls are taking men for close up dances, this time to a resident salsa band which really knows its way round. One of the older guys in the club is a professional dancer and he is with a very young girl of around eighteen. They are totally as one; the music takes them far away, to another time. He struts around with her, they are like two snakes entwined then apart.

"This is a wonderful night, my Paco", whispers Faria. "I wish we could run away from all this. It is my dream". He just smiles and looks away. Just a fantasy, *cariño*, that's all it will ever be.

More champagne arrives as the last of the bottle is drained. The two men look at each other, no words are exchanged yet each of them knows exactly what the other is thinking. Old friends, old heads on young shoulders. Sandwich is kissing one of the girls, then the other. This is *his* fantasy. For Faria and Paco, they can pretend that they are *one*. Just for tonight.

Chapter Eleven

Paco and Sandwich go mad in Ceuta

The drive from Alicante to Mucha Miel aerodrome takes you past some of the dramatic new developments which Felix and his family are working on. Once arid, agricultural land is being turned fast, oh so fast into plots for villas, hotels and apartments. The scrub on which for centuries, his ancestors had toiled was now worth millions of Euros, with banks queuing up to lend and finance new developments. Ray-Ban wearing Russians had been arriving over the past few years, armed with suitcases of street money, dirty and worn with the misery of a thousand prostitutes, a million cocaine addicted no hopers. Impoverished peasants had become Euro-Millionaires overnight with once deserted beaches and ancient fishing villages being turned into marinas and developments faster than you could say planning permission. 'Tis a grand life *with the right connections.*

Sandwich is driving the Lamborghini this morning; Paco sits beside him, dressed in customary white shirt and black trousers. Cuban salsa is blaring from the on-board Kenwood sound system, the beautiful autumn sun beats down, reflecting off the Lambo's shining waxed bonnet.

"I am using the German to take us today. I don't like that other guy. He asks too many questions. The German knows when to speak and when to shut it. My family give him some building work in Javea and he's happy. They are all happy when they see the money".

"Are we going in the old plane again?"

"He is borrowing one from the instructor so that we don't appear to be doing anything unusual. He flies all the time to Gibraltar and there we can change the flight plan to north Africa, if necessary".

He guides the gleaming Italian sports beast off the A7 and onto the aerodrome way. A small Cessna taxis around the perimeter, preparing for take-off on the sun-scorched runway as they pass through the gate and into the car-park. As they extricate themselves from the low seats and onto the dusty ground, the Cessna passes overhead, slowly inching its way up into the clear morning sky and away.

The boot clicks open and they both retrieve holdalls from within; Sandwich's Louis Vuitton in stark contrast to Paco's five Euro nylon offering from the weekly market. The boot is slammed shut, locked and then the two friends walk across the tarmac to the main building. They push the door open and walk in. Once inside, they search for the aerodrome manager. The office is empty. The control room, the same. A proper Marie Celeste job. They pass through an archway and into the bar and all is immediately revealed. The *man in question* currently has his barman's hat on, serving two young looking locals booked in for what is probably their first flying lesson. Shortly he will return to the office as he is also the traffic controller, immigration officer and fuel attendant. He smiles at Paco and pours them a thick, black coffee each, without any words being exchanged. He is of the old school. There is time for everything.

"Where is the German?" asks Sandwich, glancing around the apron for sight of anyone familiar.

"He is already here, *señor*. Checking the plane and the fuel. The flight plan is on my desk and you will find your forms for Gibraltar completed together with the returns. Also some mail for them. Raf doesn't let you down, eh?" He smiles a toothy smile; all the time, the stubby roll-up never leaves his lower lip. This is the old Spain, rusting away and stuck together with the glue of the past, struggling with the rapid advancement of the new, almost at the aerodrome gates, but seemingly miles away.

They gulp down the strong coffee and walk through to the office, collect the papers and away. Across the tarmac from Mucha Miel's 'main terminal', there are three small hangars where the Pipers and Cessnas live, together with a rag tag and bobtail bunch of rusting old relics from bygone years which still get hauled out and dusted off before being sent up into the deep blue Mediterranean skies for what could be at any time, their final flights. A tanned, blond figure is working away at the cockpit windows on of these museum pieces. He spots the two men and almost stands to attention, cloth in hand, bowing as they approach.

"Good morning. How are you both? It is very good to see you. Very good indeed. We are ready for the flight, yes?"

Paco's eyes traverse the full length of the Piper Cherokee before returning his stare towards the pilot.

"Don't worry, Herr Paco. I have been many times in this plane and she never lets me down. Only at the weekend, I was flying over Altea and I am switching the motor off, to see what is happening. I am still here, ja?" Bloody mad, the German.

"At what time do we leave?"

"I have finished the pre-flight checks, as soon as Herr Rafael is saying we can go, we go".

The boys place their bags in the little hold and return to the office. Raf is now on the radio, talking to some hapless flying instructor who wants to land and take-off straight away. They are having some sort of technical argument about wind speed and Raf is waving his arms around like a demented toreador. Just as things reach a crescendo, he flicks off the intercom and stands up, shrugging. He looks through the window and witnesses the arrival of said flying instructor. The landing's a bit dodgy, he kinds of lands a bit sideways, but eventually the plane comes to a halt outside Hangar No 2 and instructor and pupil climb out. They walk, well stride over to the terminal and in seconds, they are in the office. Paco and Sandwich look on, awaiting developments. The instructor and Raf stand face to face, like two raging bulls, then without warning, smiles emerge which quickly become cacophonous laughter. The two men embrace, which is followed by a volley of guttural Valenciana dialect. They walk out of the office in the direction of the bar, leaving Paco, Sandwich and the pupil staring at each other, totally bewildered. Outside, the German stands waiting, rolling a last cigarette before blast off. Paco picks up the signed forms and they leave, via the bar and a last good bye with Raf who is now deep in animated conversation with the instructor. A bottle of Carlos Primero sits comfortably between them, open and ready for business. Thick coffee aromas pervade the whole room. Raf waves them away in an entirely unaggressive and delightfully Spanish way. They leave.

As they walk towards the Piper, Rolf Weber is already holding the door open for them, puffing frantically on the last knockings of his roll-up before climbing in and starting up. The tiny, cramped cockpit seats six. Rolf is up front, Paco sits in the seat behind him and Sandwich brings up the rear, allowing each some more leg room and according views from both sides of the little single engined trainer. A smell of aviation fuel wafts through the cabin as the revs increase and taxiing commences. Rolf is talking to Raf over the intercom now, as they make their way towards runway one. Sandwich adjusts his Ray-Bans for maximum swagger and sits back, fastening his seat belt. Clearance comes in the form of a grunt from Raf and they're away down the runway, crabbing sideways a bit before lumbering into the clear, bright sky.

*

Hundreds of miles away, a small demonstration at a Moroccan border elicited little more than the raising of an eyebrow from the guards. 'Let us in'. 'We want to work for you'.

Fuck off, thought Sergeant Ramirez, as he wandered back into the guard house and sanctuary. Ceuta. Last bastion of Spanish hegemony on the African continent. The British have Gib, the Spanish Ceuta and Melilla. And Parsley Island. How the mighty have fallen. Landlocked to the rear, keeping the hordes at bay. Briefly on the front pages, we're just reduced to flying the bloody flag now. Grumpy old Spanish border guard. Best not go there. Not just now, anyway.

*

Out over the sea, Rolf is muttering quietly to himself and the boys are enjoying the fantastic views over Alicante and the coast. The little Piper is holding up well as he takes them higher and higher, watching for thermals, finding the ideal altitude.

"Can we use the mobile, Rolf?"

"Hah! Ze mobile. Of course you can, what do you think this is, Lufthansa? Don't believe all that bullshit they tell you. Don't do this, don't do that. You can take off your seatbelt and stick your head out of the window for all I care". He laughs outrageously and switches on traffic control, which is currently playing some rather violent salsa music, interspersed with football updates from La Liga. Occasionally, a voice is heard from Mucha Miel, *the* voice as it turns out and Rolf responds with his guttural Spanish. Mucha Miel. Now there's a thing. A good translation for the uninitiated would be 'plenty honey'. Now what sort of a name for an aerodrome is that? Sounds more like a lap dancing club. Maybe by the time the boys get back, Raf will have turned it into one, though I don't really think so. Raf and Rolf wouldn't be able to moan at each other then, which would be silly.

Raf and Rolf. How unlikely is that?

"You want to see the coast from lower down? The conditions are perfect for low-flying".

"Why not? Let's live!" Sandwich looks down at the glittering Mediterranean which rushes up to meet them as Rolf takes the Piper down to just a couple of hundred feet. The waves become really clear and the small boats travelling up and down the coast are bobbing up and down as the plane swoops over. Several people wave at them and Rolf tips his wings, fighter pilot styleee.

"Where are *ze guns* when you need them, eh Rolf baby?" Paco is playing with him now but Rolf has heard it all before. He smiles and returns to his salsa, banging the control panel with his fist.

"How long is this going to take, my friend?" Sandwich pipes up from behind.

"Are we there yet, Daddy?" Paco sniggers and pats Rolf on the back. Thumps him, more like.

"We have a little rendezvous, don't forget. You know how I hate it when we are late".

"The German will get you there. I think we have known each other too long, yes? Normally, ze Spanish are not worrying about the lateness, *hein*?"

"You just fly the plane and listen to your bloody Cuban music. We will do the jokes, *my friend*". Sandwich is playing with his passport, his phone and anything else he can lay his hands on. Just as he puts down the mobile, it buzzes into life. He hands it to Paco.

"Yes. Ronan. How are you, my friend? Business is good, yes? Good. Excellent. The noise? Oh, yes, I am on the road, we have the sunroof open. We are quite close to the ocean, yes? Felix will come to see you tomorrow. Get him one of those lobsters, if you have one. And don't let that bloody Irish cook ruin it. What? Chef?

Since when was an Irishman a chef? Bollocks. Take care, my friend". *Click.*

"It seems that not all the news is bad, Felix. The regular supplier has the lobsters again and is making a delivery tomorrow. We can try, before we buy!"

"They need to be very careful, Paco my friend. It is unheard of that the truck is returned. The British Customs never return anything. I would not use those people again. It is not good for business when the *Aduana* people are interested. Not good at all. I think we should terminate the contract".

"Ronan is thinking the same, I feel, but he is anxious to recover the merchandise before severing the connection. It will be a long time before they can be certain that there are no little presents within the truck. There is also the problem of the man onside. His contract had to be terminated following this unfortunate business with his employers. It was regrettable about the girl, but this sort of thing is inevitable when there are difficulties. We cannot tolerate mistakes".

"Who is making the arrangements to retrieve the shipment, Paco?

He is tapping his fingers on the back of Rolf's seat, the jewelled Rolex sending tiny flickers of light spinning round the cockpit as the bright afternoon sun catches its diamond bezel.

"The Irishman has his friend from Liverpool to do such things. The man Beevers will do it. The truck goes now from Dover to Ireland, via the ferry at Liverpool. Everything will be done there. *Everything*".

The German skilfully pilots the plane along the Costa Blanca, almost skimming the waves as they eat up the kilometres. He talks now and again to air traffic control, bored conversations give way to yet more salsa, yet as they get further south along Spain's seemingly endless coast, flamenco begins to take over, until they are within sight of Gibraltar and its English pop output.

Rolf is on the radio again, this time talking in English to Gibraltar air traffic. He banks the little plane and they are afforded a fantastic view of the Rock in all its afternoon glory. There is heavy cloud about half way up, then it clears for the peak to stand out, alone in the clear blue sky. The Levanta is active today.

*

Life for Sergeant Ramirez is not getting any better. The crowds at the border check point are getting bigger, becoming more agitated with the growing oppressive atmospherics of the Levanta coming straight off the hot sands of the Sahara desert. It is stifling. Some of them are chanting, pressing against the flimsy fence. The morning's press has not helped, since a statement from the Governor saying that there will be no further guaranteed immigration from Ceuta and Melilla to the mainland made the front page. From deep within the crowd, a stone is thrown which lands on the roof of Ramirez's guard house, clattering on the corrugated iron before coming to rest. The crowd jeers as Ramirez and his colleague Sanchez emerge. Some of them are pulling at the fence. At the back of the mob, several youngish looking men are donning scarves and hats, the scarves pulled tightly across, covering all but their eyes.

*

As the Piper completes its tight turn and comes in to land at Gibraltar airport, Felix is already on the mobile, chattering away in guttural Valenciana. Paco checks documents removed from his jacket once more and examines each even more thoroughly than before. Rolf skilfully brings the plane to a halt outside the customs building, a slot allocated to him by the ground controller. The engine is disengaged and slowly, the tiny propeller comes to a complete stop. Felix pats him on the back and they climb out, stretching and breathing deep; the warm, Saharan air heavy on their lungs. Behind them, a Monarch Airbus glides majestically in from London Gatwick, followed by another from Manchester.

"I think I can turn us around quickly, gentlemen. The customs man is a friend of mine, also the fuel man".

"Is there anyone who is not a friend of yours on this coast, Rolf? You seem to have many connections, no? How is it that you are still playing with building bricks in Denia?"

"Slowly, slowly. I do not like to be hurrying the life. You know this, *mein Freund*!"

"If you go any slower, the old women from the church will overtake you with their zimmer frames, I think".

"I suggest you go to the passport hut there. You can find a small café behind. It is disgusting English coffee, but there is a nice girl behind the bar". He winks at Paco and walks into the ground control office, his papers in his hand.

"Ah, the Germans. They love their papers", Felix almost spits it out as they walk towards the Gibraltar Immigration Office. As they walk in, a bored official looks up from his dusty desk and eyes them up and down.

"*Turistas?* Where from?"

"We come from Alicante and are going to Algeria. We stop to refuel the *leedle plane* and then we go. Is it possible to drink some coffee here?"

The official scans their passports and hands them back.

"Through the back. There's a sign". He returns to his Daily Mail Sudoku, as if they were not there. The two walk over to the door and Paco opens it, holding it open for his friend to walk through. They are confronted by a chain-link fence and a small gap through which they are invited to walk. 'Café Brenda this way', complete with a hand-drawn arrow. Against their better judgement, they walk in and are greeted by a girl aged about nineteen. Her bleached blond hair is scraped back in a scrunchy, revealing a heavily made up, pretty face and hooped gold earrings a show dog could jump through. She is wearing a cropped white top, hipster denim shorts and high platform wedges. Her boobs are almost pouring out of the tiny top. She gives them the once over.

"Alright, babb? What's it to be?" The broad Brummy is lost on both Paco and Sandwich but they recognise a proper girl when they see one.

"Thank you. We would like some coffee and some brandy. Carlos Primero if that is possible". Felix's eyes sparkle with delight as he stares right at the girl, his appreciation obvious. She knows this and comes back at him with a big smile.

"We ain't got much ovva choice, chick, but I've got some Remy

Martin. That's brandy, init? Some bloke left it here. In a hurry, he was". She turns around and reaches down under the counter. The boys get a face full of her perfect peachy arse, having just enough time to register this with each other before the top half of her re-appears with an unopened bottle of Remy Martin XO.

"Is this okay for you? I don't know nuthin' about brandy".

The boys nod in amazement and she opens the bottle forthwith, selects two brandy balloons from the rack and begins to pour. Very large measures.

"That's about a double, isn't it? It'll have to do. There's no measure since some bastard nicked it!"

"That is just perfect. And the coffee?"

"Oh, yeah, silly me".

She turns around and removes a pot from the hot plate and begins to pour into two Union Jack mugs.

"Milk and sugar with them, babb?" she asks, reaching for both before the boys have had a chance to say no. They are entranced by her arse, barely restrained within the confines of the tiny shorts and would probably have agreed to anything.

She plonks them down on the counter.

"Anything else? Lovelay!"

She picks up her Diet Coke and returns to the end of the bar, back to a well-thumbed copy of 'Take a Break' and chews on a knackered pencil.

Rolf walks across from the custom house and enters the passport office, exchanges a few words with the official and returns to the plane, before making some minor adjustments to the ailerons. Next stop is the refuelling depot. He walks over and removes a credit card from his small leather hand-bag and proffers it to the guy. A swift authorisation ensues and out comes the aviation fuel bowser, filling the Piper to the brim. A few more checks and Rolf's happy. He walks back to the passport control office and through into 'Brenda's'.

*

Things in Ceuta are going from bad to worse for Sergeant Ramirez. The afternoon sun is just pouring petrol on the flames, firing up the crowd. After an extremely brief discussion with the hapless Officer Sanchez, he decides to call for back-up and gets on the horn to HQ in Ceuta town.

"Put me through to Chief Delgado. No, I don't want his secretary, *imbécile*. This is Sergeant Ramirez. At the Fnideq border. Yes. We have a little problem here. Put me through. *Dios mio!*" He throws down the 'phone as the first part of the fence collapses and a couple of hundred hot and angry Moroccans and Senegalese come pouring through. They are hurling bottles and stones, some of which come crashing through the guard hut's windows. He panics and runs out, Sanchez is already there. He takes out his standard issue pistol and fires into the air, above their heads, causing them to duck and run for cover. He fires again, the last thing he remembers as a huge iron bar swishes through the air and cracks across the back of his head, splitting it wide open and sending his unconscious body crashing face down onto the dusty road. Sanchez turns to help but the mob is already on him, sensing that he has not yet drawn his gun. They beat him to the ground and the boots wade in, kicking, stamping. They are baying for blood now, the sight of the struggling policeman urging them on. Suddenly, the crowd parts, as if controlled by some mythical force. A tall, well-built hooded man comes through, carrying a huge kerb stone dug from the side of the border checkpoint. He raises it above his head, the moment is paused as if in freeze-frame, then he brings it down with extreme force onto Sanchez's defenceless head, splitting it wide open, splattering those at the front with dark arterial blood and brains. The crowd's silence turns into cheers and cat-calls as the blood begins to flow into the gutter. Ramirez is motionless on the ground; he has long since passed out from the repeated kicks and punches. More and more of the angry mob are now on Ceutan soil and it starts to move towards the town as one, unimpeded. Soon, it is gone and only the two bodies lie in the road, motionless. On the Moroccan side of the border, close to the newly constructed and hated wall, the guards look the other way.

*

"We are ready, my friends, ja?" Rolf is anxious to leave, mindful of the fact that he wishes to negotiate the journey in the light. Paco and Felix finish their XOs, leaving the coffee wisely untouched. The girl smiles sweetly at them as they go.

"You would, I think, my friend?" Paco smiles knowingly at his oppo.

"You already know the answer. Would you?" Felix licks his lips at the prospect of the chavvy blonde Brummy riding bareback on his hard cock.

"Not for me. Wrong colour, *which you know*!" Paco's predilection for petite, dusky Arabic women is well known in Alicante.

A nod to the officials and they are on the way back to the fully refuelled and recharged Cherokee. Rolf deals with the necessary communications and soon they are again clattering down the runway and up into the afternoon sky, around the rock, leaving Catalan Bay to the right and away over the Mediterranean, the white horses breaking on the surfing beach far below.

"I have made everything good with my friend. We are logged to go directly to Algeria then over the landscape of the Star Wars set. I showed them the camera equipment and they did not even show an interest. In just a few minutes, we will start to have the engine trouble and we will set down in Ceuta for the emergency landing, ja?"

"*Excellente, Rolf, excellente*. It is correct to say that you are making the good job".

"Ceuta must take us, they have no choice when we are making the Mayday call. It will be too late for the engineer to look at our *little fuel problem* tonight, so we go into the town and the plane will stay at the airport for the night. I think everything else is OK?"

"Everything else is the work for our contacts. You must ensure that the doors and catches are left open. There will be a guard for the plane, after the work is done. He will know if there is any *unexpected interest*. We will have the good time tonight. It is a pity that we cannot meet with *my* friends. That would be a serious error of judgment. I think the ending for that story is not a good one". He makes the sign of a knife being drawn across an exposed jugular, and then laughs like a hyena.

"Then I suggest, my friends, that you sit back and enjoy the view. The stewardess will be along with the drinks and duty free goods presently". Rolf laughs at his little joke, but the others' minds are deeply fixated elsewhere.

*

Click. "Gib Immigration here. Probably nothing but we've just had three men through here, Piper Cherokee index D-XFRT en–route from Mucha Miel, now routed to Algiers and back to here. Story about photographing the Star Wars set. Just a bit too glib. One for the log, maybe? Good. OK. See you anon". *Click.*

*

Ceuta Police Headquarters

"Sir, I do not know if this is important, but we had a message from border control 'D', direction Fnideq about twenty minutes ago. Said they had a problem and then the line went dead. Should we do anything? I have tried to call them back but there is no answer".

"Probably nothing. Was it Ramirez?"

"Yes, sir. Sergeant Ramirez sounding excited".

"And what is the new thing about that?"

"I…I'm just worried about them, sir".

"Send a car, just to verify the situation. If they won't answer the radio or the telephone, then we must use the car. This is very inconvenient. I need the car to go to a dinner tonight".

*

Slowly, Ramirez opened his eyes, gingerly checking the growing lump on the back of his neck. Caked blood covered his back and stained his police uniform. He staggered to his feet, then fell again to his knees, head spinning from concussion. As the stinging tears cleared from his eyes, he was met with Sanchez's twisted, lifeless corpse slumped in the road. He half-crawled, half rolled his way towards it, almost stupefied from the searing pain coming from every part of his body. As he got close, the realisation of Sanchez's horrific death became horrifically clear and he sunk again to the ground, utterly defeated. His eyes met the broken fence and events of earlier came flooding back to him. He felt for his police walkie-talkie, but it was gone. Turning around as fast as his head would allow, he saw the radio discarded on the road. He crawled towards it, desperate to warn HQ of the murder. He looked around, but he was alone, save for the bloody torso of Sanchez. The radio was smashed.

*

"D-XFRT calling Ceuta. D-XFRT calling Ceuta. We are encountering engine problems, intermittent fuel supply. Engine cutting out. Request permission to land. We are Piper Cherokee D-XFRT out of Gibraltar heading for Algiers. Request permission to divert and land. Come in Ceuta".

"Ceuta Tower. State your position please".

"Currently eighteen, one-eight miles east from you over the sea. Engine is cutting out".

"Message understood, D-XFRT. Permission granted. Approach runway one-niner. Wind south-south-east, Force Three. Emergency services notified. Good luck, Piper. Ceuta Tower out". The radio went silent and a grin from Rolf told the boys that the job was on.

"I have made some minor adjustments to the fuel line, Felix. When we land, I will cut the engine and then we will come to a halt without power. They will want to check the machine. Just before we land, I am going to switch to the reserve tank which contains contaminated fuel. That should be enough to keep the engineers busy for a few hours tomorrow!"

"You think of everything, my friend. Let us hope that the morning is as successful as today. Complacency is the enemy of the organised".

Where does he get them from, thought Paco as he went over the collection for the fiftieth time. Yin and Yang. Sometimes he was not so sure.

Rolf began to bank, ready for the approach from the sea straight into Ceuta at one hundred and thirty miles per hour. The little plane almost skimmed across the waves, nearing the flat, sandy coast.

"Ceuta Tower. This is D-XFRT. We are on final approach. Runway one-niner. Engine almost out. Please make ready the emergency services. We are three persons on board. May God be with us. Over".

"D-XFRT, this is Ceuta Tower. Runway open and all other traffic holding. You are clear to land, runway one-niner. Good luck. Out".

As they crossed the coast, Rolf began to waggle the wings, feathering the engine and bringing the nose up and down for full effect. The runway came up to meet them and then they were down, immediately cutting the engine, swerving across the tarmac and coming to a clumsy halt just in front of the tower.

"Ceuta Tower. Thank you for your assistance. As you can see, we are down. Request help to move to apron. No power, repeat, no power. Over".

"D-XFRT request acknowledged. We are arranging a towing vehicle for you. It is on the way. Ceuta Tower out".

Within seconds, the searing desert heat hit the small cabin like a wave, quickly rising to over forty degrees. Rolf opened the tiny windows but the effect was minimal. Jackets were removed and Rolf opened the cabin door to offer a little more assistance. Eventually, the small, yellow flat truck arrived and the front wheel was hooked up. Slowly, the Piper was pulled towards the hangars, finally coming to rest next to the rotting hulk of a DC9, long since retired. Rolf, followed by Felix, then Paco emerged onto the burning tarmac, ostentatiously retrieved the cameras and holdalls and led them towards the terminal building. A solitary Iberia Boeing 737 stood at rest, awaiting orders for its return flight to Malaga.

"I think it is best if you wait in the terminal whilst I deal with the technical people. It is easy because I am German. If I don't want to understand their Spanish, then I just look stupid. Maybe that is not so difficult, hein?" Rolf smiled, his fingers crossed.

"So far so good". There was a menacing tone in Felix's voice, the German's laissez-faire attitude was wearing thin. As Rolf walked away from them, his expression told everything to his partner. Coldness, even in the heat of the desert sun, was all around.

They made their way towards the terminal and air-conditioned sanity, whilst Rolf blagged his way to a repair and storage for the plane. Ceuta immigration was a formality as the men showed their Spanish passports. Congratulations were given in the form of handshakes and hearty back-slapping. News of the 'controlled-crash' had travelled quickly around the little backwater and they were given large Carlos Primeros in tribute to the *expertness of the pilot*. Studied confusion reigned on the faces of the two men and they began to ask rehearsed questions about the plane and how long it could be before an engineer would be able to attend. Their questions were met with the usual incredulity. 'Don't know. Maybe. Possible. This is Africa. Tomorrow. The next day.' Their despairing faces worked perfectly and it was not long before offers of help began to materialise from the growing throng in the small terminal building. News of the border problems, however, was a lot slower. It had not yet reached the airport.

"I think we should leave the situation now, my friend. You have the mobile number of the German?"

"Rolf will be OK, I think you will find. He is a survivor, of that there is no question. You could throw him upside down in his precious septic tank and he would emerge smelling of San Miguel!"

Nice analogy, thought Felix, but his mind was already elsewhere and his mobile was already on.

Click.

"Good evening, *princesa*, I think that your dreams have come true!"

"Well, how nice to hear from you after all this time. May I assume that you are already feeling the sand of Africa under your feet?"

"You would be correct in that assumption".

"*Perfecto*! Then you should meet me in town straight away. Are you alone?"

"Naturally, our friend Señor P is with me. There is also another but he has his own agenda. Not a problem for us".

"Let us say in one hour. Be on the corner of the Paseo del Rebellin and the Plaza. My driver will collect you. Then we go and have some fun! I have many things to tell you. Ciao!"

Click.

Fun. With Marianna, that can mean anything. Anything from a business meeting where she makes a fortune and you make nothing, to a wild night on the edge, where her adventurous desires go way beyond the perimeters of fantasy. She will go anywhere, do anything if it suits her. She has been known to have meetings in Madrid with the government, then go out in the evening to a salsa bar, dance like a dervish, then strip naked in a seedy back-street joint, taking the ten-Euro notes with her and giving them all to a street kid outside. She is *unpredictable*. She lays everything open, yet no-one knows her. Danger for her is an emotion. Something with which she trifles, if it takes her fancy. She is truly an enigma.

"All systems go, Paco. It is time to move. Tell the German that we are leaving the airport and that he is to call us if anything *happens*. Marianna's people will *fuel the plane* then everything is done. They will come in after the airport is closed. The hold is unlocked. We just have to spend the night here and in the morning, like magic, we can leave and return to Mucha Miel".

"Like magic, huh? That sounds like a dream to me. The problem with dreams is that sooner or later, you wake up".

"*Tranquilo*, my friend. Marianna has everything under control here and she also has some news for us. She seemed *excited*. I don't know what that means, but there must be a good reason for this. Never, does the *princesa* waste her breath".

"Then let us go, my friend. It is time once more to witness the delights of Africa. For too long I have not been with a true woman!" His face lights up, he comes alive at the prospect of a long African night. They walk out onto a sandy forecourt, to the taxi rank, where there is just one very old but very clean Mercedes, complete with smiling Algerian. After briefly dealing with the German, Paco aims a volley of fluent Arabic at the driver, who looks a little downcast at the fact that his passengers are going to rumble the slightest deviation in route or fare. He shrugs his shoulders, puts the holdall into the boot and climbs in.

"Where to, *effendi*?"

"To a good hotel, please. A *very good* hotel". His expression sorts out any doubt in the guy's mind and they're off. Pulling away from Ceuta airport takes you straight under the skin of north Africa, the smells, the whole being of the place is a million miles away from where they were just hours before. We're on the coast road, taking us into the town, past villas, a nice bit of colonial faded elegance as only the Europeans can do when they kind of leave Africa behind, but leave a toe in the water, if you know what I mean. The irascible old buggers stay on, pretending, hoping for some long gone world to return. Kiss it better. It's a total anachronism here, just like most of the inhabitants. Soon, they're coming into the town, along the palm-flanked boulevards and avenidas and into the older part. On the left, the bazaar; the air is thick with aromas of spices and exotic concoctions. A thousand cigarettes are lit and extinguished along the narrow street, the hookah pipes grow bright.

"Very good hotel, *effendi*! Very popular with tourists".

"You have tourists here now?" Felix laughs at this concept. He's been coming here too long to fall for that one. He pays the driver in Euros as the small holdall is removed from the cavernous boot of the Merc.

"A thousand thank-yous, my friend!" and he's off, in search of new prey.

The hotel is old and traditional, rather like the whole place. As they walk in, the aroma of joss sticks fills the air, despite the obvious Spanish ownership. They undergo the predictable searching to 'see if we have rooms available', however, the sight of Felix's black American Express card seems to do the trick and suddenly everyone's fawning all over them. Two lads are fighting over who's going to carry the Vuitton bag up to the rooms. How is it that hotel people can *smell money*? Years of practice!

The rooms, at the top of the hotel, are neighbouring and have a roof terrace, overlooking the old town. It *screams* north Africa, right down to the minaret across the square, even now calling the faithful to prayer through the loudspeakers hung round its slender tower. This is not Spain.

Felix has barely sat down on the bed to rest his legs for a moment, when a rapid knock at the door, followed by a barrage of guttural Valenciana announces that Paco is already lonely. He walks in and together, they walk out onto the roof terrace. He is armed with two ice-cold San Migs from the fridge and they stand and admire the view over this enclave of intrigue.

"They could do so much with this place. Look at it, my friend. Just a little money and they *would come*! The weather is good all the year, the travel, it is good from Europe and well, you have the girls too!"

"You are incorrigible, my dear Paco. And as for the place, do you not know that the money from *Bruselas* is already coming. They have big plans for this little place. We will be many times here, I think. But I do not understand what you see in these girls though. They are so complicated! "

"Then you have your answer. I do not understand this straightforward life of yours, this perfect clean place you come from. For me, life is in the gutter, life *is* the gutter. It is from where we come and where we will end. The soil of the field is maybe more faithful, but it is the gutter from where you get the true honesty. It is where wars are won and lost, love and sex, friendship and trust. When you come from that place, you have a reality which others cannot understand".

"I never understand a fucking word you are saying, *pequeño*! You are like that Frenchman, the footballer Cantona. The work you do is perfection, but what comes from your mouth, it is total bollocks. Do you know what I think? I think we should start drinking very heavily!"

"Then we are agreed on something! Let us finish these and then we go to a bar before meeting the *princesa*".

They drain the San Migs and leave the bottles on a small wicker table standing just under the wall. The sun has given up and the lights of the town glow bright against the moonlit sea. Cooking aromas rise into the night sky, promising much to the olfactory senses, coriander, marjoram and cumin are mixed with barbecuing lamb and beef.

Their return to the reception area is met with much bowing and scraping, but they are out and away before any taxis can be whistled up. The walk to Plaza Africa takes them along narrow alleys, lined with tiny shops, vying for the little business which the late autumn brings. There is a coolness in the air, the desert heat fast disappearing with the dying fiery sun. At the end of the alley, there is a tiny walled garden bar, with wooden tables and chairs. They pass in, under the ancient sandstone arch and sit down under a canvas awning, the warmth from the kitchens enveloping them.

They are greeted by a fat moustached old man who seems to appear from nowhere.

"*Dios mio*! Paco! What brings you to our humble city? We are indeed greatly honoured to have you here. This is a gift from Allah. On this of all days!"

"Is there something we should know? It is not a saint's day today? My mother would kill me if she thought I had forgotten a special day of the saints".

"Do you not know?"

"What, my friend, know what?"

"Today is the big news day in Ceuta. Today we have the rioting in the town, many people have been killed. Hundreds, they say!" His face is alive with excitement and enthusiasm.

"You are joking with me. I do not believe that this is possible. Everyone is too sleepy to riot. No, I will not have it. Tell me something sensible for a change!"

"Señor Paco, it is true. Some people, they came through the border at Fnideq this afternoon, they kill the border guards and then they come into the town, breaking windows and turning over the cars. The police, they try to stop them, but one has a gun and he fires it into the crowd. The police, they fire back and then there is panic. It happened not five hundred metres from here! They say it is Al Qaeda!"

"And what of the riot now? Where are all these insurgents?"

"After the shots were fired, the people, they ran into the town and away. The bodies are at the hospital and everyone else is in the jail. It is now full and this morning it was empty. Life in Africa is never simple. Since Karim el Majjati put this little place on the map…"

"You see, my friend, there is your complicated Africa at work. Do you still like it?" Felix raps Paco on the arm, half in humour and half serious. His mind has already raced ahead about a hundred miles and he is not, repeat not happy.

"My friends, the news is not good, I know but let me ease your pain with a cool drink. Some *airan*, perhaps?"

"I think we need something a little stronger than that! Two Chinchon, large ones".

Fat moustache goes back inside and quickly returns with two very large measures of what looks like alka seltzer. Cloudy, white spirit from just outside Madrid, dearly beloved in this little outpost. Both of the boys neck them down and then another. This time, they are joined by the fat guy and talk quickly turns to the future. Another ten minutes and they announce their departure by the appearance of a fifty Euro note and that's that. Quick embrace, kiss on both cheeks, undying friendship and they're away, across the Plaza de Africa and Marianna's waiting 600.

"Good evening, gentlemen. Señorita da Sancha would like me to drive you to her. Just a little precaution, you understand. Permit me to take you there". The chauffeur's sunglasses reveal little in the African night, but the size of his pecs and the sheer physical presence indicate that he hasn't been chosen just for his driving abilities. The guy is massive.

The Mercedes glides away from the Plaza and back into the narrow streets of the old town. In not more than two minutes, the car stops and massive bloke is out and opening the rear door, pavement side.

"Please, go up the stairs facing you and turn right at the top. Do not be alarmed, the Señorita is expecting you".

"Oh, we know that". Felix is out and off the street in one second, closely followed by Paco. Inside the open doorway, a soft orange light glows and powerful exotic aromas greet them. There is no sign; no logo to indicate what might be at the top. The faint sound of desert music is just audible and it draws them up. A beaded curtain greets them and they push their way through and into a dimly lit room. A veiled girl stands there, dressed from head to toe in gauzy red silk, her feet bare and covered in gold jewellery.

"Welcome, gentlemen. Please leave your coats and your weapons here and follow me".

Paco and Felix nod to each other and accede to the girl's requests. Who wouldn't? As they walk behind her, they can just make out the shape of her body through the exquisite material. Her naked body.

"Hello, boys!" Across the floor in the salon, Marianna lies decorously, propped up on large cushions, dressed also in silk. Her feet too are naked and the jewellery matches the other girl's perfectly.

"Make yourselves at home, my friends. Tonight, Marianna will entertain you like never before". She claps her hands together and two more girls appear from behind a golden curtain. They bring in hookah pipes and set them down in front of both Paco and Felix.

"Please, enjoy a little smoke before the girls take you to be bathed. I think you have had a very long and hot day. It is not nice to have the plane break down, no?" Her smile so wide, her expression more wicked than Medusa herself.

"Do you like my little playroom?"

"It is beautiful, quite beautiful, *princesa*. You truly can be royalty in here! But why the little game? We could have made our way here. You could have just given us the address".

"Haha! There is no address for here. This is the house with no name. I found it when I first came to the enclave. It was a little shabby then, not quite the place it had been before Spain decided to, shall we say, downgrade its influence here. I have simply given it my patronage and now, well you can see, it is a little heaven on earth!"

The girls sit at their feet, waiting, smiling from beneath the thin silk. Their makeup is flawless, dark, heavy eye-shadow and liner, dark red lips lined with black. Their heads are slightly bowed, giving the impression that they are looking up to the men from under perfectly sculpted eyebrows. Both men draw deep drafts from the pipes, gradually lying back on the soft cushions, the air thick with the heady smoke. Once they have inhaled sufficient, they look at each other, then at the girls and Marianna motions them to leave, taking the boys by the hand. They pass through another arch and into a galleried room. Below, down a shallow staircase, lies a steam bath, complete with Roman pillars and stone seating. They walk down the stairs to a large table at the bottom where they undress. As promised, underneath the silk, they are both completely naked, but for gold chains around neck, wrist, waist and ankle. Their navels are each studded with large diamonds. Undressing the men, they show the way into the hot bath, following dutifully behind.

"This is unbelievable, my friend. The *princesa*, she amazes me always, but this, I did not expect!"

"No, you are right, even I have seen nothing like this. I have been in some very special clubs with you all over the world, but this, this is something else".

The atmosphere is becoming dreamy and the girls' soft voices somehow distant. They sit down on underwater stone chairs, shaped to the body so that they lie down, with just the head above water level. The girls begin to perform massage but soon, their hands are well below the water, working a different kind of magic. The pipes have done their work and they are both totally out of it, conscious of what is happening but totally lost to reality. The girls are both sexual experts and soon have them both fully erect, massaging and kneading. One by one, they climb on top and are soon riding away in perfect unison, holding hands with each other. The heat is intense and steam is rising from the surface of the water, filling the room with a strange cocktail of aromas. As the heat becomes too much, the girls climb off and take each of them by the hand once more, out of the pool and up the stairs. They are guided, totally out of it, into the room and onto the cushions once more. This time, the girls take bottles of oil and begin to rub them all over, their bodies glistening bright in the flickering candlelight. They are soon climbing back on, but this time, there is a coupling going on, each girl giving of herself totally. The boys' eyes are closed, they are barely awake, yet they are standing upright like truncheons. Within a short time, they are done, the girls climbing off and sucking them to completion. All the time, Marianna is watching from a distance, licking her lips, playing with herself, a huge dildo inserted to the hilt. Her perfect legs wide apart, exposed to the world.

"That was beautiful, my little ones. You are so professional now".

The veiled girls take silk robes and drape them over the now softly sleeping Felix and Paco and leave the room, following Marianna's instructions to bring drinks and more pipes. They soon return and take small glasses of opaque fluid from a golden tray, pouring a little of the liquid over the boys' lips. Human instinct takes over and just like the scene from the Bond movie, they lick them like the good obedient boys they are! In seconds, they both come round, slowly but without any side effects. Just a little woozy. As their eyes open and focus, they see Marianna across the room, now restored and sipping a cocktail from an old fashioned martini glass.

"Welcome back, boys! How do you feel now? Totally relaxed?"

"I don't know" says Paco, he really doesn't know what the fuck's going on.

"What are these robes all about? Where are our clothes?" Paco, Paco, Paco!

"At this very moment, someone is washing and drying them for you. The jacket is being dry cleaned and everything else is under control. Any other boring questions?"

"Just that I feel fantastic and I can't remember a thing. Apart from, that is, some pipes when we came in? Yes, Marianna, that I *can* remember! What on earth did you put in there?"

"It is that which made me buy into this little place. They grow it on the roof and say it has been growing here for many generations. It is why people come here!" Her expression is one of pure mischief, God knows how she does it, but she just captivates everyone in the room.

"Now, boys, despite the rather pleasant interlude you have just enjoyed, we have a little problem. By the way, was there anything unusual at the airport?"

"Nothing the German couldn't deal with. No, we just came straight to the hotel and now we are here. Courtesy of your two girls, that is!"

"Earlier today, there was a small problem at the border crossing to Fnideq".

"We heard about it. Hundreds dead?" Paco smiled at the news.

"Not quite hundreds. Maybe a few, but the problem is far greater for us. The port is closed and we cannot get the merchandise. At least we won't be able to get it before you have to go back. If you stay too long, well, you know what can happen when you get back, *cariño*! Too many questions. I don't think anything is going to happen to change matters until the idiots from Madrid get themselves down here and 'assess the situation'. That could take days".

"So this is a wasted trip, then?"

"Not exactly wasted! I think you enjoyed yourselves? Anyway, there are other things which we need to discuss. The cartel has plans for expansion in mainland Europe and that is going to include the UK. You had better go back to Mr O'Riordan and give him the good news. I think he would like that, no?"

"A man would never truly know whether Mr O'Riordan would like anything. Even his own people don't know him sometimes".

"Aaahh! A man of mystery. If only he were a little younger. I should have to snare him, no?"

"I am sure, *princesa*, that if you wanted him now or then, you could have him".

"There, *amigo*, I think you are wrong. That is a devoted man, devoted to his wife and his lifestyle. He is like the brick wall to other women now. There is some darkness in his past, perhaps in their past which we will never know. Often, it is good to leave these things alone. There are some secrets which should never be revealed, for they are too painful. Anyway, the cartel wishes for a report, so I would like you to look into the possibilities in Alicante port for a bulk shipment to arrive. We are talking *tonnes*, gentlemen. I think your friend in the *Aduana* will help, no?"

"With her, anything is possible, *princesa*, but this is a very serious escalation in our activities, no? I think that our friend will be very concerned about what has been happening here today. Is it anything to do with Shukrijamah and Mejjati? I hope not, because we do not want too much interest from the mainland. After the bombing at Atocha...?"

"This will calm down. I already have it... *in hand*... We are going to turn things here to our advantage!"

"It would be madness, suicide, even, to try and move something from here in the next few days?"

"You are right, my Paco. For you, this trip has become one of education and planning. The cartel wishes to expand rapidly into these markets, so the faster you pass this news to your *Aduanista* and my friend Mr Patrick, then the better it will be. You will return to Spain tomorrow with a cargo not of dreams, but of untold riches for the future. We are not talking hundreds of percent increase in business, but thousands!"

Felix lay back on the silk cushions, his brain back at work. He could sense achievement in Marianna's voice, an excitement normally reserved for her moments alone. She was *sharing*.

*

Rolf Weber's airport activities had soon come to a close and he was now planted firmly on a bar stool. The heights of Monte Hacho accorded him a view down into the town. They also gave him prior warning of any undesired police activity, but there was to be none of that this night. Instead, he was joined by two leather jacketed Moroccans who toasted his arrival in Turkish *raki*, a luxury which normally remained concealed under the dark wood bar top. The German's blonde hair contrasted with their swarthy appearance and made him appear to be the sandwich filling, yet his relaxed posture and attitude told a different story. He was at all times in charge. The customer. *The paymaster*.

"There are problems, *effendi*. Problems of a new kind. We do not wish you problems, only solutions".

"Tell me, my friend, what is there here that you cannot solve for me? This is not normally something which you bring to my table. You are not losing your touch, are you?"

"The touch? No. There are forces *over there* which I do not control". He gestured towards the Moroccan side of the border, towards Fnideq.

"They do not like the new wall. They say the money for the wall comes from Europe and it is Europe which is closing them off from the jobs. Now that has been hi-jacked by Al Qaeda and their supporters and it has become all about politics, not jobs. Until recently, everyone was happy here making plenty of money from the drugs and the boats taking the Moroccans and Senegalese to Spain. Everybody money…everybody happy. Now these fucking *terroristas* spoil it for us. They don't give a fuck; just want the Shariah law, throw out the Spanish".

"And my *coca*?"

"Now they want the money to buy guns, make bombs for destroying the trains and aircraft in US. *They* want the coca business. They see how much they make from the heroin in Afghan, now they want this! Already they try to steal from the importers!"

"I think they have a big fight with Medellin, ja?"

"I think no. There is talk of many more soldiers from Spain coming here. After today, I think that is certain. Maybe they leave us businessmen alone?" The three men laughed quietly into their drinks, before moving unnoticed into a back room to conclude their business.

*

Much later, in a street running parallel to the hotel of the sleeping Paco and Felix, four hooded men dismantled and re-assembled smuggled guns, ready for the morning. They were the only ones from the border incident not in custody. Sergeant Ramirez lay sedated in a hospital bed, his memories of the heavily disguised men distant and for now, forgotten.

Chapter Twelve

Waterfront Place, Chelmsford Friday 13th October 2006

As the Bold party begins to arrive, sweeping into the gravelled car park of the Waterfront, teams of staff swarm into the 'tram-shed' as the function room is known. Since the exquisite refurbishment of 2005, business has been booming, bigger and better acts have started to appear at the venue. Tonight's attraction is a soul night with a Blues Brothers tribute band headlining, fronted by a major Stax artist from the 1960s. The great and not-so-good are out in force and tables were sold out within two days. Dean's round table for fourteen is nearest the stage. It's all a bit 'Long Good Friday'. On the runners and riders tonight are: Gina-G, a surprising appearance by the lovely Benissa, Dave and Shirley, Debra Dildo, Mick The Teeth and Mrs Mick, Town Hall and his bird Tracy, an old mate of Gina's called Lorraine, Shotgun Kev looking a bit out of place, Dean's mate from the Hammers' days called Jimmy Jag, aka 'Stanley', who, for some reason has brought his seventeen year old son Sean and last but not least, Debra's blonde mate Paula who's just come back from Cyprus sporting her new tits. On the missing list: One Language and Ali the Coat.

*

And thereby hangs a tale. The boys will know what's going down *because they are not there*. This seemingly eclectic group of chaps has been together for one hell of a long time.

Dean. You know. For some reason, everybody loves Dean despite himself, or maybe even *because* he can be such a twat. Dean the controller. Dean the top man. Dean is, well; Dean.

Dave. Lifelong friend. Of Dean. Big lump. He saved Dean many times during the old ICF days. Because whatever you say about Dave, if he hits you, you fuckin' stay hit. He's been in Dean's shadow for his whole life, which is where he likes to be. When he's not in Dean's wife. How the hell that happened is bizarre. A quick fumble one night, accidental really, but as long as it's kept quiet, then everything will be alright in the world. Just don't be around if Dean ever twigs that his missus is being porked by Number One Mate. 'Cos Number One Mate will be translated into Number One Stiff and he won't be no good to Mrs Dean then.

Mick. Ah! Mick the Teeth. Spread them all round the Smoke in the old days. Want it doing, whatever it is and if your name is Dean Bold, then Mick's your man. Ever since Dean gave him a job after he got out of the shovel and he met Mrs Mick through Gina, there is *nothing* that he wouldn't do for Dean. In fact, should Dean ever find out about Dave and Gina, it will be Mick who will sort it. Just before Dean delivers the final blow.

Shotgun Kev. Bit of a mystery man to the world is Kev. But then the world is a bit of a mystery to him. Never says much. Tends to let the gun speak for him. Incredible sense of humour has Kev. No-one ever expects him to say anything, so when he does, the place invariably goes quiet. He's done every bank from Tower Bridge to Southend and back. Always maintains his dignity does Kev, in the face of some considerable adversity during his time. He's done some bird and rumour has it that he once went a whole year in Wandsworth without saying a word. Just didn't consider it necessary. Quietened down a bit lately an' all. No-one ever really knows what he's thinking about. Except Dean.

Town. An outsider. As you know, a mate of Dean's who is just about to be made up into the firm. Contacts man. Bit of a cut above, the object of suspicion from the older members of the firm. Spent some time in the 'Ville with Ron, who vouches for him.

Jimmy. Another of Dean's ICF team. Known as 'Stanley' in those days, on account of his propensity for excessive use of Stanley knives on his victims, cutting the letters ICF into their faces before leaving the situation. Now a car dealer and limousine hire owner, Jimmy is one of Dean's most trusted and loved mates. Made his money 'the hard way' in protection, door rackets and minding. Tight as a duck's arse.

Ron. Met Town Hall when in the 'Ville. Kept an eye on him, having earmarked him as a player. The oldest member of Dean's firm, he is the quiet planner, an old fashioned hard man with a brain. Reads all the time and loves The Times crossword which he learnt to do when serving time for attempted murder. The only reason it was attempted was because the geezer in question fell into a rubbish skip having been helped off the top floor of a car park by Ron. Instead of onto the concrete.

Coat. Born Kaleburnu, Cyprus as Ali Halil. Long time friend of

Dean from when his Mum and Dad had the Wimpy Bar in Basildon. Never takes coat off. Runs a chain of kebab shops and has a hotel and casino in Kyrenia, North Cyprus which is run by his family. Very shrewd and intelligent. Worked from the age of seven as the breadwinner of his family. Came to England after the 1974 invasion of Cyprus complete with his Mum and the contents of a Greek owned bank. AKA Ali Hali.

Every team, every firm, in order to work properly, has to have organisation. It has to have the right people doing the right jobs. I mean, imagine either Mick the Teeth or Ali the Coat doing Gina. Wouldn't work. It would look, frankly, ridiculous. Plus, Dean would have to kill them, which would fuck up the firm. Proper fuck it up. So, there you have Ron and Ali. Sitting having a quiet meal on the Romford Road, E7. They're out the back, behind a partition. Might as well be on the moon. Ali sits there, coat on, Ron has the paper next to him, a few clues are left incomplete. In front of them are two of the most succulent steaks you have ever seen. Ron has a bottle of Chateau Palmer 1985 in front of him and Ali has a Diet Coke. No ice. There is as much going on when they don't speak as when they do. However, that's not going to help you and me.

"You are 100% behind this Town Hall, innit. I mean, if you say he's OK, then that's good enough for me. I've been looking at some new storage. We're going to need it. The research I have been doing tells me that if we are going large with this, I don't think even Dean realises how big it could get. The man he is going to see, this man who Hall met in Spain? Well, he is a serious man. All his references are more than serious".

He stares at Ron, who appears to be looking at the crossword. Taking a long draught of the glinting claret nestling in his huge bowl glass, he looks up at the coated one.

"Cold but with a *beast heart*. Four letters. Ends in a 'D'".

"Please, my friend. Be serious".

"I am. Cold with a 'B' start, ending in 'D'? That would be 'Bold', then. Didn't know I could make up de clues as well as solve 'em, eh, Ali?" Ron laughed loud enough to shake the foundations, before returning the matter at hand.

"We've been havin' a good run, mate. The swerve game is getting' harder and harder. The profits in this, we can afford to drop the church a few quid each time. That way, we're a hundred percent the gear's getting through. There ain't the resources in V&W no more. The smart wedge is movin' on. We got a blindin' firm 'ere. Just needs a bitta tweakin' an' we're sorted".

"Casualties?"

"Not at the moment. I've had my cousin Hassan on it for months, ever since we had that scare with Mick's brother up at the big house. Nothing. Not a trace of a grass. The only problem we've had lately was with Rainsford and that's sorted now".

*

Looks like Veuve Clicquot's shares will have gone up by the end of the evening, judging by the number of bottles Dean's ordered. Silver champagne buckets surround the Bold table, each containing magnums of The Widow, with a special bucket next to Dean's chair, full of Ruinart Rosé. He's had this Up West in Secrets and has decided that it's all he drinks *on these occasions*. Gina-G's even given a seating plan to Dawn to send over to the restaurant. This is partly so Dean's happy and partly so that she can pricktease Dave all night. Talk of the devil: Dave and Shirley arrive first, funny, because normally you can't get Shirl out of the house. She still looks like a bag of laundry done up in the middle, but the kids are staying with mates, so she's got no excuse to mess about making food in the vast Hilton kitchen. Dave hasn't even really noticed her, he's still thinking about Gina-G and her antics. Next on the list are Town Hall and Tracy, swiftly followed by Jimmy Jag and Sean. The poor lad looks a bit out of his depth. He's a good looking boy and seems happy enough at the old man's side. The Dildo has arrived on her own, but bumped into Mr and Mrs Mick The Teeth in the car-park so they make a little threesome as they walk in. Now there's a thought! Easy, tiger! Dave's on the case and he's making sure everyone's OK. The waitresses have glasses on silver trays and everyone's steaming in, even Shirley! The rest of them drift in until finally, Dean, Gina and Benissa arrive. Gina's poured her into a corset dress which, on second thoughts probably wasn't a brilliant plan, but it's a bit late. Benissa's tits are boiling over and poor old Sean's eyes are out on stalks. Gina's wearing one of her little Versace numbers, more like a gownless evening strap, teamed with some gold jewelled Gina stilettos. She looks the business, fair play. Dean's wearing an open necked white Armani shirt and a black Versace suit, teamed with black loafers and no socks. Debra's wearing a black feather dress teamed with some peacock feather stilettos she's found in a new designer shop. Won't be anybody else with a pair of *those*! The rest of the room is filling up now and Dean's party is creating a bit of a stir. Basildon comes to Chelmo via Canvey. Now there's a conundrum. Once everyone's there, Dean welcomes them and gets them sat down according to Gina's seating plan. Sure enough, Shirley's moved across the table, Dave's to her right and she's put Tracy next to Dean. Her gold glittery corset and mini-skirt should keep his eyes occupied and if all else fails, there'll be Town on hand to help him powder his nose. She's put Benissa next to Sean, hoping that at least they'll keep each other occupied and won't see too much of what's cracking off. Kids don't miss a bleeding thing. Benissa spots Sean across the room and whispers to her Aunty Debra,

"He's a bit of alright, ain't he? Wouldn't mind him getting his laughing gear round my smelly bits, eh Debs?" She shrieks with her famous ninety decibel laughter and even her mother turns round to see what's occurring. Debra's looking around the room. Her mate Paula's playing with her new tits, still a bit of a novelty and the top she's wearing could do with being a bit bigger. Jimmy's eyes are out on stalks.

*

Ali's not really one for that sort of thing. He and Ron are on the brandies now, which is Ali's moment for coming *off* the Diet Coke. A proper conspiracy.

"A lot of this is falling to you and me to sort. He's expecting you to bring in some of the Turks. Reckons you lot are professional. He's done some thinkin' on this one, fair play. I've got two geezers in mind, but until he gets back from Spain end of next week, there's not a lot we can do on the fuckin' organisational front".

"My cousin has two boys from Nicosia. Went back to work there, grew up in north London. Proper Green Lanes boys. We can bring them back and put them to work straight away. They have had a good education back home. You know that Famagusta is a free port now. Free for many things!"

"Storage and distribution. Security. Haulage. Cleaning. The whole thing, my old mate, has changed. The latter is the hardest thing to do. Cleaning several bar a week is no longer an easy matter. Flash doesn't work. They're on that straight away. Do you know the old bill are taking motors off people in Birmingham now, unless they can prove how they paid for them?"

"Fuckin' liberty, innit? There is always Hawalla, my friend".

"Which means working with the fuckin' Pakis, mate. I ain't got nothin' against 'em. Just that I don't trust 'em. *That's* my problem. Ain't you got some kind of system you can use?"

"I will talk to my uncle. He knows about such things. Let us concentrate on earning the money for now. Not trying to move it!"

"Mick's bro reckons there's a chance we can use part of the big house storage".

"What? Put the *coca* into a bonded warehouse? Haha! That I must see. Is he mad? We go to all the trouble of hiding it from the church, then we put it back in. *In full view*! I think Mr Mick is putting too much of the powder up *his* nose!"

"Think about it, Ali. Think about the *purity of the situation*! We put the *coca* into wooden wine boxes, insure it and put it into the warehouse. Then we deliver it….. *they* deliver it! Using *their* transport! It is a beautiful thing! We use a front man for the company who knows nothing. He just takes in the wine and then sends it to the customer. *Right under their noses*! Even the weight will be perfect!"

*

The lights are low now, the band's playing their second set and Dean's party are flying. Jimmy Jag and Dean have made a couple of forays into the gents and the old Colombian marching powder's doing the trick. Benissa's already taken the hapless Sean outside for some 'fresh air' and he's come back with the biggest grin on his mug this side of Essex. Turns out he's been helping the old man down the car lot and they've got just the little motor Benissa's been after. She's well impressed and shown him just how far she'll go to get the motor. Dean's talking to Town again about Spain and Jimmy's dancing with The Dildo. She has just discovered about his limo hire business and sees herself ensconced in the back of a stretch, champers in hand, giving it large. Dave and Gina are locked in what looks like conversation at the table, but you can't see Dave's hand. Thank God it was prawns for starters. Mr and Mrs Michael Teeth are dirty dancing like their lives depended on it, snogging each other's faces off.

As the band does its, "ThankyouverymuchChelmsfordgoodnight" bit, Dean, or at least the two braincells which are still functioning inside his head, decides that it's time to go. There's a flight to Murcia sitting on the tarmac at Stansted with their name on and he is not going to miss it. Gina wants the holiday, Benissa wants a shag. Any shag. Troy would rather be anywhere else, but as the old man's paying and there's no-one to look after him over half-term and nobody's taking him to Bermuda/The Algarve/Butlins with them, he'll be on the plane. Dean wants to get cracking. Town's totally wound him up about the trip last week and he's champing at the bit. He can smell fortunes.

As the house lights come up ever so slightly, Gina removes Dave's fingers from inside her and joins her old man. Benissa and the boy are nowhere to be seen. Gina's missed nothing, but she doesn't want a performance with Dean. Jimmy Jag and Debra are still locked together. Whatever.

"Cheers everyone, yeah, blindin'. See you all after the holiday". Dean's driver Vic has appeared, and they weave their way back to the car, unlock the boy from Benissa's clutches and away to Canvey. Job done.

*

Ron calls this *my time*. Once Ali has gone back to his little corner of Cyprus, a.k.a. Green Lane, to the Turkish Club, he goes into quiet mode. He's at his most dangerous when he's quiet. Even as he is pondering matters, Ali is working on bringing the two lads back from Cyprus. Making plans.

Ron reflects. Adaptability is his forté. The paper's open again now that Ali is gone but he stares intently at the window. Ordering another brandy, he lights up a Romeo y Julieta, pausing to admire the plumes of smoke as they rise towards the stucco ceiling of the restaurant. The chairs are on the tables elsewhere in the gloom, but he just sits and stares. His methods are such that even now, a picture is forming in his mind of how it will be. Ron is a careful man now, *a cautious man*. His friends are numerous, but not for them the world of Bold. They prefer somewhat more salubrious surroundings. Channels Golf Club, the yacht club in Burnham, the Talbooth. Ron will go there for lunch on Sunday. Quiet. Nice.

And all the time, he will be planning *the move* right down to the last detail. The intricacies *belong to Ron*. They are like his children.

Chapter Thirteen

Villa Gina, Torrevieja, Spain 15th October 2006 10.00am

As the bright autumn Mediterranean sunshine beat down on warm rippling waters, Dean swam strongly, his tanned figure cutting a clean swathe across the heart-shaped pool. He's risen early today, the first morning of his holiday, washing away the rigours of yesterday's flight from Stansted and leaving Gina, Benissa and Troy asleep upstairs. It gives him his bit of freedom and independence. His mind's racing in time with the rhythmic pumping of his arms and legs. Once this swim is over, he's on his way down to Doolan's. It's like a rite of passage. Pissing in the corners sort of thing.

Gina and the dustbins are off to Caprabo to stock up for the week, so he'll pick them up later. He's got an X5 out here, leftie, tints, Spanish plates, which never sees English shores and Gina-G's going to be driving the hired Laguna they picked up from Murcia airport, complete with moaning Troy and the delightful Benissa ready to moan in all eventualities.

The swim's finished now and he's out, towelling himself off, feeling the warm, Mediterranean sun heat up his back. The distant sea draws his eyes, glinting, enticing, intriguing.

A quick change followed swiftly by a glass of freshly squeezed, sweet Spanish orange juice and Dean's ready to face his day. They're all up and about now and he kisses Gina on the lips, before grabbing his credit cards, mobiles and keys. Benissa's still monosyllabic and Troy doesn't even look up from his iPod Video. Ruffling the boy's hair as he walks past yields nothing more than a teenage grunt. He laughs and strides out onto the gravel drive. Essex boys love gravel.

He climbs in to the gleaming X5 and starts the engine. He has no idea of the significance of this simple, almost involuntary act, yet just for a second, he pauses and looks across the bay towards the shimmering sands of La Manga. He wants it all. There are *clicks* in every man's life, momentous snapshots, which at the time can seem innocent, unremarkable even, yet it is these very *clicks* which can have devastating consequences.

If you are going to commit a crime and I sincerely do not recommend that you do, put yourself in the dock as the beak hands you down a seven stretch, maybe even a fourteen and work backwards. Don't EVER work forwards, through the new motors, the lap dancers, the flashy houses, the yachts, the shampoo, the hookers and the Charlie. Work from the moment just as you start to walk down the steps, the tears beginning to fall and your arsehole contracting like a prodded starfish, look back at the last time you'll see freedom for a fucking long time and decide then; *was it worth it*? If you can keep a cool head when all around you, everyone else has lost theirs, then you obviously haven't grasped the situation. If you're still comfortable, then you obviously haven't grasped the situation. Ali the Coat has a sign on the wall of his little office at home with just the word 'TIT' written on it. It stands for 'Think It Through'. It reminds him of the days back in Famagusta when he used to walk back twenty miles each weekend to his village from where he was dropped off by the fish lorry. Nine years old, working as a kitchen porter in the international hotel district, keeping the wolf from the door for seven hungry mouths is a tall order. It was the war of 1974 which changed the family's fortunes. When the Turks invaded from the north, to save their people from extinction and genocide, the Greeks living closest to the coast understandably shit themselves, not to put too fine a point on it. Hundreds, thousands of people fled their homes in the face of the advancing troops. Included in the trek south was the local bank manager. Ali knew about TMT, the Turkish-Cypriot paramilitary organisation formed in answer to the Greek EOKA and knew that they would be active as soon as the Turkish army hit the beaches. He'd grown up fast and as luck would have it, was not due on shift in Famagusta until the next day. By the time the Turkish air force's hero pilot Erçan and his mates had overflown the island dispensing summary justice in the form of an avalanche of deadly cannon fire spitting from their wings, no-one was raising heads above parapets and anarchy quickly took hold. Ali and his uncle Huseyin made straight for the bank, smashed their way in and made off with a small fortune before anything like order could be restored. Carefully concealed, it accompanied them on the boat to England later that year. There were, after all, no further shifts to be had at what was left of the Holiday Inn, Famagusta......

TIT could not have been further from Dean's mind as he guided the X5 through the narrow streets of old Torrevieja. He felt like a king, congratulating himself for being a proper chap now. A quick chat with Uncle Charles, followed by a healthy dose of Eminem's latest on the CD and he was on top of the fucking world. He turned onto the strip, wound down the window and let the cool sea breeze blast into the car. *Blinding.*

On the corner of the Plaza Maria Asuncion, Doolan's invited everyone to come and sample its Guinness and Oyster pie, fresh lobster and king prawns washed down with the finest wines of Spain. A waiter, dressed in regulation white short sleeved shirt and black trousers was sluicing down the front terrace, another watering the bright array of plants and bougainvillea which adorned the arch around the door. Dean stopped opposite and watched. Now here was a man who knew what he was doing. Town was right, for once, he thought. The place was a hive of activity, even between breakfast and lunch. The menu boards told him that the place scarcely closed. They must be making a sodding fortune. He was fortunate. Just as he was about to get out and have a stroll round, a Mercedes swung around the corner and stopped right outside. The driver's door opened and out stepped what could only be described as a giant of a man, the shock of red hair intensified by the morning sun. He's carrying a small, black leather bag and as he walks onto the pavement, another man appears from inside the bar and catches the keys sailing towards him through the air. All the time, Dean is watching. There is a purpose about this man, a determination, maybe even a hunger, despite his years. He waits for him to go in and then slowly ambles across the Plaza Maria Asuncion and sits down at one of the pavement tables, just outside the door. Within seconds, a smiling Irish lad of about twenty-two comes out and greets Dean with the traditional,

"How're ya doin' the day?" Dean looks up through his Ray-Bans answering in the affirmative.

"I'm good, mate. I fancy a nice glass of shampoo. Got any Cristal?"

Bejasus, thinks the barman, eleven o'clock in the morning and yer man's wantin' Cristal. He nods and retreats into the bar. Out of earshot, he whispers to the manager, "We've got one of them flash cockneys in again. Wantin' Cristal. At this hour of the mornin'. On a Sunday!"

Padraig overhears this and walks over to the window, peering out through the shutters and the bougainvillea at Dean's relaxed pose. He says nothing and returns to the bar counter. Sleep was not plentiful and his face betrays some of the anger which is seething below the surface. He needs to think, to plan, to come up with some fucking reason as to how forty kees of finest Colombian marching powder nearly fell into the wrong hands. The Cristal, together with some air dried ham tapas, finds its way out on to the terrace and Dean proceeds to tuck in. He is not expecting Gina and the dustbins for a little while yet and he's feeling even more on top of the world now.

*

Padraig's mobiles have been put to full use since the recent news of Newry 57 and the *incident outside Dover*. He has called a council of war with his boys. What you might call an update. Shortly, a flight will arrive from London which contains his *man in black*. Seamus Kelly, a.k.a. *The Closer*. His identity had been kept a secret for many years, yet his reputation was awesome back on his home territories of Belfast and Dundalk. Constantly moving his location from one place to another, even the British Army struggled to identify him. Made largely redundant by the Good Friday Agreement between the British and Irish Governments, with healthy input from both sides of the fence, he had found gainful employment easy. His wealth was unknown, his movements enigmatic. As fast as one tentacle of the British authorities lost interest in him, another woke right up. M15's 'Cold War' teams had also been disbanded and from 9/11 onwards, they had been switched into watching Moslem terrorists, Russian godfathers and high-tech crime. British and European gangs were being targeted, new measures were needed. Padraig's operation was moving with the times and he had taken the decision to relocate to Spain some years before. Not so *The Closer*.

Just as the plane landed a few miles up the sun-drenched coast, Dean looked up to see the huge shadow of Padraig O'Riordan bearing down on him. He already had the advantage of the drinking Dean, but kept his council.

"Mornin'. Tis a beautiful day for a man to sit in the sun, so it is".

With that, he walked on to the car, which had now miraculously reappeared, courtesy of the earlier barman, handy with the keys. Padraig's purposefulness intrigued Dean and following Town Hall's glowing reports, his curiosity mounted. Following the giant Irishman a few steps behind was his cousin and manager, Ronan.

"Now there goes a man with a plan". Ronan's throwaway remark brings Dean back from wherever he was.

"Blindin' place, mate. You part of the furniture here?"

"Ronan". He offers his hand. A rare thing for an Irishman to do. Such a sinful thing.

"At your service". He grins at this. The man does it well, when it's necessary but both of them know that it's not fooling Dean.

"Dean. So who was the giant?"

"That'll be Mr O'Riordan. He likes to spend a little time here. You could say he's part of the furniture. I'm delighted to meet you, Dean. A man of taste, so y'are. Are y'on holiday?" Ronan winks at the bottle of Cristal sitting snugly in its icy nest.

"Got the family comin' in just a sec. Thought I'd have a couple before the missus arrives. Don't want the dustbins thinkin' the old man's on the piss just yet". He grins at Ronan and gets an understanding acknowledgement in return. They're like two increasingly friendly dogs in the park. Getting on OK but still needing to do plenty of butt sniffing. The stand-off is shattered by a party of English arriving from the beach. There's a couple of tasty looking birds and some youngish guys looking a bit flash. Ronan slips straight back into manager mode.

"Good mornin'. Is is a table ye'll be wantin' or are you comin' into the bar?" The girls are obviously taken by Ronan's accent, athletic figure and tanned complexion which belie his thirty five years. He's a big hit down at Pepe's Gym, *so he is*. They take a table just across from Dean, the girls' long, slim legs coil erotically around wicker chairs. They've started early. The boys haven't noticed yet. They will. They will. Sundry others arrive at the bar and soon, it's filling up. The Spanish won't arrive till at least two pm, so they're getting double bubble. The place is a fucking goldmine.

The Laguna draws up and the remainder of Dean's family disgorges itself from various doors. Judging by the laden hatchback, Gina's bought Torrevieja out of food. They'll declare a national emergency. Essex woman causes food crisis. It's official. Dean polishes off the shampoo and calls the waiter over.

"Another bottle for us and Cokes for the kids". Benissa's face is a study, but Dean's trying to make an impression. The guy returns in a jiffy, armed with another bottle of Cristal, two fresh glasses, an ice bucket, two Coca-Colas and some rather enticing prawn and crab tempura, the light batter is perfect. Gina takes one look at this and settles deep into the plush cushioned wicker armchairs.

"Ow, Dean, this is awesome". She hands Benissa her mobile and demands a picture. Ronan spots this and does the decent thing, grateful that he's behind the camera and not trying to keep out of the picture. Aahh! The Bolds on tour. Benissa spots the bulge in Ronan's tight black trousers and licks her lips, thankfully unnoticed by everyone apart from one of the girls at the next table who also spotted it. She glares at Miss Bold, but it also goes unnoticed. Peace can reign at Doolans. For now.

"This is the place Town was on abart. He weren't jokin'. It's a fuckin' goldmine. How much would you like a bit of this?"

"Oh, it's lovely Dean. Proper classy". Troy's deep in the iPod Video again and is dead to the world.

"Dad, they've got a club here. Tonight. How can I get down there? Is it a taxi or is my lovely Daddy going to give me a lift?" She smiles *that smile* at him and he melts.

"Course, darlin'. Anythin' for my little gell. Anyone fancy a bitta lunch?"

Dean calls over the waiter again, but this time it's Ronan and he takes the ice bucket and glasses on a tray and suggests the roof terrace. Padraig's told him to give Dean the full treatment and he's not going to disappoint his cousin. *And so it goes on*. Out come the menus and even Troy looks impressed. He is appalled by his father's *uncouth behaviour*, but the old man does have something, after all. At least he *might* get a chance to practice his Spanish. That's if they speak Spanish in South Armagh these days. They probably do.

Anyway, they're just getting through the starters. Dean's on the whelks, Gina's on the garlic prawns, Benissa's on everything and Troy's on the Sopa de Pescado. He's chosen the thing he thinks his father would never order. He's like that. Suddenly, the giant is back and he comes over to welcome them to the restaurant.

"I hope you're enjoying yourselves! Is the champagne to yer likin'? Good! Then yer'll not mind having another one on the house?" The deep throaty voice, quiet but with the kind of presence that can silence a stadium, gives Dean a sense of belonging. I bet he doesn't do this for everyone. He looks up at Padraig and their eyes meet. The cool, steely stare causes a shiver to pass down his back. He is smiling, but it does not translate to this inner coldness. The shudder is soon gone. Dean does not want to acknowledge it. His sixth sense hasn't paid the entrance fee today. Gina's soaking all this up, which is not lost on Padraig.

"Tis a grand family y'have here, Dean. Y'must be very proud". He directs this towards Gina and she smiles, bursting with delight.

"They're my world, this lot, ain'tcha?" He rubs Troy's hair in that Dad/old fashioned teacher way which provides the usual shrugging and wriggling embarrassment. This is the moment both Dean and Padraig have been waiting for, though for vastly different reasons. Padraig calls the Cristal on and soon, the waiter arrives with the golden wrapped nectar, perfectly chilled.

"Will you have one with us, Padraig?

"Aye. I'll do just that, so I will". He pulls up a chair and sits down. People are drifting up from street level onto the balmy roof terrace. There are already two guys sitting in the corner, talking earnestly and using mobile phones. The gang from the beach appears, Ronan's charm has obviously worked on them too. The girls look suitably impressed by the roof garden and sit down, giggling. Three bottle blond women totter up the stairs and make themselves at home next to the roof bar, sitting under a plain, cream, very expensive umbrella. The staff appear to have everything under control, under the watchful eye of the ever present Ronan. He works the terrace like the true professional he is and the expensive bottles of wine appearing on the tables please Padraig no end. The sun beats down.

*

El Altet Airport, Alicante 12.30pm

The bored immigration official barely looked up as Seamus Kelly handed the burgundy Irish passport to him for examination. Opening it just a fraction, he handed it back and his eyes closed just that little bit more. Happy in his work. Kelly trousered the well-worn booklet and headed off in the direction of the baggage carousel, alone. Hundreds of tourists swarmed around the belts, jockeying for position. Women carrying babies, men carrying golf clubs and teenage girls carrying Chlamydia all desperate to get their cases first, before the mad dash to the car hire desks could begin. No worries for Kelly on that score. Downstairs, a small, wiry little man by the name of Martin Keenan waited patiently at one of the bar tables opposite the arrivals door, scanning each passenger as they came through, playing with car keys in one hand, San Miguel in the other. Behind him, some twenty feet away, Andy Meacher and Kim Evans stood at a posy table, cold coffees long since abandoned, watching, waiting, notebooks discreetly hidden under day old copies of The Sun, Spanish edition. Their sporadic, seemingly random observations at the airport had thus far yielded the square root of fuck-all. The morning's brief on O'Riordan had come to nothing, as it had done for days. He went to work, he came home, he went out, he came home. No faces, no drops, no banks, no boats, save his own little trips out on the Princess. Hours of getting sunburnt on the beach, binoculars at the ready had yielded nothing more than mild sunstroke. To put it bluntly, they were well pissed off. The combination of still miserly expenses and what seemed to be yet another fruitless obo was taking its toll. Just as they were about to make a move back to the hotel, they could see in the distance a black, leather jacketed figure, shades and a shock of black curly hair, going a little grey at the sides. He was walking alone, carrying a canvas grip and looking for all the world like a man coming out for a little R n' R. But this man was different. This man would raise the hackles on even the hardiest of British soldiers who had had the misfortune of serving in Bandit Country during the 1980s and 1990s. Released under the Good Friday agreement, Seamus Michael Kelly a.k.a. The Closer was walking straight towards them with not a care in the world.

Under the sun.

Under The Sun was a small, discreet video camera, steadily

rolling, taking moving images of everyone passing through the glass door and away to coaches, taxis, hired cars and the likes of Martin Keenan and his blacked out Mercedes, which currently lay in the El Altet car park, ground level. Keenan's trilby hat stood proud, along with its occupant and made its way to the open end, past the rope and towards the exit.

Andy looked at Kim, Kim looked at Andy. There was a vague look of, 'Was that anything?' before they returned to the cold, stale coffee and the throng pouring endlessly towards them. The camera rolled on.

Once outside and with not a word exchanged, perish the thought of a handshake, Keenan pointed Kelly in the direction of the car park and the sanctuary of the exquisitely air-conditioned Mercedes. He kept hold of the canvas bag, to the point of it going on the back seat of the 'S' Class, before climbing into the front passenger seat. Back in the arrivals area, the two Customs officers maintained their vigil.

"Wait until the tape runs out and I think that'll be us for today, Andy. Most of the flights are in now. We'll download this video onto the laptop and email it back to operations. See if anyone means anything to them. Fat chance!"

Just yards away from them, the Merc was through the ticket barrier and away, the driver opening up the throttle as it bowled down the slip road and onto the southbound A7. Kelly sat silent, occasionally checking his watch, as the scorched, barren countryside passed by. Bony, strong hands drummed a tattoo on the black leather of his jacket, impatient, edgy. Seamus Kelly was *always edgy*.

"Stop the car", he issues quietly, barely audible above the sound of the concrete *Autopista*. There's a service area coming up and Keenan turns straight off, up the ramp and onto the petrol forecourt.

"Park over there, under the trees". He's already unfastened his seatbelt and as the car draws to a halt, he's out, looking back, scanning the cars coming in off the motorway, *looking for anything unusual*. This man is a true professional. He's never been caught and he's known only by his pseudonym, in hushed tones at that.

He is a one-man army and you do not, repeat not, want to cross him. He removes a tiny pair of army-issue field glasses, infra red and scans the drivers filling up at the pumps. Once satisfied, he gives Keenan the nod and they are away again. Down the road to Torrevieja. To their destiny.

As the car nears the shimmering Mediterranean, Kelly is on the mobile again.

"D'ya have a rear exit to your place? I don't want to use the main entrance, so I don't. Good. I'll tell yer man here". *Click.*

"You'll be drivin' to the back of the place, so you will".

Keenan nods and within a couple of minutes, he's deviated from the normal route and is into the back streets of Torrevieja, past tiny houses and shops and into an alleyway. Kelly is expressionless, focused entirely on his hands, his face disguised by the large trade-mark Ray-Ban Wayfarers.

"This is it, Mr Kelly. Would you like me to bring your bag?"

"I'll take it".

The back door to Doolans is opened briefly and they slip quickly inside, unnoticed.

"Will you take a seat in the office, Mr Kelly?"

He walks through, silent and focused. Keenan walks through the kitchens and on into the bar, where he spots Ronan chatting to some new customers who've just walked in. The recognition is mutual and Ronan gives him the nod, leaves the punters to their menu browsing and walks upstairs. As he arrives on the roof, he sees Padraig talking to Dean and Gina. However, his arrival does not go unnoticed by the big man, who makes his excuses momentarily, before walking over to Ronan and down the stairs. Keenan sits at the bar, alone. O'Riordan walks briskly into the office.

"Seamus, 'tis great to see you today. Did you have a good flight?"

The two men embrace and for the first time, against Padraig's huge shoulder, Seamus Kelly's face finally cracks into a smile.

Eventually, they separate.

"It's good to see you, Padraig, so it is. It's been a long time".

"A long time it is. Will you be takin' some lunch?"

"Aye, that'll be grand. Somewhere safe?"

"We've a restaurant on the roof. It's not overlooked. Just follow me".

The two men walk through the kitchen and up the stairs to the roof garden restaurant. Into the bright sunlight. In the corner, Dean and Gina are tucking into the seafood, the kids are actually not arguing and the rest of the place is making Padraig look forward to cashing up time. They choose a table far away from everyone else and sit down. Immediately, a young waiter comes over and takes their order.

"Will we be meeting anyone for lunch, Padraig?"

"Not for now, Seamus. We have some people coming to see us tonight. I would really value your opinion". Kelly sits there in the leather jacket, eventually removing it as the temperature begins to rise up on the rooftop terrace.

"Then I'll have a glass of white wine. Something from your own cellar".

"Then we'll have a bottle of the Viña Tondonia Blanco, Diarmuid. Make it a cold one, it's just too much at room temperature. I don't care what the Spanish do". He turns to Seamus. "Perfect with prawns and I *do* recommend the seafood here. It's what we're building the name on. That and the atmosphere, of course".

"Are you gettin' many of the locals in, or is it just the British?"

"It's just startin'. You'll be meetin' a couple of the locals tonight, so you will. Not the regular Spanish, if you know what I mean!"

"I think I do, Padraig, I think I do".

Seamus takes a gulp of the white wine and pronounces it to his taste. The golden, slightly oxidised sensation of the white Rioja is just perfect for the warm day.

"What exactly are you hoping to accomplish tonight?"

"I want you to get a feel for it all, Seamus. I don't sense I am in control at the moment. It's giving me sleepless nights, so it is. I don't like sleepless nights. Mrs O'Riordan doesn't like sleepless nights. They make her nervous and that makes me nervous. See what I mean. It's a vicious circle and you wouldn't be wanting one of those as a houseguest, now would you?"

"I see where you're comin' from there, Paddy". No-one, but no-one calls Padraig O'Riordan *Paddy*. Unless, that is, if they a) from the old country, and b) from the boys.

"It's prabably nothin' but I just want to *know*".

A selection of seafood tapas arrives, together with garlic stuffed olives and some hot *patatas bravas*. Chilli sauce and *alioli*, the garlic mayonnaise which the Brits go mad over accompanies the first course.

"Try the bread, Seamus. The feckin' Spanish can't bake bread to save their lives, but we've got it comin' in part-baked from the old country and this lot can't get enough of it!"

"There's nothing wrong with that, Paddy. Never tasted better".

Dean keeps looking over at them, fascinated, something which has not escaped either man.

"Yer man over there. Do we have a problem?" Seamus' voice is low now, he is back in South Armagh and his hackles are vaguely up.

"You mean the fella with the wife and kids? No. I know who he is, but the feeling isn't yet mutual, you might say. He's come to us indirectly from Beevers, our man in Liverpool. Wants to do business. He just doesn't know it yet". A mutual understanding from years of experience passes between them.

"You'll be meetin' him later, but not with the Spanish ladies and gents. That'll be after. I *particularly* value your opinion on him. Beevers is a good man, but you have to keep your eye on him all the time. Bit too fond of the snow himself, if you get my thoughts on that. I'm not saying he's a bad man, but it's always good to know".

"Loud and clear, Paddy. Message understood".

*

"What do you reckon, love? Is this place the business, or what?" Dean and Gina are wellying into the Cristal now, Benissa's in on it too and even the boy's having a glass. This is the closest they've been in years. Dean's happy because of what Town Hall's told him, Gina's happy because she's got the family together and Dean's not on the Marching Powder, Benissa's happy because her Mum and Dad are together for once and Troy's happy because no-one's taking the piss out of him, *and* he's drinking.

"Nice fella, the big bloke, ain't 'e, darlin'?" Gina's munching away on her lobster.

*

As Kelly and O'Riordan come to the end of their starters, Mr O leans forward,

"I'm just goin' over to speak to your man. Just want to keep him sweet". He gets up and ambles over in the direction of the Bold party, speaking to every seated group along the way.

"Is everything to your liking? Perhaps you'll stay for one after lunch?" He looks straight at Dean.

"You stay, babes. Me an' the kids are tired, we'll get back to the pool. You relax here and enjoy yourself. Just let us know when you want picking up". Gina-G! What are you up to?

"Yeah, babe. Yeah, I'll stay for a quiet drink. I'll be back later".

The kids' eyes light up at the prospect of the pool. Benissa's still a kid at heart, despite being a proficient blow-job artiste.

"Well, that's settled, then. Enjoy your lunch!"

With that, Padraig's off on his table-tour, disappearing down the stairs for a few minutes before sitting down once more with Kelly.

"Like your style, Paddy. You've a grand setting here. The perfect front".

"I'll be honest with you. It takes a lot out of me, but the missus, she loves it out here. She's got her garden, the Irish Women's Group; same sort of daft bitches she used to hang around with back home, but she likes it and that's all that matters to me. The kids come over from Boston now and again, which makes her life worth living, so it does. I'd love to see them myself over there, but, well, you know the rules since feckin' 9-11!"

"I do that. Feckin' terrorists, what could a man be doing with them?" His grin stretches from here to Dublin, a smile shared equally by Padraig.

Their main course arrives; some grilled sea bass with lemon herb mayonnaise and saffron rice. A Vino Joven Rioja Tinto 2006 pitches up along with the food, together with a solid silver ice bucket and stand.

"Will you look at that thing! D'ya know, a fella came in here with that? Said it was from the restaurant on the Titanic and what with me being a man from the Six Counties, would I be liking to buy it? I had to hand it to the fella, with his front. 'Tis a beautiful piece of silver, you must admit. The missus was here that day and you could tell that she loved it. We settled on dinner for four and a hundred Euros for his taxi to the airport. I haven't a feckin' clue where it comes from, but it *is* silver and it chills the wine down faster than any bucket I've ever seen!"

"You're getting soft in you old age! Buyin' ice buckets from strangers! You've been away from the 'Cross too long!"

"It's a grand life out here. A man has everything he needs. And no feckin' rain!"

"But do you feel *in control* out here?"

"I'm in control of the part I want to control, that's the part that does it for me. I let Beevers do his job, the Spanish do theirs and when it's needed, I just make a few calls and things get sorted".

"Aye, nasty business. It was the only way".

"A clean bit of work, so it was. A bit of collateral damage, but that's what happens when they play games with the *right* people. And you say I've gone soft! Who did you get to do it?"

"Young man from Jonesborough. Works in a pub over in Kilburn. Got down to Dover, did the work and was back in London before they'd even missed him".

"That's what I like to hear. Operations going properly. Shame your man wasn't out of the same mould. Wouldn't have had to have done what was necessary"

"This fish is grand, Paddy, your place is getting better to the eyes and the stomach". One of Doolans' waitresses has just popped her head round the door and Kelly has missed nothing. She's dressed in the regulation black and white, but instead of the trousers, she's in a tiny mini-skirt and knee-length high heeled boots.

"She's a beauty, alright. Mother's Spanish, father's English. Name's Paquita. The boys have been tryin' for ages to get under that skirt, but no-one's made it to first base yet, so they haven't! Young boys. Not a clue!"

"You know everythin' that's goin' on here. I remember you in the old days. Never missed a trick then".

"Matter of life and death then, Seamus. Bit different now, but I never take my eyes off the ball. Not for one moment. I'm too old to indulge in Her Majesty's Pleasure now!"

"Aye, and they follow you round, so they do. We have word that all those rumours about M15 are true. There's more work going into organised crime detection than anything else now".

"And it's these feckin' things that are the worst of all", pointing to the mobiles sitting in the middle of the table. "I change mine every week and even that's not enough".

"Have you tried the satellite phones? I've heard they're very good".

"I've heard that too. I just fear anything electronic. Do you realise that there is a record of everything? Phone calls, emails, internet access. The whole lot goes through GCHQ, every last call. Now that's something the public doesn't know!"

"Trouble is, Paddy, that when things are going well, no-one wants to listen to that kind of talk".

"And *that's the time* they should be taking care. Not pissing it up against the feckin' wall, cavorting around like dogs on heat".

"I think that's going to be my theme for tonight. There's a little too much over-confidence at the moment. They're all pissed on success, so they are".

"They wouldn't be regarding Dover as a success, though?"

"Well, we didn't lose anything, besides the route, of course. *That* hurt. I'm keen to see how they'd be reacting to that one. Yer man's dead, so he's not telling tales to anyone, but we've still the driver. Sound man, from Newry. I know the family, which makes it difficult".

"Certainly does. You not going there, then?"

"I said difficult, not impossible. We have to do what we have to do, Seamus. That's never changed and never will. A man gets in the way of me makin' me livin' and there's goin' to be trouble sooner or later".

"Just say the word, Paddy. I'll be waitin'".

*

"Babe, fancy anything else?" Dean's leaning back on his chair, drained the last glass of Rioja and looked around.

"No, love, apart from you!" The kids make sick faces and Dean laughs. He's actually relaxed and looking at Gina for the first time in weeks.

"Seriously, I ain't got time for coffees. I'll take the kids back now and have a lie by the pool. Top up me tan, like. See ya later, sexy! Take your time." She gets up and leans over to give Dean a kiss, full on the lips. For the first time in ages, he responds and feels really good. The kids give their Dad a hug and then they're away.

Dean sits alone at the table, orders another bottle of Cristal and a lardy and just basks in the whole picture. Both Seamus and Padraig witness this and immediately, the guest gets up to go. They embrace and then he's gone, away down the stairs and out the back. Padraig returns from his farewell and walks across, ostensibly to speak to a party of ladies seated overlooking the sea. As he passes Dean's table, they make eye contact and Dean motions for him to come over. The nod is returned and after his dutiful host stuff is done, he does just that.

"Did you enjoy yourselves? I hope so".

"Padraig, it was blinding. I've had some lobster before, but that? That was the fuckin' business!"

"You'll be bringin' them again, I hope?"

"Too right. This place is the business! In fact, a mate of mine recommended it. Stevie Hall. Was here about, well, a couple of weeks back".

"I remember the fella. Mr Hall. Yes. Nice man. Businessman, as I recall".

Padraig's expression says it all. The unsaid passes between them like broadband on sulphate. First base down, onto second.

"Yeah. Well, Town, as we call him, is what you might call a business associate of mine. Couldn't say enough good things about this place. Once his bird Tracy got chatting with Gina, well, that was that. She had the bleedin' bags packed an' evreything. Gives me the excuse to come over and take stock, do you know what I mean?"

"Mr Hall spoke to you at length about his time here with us then? Good. Very good. Then we don't need to go over old ground then. Or do we?" He looked deep into Dean's piercing eyes, searching for something he didn't like. Nothing. Not a damn thing. Just hunger. Hunger and *greed*.

"A bit of a chat with you would be blindin'. Whenever you're ready, Padraig. Whenever you're ready". Dean raised his glass just an inch or so, as a mark of respect to his host, but the message was clear.

"If you're not doin' anything in particular the night, then you'd be very welcome on the boat, so you would. There's a few faces comin'. People you might like to meet".

"You're on. Give her and the kids the night off. Give 'em a chance to bond. They don't see much of their mum at home".

"Grand. Take a taxi to the Marina del Sol. One of the lads'll show you to the boat".

"How will they know?"

"They'll know. Don't worry yourself. I'll see you later. Got a few things to arrange. It's been a pleasure, Dean". Once more he looks deep into Dean's watery, Cristal giveaway eyes and smiles.

"Yeah, later. Thanks, Padraig".

As O'Riordan walks away down the stairs, Dean's stare follows him all the way. He is on top of the world.

Chapter Fourteen

Monday. Bold Transport, Thurrock, Essex

"Break his fuckin' legs, Kev? I'll fuckin' kill the cunt. I am not havin' some mug thinking he can take my business. Is he takin' the fuckin' piss or what?" Dave is having murders today and he's not about to ring Dean to ask his permission. On account of Dean's holiday and all that. It turns out that Rainsford has been bubbling up the whole incident with the cable ties and the drill in the boozer, since his little 'dressing down' the other week. Larging it up with some rival outfit who've got him pissed up, few lines of hooter and he thinks he's Charlie Big Potatoes. Now the guvnor of that little firm is putting the word round Canvey that Dean and Dave have lost it.

"We're going have to lift The Fixer if we're gonna do that. I know the cunt and he's always got his people around".

"We gotta fuckin' do what we gotta fuckin' do. If Dean gets back and finds out we ain't done fuck all, it ain't gonna be pretty".

"We'll need the shooters, then. Just for show, like".

"All day long, mate".

"Just give us the word, know what I mean?" The Gun grins at Dave, he's thirsting for blood. Life's been far too quiet for him. This'll be just like the old days over Millwall.

"We'll 'ave a meet. Half-five. Down the lock-up. And tell them to leave their motors in the bleedin' car park. I don't want the place looking like Jimmy's fuckin' car lot"

Kev's straight onto it. No worries. The mobile's out. *Click*. First it's Ali, then Jimmy, then Mick the Teeth and finally One Language. He's not answering his 'phone. Dean's left him instructions. Emergencies only. The Gun keeps pressing redial until his finger's sore, but still nothing from Lingo. He goes back to Jimmy. Gets through eventually. Sorted.

"You seen Lingo this' morning over the tea stand, Kev?"

The A13 tea stands are famous for meets. Never mind from Soho down to Brighton. These things run all the way from Limehouse to Southend and all ports in between. There's been more blags sorted at tea stands than in any pub you'd care to mention. You start there when you're old enough to nick a motor and you end there in your Roller with the Canvey Island Club cap in the back. Just try and stay out of the shovel in between. Lingo and the Jag use the same one just off the Pitsea flyover. Old Reg and his Missus have been there since the war. Not sure which one but you get my meaning. Ali even owns two now. Saw the potential years ago, moved in and now he's drawing a grand a week of each of them. You know where you are with a tea stand.

"Funny you should say that, but no. Nada".

"Dean ain't gonna be happy with that. It's unlike the linguist to fuckin' go on the missing list, do you know what I'm saying?"

"He was a little on the quiet side on the boat, weren't he, Dave?"

"Come to think of it, yeah. He's been actin' all strange lately. You're right, Kevin, you are spot fuckin' on. Fuck Dean. *I* ain't 'appy neither. I'm gonna keep a fuckin' eye on Ron. We can't be 'avin fuckin' wild cards wandering around. It ain't a fuckin' option".

"Where does this Bassett cunt drink? Can we lift him from there?"

"We know he uses the Circus. Goes every night. It's like a little habit he's got. His boys are all there. No fuckin' way we can lift him without fuckin' murders. I ain't up for that".

"What about his unit? Can we do something there?"

"Same hassles".

"Home? What about liftin' him from his gaff, Dave?"

"Are you bleedin' mad? And get every cunt from his manor comin' after us? Not me, bruv".

"Any enemies we can use? Few squid in the right hands?"

"It ain't exactly the fuckin' Sopranos, is it? Gettin' some other firm to sort your problems? Come on, Kev. We got to sort this. We've got to sort it today".

"It's got to be the shooters then. Why don't we just shoot the cunt when he leaves the boozer?"

"Bit extreme, ain't it? I mean, are we trying to scare the cunt, or are we talkin' *something permanent*? Bleedin' hell. He used to drink with us in the old days".

"All the more reason for ironing him out then".

"You are not wrong. Fucking cunt. We'll ave him in the car park, Kevin. Get us a motor off the estate, do the business and then torch it on the marshes. Sorted. Just you and me. Forget about the meet, bruv. Tell the others not to bother. Tell 'em we'll make it a late one. Boys night. Circus Tavern. Ten sharp. You and me bruv, we'll be celebratin'". Dave's smelling blood now, the adrenaline rush is already there, coursing through his body, winding him up to fever pitch.

Kev's on the mobile, sorting things out. There's relief from the boys at the cancelled meeting. Gives them time to get home and see the missus, before getting sorted for later. Cleaned up. Nice suit. Ready for action. *Organised*.

Dave and Kev. This'll impress Dean, for sure.

*

They meet at the Old Bell in Tilbury, off piste. Kev's been busy and outside in the car park, just round the back from the CCTV cameras, lies a nicked Astra. He's had the plates sorted and it's all clean. The gear's in the back, Kev's boy's just dropped him off and the they're picking up the shooter from a lock up in Vange.

In the back bar, they're nursing vodkas. It's quiet in the Bell at half five and they've got a table in the far corner, away from the fruit machine which holds the only other occupants of the pub.

"You're driving, bruv. I've done a recce this afters and there's the perfect place out front. Gives us a straight shot as he's cummin out, then we're away and on the old '13. Straight across to the marshes, torch the Astra, then the Teeth'll pick us up by the old farm. He's sorted a moody van from Big Phil over Hornchurch and once he's picked us up, the van's fuckin' history an' all". They drain the voddies and away, out the back, followed by a quick check to see who's about. They're both wearing black and against the dusky sky, their anonymity looks assured. They climb in the unlocked car, Big Phil's provided some moody keys which glisten in the moonlight. The car pulls away, out of the car park and onto the dual carriageway. Twenty minutes later and they are coming in to Rainham, familiar territory. There's no chance of a pass, as the speed cameras are thick on the ground along here and they don't want any unwanted attention from the local plod. Bright lights and a large maroon sign indicate that they are at the target and the Astra pulls into the car park, close to the exit, facing the main door. The plates have been treated with anti-camera glare topped off with a splattering of mud for good measure. It looks just like every other arsehole's souped up load of shit, cheapo spray on tinted windows, alloys from the market. Cunts.

Several cars move in and out of the pub car park.

"He'll have a few sherbets with the boys, then he'll sling his hook about sevenish. Matey reckons he'll either be on his Jack Jones or max another two geezers with him. We'll have to be quick, maybe only a few seconds between him coming out of the boozer and getting in his motor".

The shooter is underneath a towel, behind the back seat which Kev has thoughtfully pulled up and modified. It's been cleaned, loaded and will be sorted straight after the job.

"When this is done, we're goin' after Cuntocks again. I've had an idea for his fuckin' final resting place. A nice touch, you might say".

After a couple of minutes, a BMW X5 with tinted windows drives in and parks up against the side of the pub. Two blokes get out and go in through the main door.

There's a kind of tension in the car, always is before a job. Kev is calm. Reminds him of the old security van work, running with the Dagenham firm. There were rich pickings back in the day. No trackers, older guards, less security all round. Sweet. Adrenaline flowing free, few lines of hooter beforehand, the final planning scenario. Bit of banter, old stories. Then someone calls the job on and that's it. Before you know where you are, you're on it and then all hell breaks loose. Needs a cool head to frighten the life out of a security guard. People have been known to lose it and the whole thing degenerates into a Benny Hill sketch. You get times when you just can't break in to the van, others when the best laid plans of mice and men go to pot and there's no cash in the safe. (When did mice make plans? Bit of a poser, that one.) Kev's really reminiscing privately to himself but suddenly there's a rush of blood to the head and he starts talking. Nerves.

"I know I said I'm not much for fuckin' talkin' but I've got to tell you this one. Me and this geezer Wellsy used to do Post Offices. Yer know, small ones, on the corner, type of arrangement. We get ourselves over Hoxton way, bit off manor like. There's this little office up Pitfield Street, closed it is now. Not fuckin' surprised after what occurred. We're sitting in the motor, all ready for the Securicor to come with the pensions and that and suddenly this fuckin' old geezer comes up to the window and looks in. Wellsy's in the front and he's brought this dopey fuckin' geezer mate of 'is along for the ride. Matey's got the window open and the fuckin' sawn off's sitting in his lap. The geezer's looked at him, clocked the fuckin' shooter and started leading off, shouting,

 'Gun, gun, there's a GUN IN THIS CAR!'

Anyways, the cunt only reaches in and starts trying to grab the shooter, matey's screamin' at him to let go and trying to punch him. The old boy's right game and he ain't having none of it. I start screamin', 'Give it to 'im. FUCKIN' GIVE IT TO THE CUNT!' You will not, in a million fuckin' years guess what transpires next".

Dave's face is a study, if only you could see it in the blackened out Astra.

"Go on Kev."

"The cunt only gives it to him, don't he?"

"Claret all over the motor and everything'?"

"No, you melt, far fuckin' worse than that. He gives him the fucking shooter! Just hands it to him like it's fuckin' Christmas. I'm thinking, for fuck's sake, trying to get the motor going and the old girl's having none of it. I gets it going eventually, like and we're off down Old Street like there's no tomorrow. I take a butcher's in the mirror and the old cunt's standing in the road, looking at our fast disappearing fuckin' getaway, then he's lookin' at the shotgun, then starts scratchin' his fuckin' ed. Me and the other fella, we was pissin' ourselves laughin'. Dave's mate's lookin', well a mite fuckin' dumbstruck. 'What are you laughing at?' 'E goes. 'I did what you said.'

I goes, 'I meant you to kill the old cunt, not give him a fuckin' present, you knob'. Dave is doubled up in the fuckin' back and we're still laughing by the time we gets back to Romford".

The two of them are in hysterics now, but the job won't go away and soon they're back on watch.

"What if we hit the other geezer an' all, bruv? Ah mean, he's bound to come out mob handed, ain't he?"

"I think they call that *collateral damage*, mate. I think there was an Arnie film a while back. Fuckin' load of stuff blowing up, I recall. We'll be alright if the other geezer's not too close, like. These things are pretty accurate, as long as they're aimed proper, do you hear what I'm saying?"

"I just don't wanna create a fuckin' bloodbath, that's all. It'll be bad for business".

"This is the only time we're going public, you might say. Cuntocks is going to be done real quiet. Leastways, quiet for the general public. He ain't gonna like it one bit". Kev laughs at this comment, delighting in the knowledge that he's going to be in on finishing the geezer off.

It's quiet in the car-park and they take the opportunity to retrieve the AK-47 from under the back seat.

"Shame we're not the first to use one of these. Would've been blinding. The first geezer to use one's doin' fuckin' thirty years".

"Fuck that. I ain' doin' thirty years for no cunt".

"Relax, bruv, everything's sweet. The shooter, the fuckin' motor, the fuckin' lot. You mark my words. Cushti".

Kev's putting the AK together, checking the magazine.

"Funny old game, eh? I mean, just sitting here waiting for him.

Have you ever thought what's going on in there? He's probably sitting with his boys, larging it maybe. He might even be talkin' about the football".

"He's Hammers and all, ain't he?"

"Oh, yeah. Used to go with Dean and the boys".

He's checking the bullets now, looking down the barrel, that sort of thing.

"Think we went up Millwall with him once. Proper fuckin' tear up. New Cross Gate tube. Got chased from that boozer all the way up Cold Blow Lane. We got cornered up some fuckin' alley. Must've been fifty of them and about twetny of us. That was some fuckin' tear up. They don't have 'em like that no more. Too many Old Bill, fuckin' CCTV and all that bollocks. Takes all the fun out of things".

"Fuckin' ruined everything, that CCTV".

You could cut the atmosphere with a knife in the car now. Conversation tense, perspiration taking charge.

"We all ready, then?"

"All set, bruv. Moment he comes art of there, he's fuckin' toast".

The car goes silent. The talking's done now. Just the waiting game. A couple get out of an Astra and go into the pub. A geezer comes out with his dog, which promptly pisses against a Transit Van parked next to the entrance. Then the door opens and it's on. One of The Fixer's boys comes out first, then it's him. The man himself. Kev takes aim and then *Crack! Crack! Crack!* It's all over in less than a second. The gun's back in, the window's up and they sit stock still. The Fixer's down, he's taken three shots to the lower body. Even in the moonlight, the claret's visible flowing out over the stone steps. He's kind of on his knees, propped up against the side wall of the pub, oozing life. His boys don't know what to do. One of them's down too, but moving. They're holding him, then they're looking round for the shooter, peering into the blackness, on the mobiles, doing the 999. Fuckin' panic stations. Dave and Kev watch the proceedings, silent, *greedy*. One of the Fixer's boys runs back into the pub to raise the alarm. The geezer's screaming in agony as they try to stem the blood flow.

People come piling out of the pub and still they watch. They're all crowding round him now. Blankets have appeared from inside and they've propped him up. Someone's talking on a mobile to the hospital and they're relaying instructions to try and keep The Fixer from going upstairs. After a couple of minutes, the ambulance appears and the paramedics fair leap out and get to it. There's four of them in two units, as someone called to say that three people had been shot. Two of them are working on him, the other two are bringing a stretcher out of the back doors. Slowly, they lift him on, then two of them get in the back with him, the other one gets in to the cab and away they go, leaving the last guy to tidy up and talk to the onlookers. The other fella's on his feet now, convinced he's been plugged, but there's nothing. Just panic. The siren begins to sound its eerie screech and the ambulance races off down the A13, closely followed by Kev and Dave in the stolen Astra. They pass the police on the roundabout and take the exit towards London and the marshes. Soon, the gun will be back in its safe place, the car will be charcoal and they'll be off across the waste ground and away. Mick the Teeth'll be waiting and it's straight into his motor and gone. Burn the clobber, hot showers, get rid of everything. Forensically.

*

Circus Tavern, Purfleet

The boys arrive, already bugled up and welly straight into the beers and anything else that's going. Kev stands upright and proud

"We ain't heard nothin' so far, bruv. Do you want me to check again?"

"Chill, matey. He went down in the car park and that's that. There'll be enough grief tomorrow when the stewards' starts! Here, Mick, rumour 'as it that The Fixer could suck his own cock? Aaaaarrrgghhhh!" Dave's loving this. Just for once, he is king of the castle.

"Well, he ain't gonna have a cock to suck after what I saw. Blindin bit of shooting, bruv. All three right in the fuckin' crown jewels!"

*

"I'm afraid there is nothing further we can do for your step-brother, Mr Vare. He was pronounced dead on arrival at seven forty-three".

Kenny Vare looks down at the floor, the tears welling up and cascading down his hardened face. He is whispering Freddie's name over and over, cannot believe what has happened.

"Don't you worry, bruvva, some cunt's gonna pay for this big time". As he looks up, Sandra, Freddie's wife arrives in the A&E reception, held up by her daughter and mother in law. She is inconsolable; grief stricken, white as a sheet. She falls into Kenny's outstretched arms and he holds her up, guides her to a chair and she collapses into it. All her energy has gone.

*

"Get us another round in, you tight cunt. What do you think this is, a fuckin' charity?" You've got the picture now. Two scenes, diametrically opposed, both inextricably linked. Not one scene at a time, like you would expect, but the two scenarios side by side, just a few miles apart, going on at precisely the same moment. Dave thinks he's pulled off the crime of the century. Kenny Vare, step-brother of Freddie the Fixer, or Freddie the Fixed as he's now known by the assembled throng in the 'Circus', is now about to unleash hell. Well you didn't think he'd just let it lie, did you?

Chapter Fifteen

Ceuta

"The latest figures that we have are that nine people have been killed. One *Guardia Civil,* Officer Sanchez, at the Fnideq border, one in town and seven so far unidentified Moroccans. Taliban? Al Qaeda? Who knows? Someone was responsible for this incursion and we need to find out who, why and when they are planning it again. Until then, we remain on a maximum state of alertness. Someone will pay for the deaths of my officers". Governor Fernandez-Hierro sat po-faced at the press conference. For once, his forgotten corner of North Africa the focus of the world's press. How he wished it was not.

"Governor. Roçio Faustino, El Mundo. Is this just a border incident or are there more sinister forces at work? Could you tell us how your investigation is progressing, please?"

"Yes, Señorita Faustino. So far, we know that the incursion resulted from what appeared to be a small demonstration on the western border towards Fnideq and Morocco, next to the new wall. Police HQ received a radio request from Sergeant Ramirez at around three pm. Shortly afterwards, radio contact was lost with the border crossing and the next report we received was that a crowd of about two hundred was heading for the city centre, some thirty minutes later. By the time our patrol car reached the border, Officer Sanchez was dead and Sergeant Ramirez was unconscious. He is now in intensive care in the city hospital, under guard".

"Maria Olarra, El Dia. Do you think that Sergeant Ramirez is in danger? If so, from whom?" This produces rumblings from the floor and the Governor appears rattled.

"No...no...certainly not, Señorita Olarra. It is solely a precaution, that is all. If there are no more questions, thank you ladies and gentlemen. When we have more news, we will let you know". With that, he stands and leaves the room as fast as possible, leaving his press officer to face an increasingly inquisitive mob. Once outside, he whispers to his aide,

"What a load of bollocks. I wish I could give them more. The truth is, we have no idea what is going on. I am hoping someone from the mainland, someone from Madrid will help us. I never thought I would hear myself say those words. I think I am getting very old. Too old for *this*". He walks slowly away and into his waiting car.

Marianna leaves the room quietly from the rear door and is straight onto the mobile.

"*Ola*! I have just come from the press conference. He did not say anything but I think they are going to close the borders with an increased military presence. It does not look good for us. If they bring the Special Forces from the mainland, they will be heavy handed. We cannot afford too much interest in our operation. No, I agree. I see you tomorrow. My contact will also be there. OK, we talk again soon". *Click.*

At the other end of the 'phone, a tall, black haired, white shirted man replaces a mobile in his pocket and returns to the thudding bass of a nightclub bar.

Marianna hurries back to the press conference and searches the room with her laser eyes. Her face comes alive when she spots her target surrounded by his entourage and wanders over.

"Alberto! How wonderful to see you! And in such exciting circumstances too. What did you make of all that? Come on, a girl must have her gossip!"

Her arrival on the scene is like a parting of the seas, some to the left and some to the right. Within seconds, she is alone with her quarry.

"They are worried that Al Qaeda might be behind the incursion".

"It's a bit small time for them isn't it? I mean, after Atocha in Madrid? A few people coming over the border?"

"It's the evidence they don't give you about the killing. We know about Mejjati for sure. We even know that he was here, plotting the outrages in Madrid. We have the intelligence on exactly who we now have as house guests in our little enclave, wandering in and out at will. Whoever dealt the fatal blow knew what he was doing. One blow and the guy was dead. It was done from behind. Professional, disguised as rage. He must have picked up the weapon and walked calmly up to the fallen officer and whacked him".

"Still doesn't say Al Qaeda to me. Is it some kind of excuse to raise the profile of the security here? Are they trying to tighten things up in Ceuta, *por ejamplo*?"

"They've been talking about that for years, but nothing has ever been done. It's the budgets, you see. Madrid provides us with ideas but no funds. Empty promises. The only time we can get any kind of incremental finance is when one of the chosen ones deigns to visit from Madrid or Malaga".

"So you think that this is all going to go away with time, *cariño*?"

"Probably, though they are serious about tightening up traffic and immigration. Maybe it's just a fortunate set of circumstances which will placate the right wing. You know they would rather build ten walls around our little desert idyll".

"God knows why. It's hardly paradise".

"Well, *bella*, it's good enough for you". He smiles at her, barely disguising his admiration.

"You talk as if you have nothing to do with the running of this godforsaken place. You are the bloody Governor, after all".

"Rumour has it that I still hold onto that dubious distinction. The trouble is, my power is limited, you know that. At best, I am a foreman, nothing more. A foreman with a ceremonial sword. At least you don't find too many of those". He smiles again, a hollow, weak smile.

"What we need here is a Spanish Hong Kong. We're within three hours flight of every European capital, we're on the coast, so all we need is a deep sea harbour and the cruise ships can call. We can build golf courses, hotels, restaurants, nightclubs, hostess bars. To hell with Dubai; this place could take over in a matter of ten years. With you at the helm. All we need is the go-ahead".

"That's what I love about you, *princesa*, everything for you is so easy. You just flutter those beautiful eyelashes, stick your nose in the air and everyone just falls at your lovely feet".

"How did you know I have lovely feet? I didn't know you had that kind of thing. You *are* full of surprises!"

Alberto is covered in confusion. The post press conference drinks is drawing to a close and the crowd is getting thin. Any longer and people will talk. Ceuta is a very small place and society consists of about thirty important families. She's looking up at him. With those eyes. Sipping her cocktail and swishing around like some kind of randy schoolgirl. He's losing control.

"P…per..haps we should discuss this further. Maybe over dinner?"

"Are you asking me for a date, Governor Hierro? You naughty boy. Well, I must go. You know where I am. Call me". And she's gone. In a flourish, sashaying out of the room on her Gucci stilettos. Out of place? Without doubt. Everything about the woman was *inappropriate*, yet men were like moths to a flame. All of them.

*

Governor Hierro sat down to retrieve official paperwork, collected his old leather briefcase from a waiting secretary and walked out to the official Mercedes, waiting to take him home to his ailing wife. His mind was in a whirl. Marianna da Sancha, no less, Ceuta's most celebrated resident, back from South America for good, so she said. Her presence in the little enclave had long been a mystery to Alberto and whilst he was grateful for the income her business interests brought his stretched tax budget, his curiosity was bound to get the better of him sooner or later. Sooner looked the better bet.

*

Señorita Marianna da Sancha. Heiress. Millionairess. Lioness. Sat in the back of her chauffeur driven Merc, dialling on one of her three mobiles.

"Yes, it's me. Yes, the Press Conference has just finished. The Governor is running scared, really scared. I think I can steal a march on this. I think we are more powerful here than we thought. And that is about to change for the better. My God, but this business makes me so horny. Bye!" She stroked her stockinged leg, the high glossy sheen reflecting queues of street lights, casting a warm glow on her exquisite legs. Her hand strayed down between parted thighs and long fingers brushed against the soft pink labia unfettered by lingerie. She always went commando to formal functions, maintaining that it gave her an edge over the other women. She let a finger slide between her lips, find the clitoris, smiled at the discovery of its swollen state. Some gentle rubbing brought her on even more and by the time her chauffeur turned the purring Mercedes into the gated driveway, she was desperate.

"You may come in, Antonio. I need you to do something for me, but you will need to be quick. I have some business to attend to".

She strode into the house, throwing her coat casually across the leather armchair situated just inside the door to her vast hallway.

"I'm in the library" she called, bending over the leather chesterfield, pulling her skirt up as if in one motion. Antonio was right there with her in seconds, his trousers round his knees, his vast cock pressed against her. He began to rub it against her shiny lips, gradually inserting it bit by bit, until she could take no more. He held her rounded cheeks tightly as she pressed back against him, ramming himself deep into her gaping hole.

"I want you to cum, don't worry about the condom, I haven't time". This spurred him on and soon he could feel himself getting closer and closer, until the thick streams of semen splattered against the tight walls of her exquisite cunt.

"Yes, yes, yeeesssssss!" she screamed, as her whole body was racked by an intense orgasm just at the point of his climax. The sensation of his ejaculation tipped her over the edge and she pushed back against him, enjoying the full length of his shaft as it was pushed hard into her.

She rested her arms on the back of the sofa and then began to stand.

"Thank you, Antonio. You may take the night off. I will not be needing you any more".

"I will return in the morning at seven, Señorita da Sancha?"

"Oh, do please. We have a busy day tomorrow".

She could feel the cum dripping out of her and down the inside of her thighs as she walked across the library and up the stairs to her bedroom. The door slammed and the sound of the Mercedes leaving momentarily filled the night air. She walked straight into the enormous en-suite, slipping out of her dress and stockings and into the multi-jet shower, her tanned and toned body contrasting perfectly with the white porcelain.

*

As Governor Hierro entered his darkened hallway, the servants having gone either home or to bed, he set down his old leather case and walked into the wood-panelled study, putting on the desk light. He could not get Marianna out of his mind. She had a *presence* which he could not fathom. Of course, women had thrown themselves at him before. Power is a mighty aphrodisiac to the aspirational and sexually avaricious woman. He had turned them down easily and with great style, yet with the *princesa* as she was inexplicably known, he was like putty in her hands. He sat silent at the desk, wanting to write her a letter of apology regarding their dinner date, but it was impossible. Try as he might, he just couldn't do it, so strong was her power over him. To put it mildly, he was fucked. Silently, he put down his pen, switched off the desk lamp and left the room. The walk up a wide expanse of staircase was a long and reflective one. As he entered his bed-chamber, the reverberation of his snoring wife in her drug induced sleep was the only sound in the world.

Chapter Sixteen

Villa Therése, Torrevieja November 2006

The sun rose as a huge fireball low in the southern autumnal sky, powering its way through the morning mist. As always, Padraig was already up and about, watering his plants, collecting the few scattered leaves from the mirror-like surface of his pool. The onset of a Mediterranean winter necessitated use of a thick cream Arran sweater, otherwise he was in his trademark formal trousers and brogues. Therése was already hard at work in the kitchen as he kissed her goodbye, assuring her of his return that evening.

*

'Zulu One departed house 6.53am. Zulu Two remaining at house. Officers Meacher and Evans commencing mobile surveillance'. Kim tapped her pen on the standard black pocket notebook and closed it up.

"Well, I guess that's us for a while. Why doesn't she ever go out? I mean, like do *something*. Any bloody thing to get us away from here. I am sick and tired of these fucking *bocadillos*. And I am sick and tired of your bloody farting. What *do you live on*?"

Andy started laughing. "Bit like a game of Dutch ovens really, I suppose. I'm sorry. I guess you get a bit desensitised when you're on a job. I think it's those pepperoni pizzas I get from the take-away. They're really cheap".

"Come on. Nothing's gonna happen here. There's a little place for breakfast just down by the marina. Does great bacon and eggs. My treat. Let's get some decent food into you. We'll be back in an hour. Mrs O isn't going to change the habits of a lifetime".

Andy Meacher opens the car door for a bit of ventilation, then climbs back in and switches on the ignition. The rented Seat drives off, down the hill and away from the vantage point across from the O'Riordan villa.

*

Half a klick away, an airport registered Mercedes 300 turns into the *urbanizacion*, pauses for the driver to check his well-worn map and moves away again, in the direction of the bougainvillea covered entrance to Villa Therése. It pauses again at the electric gates. After a few seconds, the gates begin to slide open and the car enters the property. The gates slowly slide shut, leaving the morning scene undisturbed.

*

Down the hill, Andy and Kim arrive at Café Rosa.

"You are so in need of some TLC, Mr Meacher. It's about time someone took you in hand!"

"If only. I am bored with the bachelor life".

"I did *not* mean that, thank you!" She smiles at him, that kind of head on one side thing that girls do sometimes. You're never quite sure what it means and Andy is certainly none the wiser.

Over breakfast, they discuss the case and particularly the other members of the team. Following the Thistle Hotel meeting, they have all gone their separate ways, their only contact now via Stubbins at Custom House.

"What do you make of Janet? Seems like a woman on a mission. Do you think she has, you know, a life?"

"I think she's on the other bus, if that's what you mean. She almost came from nowhere over the Metro Bond case. She was like a thorn in everyone's side and since the demise of the last Head, her rise has been meteoric. Some say she's going all the way".

"Bit too much information for me, darling", replies Andy.

"Did you always add *double entendres* to everything anyone says to you?"

"Sorry. Sorry, I just said sorry again. Sorry. There I go again". He laughs, his eyes twinkling as he watches her sipping her freshly squeezed orange juice. His mind has just woken up.

"You're funny", she smiles. "Let's order".

*

O'Riordan has arrived at Doolans. The boys are out washing down the steps and the chef is seeing in a delivery of fresh lobsters, crayfish tails and *carabinieri*, ready for the day's happy punters. Inside, he sits down at the bar and is straight on the mobile. As he dials the number, Ronan appears from upstairs.

"Mornin', boss. I've some new coffee samples. Would you be tryin' one with me, or is it the usual? Oh, and there's a message. A lady called, very Spanish sounding, said her party for lunch is increased to six. We have no-one booked under the name she gave. I said it was OK".

"Cheers, Ronan. Just the usual. I don't want any surprises today".

He goes back to his dialling.

"Hello? Can you make it earlier? 'Bout eleven? No, not here. On the boat. We'll be three hours, no more. Yes, OK". *Click.*

Click again.

"Is she there, then? Good. One of the boys'll come. Take care". *Click.*

"Ronan, get Kieran or one of the others to go up to the house. There's a woman there needs to go to the boat. Take the Audi with the tints".

*

As the waitress brings the bill, they are still laughing, finding the situation rather comical to say the least. Two senior British Customs officers bunking off to eat an English breakfast in a Spanish bar and spending most of the time trying to find a diet which will curtail Andy's farting. She pays the bill with a credit card and they're away. The morning traffic has increased and they sit patiently at the lights, whilst a refuse truck collects last night's fun from overflowing skips. He's thinking how much he enjoyed it and she's miles away, listening to a Cuban Salsa station on the radio. Soon, they're back in position, just across the valley from Villa Thérése. Shortly after they arrive, a green Audi draws up outside the gates. Andy quickly raises his binoculars and homes in on the plate.

"It's the car from Doolan's. Can't see who's driving. Probably making a delivery to Mrs O".

The gates open and the Audi glides slowly into the drive and out of view. A few minutes later, the gates slide back and it re-emerges, driving slowly down the hill and back towards town. Back towards Emily and Joe's vantage point on the beach near Doolans. Via the marina.

"Doesn't anything ever happen at this villa? Down on the Costa del Sol, it's the houses where it all cracks off".

"I didn't know you'd worked down there?"

"There are a lot of things, Mr Meacher, that you don't know about me!" She winked at him and all thoughts of a dull day just melted into nothingness.

"Have you done a lot of surveillance work? I mean the long-term obs?"

"A fair bit. Some of it's been amazing, you know, comings and goings at all hours, pick-ups, close range camera work, railway stations, following people, that kind of stuff. I guess because I'm a woman, I get chosen because Zulus never expect to be followed by girls".

"Apparently, we're getting an updated Zulu list. There have been developments in London, so Graham said".

"What do you make of him? Bit of an old dinosaur?"

"Maybe. He does rather echo the old Metro Bond days. Thinks he can get away with anything, even after that fiasco. I'm surprised someone as squeaky clean as Janet wants him around at all".

"I think it's precisely because he's old school that she tolerates him. If this falls over on its arse, at least she'll have someone to blame".

"I hadn't looked at it like that". Andy's look was rather quizzical.

"Well, if nothing *does* come of this, then someone's bound to be for the chop. I just don't want it to be me. I'm in the service for the duration".

"Are you having a laugh? Do you really expect me to believe that you think this is all there is? I mean, what about seeing the world, making some money?"

"Who says you can't make money in the service? I mean, we wouldn't be the first and won't be the last, that's for sure".

"You are so having me on, Miss Evans!"

"You think what you like. I am ambitious and I want to get on. There *is* a future here. You just have to find it".

*

Down at the marina, Ronan's shining green Audi has just arrived and the boat is being prepared for sea. He walks along the jetty and onto the rear deck, holding on carefully to the bright, white guard ropes which lead him to comparative safety. He does not like the sea, on account of the fact that he can't swim and it is *very apparent*. He checks the inside of the boat, then returns to the deck to give Pilar Estravados and Marianna Benitez da-Sancha the signal to come aboard. The two ladies extract themselves from the comfort of the Audi's leather seats and teeter across the jetty to the boat. Ronan is on his very best mine host behaviour and welcomes them aboard with aplomb. He seats them in deep cushioned cane armchairs and produces freshly brewed coffee from the on-board Gaggia espresso maker, served in bone china cups. The silver is from O'Riordan's farm back in the old country, the china from his grandmother's house in Monaghan.

A quiet word from the deck hand announces the arrival of Messrs Alvarez and Reyes, shortly followed by the man himself, accompanied by one Donald Beevers. Once he is on-board, the huge Merlin marine diesel engines burst into life and the captain eases the boat out of the marina and onto the open sea. Coffee is served to the remaining company and they settle down to business.

"Thank you. Thank you very much for comin' at such short notice. I know that you, Marianna have made big sacrifices to come here today. I would like to welcome you, Pilar and you, Felix. I must not forget my old friends, Don and Paco. Ronan, how long before we are out of range of the coast?"

Ronan appears from the for'ard section and wipes his brow, uncomfortable to say the least.

"We'll be about another ten minutes before we dip below the horizon, boss. I think then that we'll be as safe as possible".

"Which is never safe enough for me", he growls, his grimace gradually evolving into a reluctant smile. "I guess it'll have to do, so it will".

"Marianna, your news from yesterday is, to say the least, not encouraging. What on earth has been going on in your little corner of the world?" Felix's question brings everyone to attention.

Marianna explains the ins and outs of Ceutan politics, followed by an update from the Governor himself, a close personal friend. The borders are to be closed until further notice, all non-Spanish citizens are to leave and the army has been put on full alert. Additional Special Forces are on the way from Madrid and the police have been given extra powers. The habeas corpus act has been suspended.

"Most important are the new restrictions on shipping which have been introduced today. These alone, make our position almost untenable. From the conversation I had with Carlos yesterday, and I have to say it was remarkably anodyne, I believe that the measures taken will be short term and temporary. Madrid does not have the stomach for either a fight or the money necessary to make this bloody business go away, so once the world's press has got tired of our little desert paradise, things should go back to normal. Business, gentlemen, as usual".

Felix sits quietly, contemplating her news. Turning in his seat, he looks across at her.

"How long is this going to take, *princesa*? It could be devastating for business. As you well know, we do not currently have another route available".

"This is one of the reasons for bringing Pilar here today, at great expense. We cannot afford to leave ourselves exposed to the cartel. We are currently enjoying the very best relationship with Señor Montoya, but if we dry up, then everything will go back to normal and then we will need to begin again".

"Are we out of sight yet?" Ronan nods, checking the horizon with his army field glasses, long since retrieved from a dead Para just outside the Cross'.

"Where are the weak links in all this? We haven't done a stock check for a long time. I feel the need for a cost/ benefit analysis. It's time we chopped out some of the dead wood. It worked in Belfast and it'll work now".

Padraig has been silent throughout, yet his soft brogue carries formidable weight and they turn to face him.

"OK". Eyes are steely cold now, mentally he's back in the old country. "Marianna. You have some problems to resolve over the water. That's beyond your control, so it is. Just keep us informed when you have an update. Don, I think that operationally, we need to tighten up in the port so that you are in a position to identify new markets. How is the research on the gentlemen from Essex?"

"They're a tight little firm. Ambitious, I'll give 'em that. Word from our man in London is that everythin' the fella said was pretty much bang on. They lack a bit of experience, but they've got a hell of a lot of front. Fair play".

"Do they have the collateral, Don? I mean, ten keys is easy for anyone to finance but what's going to happen when they raise the stakes?"

"We know where they live", Beevers grins and winks at Padraig.

"*Cariño*, we know where everyone lives". Marianna's expression is one of deadly seriousness. "It still doesn't guarantee the payments which I in turn guarantee to the cartel. Señor Montoya is very concerned about the developments in Ceuta. He feels that we do not have things under control, despite my assurances".

"Fuck me, who does he think we are? The feckin' Spanish government? Jesus, Mary, Mother of God, I mean, we're powerful but no-one's got that kinda feckin' muscle". Now Beevers is animated, nervy.

"Sadly, Señor Montoya *does* have that kind of power. He expects everything to run smoothly. When things like this happen, he gets nervous. He's awful when he's nervous. People go on holiday then. Permanently". She looks across at Beevers with a resigned yet confident expression. She has her feet in so many camps.

"Pilar, is there really a prospect of our bulk shipping programme succeeding? How close are you to giving an informed opinion?" Felix's calm manner helps to soothe the growing tension.

"It is realistically another month away. The South American end is almost ready, together with the shadow compartments and ghost shipments. We have a complete false trail prepared which in itself is being kept highly secret until the moment when the leak will occur".

"And your own situation? How reliable is the information filtering through from your teams?"

"Currently, they are concentrating on the small boat business. British Customs, as you know, rely very heavily on Gibraltar and the Royal Navy for their information and observation. They are still obsessed with the old Costa gangs of the 1980s, like they all had children and just carried on. Whether they are influenced by the current crop of gangster movies and books in the UK is anybody's guess. Who will ever know what goes on in the minds of Her Majesty's Customs & Excise?"

"But what about the talk of increased co-operation between your people and the British?"

"Thankfully, in my position, I am the first to know. We have been expecting overtures from them for some time now, especially since the recent seizures at Altea Marina. However, it takes a lot for them to ask for help and until they change at the top, they will always have their secretive British way of doing things. And, when all is said and done, they still believe in James Bond".

"And probably Doctor Bloody Who!" Even Padraig smiles at this interjection from Ronan, who stands at his side, listening, learning.

"They have their funny little ways, so they do, but they can be extremely effective when they want to be and they're not afraid of breaking eggs when they need to. Jaysus, we've paid by underestimating them in the past". Back to the old Padraig now, sombre, cold, chilling.

"Pilar, how effective do you think this *diversionary tactic* can be? How big a window do you think we'll have with the container ships?" continues Felix.

"The information which will arrive on my desk will confirm a change in tactics. The Russians, the Chinese, they're all becoming *of interest* to our Department. The traditional focus west may well turn eastwards. We have limited resources, gentlemen. Long may that last!" She sits back, her little soliloquy over for now. Marianna regards her with great interest, looking for any kind of indication which way this is likely to go.

"And your bosses? What will they make of your little *diversion*? Surely they will want more than a few concocted intelligence stories?"

"We have, what you know as registered informants. The curse of our business in one way, but very useful to us in another. Once they are on the payroll of the Government, they are seen as true sources, *trusted* sources! Most of them come from the industry anyway and they know the game well. Some of them are failed dealers, others disaffected employees. Others are just fuelled by greed! They want their cake and eat it, as you English say".

"We'll have less of the English, so we will!" Padraig stares straight at her, but soon there is a smile playing around his lips. He can hold out no more in front of the ladies and winks conspiratorially at Marianna, which Pilar picks up on smartly.

"I am sooo sorry! As you *Irish* say".

"There's nothin' wrong with the English. Just the fuckin' Mancs!" Beevers joins in the banter and for a moment the whole atmosphere takes on an almost surreal aura.

"I just need to know that we're not goin' into uncharted areas here. One mistake now and we could be staring at a lot of bird! An' I ain't doin' that for no-one".

"Padraig, you know what will happen, I think. At the moment we have nothing yet in a week we could have all the scenarios working just right. We do not wish to hurry matters for the sake of just a little more time".

"What about your Señor Montoya? You said he was impatient".

"I said that he was nervous when things do not go to plan. He is a very methodical individual. That is why he is head of the cartel and is not lying two metres under the ground with his dick in his mouth".

"He certainly sounds like a fascinating man, your Señor Montoya. You should bring him over some time, so you should".

"Señor Montoya does not travel. People travel to *him*. That is why it is best that I continue to negotiate with him as before. We have a little *understanding*. It comes from the days in the colonies".

"I think you Latinos stick together, Marianna", says Pilar, her nose held mockingly in the air. "It's no surprise that you continue to live outside Spain. I think we are too sophisticated for you now, no?"

"Not too sophisticated for our money and our expertise in certain *matters*? No, I don't think so. I think you do your job and I will do mine. I like it that way! What is it that the French say? *Vive la difference*? Well I agree".

"Isn't tha' something about men and women? I' learned that when I was…..when I was at school".

"You were never at school. You were too busy taking the wheels off of the cars, so you were, you little gobshite!" grins Padraig.

"Good one there, Mr O! Too fuckin' shay!"

"When are you going back to Liverpool? Is everything ready there, Don?" asks Marianna.

"Everything's great. Just waitin' for the all clear with the slaughter and the facility, like".

"And the samples, Don, did they like the samples?"

"What do I know about wine? All tastes the same to me. Yes, they fuckin' loved 'em. The company's cock on to buy. What about your end?"

"The bottling plant is finished and the special packaging is perfect. Almost *too* perfect!"

"No such fuckin' thing. The moment we think that, we might as well hand ourselves in and save the fuckin' bizzies the trouble. Tell, me, Padraig, do you ever worry there's too many heads in this fuckin' trough?"

"What would a man be meaning by that?"

"We've go' the cartel, the Princesa, Paco and his posh mate, your boys, me and now half the fuckin' cast of East Enders. All we're missin's the Carry On team and fuckin' Daniel O'Donnell else we've cracked it".

"Better having Pauline Fowler than Robbie Fowler, eh scouse man?"

"Fuckin' hell, that was a bit below the belt! Ah' least Robbie can score!"

"Surely you are not suggesting that we get rid of some heads, Señor Beevers? Perhaps we could start with you?" Marianna sits there with those legs, just looking him straight in the eye, her face devoid of expression.

"Jesus, Marianna, I was only fuckin' jokin'! Anyways, where would you find your bit of rough then, eh, eh?"

"The streets are full of rubbish, Don. It is not hard to find". Still the dispassionate face.

"Yeah, but not this quality of rubbish!" This time he starts to smile, breaking into that bloody infectious Mickey Mouse thing he does, what he's always resorted to in these situations, unless, of course, he's got a shooter and his mates behind him. In which case, find the nearest window and jump straight through it. And don't pass 'Go'. And give him his £200 back on the way. Because Don Beevers and his little team of scallys back home don't let you off. Never. Ever.

"All I'm sayin' is we need to look at the whole operation again now that this sort of thing is happening. We're getting bigger, we're all movin' up and that's the time that we get into the bigger league of fuckin' bizzies. Do you know that since the fuckin' cold war ended, even MI5 are lookin' into the game? They're takin' over a lot of the work that the Customs was doin'. Add fuckin' GCHQ to that and the whole fuckin' game's got a hell of a lot harder".

"You are beginning to sound rather negative, Don. This is not like you".

"It's not like me to keep havin' me mates banged up, neither. I tell you, this game ain't no fuckin' joke no more".

"Do I detect a note of retirement? Surely not, Mr Beevers?"

"I'm already takin' steps to sharpen things up at my end, lady. Don't have no sleepless nights over me, whatever you do. The Beevers is on the case. Proper on it!"

"I'm very pleased to hear it. Señor Montoya will be pleased to hear that also. He has concerns, as I said".

"Well he can keep them to himself".

Ronan's timely return from the galley breaks up the conversation and the drinks seem to quieten things down. The boats powerful twin diesels are switched off, the only noise the occasional slapping of water against the gleaming hull. The sea is flat calm, the coast no longer visible and to all intents and purposes, they are alone.

"Tell me about Ceuta, *princesa*. What is it like there?"

"It is a den of iniquity, I think you call it. Where Europe finally gives way to Africa. A place where you can be anybody. The traders come up from the centre, bringing God knows what with them. It feels different, smells different. The cuisine is Andalusian/Arabic. This is where the Moors came from to invade Spain. They swept across north Africa and then saw what was across the way. You see their legacy in Alicante every day. Spain and Africa are not *so* different, you know".

"Well they can keep bloody Africa for all I care. And their bloody Al Qaeda".

"You are not wrong there. Since the Madrid bombings, we have had considerable interest from the Spanish authorities, but I feel that this little problem which has recently surfaced will soon go away. Madrid will not want to soil its soft hands in our filthy African dustbowl".

"Al Qaeda is flavour of the month at the moment, *cariño!*" Felix leans across to make eye contact with her.

"Yes, and for one bombing in Madrid. For how long have we had ETA? How many times have they killed and maimed in the name of *Batasuna*? Still the people, they go to Bilbao, to La Rioja and to the Atlantic coast. Trust me, my friend, soon they will tire of us and leave well alone. *Then* and then, we can begin to put little Ceuta on the map, but it will be a *secret map*! There are good times ahead for us, for the cartel and for business!"

Ronan comes back into the rear cabin.

"Boss, I think we got company. Take a look". He hands the binoculars to Padraig who scans the horizon intently.

"There's something there, so there is. Is it comin' this way? I can't really tell. Have a look on the radar. See if you can plot the devil's course. And start those engines".

The twin Perkins diesels burst into life as Padraig trains the powerful lenses onto a fast moving craft just in view. The sun keeps reflecting on its bow.

"I think we'll take this as our cue to move on, so we will. We'll not be doing anything for a week anyway. I think we all know where we stand, what we're doin'?"

"Boss, I've gotta name on that boat. I'll get it checked out. Might be nothin' but we can't take no chances".

"Grand fella, Ronan. See to it that we have no more problems with that".

The boat gradually picks up speed and soon the coast is in view.

"Take us down the coast to that new marina. Drop the others there. Call Keenan on the radio and get him to send the Voyager down to pick them up. You hang around and I'll take the boat back to Torrevieja. If it *is* our friends, then all they'll see is an old Paddy with his boat, comin' back after an afternoon's fishin'. Come to think of it, get Keenan to pick up some fish on the way down and

I'll give it to those two muppets who watch the bar every day. That'll give 'em somethin' ter think about!"

Padraig's face says it all. He is once again alive with the *craic*. The boat moves closer to the shore, whilst its only company on the sea keeps a discreet distance.

Chapter Seventeen

Canvey. The Hilton House

Dave just sits there, staring. In all his puffed up glory.

"Darlin', I thought you and Dean was going up town today, now he's back from Spain? Ain't you gonna be late?"

"No. Got loads of time. I ain't in no hurry. Besides, he don't need me to wipe his fuckin' arse".

"Dave, please! Not in front of the kids. You was being really good. I don't know what's got into you lately. It's the company you keep, I suppose". She returns to her usual resigned and pragmatic state.

Dave repeats her words silently to her back, exaggerating his face so that the kids see him. The eldest laughs. As Shirley turns around, he gives her one of those Hilton smiles.

"I ain't stupid, David Hilton! What am I going to do with you?"

"You're gonna love me like you always do, my little precious. Love of my life". He walks over and grabs her from behind, no mean feat these days.

"Get lost, will you. I'm serious, Dave. You got to start behavin' more responsibly. It's parents' night tonight. You ain't forgotten, have you?"

"I was gonna talk to you about that. Sorry, love, but I ain't gonna be able to make it. Bit of work come up".

Her face, up till now, was jovial and resigned. Now, it looks like the bottom's fallen out of her world. No anger, no fight there, just sadness.

"Dave, I begged you. Three weeks ago I told you about this. You promised me".

"Look babes, drop me out will you? I ain't feeling so good this morning. Must've been something I ate last night".

"I'm surprised you can even remember comin' in the house".

"I've had enough of this. Laters".

He storms from the kitchen, without even a kiss for the kids. No matter how hard she tries, Shirley can't hold back the tears and the elder daughter gets up from her Shreddies and comes over to comfort her. The other kids just look on, not knowing what the hell is going on, just that it's not at all a good thing.

"It's alright, my darlins. Daddy don't mean nothing. He's just very busy at the moment. You'll see him later". She's really stifling the tears now, struggling to keep a brave face on it. She clears away the breakfast things and thanks God that it's not her turn for the school run today. The doorbell goes and the kids give her a quick kiss before running to the car, closing the door behind them. *Click.*

Now, the floodgates can open. The silence of her house somehow makes it even worse for Shirley and after having a long bawl, she mopes about for an hour before going upstairs to dress. Walking into the large rectangular bedroom, which overlooks the garden, she is confronted by Dave's 'last night' clothes, strewn all over the floor. Clothes she had lovingly chosen for him just chucked around like confetti. Bad analogy, Shirley. The confetti went out of your marriage a long time ago.

Slowly, very slowly, she starts to clear up the mess, after making their huge four-poster bed. Some use that is. She catches sight of herself in the mirror and starts to cry again. *Is it my fault? Is it me that's the problem? Oh, my God, what have I done? I've fucked up, haven't I?* She sits on the edge of the bed, still in her dressing gown, looking a little grubby at the edges. *Why, Shirley? Why? After all these years, why now?* This time, she drags herself to her feet and continues with the tidying. His beautiful kid leather jacket lies crumpled, one dirty shoe actually on top of it. She puts this to one side and picks it up, walking over to the wardrobe as she brushes it down. Brush away those stains, Shirley.

As she reaches up to hang it on the rail, she stumbles and it misses, landing on the floor.

"Oh, for fuck's sake! WHY ME?" she yells out in desperation. Sadness turns to anger as she bends down once more. At the back of the walk-in wardrobe, behind the shoes, something catches her eye. Something she's never seen before. It's a small red holdall. She looks at it for a few seconds, almost leaves it where it is. After all, that's what she would have done before. That was then and this is now. She reaches in and tries to lift it, but it won't budge. She puts the jacket down and tugs at the bag with both hands. This time it gives way and she tumbles back onto the shag pile. Once she's recovered herself, she opens the zip and looks inside. On the top, there's an old hoody, a baseball cap and a West Ham scarf. She lifts these out, almost reluctantly and cries out at what she sees. Underneath, wrapped in an oilcloth, is one shining Smith and Wesson revolver, persons for the killing of. *Very successfully*. The gun is a work of art, truly a masterpiece. Next to it, is another, smaller gun, an automatic. There are three boxes of cartridges, brand new and sealed. Once she has taken this on board, she lets the bag fall to the floor, falling back against the bed, totally shocked. She's Dave Hilton's wife, but she's never seen anything like this before. She knows her man, granted, or at least she knew her man, thought she did. She's terrified now, really bloody frightened. Who knows about the gun? What the hell is it doing there? *What is he involved in*?

"Oh, Dave, my Dave, why can't we go back to how it was, darlin'?" She is shaking with fear now, yet within a minute, she has her composure back. The Basildon girl returns. Her mind is in a whirl. She doesn't know whether to curse him or pity him, the stupid big lump. What the hell is he playing at, bringing a shooter into the house? She sits and stares at the guns for ages, until she drifts off into some kind of trance. Her head falls back against the soft duvet cover and she is transported to another plane, where she is at peace with the world. It is like a former time. She and Dave are lying on a beach, Greek Islands, on their honeymoon. She looks around but of course there are no kids. Everywhere is peaceful. Idyllic even. Her anxiety is allayed by Dave's behaviour. It is tender, even in his oaf-like way, he looks after her, gets her a cocktail and shades her from the fierce Mediterranean sun. He looks fit and healthy. Though she cannot see herself, she knows that her body is good, slim and curvy. Sexy. They lie there in the lee of a steep cliff, the shimmering sea beckoning them into its warm waters. She wants to stay, but Dave drags her up to her feet and races off down the beach, calling for her to follow. Obediently, she does so and soon they are frolicking in the gentle surf, acting the goat. Their eyes meet and soon they are kissing. There is no-one around and he unhooks her bikini top, letting it fall into the foaming water. He begins to lap at her firm breasts and soon she begins to sense the wetness growing between her tanned thighs. Her eyes are closed to fully experience this sultry arousal and his kisses taste like honey. She begins to feel agitated and lets her eyelids open for a second. They are no longer alone. On the beach, a woman looks at them. *Stares at them*. Shirley cannot make out her face, yet it looks somehow familiar. Her mind is less and less on Dave's talented love-making and more on the interloper. The more she stares back at the woman, the clearer her visage becomes until it is apparent that it is Gina. She is more beautiful than ever, her figure exaggerated, her breasts larger, her waist slimmer, her legs longer. A mane of golden blond hair cascades around her shoulders and she seems to be saying something. Panic begins to take hold of Shirley's mind and with this panic comes an awakening from Dave and he too opens his eyes. Turning around, he sees Gina and instead of turning back to his bride, he disentangles himself from her and begins to walk towards the mythical Gina. Shirley calls out to him but he cannot, *will not* hear her. Gina holds her open arms out to him and as he reaches her, *touches her*, he turns to face Shirley and laughs at her, mocking her inferior body and looks. He takes Gina's hand and they walk off up the beach and out of view. Poor Shirley is left rooted to the spot, the tears beginning to flow freely.

She awakens with a start, yet as she brings her hands up to her face, she realises that the tears are genuine and reaches for a tissue. She is terrified by what has just occurred, cannot explain it. Her heart is racing, her palms sweating freely. She looks down and her tears have fallen directly on the gun barrel, making it shine brightly against the dull oil cloth. The light is reflected in it, twinkling, teasing, *calling*.

What the hell is going on? She is very alarmed. *Was it a dream, a vision or something worse? Dave and Gina? What is that all about? Not my Dave. No way!* Yet she starts to recall more tangible events. She starts to think back over the preceding months and cannot get Gina out of her mind. Dave is out. Dave is late back. Dave is not at the office when he is supposed to be. Dean doesn't know where he is. Nobody knows where he is. Gina is not at the salon. Come to think of it, she's never at the bleeding salon.

Calm down, girl, for God's sake! They'll be sending the men in the white coats for you next. Slowly, practical, mumsy Shirl takes over and she starts to pack up the guns, replacing them in the wardrobe, before going to the en-suite to have a shower. As she lets the gown fall to the shag-pile, she looks herself up and down in the full-length. Not a pretty sight. The pounds have been gradually applied, a few here, a few there. They all add up to a whole lot of Shirley. She's gone from a ten to an eighteen in four years. The love handles he used to joke about look more like something you could moor a ship up to now. Her calves are nearly as big as her thighs used to be. *Your tits are not too bad, girl, but look at the rest of you!* She looks herself straight in the eye and makes a vow, then climbs into the shower, something she *never does at this time.*

Once out, she goes to her wardrobe and selects a trouser suit she looks OK in, puts on her best lingerie, chooses a silk blouse to wear and then goes to apply the war paint and the false nails. They haven't been out of the packet in years. All around her is mayhem and debris, the mess that would normally have long been cleared up by now. She ignores it. It can wait.

Click. "Hello, darlin'! You still in the office? Everything alright? Listen. I've had an idea. I'm in Basildon doing some shopping. Yes, me shopping. Fancy that? Why don't we go down the pub an' have a bit of lunch. We ain't done that in ages. Yeah? You sure, babes? Not doin' nothing else? Right, that pub on the roundabout with the big garden. The Watermill. Yeah, that's the one. See you at one? Love ya'." *Click.*

That was a bit too easy, but no matter. Not to a woman on a mission. She returns to the makeup mirror and really starts to go to town. She hasn't had this much fun in years. She goes to the shoe cupboard and looks at all the disappointing flatties. Not a heel in sight. Then she returns to Dave's wardrobe just one more time and reaches in. Her mind is made up along with her face and within ten minutes, she's on her way into Brentwood, to the shop Gina uses for all her ridiculous stilettos. It's time *I* had some of those. Four hundred quid later and she's kitted out in a pair of Jimmy Choo's. A five-inch heel and a strap is about all there is. Perfect!

She parks herself up just along from the pub and waits for Dave to arrive, which the silly sod does bang on time. She checks the contents of her bag and then her makeup just once more. He parks up the M5 and goes in. She waits just the requisite five more minutes then climbs carefully out of the car, making sure not to scratch the works of art which now adorn her feet.

The big daft lump is waiting in the corner bar, smiling like he hasn't a care in the world. But then of course, he hasn't. She walks towards him, well, more stalks towards him really. The Jimmy Cs are already killing her but that's not going to take the smile off her face. The bar is quiet and as she walks deliberately towards him, she reaches slowly into her handbag. As he gets up to greet her, smiling, her hand closes on the surprise and she brings it out, thrusting it towards him. As he looks down, he jumps back in surprise.

"Hello, babes!" she calls out, placing in his hand a photograph. "Look what I found today". It is a honeymoon picture of the two of them on the beach in Greece. Happy as Larry.

"Blimey, ain't seen that in a long while. Where the bleeding hell did you find that?"

"I was thinkin' about the old days and something made me think of it. We *was* 'appy then, weren't we?"

"Course we was, babe. What's this all about? Memory lane? Cos if it is, I got work to do".

"No, darlin' it's not about that. It's about you an' me having a bit of time for each other. No kids, no house, no problems. Just a bit of lunch, a glass of wine and a proper old fashioned chat".

Dave's face is a study and he's already shifting around in his seat. She looks at him from under the false eyelashes. Fair play, she looks the part, but the big daft lump can't see that.

"Well you've certainly surprised me, girl. You're usually doing house work now. What's happened to that?"

"It can wait. What I was really thinkin', Dave, was why don't we have a little holiday again, just you an' me. It wouldn't hurt, would it. We could even go during term time so that the kids are OK. I could get me skinny or Deb to look after 'em".

"You had some kind of lobotomy, girl? Am I with the woman I left indoors this mornin'?" He's grinning at her now, that look which she always used to love.

"Just thinkin', that's all. Sometimes people just lose their way, don't they Dave? You see, look, well…". Just at this moment, the waitress comes over and tells them that their table's ready, so they get up from the bar stools and walk over to the restaurant level through the little archway.

Once they're sat down and the girl's brought the remains of a bottle of Australian Chardonny over, she resumes.

"You see, Dave, the photo wasn't the only thing I found this mornin'." She pauses for effect and looks at him, watching for any kind of giveaway sign. Nothing forthcoming so far.

"I went up to the bedroom to clear up, like I do, an' your clothes was all over the floor, as they always are". She gives him that look of loving resignation which women who are married to big daft lumps like Dave do.

"Anyway, I starts putting it all away and there at the bottom of your wardrobe, well, Dave, there's this bag!"

At last, his face begins to register some kind of awareness of where she's coming from.

"Well?"

"Well, that's the point, isn't it? I was puttin' away your jacket and there it was, or as I should say, there they were. Guns, David. Why have we got guns in our house?"

"Listen, babes, it's not how it looks".

"What do you mean, Dave? Are we just keeping them for a friend, is that what you are sayin'? Cos if we are, do you think you could get this friend to get them out of my fuckin' house, David? For God's sake, my children are in that house. *Our children*. There's bullets and everything in there. What happens if we get a raid? And don't say to me it won't happen, because it's happened before. You're not bleedin' invincible, David Hilton. You might think you are, running with Dean Bold and the rest of your bleedin' gang, but I see you for what you are an' you ain't foolin' no-one".

"Babes, babes, don't go gettin' yourself all upset. It ain't what you think. They really are just there for a couple of days and then they'll be gone".

"I want 'em gone today. I ain't negotiatin', neither".

"Alright, alright! I'll get something sorted. You didn't need to go to all this trouble just to tell me you wanted rid of the shooters, babe".

"Oh, that ain't the only reason why we're 'ere. What I said earlier stands. We need to spend a bit more time together. Work things out. I know I ain't been much to look at lately, what with the kids an' that, but that's gonna change now. We're going to be more of a family but with all of us, not just me and the kids. We was just you and me before they came along".

He's sitting there looking at her. *You're not wrong there, you dozy mare*, he's thinking. *Course we was on our lonesome before the dustbins. Who else was going to be there? What would Dean do?* Probably give the interfering cow a good slap. He looked at her, looking a bit like mutton, but at least she'd made a *bit* of an effort. *What the fuck does she want, anyway?* Last thing *he* wants, is to have her booting off at the slightest thing.

"Alright, babes. I'll fuck 'em off. Get one of the boys to come and sort it. Don't you worry about a thing". He smiles that big, daft grin at her. Looks like it's working.

"Look, what you do is what you do. I've turned a blind eye for years. Always knew what kind of man you was, Dave, but this? This is more than I can handle. I can't sleep at night with shooters in the bleedin' wardrobe. The old bill don't fuck about no more, Dave. You'll be staring at at least an eight, even if the bleedin' things ain't been fired. God knows if they have. You'll never see the kids. They'll be grown up by the time they let you out".

"D'you remember what it was like, you know, before we had the kids? Maybe you're right, girl. Maybe we should have some kind of holiday. Get away. I could have a word with Dean, see if we could have the villa like. Just you and me, babes".

"Oh, Dave, could we? That would be nice. Just a few days would do it. I'm going to sort myself out an' all. No more lardy bird for you. I'm going to join the health club, get back to how I was".

"You do that, princess and there'll be a nice little treat at the end of it".

The food arriving brings a welcome break for both of them. Dave's steak and kidney pud contrasts with Shirley's salad, though the wine's still flowing like it's going out of fashion. Dave calls on another bottle, almost like he's forgotten himself.

"I thought you an' Dean was goin' up town, anyway. Leaving it a bit late, ain't you, darlin?"

"No. Something's come up. We ain't goin'. I won't be home later, neither. Got a bit of business to sort. Might be a late one".

Shirley's hackles are up at this news, but she keeps it to herself, knowing that one slip could give the game away. She munches away at the crispy radicchio and sips her Chardonnay.

"Alright, babes. Do you want me to wait up, or do you want to wake me when you get in?" She opens her eyes wide, the lashes flickering in the half light of the pub. Dave's getting well pissed and now he's horny.

"Don't wait up, princess. I'll give you something to do when I get in, eh?" he winks at her and returns to the fast-disappearing kate n'sidney. Shirley's list of mental notes to do later grows by the minute.

"Do you want me to give you a lift anywhere, babes?"

"No. No point. I'm meetin' Dean over Canvey. Might need me own motor".

"No worries, babes", she looks at him. "No worries at all".

Chapter Eighteen

Later. Dean's Boat, Canvey November 2006

"Dean, bruv, we're gettin' stretched".

Dave sits opposite Dean. It's early evening. Dusk. He's got a face like a smacked arse. Well smacked.

"Chill out, matey. Deano's got everythin' under control. It's just teething troubles. Plus, I have to say, whackin' an old mate the other night did rather stretch us even further, *BRUV*!"

"He had it coming. I weren't havin' him leading off like that about us. No fuckin' way. I'm havin' it with the other fella again an' all. Time that cunt got ironed out."

"What is it with you, Dave? You been watchin' too many films? You on some kinda mission? And anyway, who's calling the fuckin' shots?"

"Just doin' what's right, that's all. The cunt's takin' the piss. I'm only finishing what we started down the fuckin' unit, anyways. We gotta do it. It's a matter of fuckin' pride. For the firm, like".

"For once, bruv, you're fuckin' right". The hooter is kicking in again and he's got his dander up. "I ain't fuckin' having it neither".

The two of them sit opposite each other, making some serious decisions. Dean's a bit precarious. He can't really see where all this is going and yet his sheer ambition is getting the better of him like nobody's business.

"I was thinking about one of them Baby Bentleys. That'd look blindin' on the fuckin' drive. Proper".

"Sounds good to me. Fancy a new motor myself, like. Something a bit more, in keeping' with my status in the community. I want to right fuckin' blend in".

"You couldn't fuckin' blend in nowhere on national fuckin' blendin' in day, you cunt". He laughs and punches Dave on the arm, opening another can of Stella.

"We've got some serious fuckin' decisions to take today. I'm gettin' sick of all this bleedin' talkin'. It's time we had some fuckin' news from Spain. However, first decision is, do us a favour and sort out the Porsche for us? It's making a moody noise from underneath and I ain't having that. Not at Christmas. Plus Gina's giving me fuckin' murders. If I get a fuckin' Bentley, it's extras. I'm keeping the Porker and the Range Rover".

"No problem, bruv. I'll take it tomorrow and have it back to you in a couple of days. Use the four-by-four if you want. Shirl can give us a lift to the unit".

"You're a star, matey. I take it all back. What's the latest on cuntocks anyway? He won't be coming back to the office in a while".

"No cunt's seen him since the little matter at the warehouse".

"That was fuckin' blindin'. Took me right back that did, Dave. Nice touch, real bit of nostalgia".

"Kev ain't lost his touch. A real craftsman with the KD, eh? And Ali. What can you say about Ali the Coat that's not already been said? That geezer fuckin' frightens me, the cunt and I'm on is bleedin' side!"

"He's your classic psycho, I reckon. Loves 'is Mum an' all that, but when it comes to the crunch, what he really likes is tuning cunts up".

"I can relate to that. There is something pure, something well, *creative* about tuning a geezer up. You ask any of the old ICF, the fuckin' boys. They'll all say the same. It's the sheer fuckin' inevitability of it. Yer get a geezer away from 'is mates, up some fuckin' alley. There's about six of you, one of him. It ain't fuckin' Pimms o'clock, that's for fuckin' certain". Dave's pissing himself laughing.

"So you've gone in with the Doc Marrtens an that, the cunt's beggin' for his life and just when he thinks he's onto a winner, out comes Uncle Stanley. What would we have given for one of them camera phones then? These little bastards have got it cushti now. Not just snaps, fuckin' videos an' all. So you're goin' to work on the cunt's face with the blade, the claret's spillin' all over the bleedin' place and then he's gone. Once they've passed out, the fuckin' fun factor's right art the fuckin' window."

"Happy days, bruv, happy days. I thought I was supposed to be the fuckin' psycho! You on something' I don't know about?"

"I miss it, Dean, have to say, I fuckin' miss it. I mean, all this fuckin' about with houses, fuckin' school fees an' all. What the fuck's that all about? Think of it, mate. Think back to the 80s. Millwall away, Chelsea, Cardiff, Birmingham. Fuckin' Baker Street tube. Right old fuckin' tear up. We was wanted by every fuckin' force in the land. All Stanley'd up, the calling cards. Even takin' a fuckin' pasting! It weren't all that bad. It was *proper*. Meeting in the boozer, get the boys together, down Mile End, bit of bugle and away. The fucking boys on tour. Hear what I'm sayin'?"

"All day long, bruv, all fuckin' day". Nostalgia is getting the better of Dean too.

"Do you remember the eighty-five, eighty-six season? Blindin'. Nearly did it too. Didn't miss a fuckin' game all year. Had some right fuckin' tear ups and all. QPR, Chelsea. And Luton. Luton was the fuckin' business. Must've been a hundred of us. Took the lot of 'em, we did. That fuckin' road was red after Uncle Stanley had paid the cunts a visit. Didn't need no calling cards that day!"

"There's a lot of the boys gone back in now. Just 'cos we are in our forties don't mean we can't fuckin' mix it. I'm itching to cut some cunt".

"There's always cuntocks".

"Too easy, mate".

"Not if *we* do 'im. Just you an' me, like the old days. Take 'im up Tilbury Fort, proper job. Give him a chance. Bit of sport, like".

"Hang on, me phone's buzzin'" Dean answers his phone.

"Hello, mate. Yeah. Blinding. Yeah? The bollocks. You'd better come over. Yeah, on the boat. We're taking it down Southend. You can come along for the ride". *Click.*

"Town Hall's comin'. Reckons he's got some news. Good news

an' all".

"You sure about him? I mean, the other day, some of the boys was a bit, well, reticent. He makes them nervous. He's not like, well, *one of us*".

"Well you couldn't call The bleedin' Coat one of your own and he's as sound as a fuckin' pound. Dutch Frank's a mate of his anyway. Always goes through Tarn. Trusts him".

"Yeah, well, that's as may be. Fact is, the Coat's different. He's been around since the beginning, ain't he? He provides things, like".

"Yeah, well, Town's been a mate for years an' all. Just ain't been right on the scene, that's all. You said the same thing about Ali when I brought him on board".

"True, true. But if he's comin' in, we need to know he's proper sound. Maybe we bring him in on the Fort job an all. Let him cut his teeth. Nothing like the first time you watch a new geezer cut some cunt. Almost as good as doin' it yerself".

"You sure? I don't think that's his cup of tea".

"It's like a rite of passage, ain't it? It's got to be done, bruv".

"Yeah, maybe you're right. It's not like it's anything major".

Dean walks to the drinks cabinet and gets out the Remy Martin. He takes two large crystal glasses from the unit and pours out huge measures for him and Dave.

"We'll do it without the others, just for old times. He's just about recovered by now, so it'll be a fuckin' scream to tune him up again". Dave's warming to this idea, big time.

"We'll have a little chat, like on the way to Southend. Give you a chance to get to know the geezer. He'll be here in a mo."

Dean takes out a bag of the white stuff and chucks it on the table.

"Come on, mate. Few little diamonds won't fuckin' do you no harm and all".

"I ain't touched the bleedin' gear in ages, bruv!"

"You're 'avin' a fuckin' laugh! Well, all the more fuckin' reason to have some now!"

Dean starts chopping up the wares and soon has four nice big thick diamond mines all set up, two for him, two for Dave. He takes out a spanking new nifty and proceeds to get sorted, passing another to Dave. He is a little reticent, but with Dean's encouragement, he's straight back on it, snorting like a good 'un.

"Oh, mate, that is *blind-ingggg*! Is this some of Town's?"

"Do you know what I'm saying? He ain't such a bad lemon. Talk of the fuckin' devil, he's here".

Dean looks across the marina towards the car-park and Town Hall's BMW M5 which has just pulled up. He climbs out, grabs a holdall from the boot and starts to walk over.

"Funny, ain't it, watchin' someone when they don't know you're there?"

"Better not be no-one watchin' us, bruv".

"Get the engines goin', mate. You'll make me fuckin' paranoid!"

Town's at the jetty now, comes aboard carrying the tools of his trade.

"Alright, mate?" yells Dean, already casting off. Dave stands rock steady at the wheel.

"Rough as arseholes, chavvy. Rough as fuckin' arseholes. Blindin' night. Went with them birds from the club in Chelmo again. That Natasha! Fuck me, can that bird suck! Her and that Anastasia or whatever her name is put on a little show for me, lesby friends stylee. Oh, man. I was running round the room like a fuckin' tripod, trying to stick it in. Fuckin' anywhere would've done. I tell you, three Viagra and them two and you could've cut fuckin' diamonds with mine, no worries!"

"You dirty cunt! Fuckin' slidin' off like that, fuckin' sly! What about your mates, then? Cunted right off!" Dean cuffs him right on the shoulder, giving him a momentary dead arm.

"So how much are them two costing you then? Them Russian birds ain't cheap no more. They cottoned right fuckin' on!"

"Monkey each for the night. Full on for that, mind". Town gives him the look, bends over and smacks his arse loudly.

"You dirty cunt! You doin' em up the arse an' all?"

"I should fuckin' coco an all, for a fuckin' monkey!"

"And they say it's always the quiet ones!"

Dean's pissing himself laughing, shaking his head. He walks over to the cockpit and takes over from Dave, revving the powerful diesel engines. A throaty roar comes from the stern as the twin Perkins roar into life.

Across the other side, just for a second, the light catches a pair of binoculars, trained fair and square on the boat. Behind the lens, a leather jacketed thick set man stands hidden by a low wall. Next to him, his heavily scarred colleague makes notes on a small pad. As Dean opens up the engines and the boat disappears beyond the harbour wall, a camera clicks merrily away on multi-frame mode.

"Blinding performance, mate. How much can it do?" Town looks like a teenager in a sex shop. Wide-eyed.

"She, Town, she. You have to call a boat she. It's the rules!"

"Rules. What fuckin' rules to you adhere to, then?"

"Why the book according to Dean Bold, that's his rules"

"You lairy cunt, Dave". Part of the furniture now, Town.

"Say what you see, bruv, say just what you see".

"What is this, fuckin' Blockbusters? You fuckin' mug!"

Town walks over to the fridge, getting out more Stellas.

"So why all the secrecy, then? I mean, we ain't fucked about with all this cloak and dagger stuff before".

"We're gettin in a different league now, Dave". Town's taking over now, he senses the opportunity and grabs it with both hands.

"These guys in Spain, there proper fuckin' professional. It's like everything's run like a fuckin' multinational. Board meetings, fuckin' structures. If we're gonna become part of this, we've got to get right up to speed. I ain't joking mate. The profits are much higher but the fuckin' risks are Premier League and all".

"Mate, I hear there's bin a bit of bother south of the river. You heard anything from Simon?" Dave's had enough of Town's lectures and changes the subject.

"What, old Selhurst Simon? Fuck me, he's bin of the missing list for a while".

"He's just got out after a four and a half stretch. Got his jam roll an that, but he's keeping 'is head well down".

"Wasn't that the Deptford job?"

"Yeah. One of your own, Simon. Seen his fuckin' interviews? Proper. Don't say nothing to the cunts for ten hours. He just sits there staring at a dot on the fuckin' wall. Don't even give 'em the dignity of a fuckin' *'no comment'*! I'd have him on the fuckin' team tomorrow, if he weren't from down south."

"Fuck's sake, Dave, your turning into a right fuckin' nause. This ain't the fuckin' seventies. People do talk to each other now. Blimey, mate, if you had your way, we'd be back to going over the bridge and having it with them, just because of which fuckin' side they live. Play right into the hands of the filth".

"Just sayin', that's all".

"Who's this Simon, then", asks Town Hall, all intrigued. "'Another one of your old Hammers mates?"

"He'd fuckin' kill you if he heard that. South London Hammers fan? Ain't gonna happen, not in our world. He's fuckin' Palace. Here, Dave, remember the fuckin' play off final in o-four? We're all down there in Cardiff, fuckin' name's on the cup, all we gotta do is turn up, an' that cunt Shipperley fuckin' pops up and puts it in. Their end's gone fuckin' mental and we're all at a fuckin' funeral. I tell you, the walk out of that place was a fuckin' tragedy. Shakespeare couldn't have wrote it better. Everyone's calling for fuckin' Pardew's head. He's ex-Palace an' all! Look at us now. Last season, fuckin' two minutes from winning the Cup, till fuckin' Gerard hits the fuckin' goal of the season, tenth in the Premiership. This year's gonna be even better, now we've bought the Argies". Dean's on a roll now, shouting from the cockpit as he puts it on automatic pilot. He walks in and sits down, couldn't give a shit where they're going. Just knows they're going to get there.

"Anyway, we're out of the ground, walkin' back through Cardiff, keepin' an eye out for the Taff cunts, to the cars, feelin' like we've lost a pound, an there's this voice, 'Oi, Deano, you cunt!'. It's only fuckin' Selhurst! He's there, about nine-handed, outside a boozer. All Palace. Get your arse over here.' There's one of those moments, you know, when it's like everyone's lookin' for a lead. Some of 'em's thinkin', 'are we having it with these Palace', others are just trying to get home and I'm thinking 'Fuck me. It's Selhurst Simon'. Very emotional moment, Dave, weren't it?"

"Poignant, bruv, poignant".

"So, after that, we wanders over and he's all emotional, proper greeting and everything. Introduces us to his firm an then the beers come. Fuckin' surreal. Actually drinking with the enemy. We was having to pinch ourselves. The fuckin' Palace an' us, gettin fuckin' wankered together. Fuckin' bizarre". Dean's all emotional now, he's got that far away look in his eyes, like he's having some kind of out of body experience.

"You talk fuckin' highly of this Simon. Can we bring him in? Sounds like we could give him something to do?" Town's getting really interested now and his eagerness is infectious.

"Dave, have a word with Big John down the fruit market. He always knows Simon's fuckin' habits. If he's only just come out, he's going to be plotted up somewhere quiet. He's over a four, so he ain't on a tag. Be great to see the cunt".

They're way out in the estuary now, heading towards Southend-on-Sea, lights on. There's a little rendezvous with a boat from Holland. Dave and Town settle back for the rest of the ride and Dean's back in the cockpit, the music's blaring, bit of R&B. He's chopping up a couple of lines for himself and the boys with one hand, the other's on the wheel. The boat is ploughing through the choppy sea, rain's started lashing the windscreen and Dean is just loving it. His boat is the one thing he does where he gets out of himself, kind of communes with nature in a Perkins Diesel sort of way. He's finished the coke chopping exercise now and calls the boys over. They line up for their lines. (Sounds like school. No relevance there, then). Town's in first, then Dave brings up the rear, bit slower but very methodical. Dean's flying now. He opens up the Perkins to full power and they're hitting thirty knots.

"Get out the back, Town and have a look at the fuckin' stern wave. Fuckin' symbolic".

"You sure? I ain't gonna fall out, am I?"

"You fuckin' wuss. Get out there, you cunt. Get some fresh air in them lungs!"

Town opens the double-glazed sliding door and goes out. As the door closes, the word 'Cunt' is heard from the cockpit. Dean's grinning face is reflected in the windscreen as he takes the throttles up to maximum speed. Dave looks out the back.

"Good work, bruv, but the cunt's still with us!"

"What sorter person do you think I am?" He's pissing himself now as a drenched Town Hall staggers back through.

"Close the fuckin' door, bruv. A bloke could freeze his bollocks off!"

"Fuck me! It's like the bleedin' Antarctic out there."

"That's why we're in here, you mug!"

In the distance, the Southend lighthouse comes into view, then through the spray, the dark pier just becomes visible, its mile of lights still a faraway glimmer. Dean eases off the power, taking her down to around twenty knots and they head towards the Southend Sailing Club.

"How do we know he's there, Town?"

"He'll be there. Most reliable man I've ever met. Ask him

something and if you ask him again, he gets the right hump, cos he's already done it".

"What's he in?"

"He comes over in one of them old Lugger things. Like Maldon. Uses the engine to get here and then sails for the last bit. They love him in the Club here. Think he's some kind of eccentric! You'll see his old fuckin' rust heap when we gets in".

"They're all fuckin' weird, the Dutch. Me an' the Jag met a right cunt the other day with poor old Piet. He's got him workin' the fags game over there. Right moody cunt an' all. Gotta bad feelin' about him. I can spot back-dooring a fuckin' mile away and that cunt's got it in indelible fuckin' ink right across his boat".

"Piet lost his marbles? It's not like him to hire a wrong 'un".

"The geezer ain't too well, Dave, do you know what I'm sayin'? He's still on the Bacardi Cokes but he can't eat fuckin' solids no more. He's tried, but you know he's chuckin' it all up in the fuckin' karsi later. Only thing the cunt can eat is that fuckin' broth he gets in his bar in Antwerp. Do you know what Antwerp means, Town?" Dean's off on one.

"No, Dean".

"Means 'hand-throw'. Like, you know, throwin' your hand in. Must've been a poker playin' leper colony. Geddit, Town? Aaaarrrggghhhh!" Dean's got the laughing gas again and he's off. Off his head, more like.

"You really are a mine of useless fuckin' information, Dean!"

"Just tryin' to educate you cunts. Get you up to speed!"

The boat is crawling along now, just past the harbour wall and in, the low bass throb of the Perkins barely audible above the November rain pounding Southend. Dean guns it slightly, just to announce their arrival.

"Can you see it?" Town's voice has an urgency to it, like he's a bit nervous.

"See it. I can't even see the fuckin' end of the fuckin' boat!"

The lights are on full beam and he can just about make out an empty berth which he slowly aims for. The engines are engaged in reverse and slowly but surely, he inches in towards the jetty. Despite everything.

Gradually, it comes to a complete stop and Dave's already out, chucking the for'ard ropes to a lad who's wandered over, dressed from head to foot in yellow all-weather gear.

"We are going to get fuckin' soaking, bruv!"

"Not with this lot we ain't" Dean points to a box in the corner.

"Have a butchers in there. You know Fat Cheryl, down the market? She got a load of this gear off some geezer in the docks at Tilbury. Proper it is an' all. I didn't wanna look a fuckin' gift horse in the mouth now, did I? Ali mentioned it the other day. Never one to miss a bargain is Ali".

"All day long, bruv". Dave's back in now after tying up the boat, soaked to the skin, whilst Dean and Town are getting into the waterproofs.

"Oh, that is nice! Wait till I fuckin' get outside, then put all that fuckin' gear on. Why didn't you tell me, you cunt?"

"You never asked" Dean replied, doubled up with laughter at Dave's appearance.

"Quick, go and get changed. We've gotta fuckin' appointment!"

Wet Dave shuffles off to sort himself out and Dean prepares to lock up the boat. Town's buggering about with his bag.

"He'll be here by now. Probably in the bar, on the JayDee. This'll be a long night. We'll do the business an' go into town".

"I ain't havin' the fuckin' gear on the boat all bleedin' night. No fuckin' way".

"Chill, bruv, the Dutchman ain't like that. It'll be on a rope underneath the stern, knowin' him".

"S'alright then. Dave, you comin' or what?"

"Give us a bleedin' chance, bruv. Ain't got me kecks on yet".

"Hurry up. We're missin' fuckin' drinking time".

Dave appears, still doing up his Calvin Klein belt, his new Gucci deck shoes shining in the cabin light.

"Fuck me, bit bright, ain't they? Wear 'em in a bit next time, for God's sake!"

"Give us a chance, bruv!"

"Come on. This rain ain't stoppin'. We might as well go now".

Dean opens the doors again and they force their way out through the gale and onto the stern deck. The rain is coming down sideways, the wind is lashing the whole marina and a boat has already broken its moorings, bobbing about like a cork in the middle, with two geezers in a small motor boat trying to get on board.

"Fuckin' mission!" Dave's laughing now, happy someone else is getting wet.

Dean locks up the doors and they're away, up the ramp and onto the jetty. He goes off to the office and checks in with the harbourmaster's clerk, shows him his papers and that's that. The walk up to the sailing club is thankfully short and soon they're in the warmth of the bar, the aroma of smoke and beer thick around them. The bar's quite full, despite the weather and it's a couple of minutes before they spot the Dutchman and his boys, in the far corner.

"Frank, good to see you". Dean and the Dutchman embrace, he gives him a kiss on both cheeks, then it's Town's turn for the same and then it's introduction time.

"Dave, this is Frank, an old friend".

"Not so old, yes?" He's got a kind of smile playing around, but his eyes are as cold as the grave.

"Dean, Stephen? These are Rudi and Yakob". Quick handshakes then it's time for drinks. Dean's on the vodka and tonics, Dave's on the brandy and coke and Town's on the old Bombay Sapphire.

The Dutchmen order Hendricks and tonic. You can tell he gets a lot of Dutch by the amount of it behind the bar.

"Good trip?" Town's straight into the small talk and you can tell that the Dutch are used to this. They chat about this and that, and Frank seems mainly interested in his house at Knokke and the local vandals. He's moaning about *this* and *that* and then it's down to business.

"Everything for you is under control, yes, Stephen?" Now you don't know if this is a question, if *he's* got it under control, whether *Town's* supposed to have it under control, or what. Is it the gear, the scratch or what?

"There's a geezer nearby with what you need. You got what I need?"

Now we all understand. Stephen. No-one *ever* calls him that no more. Almost wonder who they're on about, till you realise it's good old Town. And he soon will be old Town an' all. Been in this game a long time, never mind his little spell in Winson Green. From Soho down to Brighton……

"Is your man in a hurry, Stephen? I don't think we are going back to Holland tonight, not in this weather".

"You was never going back tonight, you dodgy cunt! You're here for a bit of r n'r and you always were. Bit of jiggy jiggy? Well it just so happens that Uncle Stephen's already got it well under control. You like Russian, Frank?"

"In our game, my friend, everyone likes Russian! Natashas, Ludmillas, Natalias, Olgas, they're all the same after a while".

"Not what I've got for you lot. This is a bit of *real* Moscow muff! I hope you got plenty of product with you, cos' I got eight of 'em comin!"

Dean's face lights up at the thought of the charlie and he's downing the vodkas like nobody's business. Dave's talking to one of the Dutch geezers and the evening's off and running.

"Stephen, I know we talk about this, but your orders, they are getting bigger and bigger. Soon you will be my biggest client. Are you growing more noses here?"

"Nice one. No bruv, we're just movin' inter new markets, shall we say. We've had a bit of a change in direction, so to speak, ain't we Dean?" Before he can answer, Frank is in again, "So you and Mr Dean are formal partners now? This is good for business, I think".

"We've a little understanding now, eh Dean?"

"Basically, Frank, we've been the other game for a long time. It ain't what it used to be, what with the church beaking in all the fuckin' time. Time was when a bloke could have a good earner on the swerve, but it ain't like that no more. Too much fuckin' checkin' up".

"We know this too. In Holland now, the FIOD are very busy. The cigarettes game is a joke now. But I think things are still the same with the prison sentences, no?"

"That's put a right fuckin' downer on the proceedings. Last thing we wanna talk about".

"Holland is a much more civilised country. Not for us, these long times in the jail, eh? Forgive me, I am being too serious. We can supply you with good quantities, either in this way or another way if you want. We have a small shipping company which can bring larger amounts to England, carefully hidden. We just need to have the address of your slaughter and then we can making the preparations. Of course, the price, it would be different".

"Different price? Different fuckin' price? What the fuck's that all about?"

"Well, we bring the merchandise all the way to you this time, Mr B. You tell us where you are wanting it, we supplying, yes? A kind of complete delivery service".

"What we talkin' about, Frank?"

"Like me, Dean, I am sure you would not like to talk about such matters here. Perhaps your boat is safer?"

"Blindin'. Town, what time are the brasses plotting up?"

"They're on standby, bruv. One little call and they are here!"

"What's the time now?"

"It's a little after nine, my friend".

"Get 'em down for about elevenish. We'll have a few sherbets an' then a bit of business on the boat before they get here. Got any good clubs where you are, Frank?"

"In Rotterdam and Antwerp mostly, the clubs are very good, but in Antwerp now, things are not so good. One of the best ones was closed for problems with the girls; too many illegals and one was closed for too many drugs. In Holland it is different. The clubs are a little more free but the problem is more with the Aids. Some of the girls, they come from Africa and the Dutch West Indies and they do not have the same kind of clean health than we".

"Fuckin' spooks. You ain't gettin' me near no fuckin' egg an' spoons". Dave's face confirms that there is no way that's going to happen.

"You know what they say, Dave. Once you've had black....."

"Not for me, bruv. Give me a nice little Thai bird any day".

"Yeah? Trouble is, vey might be able to shoot fuckin' ping pong balls out of their fannies, but come the end of the fuckin' night, an' you find she's fucked off and you get more than you bargained for in the downstairs department with the fuckin' replacement! Fuckin' lady-boys. What the fuck's that all about?"

"They are coming also from Brazil, I think?" Frank seems to be a bit of an authority on this.

"Did you see that lot on the telly the other night, Dean? Fuckin' plastic surgery an' all. I couldn't fuckin' adam n' eve it. Fuckin' geezers avin' their fuckin' cocks turned inter fannies, fuckin' tit jobs..."

"Tell you what, though, bruv, that Debra, you know, Gina's sister, fuckin' blindin' job she had done in Cyprus. Best fuckin' three grand she's spent in fuckin' ages! What size are those charlies?"

"Dunno, mate but they're fuckin' big. About the same size as Jordan's?"

"Reckon you're right there, bruv. You ever fucked a bird with tits like that?"

The tit conversation has them all sucked in and lapping. More drinks come and go. It's one of those conversations where no-one who could remotely be identified as a wife/girlfriend/partner is being talked about, so everyone feels safe to come out with whatever bollocks they see fit and everyone else just goes with the flow. Bit tit stories turn into strange fannies, strange places and within no time, the boys are all asking about the brasses.

"Time to go, I think?" asks Frank. It's that time of the night and if they don't go now, the few brain cells that are still functioning won't be too chuffed in the morning when they realise they've totally forgotten about the real fucking point of the trip. Business. Big fuck off importation of Class A drugs. Proper.

Dean leads the way, followed by Frank, Town then the two Dutch boys with Dave the Rave bringing up the rear. He's thanking his lucky stars no-one mentioned Gina-G, but then she *is* Dean's trouble and as such is off limits to all who want to keep their noses intact. Just the thought of her and he's got the raging horn. Some girl's gonna get it tonight. Town's busy sending Natasha a text.

The rain's stopped now, but the wind has got worse and they're almost blown off the jetty walking along back to the boat. Despite its size, it's bobbing up and down.

"Wait till the fuckin' brasses get' ere, then you'll see it move!"

Dave nearly falls in and it's only the speed of Rudi that stops him ending up in the drink. They get onto the deck and Dean opens the door, switches on the cabin lights and they're in. Across the marina, in the immigration office, two hooded fleeces are making notes and taking photos with a long lens camera. Dean's curtain closing exercise puts a stop to that, but they already have enough. One of them begins to dial on a mobile, the other completes his notes.

"Dean, bruv, they'll be 'ere in about twenty minutes. There's only seven of them. Should be enough, eh boys?" Town's coming into his own now and retrieves a large bag of the Colombian marching powder from his holdall and starts serving up on the dining table. Soon, there's a dozen lines all neatly sorted. Frank's in first, then they all take their turns and the party begins. The Stellas are in full flow, the champagne's coming out now, the Jack Daniels and the Zubrowka vodka bring up the rear. Dean's on the case with the music and the room's filled with Ibiza sounds from the summer, courtesy of his iPod. Banging tunes? I should co-co.

Town's mobile's going off. The girls are at the marina and want to know where the boat is. The boys are getting excited, the coca is making them fly. Next minute, there's a tap on the door and Dean opens it to reveal seven tall Russian girls, very windswept and very pretty. The sight of the champagne and the charlie works wonders and in they come. Natasha's the first one. She stalks in on her five inch heeled patent leather thigh boots and whisks off her coat to reveal….nothing at all. She's got a gold chain around her waist and apart from the black stiletto boots, that's it!

"Good evening, boys. Let me introduce my ladies to you". The boys are whooping and cheering as the girls parade up and down in front of them. One by one, they take off their coats. They are all dressed, save Natasha, but some of them are in lingerie and one of them is wearing a black PVC minidress, her huge boobs spilling over the top.

"Fuck me, look at them puppies!" The comments are coming thick and fast. Dave's up already and dancing around the room with Natasha, his hands are round her waist and she's running a finger over his mouth, dipping it in the coke and putting it into her own. She is not a girl for wasting time. Her ultra-slim body fits snugly into the soft leather boots and the waist chain shines bright against the darkened cabin. The hooter's getting served up all over the gaff and the music's going up and up.

"I think we have a long night, my friends". Frank's already down to his shirt and cacks and one of the girls is stroking his chest with her talons, flicking her tongue in and out at him and rubbing his cock. One by one, the girls start pairing off with the now ecstatic firm, except for two of them who look alarmingly like twins. They get down on the carpet and proceed to go down on each other. This stops the boys in their tracks and soon they are standing in a circle, cheering the pair of them on. One of the other girls acts as director and keeps pulling back the flowing golden mane so that the boys get a really good eyeful of waxed pussy. They are going at each other like wild animals and you can tell it's not going to be long before the tell-tale screaming starts.

"Where the 'ell did you get these lot from, Town?" Dave's got his arm round Natasha, idly stroking her erect nipple as they watch the little act.

"Blinding ain't they. It's like one thing led to another really. Met your one and turns out she's got lots of mates. Bob's your uncle, you might say, old chap!"

"Who's their fuckin' uncle? Bet if they 'ad one, he'd be fuckin' shocked at this little scenario! Bet they don't teach this at the fuckin' Bolshoi!"

The girls are really going for it now. The one underneath is arching her back and she's got the other one's finger up her arse. It's wiggling about and suddenly, she cums all over the place, screaming like a banshee, in Russian! I ask you.

She collapses back onto the carpet and she won't be doing anything to anyone for a while. The one on top turns over and lies there, her legs wide open.

"Would somebody like to finish me, please?" There's a rugby scrum, followed by a load of cheers, as one of the young Dutch boys is quicker than the rest and gets straight on with a bit of tongue action on the wanton girl. Looks like he's done it before. Soon, she's pushing against him with all her might and then she cums. Bit quieter this time, but lots of pushing and heaving tits. Someone's already giving the other one a good seeing to. The sight of wet open girl is too much for any red blooded male and after all, there is national pride at stake here. Dave's left Natasha to Town who is giving her tits the licking of their life. He's down on the twin and straight into her, without delay. The Laurent Perrier Rosé champagne is flowing in rivers, as is the girl on the floor. The old Dutchman's got hold of two of them, he's doing one from behind and stuffing his podgy fingers into the other.

Suddenly, up stands a very willowy girl with very good implants. She is in the middle of the room, wearing just a pair of black patent pole-dancing stilettos. Her hands are on her hips and she looks like she means business.

"Boys, boys! If you want, we can have a little competition? My name is Anastasia. There are six of you and seven of us. We bet you that if you do each of us in turn, none of you will get to last girl before coming. I will be referee and prize is......well the prize is that winner gets to take me up the arse".

"Michael fuckin' Winner?" grins Dean, his cock buried in one of mother Russia's finest.

The whole room has gone silent, they've never been spoken to like this by a brass before, but she's so stunning, they're like lambs. The girls lie down all over the cabin.

"The rules are five minutes with each girl, then you must change. It is a game very popular with Russian teenagers. We have to find something to keep us warm in the winter, no? So, boys, choose a girl to start with and off you go!"

The girls know exactly what they are doing and after a couple of turns, the younger Dutch lads are out, totally mugged over by a combination of skilful use of muscles and the old finger up the arse trick which works pretty much every time. The two empty girls are fingering themselves and being cheered on by Anastasia, who stands there like a modern day Boadicaea. Just give her a whip and she'd be cracking that! Now a side-competition has developed and the girls are wanking furiously to see who can come first. The two lads have a bet on as to which one it's going to be. Just before anything happens, it's time to change and now two other girls are empty. It's Natasha and Orla from the other night and they take over the gusset typing competition with gusto. Town looks up from his work and sees Natasha with her head back, her long slim fingers frantically working away at her clit and that's it. He shoots his load right into a little curvy piece with blond permed hair and huge nipples. Three down, leaving the old Dutchman, Dean and Dave. Dean goes next via the old finger trick and a lot of lip licking and eye contact with the fiery little slapper he's up. It's a straight fight now between Holland and Essex and as they go on to the next girl, it looks like it's neck and neck. Dave's got his eyes shut and unbeknown to everyone else there, is trying not to think about Gina-G. Images of her lying on the back seat of his four by four, one leg stretched over the front seat, the other pressed tight against the back as he pumps her full is too much though, he just can't get her out of his mind and that's it. Game over. Holland 1 England 0, Ronald Koeman, late free kick. Or was it cock? There's loads of cheering and abuse, the boys are getting ready for seconds and the girls are serving up more charlie and champagne.

"Anastasia, I take my prize at end, okay? For now, we play!"

"Who wants to play another game? Yes?"

She's greeted by noisy shouting and cheering, the girls are really in the spirit of it and they're winding up the boys like nobody's business.

"OK. I think we play another, yes?"

It's off again and the boat's rocking with the movement of thirteen coked up bodies heaving around. The music's up high, the girls are high up. Dean's snorting like it's going out of fashion at midnight. He's on top of the world, the last sensible bit of him looks around the room at his boys, just before the lid blows off and he's back on one of the girls, not caring who it is.

"We have some blindfolds for you here. You will all lie on your backs on the floor. We will tie them on and then each of us will place our pussies over your face and you must guess which of us it is. When we have done that, we will each ride you and you must again guess which girl is fucking you. The winner will have a *special fuck* from all six of us! You like?"

The scene descends into chaos, cheering, clapping, whooping. The whole shebang. They're so into the whole game thing now that they're almost fighting to get the blindfolds on. The girls are trotting round in their stilettos, arses wiggling, laughing, giggling.

Outside, the rain is still lashing the boats. The immigration office is in darkness, having been locked up for the night. With the exception of the boat party, there is not a soul about. Frank's lugger is thrown from side to side by the strong, white waves. A shadowy figure moves around on the deck, searching, prying into the tarpaulin covered boxes. He has already been below deck. His infra-red glasses show up an eerie night, compounded by the driving rain. The brightness of his colleague's eyes shine brilliantly against the murky backdrop of the marina. He in turn, keeps watch on the *Benissa Costa* using a pair of night-glasses, before returning to check out his searching fellow officer. The hunt becomes more frantic, the longer his quest goes on. Eventually, he leaves the lugger and returns to the shore.

"Without disturbing anything more, there is nothing I can do. I am certain that there is nothing on that boat. Absolutely certain".

"We had better go then. We are already running a great risk of discovery and that is not the purpose of this exercise. I think we will call it a day". They put away the infra-red gear and walk quickly to the opposite end of the marina, into a waiting car and away into the foul Essex night.

Back on the boat, the whole thing has turned into a right old carry-on.

If you walked in on it, the first thing that would hit you is the *smell*! Seven girls, horny as hell. Hot and sweaty. There's harry monk all over the fuckin' place, spilt champagne, the Dutch boys are doing twos up on Orla, one up and one in her mouth. She's on all fours and they're kneeling opposite each other as she sucks hard, champagne in one hand, joint in the other. Frank's lying across the couch, lighting up the biggest J you've seen this side of Trenchtown. He's got Anastasia on one side, half asleep, her legs wide open and the curvy blond on the other. She's playing with herself, just can't get enough. A girl called Raisa lies flat on the floor, Town Hall's serving up fresh lines on her flat-board belly. Dean's lining up for some more of the Colombian and the sight of the uninhibited Russian is giving him the horn again. There's a kind of lull in the proceedings. Dave's trying to drag one of the girls off to the bedroom which she eventually agrees to and that's them for the night. The Dutch lads have finished doing Orla now and have collapsed on the floor, totally shagged out. Two of the girls are in each other's arms, kissing. Very nice. Very *tasteful*.

*

Morning brings harsh reality to the carnage. The place looks like the battle of the Somme. Sleepy girls lie amongst cast-aside empty champagne bottles. Unused lines lie still on the table. All too much. Frank's the first awake at around six. It's still dark outside as he pulls on his clothes and makes his way across the walkways to the lugger. The lowered anchor rope is still in place, just where he left it last night. Excellent! He climbs onto the deck, undoes the rip's mooring rope and climbs in. The anchor rope is now tied to the back of the rip and he slowly paddles his way across the now flat calm waters of the marina and to the back of the *Benissa Costa*. There is not a soul about as he works quickly on the knotted ropes, untying and tying again, speedily, swiftly, like his life depended on it. Once completed, he slips the blade of his single oar into the lapping water and eases his way back to the sailing lugger, ties up and walks back to the *Benissa Costa* pausing only to roll a cigarette. Dawn breaks just as he steps onto her rear deck. The sound of stirring comes from the cabin. Twelve hung-over, coked out and proper fucked bodies begin to wake, to focus, to wish they were somewhere else.

"Rudi, make some coffee for these poor people. Especially the uncivilised English, yes?" He laughs like a drain at the poleaxed state that the waking Dave finds himself in. Town looks the best of them, closely followed by Dean who is already making eye contact with Frank. The mere flicker of recognition on his face reassures Dean that the work is done. Mr Bold gestures towards the for'ard cabin and the Dutchman nods.

"Come on ladies! Time you wasn't 'ere. We'll let you know when you're wanted again. It's been a pleasure. Ain't it, gentlemen? A right fuckin' pleasure".

Slowly, the girls make their way out, Natasha giving Town a chaste peck on the cheek before grabbing his cock and squeezing it. She laughs, slips her heels on and stalks out of the rear cabin doors, up the walkway and off, into the misty Essex morning. Dean returns from the cabin with a holdall which he leaves at the feet of the big Dutchman.

"Give it some thought, what I said, yeah? We're goin' large now. I'm talkin' London, Birmingham, Manchester. Our contacts are ready and waiting".

"Then we give you price later today".

"An' I don' want no fuckin' shit neither, Frank. None of that five times cut bollocks. We want proper full on Mother of Pearl".

"For that, Mr B, the price is the highest. You know this".

"Frank, just give me the fuckin' scenario. Tell me. This afters, yeah".

"You will have everything you are needing to know this afternoon, Dean. You having my word on this".

"Okay. Scenario One. Usual deliveries here and Tilbury. Scenario Two. London Postal area, we supply the address. Same for Birmingham and Manchester. Ten kees, fifty kees, hundred kees, two hundred kees. Weekly. When we got viss on fuckin' track, we can start lookin' at bigger volumes".

"This is a big departure for you, Dean. We are looking at the finances too, I think. Five million pounds for one shipment is much money".

"You can do it, bruv. I got every faith in you. Come on Frankie, you're a fuckin' geezer. You ain' worryin' about a few quid. I'm gonna make you a fuckin' lotta dough 'ere. What we done in the past? Fuckin' chicken feed. Drop in the fuckin' ocean".

"Then we wait till later. I contact you this afternoon".

Dean reaches into the holdall at the Dutchman's feet and lifts out two mobile phones.

"New basher for you, new basher for me. Just for this, yeah? Just the one number in each one. Choose your weapon, cloggie!"

He leans across, takes one of the Nokias and trousers it.

"In the bottom of the bag, you got a little packet with some more bashers. Each one's numbered, one through five. Each time you bell me, throw the used one away. Just once, yeah. I've got the corresponding ones with me. No other calls, no cross contamination. When you finish with each one, it's chip out, battery out. Smash it up, get rid in separate places. No fuck-ups, Frank. No mistakes".

The Dutchman is staring down at the holdall. Slowly, he looks up and stares Dean right in the eye.

"I am impressed, Mr Dean. Very, very impressed. It seems that you have thought of everything this time".

"I fuckin' hope so, mate. Listen, bruv, we better be goin'. You an' all. Laters, bruv".

He gets up and the pair of them embrace and kiss on each cheek. Town then does the same, followed by Dave. The two Dutch lads shake hands sheepishly and make their way back to the lugger, followed by the loping gait of Frank.

As Dean starts up the engine, he does not see the rising sun glint on a camera lens across the marina from them. A newly arrived camera lens, behind which is a thick-set, leather jacketed man, clicking away for all his life's worth. Beside him is a small walkie-talkie and a long, black flight case. His camera clicks away, recording the departure meticulously. Soon, the *Benissa Costa* is away and onto the open sea, Canvey bound.

Chapter Nineteen

Custom House, Lower Thames Street, London EC4

"Get me a meeting with the Departmental Head of Investigations in Alicante port. Don't care how you do it. This has just got one hell of a lot bigger".

"Why can't we just go it alone? We've got the clearance to be on Spanish soil for as long as we want, subject to all the renewals".

"Graham, I know you want to do this the old fashioned way, but those days are gone. We absolutely have to do it this way".

"How do we know we can trust the Spanish? I mean, they haven't exactly been co-operative in the past. It took years to bring the bloody Frogs round, how long are that lot going to take?"

"I thought it was going to be easier than this with you. You're like something out of the ark!" She smiles wickedly at him, pressing buttons she knows will get a reaction.

"And you are like a kind of brand new squeaky clean idealistic danger woman. What the hell do you think you're really going to achieve? Some sort of new brooms, all singing, all dancing service? Life doesn't change overnight. The bloody law doesn't change overnight".

"Look, Graham, I brought you into this, kept you in this, because you are a bloody good operator. You know the way these people work. You had a good team with you. All you lacked was the funding. Now we have that funding, we have the resources to run cross-border co-operative observations".

"For God's sake, you even come across like a bloody sound byte. Wake up and smell the coffee, Janet. Be *realistic*".

"I *am* the realistic one. You are living in the past. I am convinced that part of you wants to come with me on this, but you're holding on to what didn't work before. It didn't then and it won't now. Please, Graham, give this a chance. It's going ahead with or without you. Let it be with you".

"You give me no choice, but I am warning you now. The moment you bring foreign services in to work with us, you dramatically increase the chance of compromise. The chance that we will be discovered and our targets tipped off. Just think, all this work will be for nothing. They will just go to bloody ground".

"You talk as if you *believe* this will fail. Is there something you're not telling me?"

"You know that could not be true. No-one is more committed to catching these people than me".

"Join with me, Graham. Work with me and we will get some results. Don't just be a part of this in name alone. I am totally committed to this course. If it fucking well kills me, we will throw some heads in".

"Of course I will stay with you. I don't want you to go in with your eyes closed. Be careful. Don't lose sight of the fact that this is *our* operation. It's not some kind of bloody pan-European bun-fight which will increase the PM's kudos with his cronies in Brussels and the G8. It started with my operation last year and should end with yours. Don't let them hi-jack it".

"We have to move on from this now. I take your points Graham but you and I should not be arguing. We have a wealth of information and obs to go through as it is. Shall we?" She stands firm in the middle of her office. Not a woman to be trifled with. Stubbins' resigned expression told her everything she needed to know. She had won.

"I do need your opinions on the way the teams are working. How are the team leaders coping? Do you think we've got the right ones in the job? Because if we haven't, then I can have them moved inside twenty four hours. This is vital for me, Graham. I am not playing games".

"Torrevieja seems to be doing very well now. I sense that we are about to move the investigation much further on. I am convinced that O'Riordan is our man. We're just not getting at the tentacles at the moment. That could change at any moment".

"And what about the new Zulus? How much information do we have, over and above the photos? I take it we were never close enough for DNA profiling?"

"O'Riordan's place is like Fort Knox. We just can't seem to get in there. He won't employ anyone without serious credential checking first and the way he does it, our people wouldn't stand a chance. Most likely end up as fish food in the bay. He just puts in a call to the Old Country and that's that. You know what happened in South Armagh the last time we tried anything".

The South Armagh fiasco, it became known as. Not a good choice of word, but it was used to hide the real significance. Two officers, good ones at that, sent in to assess a fuel tax loss and check on cross-border activity. Too little and far too soon. The pair of them wound up in the Liffey of all places. The south takes its detritus to the north and just for once, the opposite occurred here. Heads and torsos in separate bags. Both had been tortured. Slowly. Methodically. *Expertly*.

"How the hell are we going to get them in, Graham? You're the ops and obs man".

"There just isn't an easy answer. The guns and bombs may have long gone, but they have been replaced with a far more fascinating carrot. They may hate Her Majesty, but you show one of the bog-trotters her head on a note and they can't get enough".

"Graham, for God's sake! Not even in fun, do you use that kind of terminology. You'll get me shot, if anyone hears you expressing those kind of views. The service is multi-racial and multi-cultural. You're like some kind of dinosaur, re-invented and wound up ready to go".

"Sorry, ma'am. I am afraid I'm one of the old school".

"Well start acting like an old school obs man then. Come on Graham, there has to be a way to prise open that secrecy surrounding O'Riordan".

"We could try posing as customers, see if we can flush him out that way. Trouble is, we just don't know whether he actually *is* doing anything. Worst case scenario here is that we go to all these lengths to unravel the world that is O'Riordan and find there is nothing underneath".

"There has to be. *There must be*".

"You don't think that you are making this too personal, ma'am? I mean, it wouldn't be the first time that private feelings have got in the way of an investigation".

"I *never* make things personal, Graham. This is all about cracking one of the biggest thorns in the side of the service. More than that. O'Riordan and his kind are like a cancer eating into the very structure of this country. His time has come and I *am* going to be the one to do it".

"Is there any way he could play the dual nationality card with us?"

"I don't really think that's on. The CAB in Dublin would love to nail him, so I don't think his friends in the south are going to be of much use".

"What about the Creaven case? NCIS thought they had him with Operation Fulcrum and look what happened there. Even the Irish finance ministry were laughing in our faces. People have long memories".

"We have learnt from that. Things have changed forever".

"Oh come on, ma'am. This is me you're talking to, not the press or some bloody nosy judge. Damn all's changed, just the names".

"You old cynic, Graham!" She looks out from over her severe glasses, a wicked grin playing around her mouth.

"You really should keep these thoughts to yourself, though. People might start believing you, and then where would we be?" Her tone takes a sharp reversal.

"I will *not* have this investigation, this *project* ruined! I kept you in this because you know the field. You have a great reputation as a closer. Don't make me feel undermined. I can have you off this before you've left the office. Don't fuck with me!" Her eyes were on fire, her face flushed and burning with anger. He had never seen this side of her before. Her reputation had become legendary since the Metro Bond debacle and for the first time, he felt the full force of her venom.

"You know I wouldn't do that, ma'am".

"I don't know anything any more. You are in serious danger of destabilising my future".

"*Your* future, or the future of this department?"

"What's the difference?"

"Oh, I think there's a hell of a lot of difference, *Janet*! I think you see this as your short cut to the top and bugger everyone else who gets in the way!"

"How *dare* you say that to me! Who the hell do you think you are, little man? You come in here with your *bloody* attitude. I make one simple request of you and get it all thrown back in my face. *One bloody request*, Graham. You are torpedoing me at every turn. I sometimes wonder whose side you're on. You are on our side still, I presume?"

"Oh, I get it. Let's marginalise Graham time. How many people know you've had this planned? In fact, you've been planning this for ages haven't you? Drag the old ops man in, flatter him, then just when he thinks he's safe, cut the old bastard adrift. Good God, woman, if this was Japan, you'd have me watching bloody windows! I'm not some old horse you can just put out to grass you know".

"*I* can have you put out whenever I want, Graham. You have no idea how high the authority goes for this operation. Not a fucking clue, have you? No, because *you* aren't privileged, that's why. I *am* this bloody operation whether you or anyone else likes it".

"You are one conceited bitch! You really think you're bigger than all this don't you? This service, as well you know, has been in existence for five hundred years and one self-important bloody rug muncher like you isn't going to make one joy of difference in the long run. You…"

"You bastard! How *dare* you bring my sexuality into this, as if it's some kind of fault. I do *not* bring my personal life into this office and you have no right, no right at all to even comment on it. I could report you for that. Your precious bloody union wouldn't even support you. Get out, out of my office now, while I decide what I am going to do with you!"

"With pleasure, *ma'am*."

Stubbins turns on his heels and is out of the door before she can think of something else to say to him. The walk down the corridor is a long one and it seems like a lifetime before he is into the lift and down to the ground floor. He walks out, practically throwing his pass at the security officers on the desk. Outside is bright sunshine and he walks over to the railings, between two obs Renaults. He stands stock still for a moment, surveying a sight so familiar to him. A sight he has witnessed for some twenty-five years, which suddenly seems so black and white, despite the beautiful glistening Thames flowing stately by.

"Fuck it", he says out loud and walks along the embankment wall, past the security hut and up Sugar Quay towards Lower Thames Street. He crosses the road and walks straight into the East India Arms by the Fenchurch Street railway arches.

"Pint of Green King IPA, please. And a whisky chaser". One of the old school, Graham.

*

"Find me the name of Departmental Head, Alicante Aduana. Call me back as soon as you have it. Call the Embassy in Madrid if you need some support". Weatherall drummed her fingers loudly on the mahogany desk, seething with anger. She stood up and walked to the window, looking down into the car park and across to the embankment gardens. Where Graham Stubbins had stood alone, cut adrift, a sad figure at the end of his career, there was just emptiness. And that was how it would stay. She would see to that.

*

He sat down at the one vacant table adjacent to the bar, staring into space. The IPA tasted great, just slipping down, helping to rid him of the Weatherall. The chaser had already gone in, long since working its magic on his mood. Getting up and ordering the same again, knowing that soon he's not going to give a fuck about her, the service, Operation Watchtower II or any other bloody matter.

*

"Ma'am? I have the details you requested. Operational Head of Investigations in Alicante port is one Pilar Estravados-Lopez. Her number is 0034 96 500 0100. Would you like her email address as well?"

"Send it to me, please. And thank you"

Weatherall sat and stared at the number she had just written down. This is seriously going out on a limb, she thought, then dismissed the notion for ever. May you live in exciting times, Janet. She dialled the number. No secretaries this time. *Direct action.*

*

As one pint followed another, Stubbins realised the irony of the situation. His bravado and rebellious nature had finally got the better of him. There was no room for two mavericks in the operation and he had just come a poor second. What now, he pondered? Muswell Hill suddenly appeared rather attractive. So be it, he decided. Another pint was called for, then it was going to be straight home and into a long bath. Who knows, I might even slip below the water forever. To sleep, perchance………….

*

"*Buenas Dias*. May I speak to Señora Estravados-Lopez, please? Thank you".

Mindless holding music droned in her ear as the receptionist attempted to locate Mrs Estravados, giving her that last opportunity to hang up and return to sanity. It was not to be.

"Señora Estravados? Good afternoon. My name is Janet Weatherall from Her Majesty's Revenue and Customs in London. My credentials can be established via the British Embassy in Madrid or via the Consulate in Benidorm. Please forgive my direct and somewhat unexpected approach, but I am making a trip to the Costa Blanca this week and would very much welcome the opportunity to make a courtesy call to you, really just to say hello and to introduce myself. Yes, it is rather short notice, but I hope that as one department head to another, we could be of mutual assistance? Good! Yes, I would welcome a tour of your operations and a chance to have some lunch with you. How kind! I will be in touch with my hotel co-ordinates shortly. Could you give me your secretary's details perhaps? Thank you so much. Yes, my email address is janet.weatherall@hmrc.gsi.gov.uk Oh, I would appreciate it if you would keep this visit confidential, in view of the fact that I am not on official business? Thank you. You are most kind. Good bye".

She sat back in her chair. A woman! Intriguing.

*

Stubbins' trip home on the Tube was seemingly as normal as ever. He walked up the broken escalator at Highgate Northern Line and up the hill, right into Muswell Hill Road and stood at the bus stop. Three stops and a child who threw up on the bus later and he was walking down the hill towards his flat in Linden Road. His sad bachelor existence lay silent and cold as he walked up the two flights of stairs.

"Good evening, Mr Stubbins. You're home early. Anything wrong?"

The old girl downstairs squinted up at him. He closed the door, sparing her his gloom. Inside the flat, the morning's post lay on the mat; bills, bills and junk mail. He trod them hard into the carpet and went straight into the kitchenette. Straight to the fridge, in fact and to the bottles of Bishop's Finger which were reserved for home time after a difficult day. He opened four and carried them into the little sitting room which overlooked Wood Green and beyond. His window on the world. The room had a kind of musty smell and he opened the sash to let in some fresh air, leaning out to take in some fresh breaths. But all he got was a mouthful of lawnmower fuel. The bloody fellow next door was only giving it a service. In November, for God's sake.

"Don't you ever do the right thing, like go down the pub, you arsehole!" he yelled, awaiting a response which would never come. The chap is wearing his iPod and can't hear a thing above Dire Straits. *Dire Straits*. If only Stubbins knew what he was listening to. The quiet suburban atmosphere of Cranley Gardens forced him back inside, back onto the moth-eaten sofa his wife had left him when she finally rebelled against his moods and sloped off one day when he was at work. He hadn't even revealed that at the office. Not that it would have mattered. He never got invited to anything where her presence would have been required anyway, these days. He flicked the TV on, to reveal Noel Edmonds' smiling face as yet another red box was opened. The remote flicked across the channels; Paul O'Grady (twice), Cash in the Attic (second time today) and Ben Fogle doing underwater basket weaving for beginners, whilst rowing the Atlantic cuddling a lion. For heaven's sake. Hobson's Choice.

He ambled aimlessly into the bathroom and turned on the taps. Slowly the hot became scolding and the bath began to fill. He just stood and stared as the water swirled and splashed up the side of the bath. Washed up.

He removed his shirt first, then his trousers and underwear. Walking back into the living room, he picked up two more bottles of Bishop's Finger from the fridge and switched on the aging CD player. The sound of Free's 'Wishing Well' filled the whole flat, resulting in immediate banging on the ceiling from old Mrs Wisbey downstairs. This time, as opposed to all others, he just ignored her and returned to the now almost full bath. He climbed in, sliding beneath the comforting heat of the water. The beer slipped down his throat, warming him from within. Once the water had reached his chin, he turned off the taps and just lay there, still, his eyes closed, reflecting on this crossroads.

As his skin temperature becomes as one with the steaming bath, he drifts off into a kind of stupor. Pints and whiskies, whiskies and pints take their cotton-wool control of his self-preservation and the beer bottle falls from his hand onto the bathroom floor, its contents flowing freely out all over the threadbare mat. Slowly, his head drops below the water level, the tiny bubbles rising slowly to the surface. Suddenly, he is fighting for breath, his arms flail wildly against the sides of the bath as his lungs struggle to expel the water from his throat. He manages to sit up, coughing, spluttering. His face is bright red from the trauma and he is gasping for air. His lungs feel tight, he cannot breathe. His hands are now flat against his chest, trying desperately to relieve the pain. There is no respite, save the drumming of his feet against the end of the bath. He can feel the life ebbing slowly away as the pain in his chest intensifies. He can hear the knocking at the door, getting louder, yet as he tries to answer, the words just won't come out. Instead, there is just a rasping, hollow croak, as once more, he sinks back into the warm glove of the bathwater. The heat helps to relieve the pain and he surrenders to its cocoon.

Outside, the neighbour bangs and thumps at the door. She is joined by one of the students from the ground floor and he stands back before booting the door in. The stench of the spilt and stale beer hits him as he stumbles in. As he rushes around the flat, the old girl walks into the bathroom and lets out a blood-curdling scream. He runs from the kitchen, his huge frame knocking ornaments flying around the sad little flat before getting into the bathroom and the sorry sight that greets him. Stubbins is lying half in, half out of the bath, his eyes have rolled and he's not moving.

"Quick, call the ambulance, do it!" He picks him up and tries to lift him out of the bath and onto the floor, which he eventually manages after a hell of a struggle. He turns him on one side, trying to get the water out of him, then onto his back. Starts giving him the kiss of life, then the chest pumps, alternating between the two. The old girl returns from phoning, stands over him, just staring, incredulous. As his strength begins to diminish, the result begins to become apparent, just as the ambulance siren becomes audible.

He collapses, exhausted against the bathroom wall, his energy gone. Stubbins' hasn't moved.

The ambulance men are soon at the door, soon in the bathroom. They take over and send the two neighbours out. The work continues unabated. They too become more and more frantic, until it becomes obvious that there is no hope.

Chapter Twenty

Ceuta, North Africa December 2006

Marianna strode into the offices of El Mundo in Ceuta town, armed with news of an article in a radical Algerian broadsheet.

"I want to see Señor Jauregui. I have news for him about our problem. Tell him that Señorita da Sancha is here to see him. *Roberto* Jauregui, you silly girl". She barked the orders at a bored looking receptionist and sat at a low table, her slim legs coiled around each other in a very 'I am in control here' way. The girl eventually ceased her perusal of *Ola* magazine and put a call through to the editor. Seconds later, a stressed looking man hurried from his office and entered the foyer.

"Marianna, this is an unexpected pleasure. Ceuta's first lady of leisure twice in a week is more than a man can cope with. I trust you are well?"

Marianna remains seated, her legs providing more than enough eye candy for the sweaty editor.

"Roberto! Aaah. Lovely Roberto. I too am delighted to see you. Shall we go into your office? I have some news for you".

As he looks down at her beautiful form, she uncoils herself from the sofa and extends her perfectly manicured hand in his direction. He takes it and leads the way towards what passes for the editorial suite.

"This really is a pleasure to see you in our humble office, Señorita da Sancha. If only we could see you more often".

"Oh, cut the crap, Roberto. I don't have time for coffee talk. I am here on business. Shall we say, a coup for your little paper, Ceuta edition of course. Tell me what you think of this". She hands him a rather crumpled copy of an Algerian newssheet, torn but with the headline intact.

"I…I'm afraid I can't read Arabic".

"*Dios mio*. Can't you do anything? Give it to me". She grabs the paper from him, knowing already that his comprehension of the language was very weak.

"Ceuta to close border. Official Report. It goes on to say that there have been attacks on Algerian nationals in the enclave, that the Governor is planning compulsory repatriation and that the production from the fruit packing factory is to transfer to the mainland. Altogether a complete undermining of the Governor's authority. THIS is what incited your riot, Roberto". She threw the newssheet back onto his desk and stood facing him, elegant hands placed provocatively on sculpted hips, nostrils flared.

"But our news is that it was something that had been planned carefully and tactically. Something with possible Al Qaeda connections".

"Al Qaeda? Don't make me laugh, *pequeño*. What on earth would Bin Laden want with our little godforsaken corner of the earth? This is not even a titbit on the banquet of Al Qaeda. Not even a bloody cashew nut, *idiot*! I suggest you get your presses rolling and get on with it".

"But what about Mejjeti? It was proved that his cell which planted the bombs in Madrid was based here".

"Exactly, my Roberto! Was! Al Qaeda cleared out of here long ago. Ran for the hills".

"I will have to have the story checked, Señorita da Sancha. According to our sources..."

"WHAT sources? What *fucking* sources do you have that a worth one leedle Euro cent? *Dios mio*, I have found out more in three days than you will uncover in a lifetime. You are here to write the news. Now WRITE IT!"

A terrified look comes over the editor's face. He is shaking with fear, whilst Marianna stands cool and resolute.

"And when you *have* written it, we will have another of these....little chats. Good bye, *Señor* Jauregui". She turns on her five inch Manolo Blahnik heels and stalks out of the room, papers flying everywhere. As she leaves the tiny office and the door slams behind her, she breaks into laughter. A Mercedes waits at the corner of the crowded back street, the V8 purring. The chauffeur is out and opening the door as she approaches. As she climbs in, the flouncy silk skirt rides up, revealing just a glimpse of exquisite leg, covered in lace-topped cream stocking. Then the door is closed and she is gone.

Jauregui calls his sub-editor and chief reporter in, hands him the Arabic newspaper and tells him to get the story out as soon as possible.

"Make sure you play down the Al Qaeda connection. It is obvious to anyone other than a fool that there is NO truth in it. This is a non-story. There never was an organised incursion".

"But the reports we had. The arrested rioters. The police report itself. All pointing to there being a connection".

"Rubbish. All of it. Obviously, there are certain individuals in the ethnic population who like to propagate this kind of bullshit. I will not tolerate this kind of thing in my newspaper. I want this…this… rag copied and used for the lead story. I want it denounced. It is very bad for business here to have this kind of thing going around. The Governor has been talking about closing the port and the border. This place will die without that, and your job with it. Now GET ON WITH TOMORROW'S HEADLINES!"

Jauregui stormed back into his office and closed the door, striding straight to the drinks cabinet, extracting a bottle of Carlos Primera and taking a large gulp. He sat down in the tatty leather armchair opposite the desk and closed his eyes. Visions of border crossings followed container ships, Osama Bin Laden being sworn in as Governor of Ceuta and murdered policemen filled his head, swirling round and round, until gradually it cleared, leaving just Marianna's face, shouting at him, arousing him. Slowly, he drifted off into a peaceful idyll, then *just blackness*.

*

The Mercedes drove out of town and into a small suburb with palm tree lined boulevards, bougainvillea covered walls and electric gated haciendas. Deserted roads reflected the heightened fears of residents, private security guards patrolled from red and white striped sentry boxes. The da Sancha villa came into view and the car swept into its driveway, the gates closing behind. The Mexican colonial style house dated from the 1800s when Spain's world presence was high, its spheres of influence spread far and wide. Now it was a stylishly anachronistic pile, reminiscent of its owner's family history in Latin America. The chauffeur pulled straight into a covered area, which led around the side of the house to a walled garden, ponds and a further Japanese formal garden. Marianna climbed out of the Mercedes and across the terraces to her favourite spot, where she could survey her entire estate, leading down to the sea. Mature palms swayed in the autumnal breeze. She lay down on a deep padded sun lounger, arranging her legs as if for a once oh-so-familiar photo shoot. She rang a little brass bell which sat on the stink-wood table beside her. After a short period, a uniformed flunky appeared.

"Get me some coffee and a telephone. And prepare lunch for two pm. I have a guest coming". She waved him away. Shortly afterwards, both appeared, in the form of a satellite phone and a pot of freshly brewed Colombian dark roast.

Her slim, taloned fingernails tapped out the number on the sat-phone and after a short while, she heard a ringing tone in the earpiece.

"*Si.*"

"*Buenas Dias. Losiento para la hora, pero tengo noticias de patria.*

"*No pasar nada. Estoy siempre despierte temprano*".

"*Penso es mechor desde dos, tres dias.*"

"*Penses? PENSES? No es suficiente. Quando tienes hechos, despues voy a escuchar a algo. Hasta!*"

Click.

Facts. I will give him facts, alright, she thought as she sipped the thick, black Colombian. Picking up her mobile, she looked across the bay at Ceuta town, her mind racing. Her talons pressed the tiny keys. A rich burst of South Armagh answered.

"Good morning, *amigo*. We have *some* improvements here, but I need news of the *direct proposals*. I do not wish to put pressure on, but we are in a strong position now. Our kudos has, shall we say, gone up with my rich-roasted friends over there".

"Good, good. We need your option open and running again as soon as possible. There is an animal on the loose and very soon, it's going to need a cage, *so it is*".

"If this place is still quarantined, can we be certain of finding a home with you?"

"Certain is a strong word. There is a meeting today. A *strategy* meeting. Diversion is the key word".

"Mmmm! I like the sound of that. Keep me informed, *cariño*! Ciao". *Click.*

Marianna clapped her hands together, wiggled her bottom on the lounger and smiled. Progress at last! She picked up another mobile and dialled again.

"*¡Buenas! ¿Algo nuevo para mi, cariño? Dos horas? ¡Vale!*"

Two little hours until Pilar's Customs strategy meeting would come to an end and she would finally have her update. The consequences were just too exciting. She could feel herself becoming aroused, her heart was pounding, her palms becoming damp. Once more, she rang the little brass bell.

"Some champagne, I think, Raul. Bring me the Charles Heidsieck Rosé. And two glasses please".

Her number one mobile rang.

"*Si? Buenas Dias, Señor Gobernador. ¿Cuando esta aqui? Ahora? ¡Fantastico!*"

She replaced the mobile in its cradle on the side and checked her makeup, applying some fresh Dior rouge-noire lipstick, matching her long nails perfectly. Her butler appeared with the champagne, setting down a silver ice-bucket together with two super-slim elegant plain crystal flutes. Silver bowls of nuts and nibbles accompanied the salmon pink champagne. Slowly, he uncorked the nectar and poured a few drops into her glass, waiting whilst she tasted it.

"*Perfecto!* Pour it, please Raul. I am in need of refreshment, *really in need*! My guest will be arriving by car in just a moment. Please let him in".

Once the excellent Raul had disappeared, she lay back on the lounger and awaited the arrival of her lunch guest. A few minutes later, the sound of a horn announced this, followed by the sound of the gates sliding back.

She peered over Chanel sunglasses at her guest. He was clad in a blue linen jacket and cream chinos, an open necked Armani shirt and Gucci Loafers, a gold Rolex Oyster day-date dangled on his left wrist. A pair of Wayfarers peered out of his top pocket.

"*Cariño!* How delightful. So much better than meeting in town, don't you think? At least the food will be edible. And of course the surroundings are more...suitable". She giggled, observing his reaction with curiosity.

"Marianna. So beautiful. As always. *Señorita*, you take my breath away!"

"Champagne, I think".

Raul appears as if on cue and pours a second glass for Marianna, a first for The Governor of Ceuta, Señor Alberto Fernandez-Hierro.

"So, Berti, tell me what is new in your world. My life is so boring stuck here in this palace. A girl needs some excitement now and again, or she will simply fade away".

"I think you are playing with me, Marianna. You are so naughty. You should be in politics".

"Oh, I couldn't do what you do, Berti. It just simply wouldn't do". She waved the butler away to prepare the starters and returned to staring into The Governor's eyes.

"In another world, Berti, we could have been anything, you and I. Who knows, perhaps we could even have been king and queen. How exciting! Here's to marriage and more!" She raises her glass to his and they chink, chink. She returns the glass to her lips and just for a split second, shows him her tongue, licking mousse from the rim. He swallows deeply and takes a large gulp.

"So tell me, where are you today? Or should I say, where are you supposed to be today? Surely not here." The wickedness of her smile says it all.

"Er, I was at a meeting this morning which has gone on through lunch. I have a few hours to spare. Mmm".

"How thoughtful of you, Berti. Always thinking of me. I *am* flattered. So, what's the latest with the little riot which enriched our outpost so much? Are we to close our borders and isolate ourselves from the rest of the world? I do so hope not. Life would become simply intolerable".

"Since the discovery of the Arabic newssheet, I am expecting El Mundo to do its best to play down the Al Qaeda connection. God knows where they got that from in the first place".

Marianna's enigmatic smile said it all, though it went unnoticed.

"I have to say, since that happened, we have done a re-appraisal and are having a review conference call with Madrid tomorrow. Can you believe that? They're not even sending a representative to the fucking meeting? If I didn't know my place before, I certainly know it now". His face is contorted with anger.

"Berti, Berti, there's no need to be like that. You know they think very highly of you. This is a difficult job for anyone. We are the only bloody Spanish enclave in Africa after all. Well, apart from Melilla, that is. And Parsley Island". She giggles once more and his face relaxes. "It is a good thing that no-one comes from Madrid. I do not like it when they send people here".

"To Ceuta and all who sail in her!" They drink more. The afternoon sun crosses the beach and casts long, beautiful shadows across the garden. The starters arrive, tiny tapas selections produced by Marianna's chef, followed by lobster flown in from the mainland that morning, with crab, crispy salad and a *piccante* rice dish, topped with chef's own recipe dressing.

"Do have some bread, darling. I have it baked here, you know. Can't bear the local product. No taste!"

"You have, as always, *princesa*, perfect taste! I am at your feet in admiration".

"Berti! That's the second time you have mentioned my feet this week. You naughty, wicked boy". She slips off her Manolo slingbacks to reveal perfectly manicured and painted toes, just visible under the glossy cream Dior stockings.

"Is that better?" she purrs, wiggling her toes in his direction. His discomfort all too apparent, to both of them.

"Erm, I....I...don't know what to say. It just sort of....slipped out". He is covered in confusion.

"Well, perhaps we should eat some of this wonderful food which Raul has brought. We don't want to upset chef, now do we? There's a good boy!"

She uncoils herself from the lounger and proffers her hand to Alberto, which he readily accepts. They walk over to the table, set ready for lunch. A bottle of Le Montrachet 2000 lies in the frosted ice bucket, which he takes out to pour.

"Oh, you taste it, *cariño*. You must do *some* work for your lunch, after all!"

As she sits down, he can see her perfect legs through the glass topped table, her foot just centimetres from his leg, playing, teasing. He makes a shaky attempt to taste the mature chardonnay then pours some into her glass, ready for her approval. Its viscosity slides around the shining crystal, enticing, teasing. She ignores it.

"Tell me, Berti, what will be the future of our little paradise now that this awful business has occurred? I mean, what should a girl living in a place like this do? Is it safe?"

"It is firmly our belief that what occurred last week was a one-off incident. An embarrassment, admittedly, but no more than that".

"But what of the poor policeman and his colleague? What will become of *that* news? I mean, the widow, the children?"

"We are going to mount the correct response. There has already been a collection for the family, the police federation are going to honour him and within a couple of weeks, everything will return to normal".

"Can we be sure that there will be no more of this sort of thing? It is terrible for business, Berti. Such acts cannot go unpunished, surely?"

"We do, of course, have some people lying in the jail at the moment. We do not yet have the murderers, but we do have some of the rioters. Ceuta is a small place, as you know. If they are still here, then we will find them, hunt them down like dogs".

"I feel that a gesture is needed, *cariño*. A swift and public trial which shows these people for what they really are. We cannot have our precious little home ruined by a lunatic fringe from the Arab world. It would not be right and would send out totally the wrong message to that world. We are not soft and we must be seen to be harsh and swift. Harsh and swift, Berti. The people will want blood".

Marianna's eyes are aflame, her voice raised, her face flushed. She is sexually aroused by the thought of blood and wants him to know. She sips the Burgundian nectar this time, briefly allowing her tongue to once again touch the edge of the glass, visibly play around the rim as she peers seductively out from over her Chanel sunglasses.

"We must still adhere to the process of law, *princesa*".

"Fuck the law", she whispered, almost spitting venom through her clenched teeth. She could sense her pray was about to become her victim. She was tearing at the lobster now, ripping it from the shell, dressing dribbling down her chin. Her tongue was circling her lips, licking the oily residue and all the time maintaining eye contact with him.

"This……is business. We cannot allow the law to get in the way, now can we?"

She has deliberately allowed her skirt to ride up, revealing deep lace stocking tops and cream, satin suspenders. Alberto's eyes are out on stalks, he is so aroused now. Her voice is saying one thing, her whole body another. She slowly uncrosses her legs, just for one second exposing her waxed vagina to him.

"More wine, please, Berti. I am insatiable today". His hands are shaking now, he is totally out of control and can barely remove the bottle from its cradle. As he leans over to pour out the golden nectar, she tears a large piece of succulent flesh and puts it to his lips, her fingers stroking his face.

He whispers to her, "*Princesa* this is insanity. What will happen if we are discovered?"

"Oh, Berti, my dear Berti, always worrying, always thinking such *sensible* thoughts. Banish them, Governor Hierro, show me some of that *iron strength* of your name. Pleeeeeese?" She looks up at him, cat-like and fecund. Her legs are slightly apart now, a drop of dressing lies on her lips, she is a wild animal, desperately in need. He is beyond caring now, she pulls him towards her and their lips meet, harsh and strong. Her tongue flicks in and out of his mouth, teasing him to distraction. He takes her shoulders in his strong hands and lifts her towards him. They are standing close together, their kisses hot and raw. He presses himself to her, making her feel his hard erection against her soft body. Their hands ravage each other, groping, grasping at clothing, at flesh. He takes a hand full of hair and pulls her head back, forcing his tongue deep into her open mouth. She is fumbling with his flies, desperate to release him. Her fingers expertly undo his belt and then her slender fingers are upon him, stroking, teasing his engorged manhood. His hand is under her skirt, up and over her rounded bottom, kneading the flesh. Hard, harder until his fingers force red wheals in her, digging in. He holds her close, their dance one of caged animals suddenly freed, a celebration of what is to come. She puts her arms around his neck and wraps her legs around his waist, squeezing hard against him. He walks them over to the sun-lounger and lays her down. Her skirt is around her waist, her legs are wide apart, a foot on either side of the bed, inviting him in. He lowers himself down on her, his finger running down over her clit, across the puffy, swollen pink labia and into her gaping hole, drawing out dollops of juice, which he licks hungrily before returning his finger once more.

"Fuck me now. I want it harder than you have *ever* fucked a woman". She scoops a hand under each thigh, opening herself to the maximum. He removes his trousers and lowers himself down onto her, *into her*, forcing himself right up to the hilt. She squeals with pain and delight, wrapping her legs around his back and drumming her heels against his exposed bottom. His fucking is hard and rhythmical, the noise of her juices loud against his pumping thighs.

From within the house, Raul watches with increased interest, as his mistress' legs play their dance across the Governor's back. He smiles and looks away, checking the settings on his digital camera, before pressing the trigger to rapid frame. The bougainvillea makes such a nice frame for the photographs, he feels. Once the memory stick has its one hundred and forty frames, he walks away from the balcony, continuing with his chores.

"Harder, HARDER, damn you! Fucking split me, you bastard!" Alberto's athleticism cannot be faulted. He is going at Marianna like a steamhammer, his cock pulling out all the way before once again plunging all the way into her gaping cunt. The air is thick with musky aromas, as she places her hands on her belly, pressing hard down on herself, feeling his hairy torso crash down on her with each penetrating thrust. She can feel her orgasm coming, feel herself tightening. Her voice is low now, her body is starting to shake and shiver. All of a sudden, he feels her muscles tighten and he can no longer go in. She lets out a blood curdling scream and a huge jet of liquid squirts out from between her legs.

"Fuck...fuck...oh FUCK..fuck...FUCK!" She is spraying all over the lounger, all over Alberto. He kneels between her legs, totally absorbed by what he sees. Every shake of her body yields another huge powerful squirt, until he is soaked to the skin, his shirt streaked with her pungent juices. She pulls him to her as the orgasm ebbs, he is again accorded entry and plunges himself back in to her soaking hole. Deep fucking starts once more and she can feel he is close, so aroused by what he has just seen. He pushes harder and harder, further intensified by her long talons gouging his back. Her tongue licks at his neck and shoulders, bringing him ever closer to climax. He looks down at her beautiful face and she reads him totally, her tongue flicking in and out like a predatory serpent. He clasps her to him and feels the first cum hits her cervix. Thick, hot cum spurts out, jet after jet. She closes her mouth over his exposed shoulder and bites him as hard as she can, her teeth effortlessly breaking the skin and drawing sweet blood. Her tongue continues to lick him as the teeth go in further and further, her mouth wide open. She can feel the blood pass down her throat and she clasps her legs tight around his back. As his climax begins to slow, she closes her mouth and looks up at him, a tiny trickle of blood oozes from the corner of her mouth. Her eyes are on fire, yet she is sated, for now. He lies heavy on her, his large frame dwarfing her slim, elegant body. She snuggles into him, protected by his presence, her long legs wrapped tightly around his back.

After a short while, he opens his eyes to see her watching him.

"Mmmm! Well, Governor, you DO surprise me. There aren't many men who can make me squirt on the first visit. We must do this again!" She pushes him away and lifts herself off the lounger, removing her skirt and blouse as she goes, revealing exquisite satin La Perla suspenders and brassiére.

"Come on, it's time for a little swim. Clothes off, there's a good boy!"

She skips down to the oval pool and dives in.

"If you're quick, I'll let you remove all this", she shouts, giggling like a schoolgirl on her first date.

He is down by the side of the pool in seconds, fighting to remove all his clothes. Soon he is totally naked and in with her, his blood forming little streaks across the glistening surface of the water. She puts her arms around his neck and whispers, "You poor angel! You're bleeding. What a naughty girl must have done that. Why, not a girl, an *animal*! Shame on her, the cheap whore!" She giggles again, turning tail and swimming across the pool to the other side. He follows obediently, sensing and liking her little game. She is out of the pool in a second, slipping off her soaked lingerie and stockings.

"Too slow!" As he swims towards her, she extends her feet towards him.

"Lick them. You've been wanting to do that for ages, you naughty boy. Lick me". She splays them and he obligingly slips his tongue between her still hot toes, arousing himself immediately. She looks down into the water to watch his growing erection.

"More work for you, *boy*!" She lays back on the warm grass and opens her legs wide.

"Now you've got your tongue working, you can go down there!" she points her long fingernail right at the swollen button of her clitoris. He obligingly goes straight to it, extending his tongue fully before applying it to her pink clit, pressing hard in a circular motion, bringing moans of delight from Marianna.

From an upstairs balcony in the hacienda, Raul's cameras are working hard again, video and still, at the perfect angle to record the proceedings. Her arms are back over her head, her legs stretched wide open, her skilfully augmented silicone breasts lie perfectly upwards, the almost black tanned nipples fully extended. Alberto's head is rocking up and down with each pressured lick of Marianna, his skilful tongue working its magic, leading her up the hill once more to a different kind of completion.

"Mmmm," she purrs, "mmm, that is sooooo good. Berti?"

"Uhuh?"

"Have you ever performed *feuille de rose*?"

"What is that, *princesa*?"

"Well, if you move your tongue down a little, like that....mmmm, very nice, but that's not really where I meant. A little....*further*. And a little more. Mmmm, that's it! Now put your tongue up inside, like a good boy. Is that nice? Do I taste nice there? Mmmm. I thought so!"

"Oh, *princesa*, that is wonderful!"

"Well, now that you have discovered it, I don't think we need any more talking!" She pushes his head down and once again gasps at this *petit invasion* of her anus. Her bottom begins to writhe around and her moans intensify the deeper Alberto's tongue penetrates. When she can stand it no more, she grabs a handful of his hair and pulls him back to her clit.

"Mmmm, oh, baby that is just what I want! Make me cum".

The Governor of Ceuta obliges and his tongue is focused on her for the final climb to the top, teasing, pressing, *forcing* her to orgasm. He feels her thighs begin to tighten and as she gets closer, he slips a finger into her anus, locates the prostate and presses hard to help her reach her goal. She moans louder and louder, until once more she is thrown over the edge into oblivion.

Her orgasm is captured in all its glory for the cameras, with some excellent face shots of the Governor from the perfect angle. They both collapse onto the soft grass, into each other's arms. Her hand wanders down between his legs and begins to massage his swollen erection, guiding him between her puffy wet labia. She is flat on her back, the soft grass forming a warm bed against her rounded arse. He begins to pump her, slowly at first then faster and faster, harder and harder, the more she encourages him. Her fingers dig deep into his shoulders, his back, she tears at his hair, pulling him down and in deeper. His eyes are closed in ecstasy, his face just inches from hers. She flicks her tongue out and licks his mouth, making his eyes open. She fixes him with a stare, her eyes narrowed, cat-like. The huntress. He stares back deep into her mind, but discovers nothing. It is as if she is impenetrable, yet her legs are wrapped around his back, her cunt wide open. She leans forward and closes her mouth over his left nipple, tongue flicking and teasing, he can feel the sap rising. She returns to his mouth and can taste his closeness. Her fingers dig deeper into his back and suddenly, he is there, pumping her full. Her feet press hard against the back of his calves, holding him in as the jets of cum splatter against the walls of her cunt. Her vaginal muscles hold him in and she squeezes every last drop from him. His body starts to become heavy and she knows that he is hers now. Her arms wrap around his back and he rests his head on her shoulder. She smiles, a wicked smile up at the camera. Her eyes narrow as she fixes her manservant with a harsh stare. The Governor is lost to all but her now.

Chapter Twenty One

Canvey December 2006

"Babes, listen to me. Just listen. I gotta see ya. This ain't workin'. I have to…"

"Dave, it ain't gonna happen". Gina interrupts him, shouting loudly into her pink Motorola Pebl. "I've told you. It's over between you an' me. I can't cope with him and you. I'm gettin' torn in two and it ain't fair. I've got the bleedin' kids to sort out, e's drivin' me fuckin' mad with his moods and then there's you. Go home to Shirl. She bleedin' worships the ground you walk on. If it's shaggin' you need, there's hundreds of girls on the island would have your pants off in no time, successful fella like you. It's just too close to home. I ain't shittin' on me doorstep no more, Dave".

"But, babes, I luv ya and I know I mean a lot to you. This ain't some bleedin' teenage crush. We've been through a hell of a lot together, you an' me and I ain't givin' it up just 'cos fings is getting a bit warm with 'im".

"What do you mean, we've been through a lot? We ain't been through nothing, Dave. We've had a few shags, nice ones granted, but that's all. You know I can't keep me legs closed for more than five minutes. You'll never be the only one. I need cock and I need it regular. He ain't gonna give me no more, he's in love with is Uncle bleedin' Charles, that's half the problem. If he catches us, it ain't gonna be no kiss an' make up. It'll be the fuckin' high jump and we ain't gonna get over".

"Look, babes, I can't talk to you on the mobile. Just meet me for half-hour. You ain't got nothing to lose. I promise I won't try it on. Just wanna talk".

"Dave, there's no point".

"There's every point. We can't leave it like this".

"Alright, but just a few minutes. I've got to meet the girls in the wine bar. They'll notice if I ain't there".

"Don't worry, babes. I'll have you there in no time".

"Pick me up in twenty minutes. Round the corner from the salon".

Click.

*

Six miles away, a man sits waiting in a blacked out Impreza. His fingers tap out a repetitive rhythm on the steering wheel. A magazine lies on top of a leather coat. The leather coat lies on the front seat. Between the coat and the seat lies an AK-47 assault rifle, its long flight case on the floor. On the dashboard, a basher goes off, a text.

'Vee go. Option B, *ja*'.

*

Dave collects the Porsche from Hutton, paying in cash and giving the girl on reception a nice crisp nifty.

"Get yourself something nice, darlin'". He's away, out the door and onto the forecourt, swinging the fob around his wrist as he climbs into the driver's seat of the silver 911. A turn of the key and the car roars into life. He switches on the six speaker system, bathing in its sensuality. Full-on Sylvester. Mighty Real. The bass is building as he turns onto the A12.

*

A walkie-talkie crackles into life.

"Target moving off from Location Seven. Suspect returning. Over"

"Follow and intercept at Location Nine. Repeat, Location Nine. Out"

*

Dave's flying now. He's putting the 911 through its paces along the A12, overtaking like a maniac. He slips it down into second and blazes away from the roundabout on the A130 and he's up to ninety before anyone else is into third. He's at the thirteen in no time, then it's off down the Canvey road and into the town.

As he slows down for the crossing, the brakes lock a little and he begins to skid, but the Porker's having none of it and he's soon back in control, turning the corner and stopping by the flower shop. He nips in and picks up a large bouquet, bungs the girl with more cash and he's out. Just as he's putting them under the bonnet, Gina comes round the corner and sees him. She's wearing a silk leopard print top and shot silk Nicole Farhi mini-skirt, trade-mark Gina sandals and a face like a robber's dog.

"I ain't stayin'. What you doin' with Dean's motor?"

"Hello to you too, babes. I just picked it up from the garage. Had some kind of problem. It's drivin' proper quick now. Hop in". He holds the door open for her and she slides herself onto the soft cream leather seat. Dave runs around the other side and jumps in, almost crashing against her.

"Dave, I'm tellin' you. Keep away. A quick chat, that's all you said. And that's all you're gettin' and all. Drive".

He drives. Up to the end of the street, then a double back to the dual carriageway and off.

"I'm achin' for yer babes. My cock is just dyin' for yer one more time. Big and hard, fillin' you up. Just once, then I promise I'll leave you alone. Scout's honour".

Gina looks across at his bulging trousers and well, you know Gina. She just sort of melts. Leaves a puddle on the seat kind of melting.

They drive towards the Basildon roundabout, Pitsea flyover. He reaches across and puts his hand on her thighs. She parts them slightly, just enough so that he can massage her clit through the thin material. She always did play hard to get.

*

"Still in pursuit. IC1 female now in car, *ja*? Blonde hair. 30s. She must have got in the car whilst I was pulling into C. Over".

"That will be the wife. Continue pursuit. Original plan now. Do not, repeat do not allow to return to base, unless absolutely unavoidable. Out."

*

Dave pulls into the car park behind the Dog and Fox. They are out of the Porsche and up against the wall. She's fumbling with his flies and he's got his hand inside the Nicole Farhi, working her clit like a brass-rubbing. She gets out his fully erect cock.

"Fuck me, fuck me good and hard". He pulls down her thong and she slips out of it. Hoisting her up, legs around his waist, he plunges deep into her gaping cunt and power fucks till she screams louder and louder. At the end of the lane, people are walking past, yet the entwined couple are beyond caring, totally wrapped up in their final twisting dance. He pushes in up to the hilt, burying himself deep and then she feels his cum flood into her hole, ramming hard, harder, hardest. Eventually, he is spent and he lowers her down, staggers back against the opposite wall, finished. She picks up her thong and silently puts it back on. After a few seconds, he has his breath back and looks hard at her.

"OK? I'll give you a lift back to your mates. Drop you off round the corner, like".

"Yeah, whatever". She's miles away already, totally oblivious to Dave's desperate cow eyes. He's been fun, but there are a lot more cocks to play with in Essex and this one's just lost the plot. I mean, what sort of a man begs a woman not to leave him? *Not the sort I want*, she muses. She looks down at her highly tanned legs. *Lookin' good, babes, lookin' good. Time for a new beau! Still, quite sexy to be driven home in the old man's Porsche with your dumped lover at the wheel. What are you like, girl?* Her fingers wipe jizz from the inside of sweaty thighs. She smears it all over his trousers and smiles sweetly at him. Weak man. They return to the car, he holds the door open for her. *For the last time*. She climbs in and he goes round to the driver's side, jumping into the Recaro like a racing driver at Le Mans. *Click.* It's all bravado. They look just fleetingly at each other as Dave leans forward to turn the key, there's a little connection made, then it's gone. *Click. Click.* Gone forever, just as the volley of bullets smashes through the driver's side window and into them, spraying blood and bone all over the polished cream interior. Then blackness.

*

Across the car park, a tinted window slowly climbs its way up the door frame, the car well on its way out and onto the high street. Inside, the gun is already being dismantled. Seventeen bullets have been fired in rapid mode, the barrel is red-hot. The driver is already on the walkie-talkie.

"Targets down, repeat, targets down. Am returning to base. Out".

The black Subaru makes its way down past the market and out onto the A13 towards Tilbury Docks. By now the gun is totally in pieces and the balaclavas are off. It stays just within the speed limit and arrives in the port within twenty minutes. The driver selects the sign for 'Euro-Container Port', all the time driving unobtrusively. As he follows the arrows to the car park, his passenger is on the WT again.

"The letter has arrived. Repeat the letter has arrived. Please open the envelope. Over".

"Second class post, repeat, second class post. Out".

He looks up at the signs and eases across to the left lane, ready to take the turning for container wharf 2. The rain begins to pour down through the afternoon gloom onto an increasingly rough sea, creating an eerie atmosphere. Ahead, a uniformed man steps out from his guard hut and raises his hand, causing the Subaru to slow to a halt. The window is lowered, rain is now lashing the car.

"Take the third aisle on the right. Blue Maersk Lines container. Drive slowly in, watch your tyres". He is shouting to make himself heard above the storm. The window is raised once more, for the final time. He follows the instructions and moves off. As he turns into the aisle, two figures are barely visible at the end, both wearing yellow waistcoats and sou-westers. One of them beckons him on and he creeps slowly towards the open 20` container. Each is holding a heavy metal door back against the gale, fighting to keep it open. The car inches forward, into the container. The doors slam behind them. Then blackness.

*

"What the fuck was that?" Outside the flower shop across the road from the pub, a large glass vase has just shattered, sending its contents flying across the pavement and over passers-by.

"Roy, there's bleedin' glass everywhere out here. Must 'ave been one of them little bleeders from the estate. I've just about 'ad enough of this". She looks up and around, trying to see where they've gone. The street is quiet, bar the usual few pensioners wandering up and down. After all, it is Thursday.

Suddenly, she screams. And she won't stop. It's a despairing, hopeless scream. She starts to point across the road at the side of the pub. The passenger side window of a silver Porsche Carrera 911 is down. An arm lies limp, dangling down against the door metal. Blood is running slowly down the polished paintwork and drip, drip, dripping onto the tarmac. She's got hold of her husband now, grabbed him by the arm and she's gesticulating across at this gory play unfolding before her eyes.

"What, what the hell am I looking at. All I can see is the bleedin' pub car park. Fuck me that place needs a tidy up".

She's trying to get the words out, but they just won't come. Her pointing becomes more desperate and she starts to cross the road towards the car. All the time, she's holding on to Roy's shirt, tugging, *dragging him* across the road. As they cross, a car swerves to avoid them, a volley of abuse comes from the driver's window. She is totally oblivious. Just as he is about to turn round and give the driver the usual 'wanker' signal, his eyes finally focus on the car. *And the arm*. "Fuckin' 'ell". He starts to run, she's still holding onto him. As they reach the open window, the sight of Dave and Gina makes him throw his guts up all over the ground. Dave is slumped over the steering wheel, the back of his head almost blown off by the two bullets which followed in quick succession, skimming his hair line. There is glass everywhere. Gina's head is tipped back against the head-rest. Her nose is smashed all over her face, her forehead is oozing life.

They stagger round to the other side, to Dave's side, all the time he is wiping vomit from his mouth and the sheer reality of what has happened hits him hard. There are bullet holes in the driver's door, the front wing, even the tyre's gone.

"Call the ambulance. CALL THE FUCKIN' AMBULANCE FOR CHRIST'S SAKE!"

She is just standing there now, in shock. Her body is shaking, yet her eyes are still, transfixed by what she sees. He spins around, looking for help. Others have heard the shouting and come running over. "Go in the pub, get them to call the ambulance, police, everyone".

"Should we get them out, Roy?"

"Don't do nothin', girl. See if the woman's breathin'. I can't move the bloke else his bleedin' brain'll fall out". Miraculously, the back of Dave's skull has shattered all over the front seat, leaving the intact grey brain looking like something from a specimen jar. He lifts up Dave's arm and feels for a pulse. He can't even tell if there is anything there. In the distance, a siren is heard. Someone else saw the whole thing and already called them out.

"Mate, can you hear me? CAN YOU HEAR ME? Just squeeze me hand if you can".

He's holding Dave's right hand now, trying to find any sign of life. She's stroking Gina's left arm, trying to talk to her. Blood bubbles are coming from Gina's shattered nose and mouth. The exit wound in her left cheek is huge, leaving the inside of her mouth looking like a laboratory experiment. A man runs across from the pub.

"They're on the way, apparently they've 'ad loads of calls. People heard the shots".

"Well, they'd better be quick, else it'll be the mortuary. I don't think these 'ave got a fuckin' 'ope in 'ell".

Gina moans quietly, tries to move her head but it just won't happen. She passes out again. The screeching siren announces the arrival of two Essex Ambulance Service vehicles. The rain is starting to come down heavily now, umbrellas have been produced in an attempt to shield Dave and Gina from the driving water. The paramedics jump out and run over to the bullet-ridden Porsche. One look inside and they are on the radio for specialist help. They clear the area and begin to attach breathing equipment to what is left of Gina's face. Blood is all over the inside of the car, impossible to say from where it has come. One cradles Dave's head, placing a pack behind to hold his brain in. The other attaches an oxygen mask to his face and checks his pulse. The stretchers are placed either side of the car and the mammoth task of getting them out begins.

*

Click. The dashboard light is on in the Subaru. The walkie-talkie crackles into life once more.

"You will be on the move shortly. Estimated departure 7.00pm. You are in final ten. Congratulations. Out".

They climb out of the car, squeezing between the door and the damp side of the container. A large box lies in the corner, containing food and provisions. Once this has been opened and examined, they return to the car, recline the seats and await developments. Shortly afterwards, a loud bang emanates from outside the box and the sound of scraping is heard, followed by voices. Then the container lifts up and swings around before coming to rest once more. Both men are totally relaxed. More voices come from outside the container, this time they are foreign, sharp, guttural. A ship's hooter sounds loud and clear. The container muffles outside sounds, yet the silence within seems to augment the clarity of what is going on. Another container is heard being placed next to them, then silence once more.

"*Da gibt's Bewegung. Wir sind auf See*".

"*Genau. Hoffentlich gehen wir bald wieder an Land. Es gefällt mir nicht*".

"*Die Beide. Umgebracht?*"

"*Ich glaube so. Jedenfalls ist es mir völlig egal. Dreckige Fotzen*".

"*Möcht's mal fressen?*"

"*Warum nicht. Ich habe immer riesen Hunger danach*".

They break open the food containers to reveal chilled seafood salads and black bread, rollmop herrings and bottles of Becks. They settle down to a post-murder feast, unaware of developments on land.

*

As the two ambulances arrive at Accident and Emergency in

Basildon & Thurrock Hospital, the paramedics are working frantically on both Gina and Dave. At first sight, Dave has three bullet wounds. The first has hit him in the thigh, having passed clean through the door, shattering the femur and causing extensive bleeding. The second, more serious wound is in his neck, narrowly missing the jugular, but dangerously close to the spinal column. The final and most serious is the one which has taken the back off his skull. As the assassin's bullet left the AK-47 and travelled its short journey across the car park, he was already leaning forward to start the ignition. It came straight through the glass and across the back of his head. Millimetres either way and the outcome would have been so different. To the right and he would have died instantly, to the left and it would have missed him completely, Gina too. For the slight deflection ensured it veered off course just enough to travel across her forehead, out of the open window, across the rest of the car-park, across the road and smashing into a glass vase outside Sheila's Blooms. It is now embedded in the door frame, where Essex Police forensics will find it that night. They will identify it as *unknown*, from an *unknown source*. The gun was last fired in Chechnya during the uprising and was stolen from Russian Army Intelligence in Grozny shortly after it was recovered from an ambush. It was purchased in Antwerp for little more than the price of a fine steak tartare dinner. Which is what Gina's face looks like. Besides the bullet which travelled across her once smooth forehead, she has taken one in the shoulder and one which has entered her right cheek and exited through her left, causing a huge exit wound the size of a golf ball. Her blonde hair is matted with blood and flesh.

The staff remove the two stretchers from each ambulance and they are taken quickly, straight into two neighbouring operating theatres. Two dedicated teams go straight into action, stabilising them and carrying on from where the paramedics had done their best. Dave is on his side, the pressure from his brain too great against the special pack which is holding him together. The tubes are going in now. He has not recovered consciousness. Gina has been coming in and out and is now sedated ready for the operation to remove the bullet lodged in her shoulder. Dave's leg resembles Smithfield Meat Market on a bad day. They are working frantically to stop the arterial bleeding as he has already lost two pints.

*

"Does anyone know who owns the motor? I ain't seen it before. Couldn't tell who they was anyway. Too much blood. Never knew there was so much blood in people".

"Probably asylum seekers. You know what THEY'RE like".

"What? In a bleedin' Porsche? Your havin' a laugh, girl".

A huge crowd has gathered around the bullet-holed car and the police are having a hell of a job keeping them back. The place has already been taped up and forensics are at this minute belting down the A13 from Chelmsford. Special forensics.

*

Knock, knock.

"Yeah, what do you lot want?" Benissa stands squarely at the front door, facing the two Essex police officers standing there.

"Is Mrs Bold here please?"

"No, she'll be down the salon. Or in that wine bar she goes to with her mates. Why? What's the problem?"

"We really need to speak to Mrs Bold".

"Well I'm her bleedin' daughter. Don't I get a say in the matter?"

"I'm so sorry. I'm afraid there's been an accident".

"What kind of accident? Is it me Dad? What's 'appened to him? Oh my good God. What the bleedin' ell's goin' on? Tell me. TELL ME!"

"I am afraid that Mr Bold is in the Basildon and Thurrock. We, we really need to speak to Mrs Bold too. Could you give us the address of the, er, salon? Is that where she is today?"

"She owns it". Benissa is already grabbing her coat and is off out the door, leaving the Police standing on the step. She climbs into her new Z3 and a screech of engine and a volley of gravel later and she's off down the road to the hospital. *Click.* She's dialling her Mum as she goes. The phone begins to ring the other end and she slows down to take the expected response. It rings and rings. She starts to cry and the thick, salty drops flow down her face. She's driving like a nutter, can't see through the mist of tears, yet she presses on towards the main road. Within ten minutes, she's somehow got to the hospital, screeching to a halt right outside and rushing in to A&E.

"Where's me Dad? Where the hell is he?"

"Could you come over here, please Miss? Maybe I can help you?"

She runs over to the desk, close to panic now.

"It's me Dad. There's been some kind of accident? He must be in 'ere somewhere".

"Could I have your name, please?"

"It's Bold. Benissa Bold".

"Ah, yes, we have someone of that name. If you go to the receptionist at the end, down there, she will be able to help you. Just there at the end, under the sign marked *Reception*".

She runs off down the long, white, endless sterile corridor. It's like everything's gone quiet, there's just the sound of her feet on the tiled floor. People are looking at her.

"Bold. Where's Mr Bold?"

"*Mister* Bold? We have a Mrs Bold here".

"What? What's me Mum doin' 'ere? Where's me Dad? Oh my God, what the fuck is goin' on?" She collapses into a chair, her head in her hands, sobbing her little heart out. The receptionist comes out from behind her desk, puts her arm around Benissa's shoulders and holds her tear-stained hand.

"Are you Miss Bold? Your Mum's in the operating theatre at the moment. She's a very brave lady. It will be a while before you can see her, but they're doing their best for her. Don't worry, pet, she's in good hands". Her soft Geordie accent is reassuring, but Benissa's having none of it.

"Theatre. What the hell's happened? How bad is this accident?"

"The CID will be here in a minute, pet. They'll be able to talk to you, tell you what it's all about".

"I don't understand. First it's me Dad, now it's me Mum an' now it's the Bill. Is somebody having a laugh?" She certainly isn't and her face tells it all. Makeup is streaked all down her cheeks and her eyes are red-raw.

"We've managed to get hold of your Dad, Miss Bold. There seems to have been some kind of mistake, pet. He's on his way from the warehouse now".

*

"Sarge. There's someone here who thinks the shots may have come from a car".

"Bring him over".

The Sergeant is waiting for more backup from colleagues and is still concentrating on keeping back the crowd. The rumour mill is working overtime and by now the news is all over the area. It's already on Essex FM and Dream 107.

"This is Mr Braintree. He thinks he may have seen something".

"Roger Braintree. I work in the charity shop over there. I was just looking out at the weather when I saw this bright light, over in the car-park. It flashed, you know, like a torch. Loads of times. It came from a car over there. It was black, looked a bit like a boy-racer car. You know, with one of those spoilers on the back. I thought it was kids messing about. You know, with one of those laser pens. Something like that".

"Did you see the car move away at all?"

"No, I'm afraid I didn't. I had a telephone call you see and I had to answer that. It might have been head office".

Great, thought the Sergeant. Biggest thing we've had in years and this silly old fool has to go and answer the fucking phone.

"Did you see anything else? Anything at all?"

"Only that when all the shouting started outside that the car was gone. See there's two entrances to the pub car park so they could have gone out of either of them. If you see what I mean".

"Thank you, Mr Braintree. You've been most helpful". *Not*. The Sergeant looks up to heaven. Maybe some divine inspiration? I don't think so. This is England on a wet afternoon. Have you lost your mind?

*

"Why don't you try your Dad again, love. Perhaps he'll answer his mobile this time?" Benissa sits in reception, expressionless, swaying slowly from side to side.

"When can I see me Mum? I wanna see me Mum, *please*".

"I'm afraid she won't be out of theatre for a while yet. She's lost a lot of blood and they have to be very careful. The doctor will be out to see you soon. I expect your Dad will be here soon".

"But the Old Bill said it was me dad in 'ere? I'm so confused. Oh my God. What about Troy. Me brother. He don't know. He's at school". Her fingers frantically tap away at the mobile. A ringing tone. A voice. A friendly voice.

"It's...it's Benissa Bold here. Troy's sister. Oh my God, it's awful. There's been an accident. Me Mum's been hurt. She's in the Basildon and Thurrock Hospital. Can he come out of school? I'll get me Auntie Debra to come an' pick him up, if that's alright? Yeah? Thanks, Miss". *Click.*

She's straight on the speed dial to Debra.

"Auntie Debra, it's me. Listen, me Mum's bin hurt. I don't know what's happened but she's in A an' E in the Basildon and Thurrock. What? YOU WHAT? And she was with you lot? Where did she go? What do you mean, *she was actin' strange*? Me mum don't act strange for no-one. Listen, can you pick Troy up from school and get him over 'ere? Yeah. Oh, Debra, what's goin' on? I can't get me 'ead round this. I'm scared. Come quick, please".

*

In theatre. Dave's in one, Gina, of course is in the other. There's about twenty people working like crazy trying to keep the happy couple from meeting the big man. Strange isn't it? A few bullets, only one of which does any real damage to the pair of them. One gun and now all this just to keep them going.

Dave's wired up to the monitors. Amazingly, he's not lost enough blood to be life threatening and they're working on the back of his head. He's face down on the table and you can see his brain clearly through the tennis-ball sized gap in his skull. He'd obligingly shaved his head only this morning, so at least something's gone right today. They've got the bullet out of his thigh and the scan has shown up the one in his neck is lodged dangerously close to his spinal column. It's totally missed the jugular, by some sort of miracle and now they're having to stabilise him. He was knocked clean out by the bullet to the back of the head and has not recovered consciousness. Gina, on the other hand is in serious shock and her body's showing it.

*

At the end of the corridor, Shirley Hilton comes bursting through the double doors, her face tear streaked. She runs into Dean, coming the other way, throwing her arms around him, sobbing her little heart out. He holds her close, closer than he's ever done. They've never really got on that well, bit like a lot of people and God. Until they need Him. They cling together, the tears flow like rain. It seems an age before they can speak.

*

The ship's well out to sea now, the gentle motion of the waves rocking the container from side to side, barely noticeable. Inside, the meal's finished and they are wellying into the Becks. A mobile rings.

"Congrats, boys. A first class job. The Guv'nor's very pleased with you. We may need you again".

"Senk you. Zis voz just introductory price, though. Vee are not doing, buy one, get one free, no?"

"Yeah, alright boys. I hear you!"

"I hope you are happy vith ze service. Do you haff any after-sales feedback?"

"'Fraid not. Nothing I can talk about on here. You will hear soon enough".

"I sink ve vill. Until zen. Good bye". *Click.*

*

Dean sits in reception, Benissa on one side, her arms wrapped tightly around her Dad's waist, Troy on the other, his head in his hands. Shirley is pacing up and down, incredulous.

"What is goin' on, Dean? What kind of people are you involved with?"

"He'd only just picked up the bleedin' motor. *My* motor, for God's sake. Just bringin' it back ter the unit".

"Dad, I'm really scared. I've never felt like this before. Mum's going to be alright, isn't she?" Troy's clipped private school tones seem strangely out of place all of a sudden. Everyone takes the piss normally, but this is neither the time nor the place.

"Yer mother's a strong lady, Troy. If anyone can pull through this, she can". He tightens his grip around the pair of them. Shirley's pacing up and down still and her face is covered with new tears.

"Oh, Dean, what the bleedin' 'ell am I going to do? Dave's all I got. Him and the kids. Bleedin' shot in a car park. What the hell was he doing there anyway?"

"All I know is that he was bringin' the Porsche back, love. Just asked him to pick it up. That's all. What the fuck is goin'on?"

"I dunno, Dean Bold, but I am gonna find out. I am *so* gonna find out. And what the hell was Gina doin' in the car?"

"Perhaps he were givin' her a lift home. How do I know?"

"Mum was at the salon this mornin'. She was meetin' her mates for lunch. Maybe they was planning something nice for you or Dave, Dad? You know Mum's always doin' stupid things for you".

"She's a wonderful woman, your mother. She's gonna pull through this. Don't you worry about that. She's always been strong. Now's the time to prove it. Dave ain't no pushover. He was always the one who'd come and get you out of a row".

Shirley's still pacing up and down. She's there alone, the kids are with her sister and she's focused.

"Was this an accident? I don't bleedin' think so. So, who was they after, Dean. Was it Dave, was it Gina, or was it you? It was your bleedin' motor, when all's said and done. Or I suppose the bullet just happened to find its way into my Dave, is that what you mean?" She's ranting now, doesn't know what she's saying. Yet the truths are coming out thick and fast.

"I just don' know, love. I'm at a right fuckin' loss".

"This isn't just about you an' Dave, you know. *Life*, isn't just about you two an' your football an' your business an' your fuckin' drugs. Yes, Dean, I know everything. I know about you and your fuckin' cocaine. Gina was so worried about you. She don't know what to do, Dean. She says you're not the man you was".

"Steady on, Shirl. We're sittin' 'ere, the people we love are in there, fightin' for their lives, an' we're out here, fuckin' arguin'. It's not what they'd want, is it girl?"

"I'm just so frightened, Dean, I ain't had nothing like this happen before. I know I'm obsessed with the kids and I know people laugh at me behind me back 'cos I'm not a bleedin' size 8, but I love that man. I love 'im so much. I don' wanna lose 'im".

"Come on, babes. You ain't gonna lose Dave. He's too strong for this".

"Too strong for bullets, Dean? Is that what you're sayin'? 'Cos they ain't invented no-one who's that".

"We got to deal with this in our own way. Please, Shirl, your upsettin' the boy". Troy has his head in his hands and is weeping quietly. His sister has her arm around his shoulders. She looks down at him and the realisation hits her like a train crash. She sits down on the other side of Troy and holds his hand.

"It's alright, Troy, love. Your Mum'll pull through. She's a strong lady an' all. Loveliest Mum of all, ain't she?" The boy's head stays buried. His hands grip Benissa and Shirley tight and all of a sudden, Dean is the interloper. He stands and stares. Terrified.

*

"Wie lang dauert es vor der Ankunft?"

"Ungefähr zwo n'zwanzig Stunden. Am besten schlafen wir. Gibt's gar keine zu tun!"

"Du hast rechts, Arschloch!"

"Verpiss dich, Schwein. Bis Morgen".

There is, indeed nothing else to do. The cramped Subaru changes into a hotel this time as they put down the seats and settle for what will be a long night before they reach Hamburg. The temperature begins to drop as the ship heads towards the oilfields of the North Sea. In the distance, intermittent flames shoot high into the night sky, part of some devilish game, in which the assassins are, yet, not party to. Slowly, the ship is steered between the rigs, as the fog banks sweep down, circling and swirling between giant steel platforms.

*

"Any news, love? I ain't copin' well with this".

"We're hoping to have an update for you very soon, Mr Bold. I know it's very hard for you, but the doctors are working very hard. Your wife is in very good hands. Your husband too, Mrs Hilton".

Shirley has somehow acquired an exterior toughness which belies her size and demeanour. She stands, staring at the sister.

"You *must* have some news by now. Anything, just so's we know they're OK. I can take anything just so long as we hear something. This no news is killing me". The pun is thankfully lost on everyone, the nurse included. No-one's laughing there.

Dean has totally gone into himself now. He starts to reflect on the past few weeks. His mind tells him he needs a few lines, but he just can't bring himself to leave the kids. What a fuck up.

The retribution and scapegoating seems to have abated, to be replaced by a hollow hopelessness. They are fearing the worst now, still haven't been able to see either Dave or Gina. There is a hell of a lot of coming and going, even though they are nowhere near the operating theatres where frantic work is taking place. Infrequent nurses rush to and fro, performing seemingly trivial tasks, all of which is contributing to the overall panic in the Bold and Hilton camp. It's famine or feast. Dean goes off to get some coffees, taking Troy with him, leaving the girls to comfort each other. Benissa has taken on a kind of maturity he's never seen before. He is starting to hate himself and the atmosphere is now extremely strained between Shirley and him. He wants to give her the old, 'you loved the money in the good-times' routine, but somehow, this is neither the time nor the place.

Suddenly, the swing doors at the end open and an exhausted doctor comes through, clipboard in hand. He walks towards Benissa and Shirley. As he gets nearer, they both look up. Shirley knows, she *just knows*.

"Mrs Hilton? Miss Bold? Is your father here? We need to speak to him".

"Oh, God, oh my God. Is she alright? Me Mum, is she goin'to be OK?"

"I really do need to speak to Mr Bold".

Just at that moment, Dean and Troy come back through the other doors with the coffee. He sees the doctor, drops the coffee in a state of total fear and runs towards the huddled girls.

"WHAT! WHAT IS IT?" He is screaming across the corridor, trying to get to the doctor.

"Mr Bold. I have just finished operating on your wife, er, your mother, Miss and Master Bold. I am afraid that she's a very poorly lady. However, there *is* some good news. Mr Bold, are you happy for me to talk in front of the children?"

"Yeah, yeah. Just le' us know, Doc. She's gonna be alright, ain't she?"

"Your wife has lost a lot of blood, but we have managed to

stabilise her. The bullet passed across her forehead, before glancing away. It did not, thankfully enter her cranial cavity, er, her head. However, there was a second bullet, which entered through the neck, narrowly missing the jugular. This bullet is now lodged at the top of the spinal column, resting against the C2 vertebra. There was a third bullet which passed through your wife's right cheek and out through the left one. She is a very lucky woman. The low calibre used means that the exit wound is relatively small, compared with what could have happened. She must have had her mouth open when the bullet passed through".

"Thank God! She's always talkin', my Mum". Benissa's remark momentarily lightens the mood. Troy laughs nervously.

"This bullet in her neck. What can you do with that?"

"For the moment, Mrs Bold has suffered far too much trauma for us to operate now. We are going to stabilise her and then transfer to the intensive care ward".

Shirley just sits and weeps, totally silent. No-one is even looking at her, they're just listening to the doctor's soothing words. A small wailing sound emanates from between her silent suffering. Dean spins around and looks at her; utterly destroyed.

"'Ave you gotny news for *her*? She's desperate".

"My, er, colleague will be with Mrs Hilton shortly. They are still with Mr Hilton in theatre. I am afraid that I haven't any other news for you, I am sorry".

Benissa bends down and holds both of Shirley's hands.

"It'll be alright, Aunty Shirl. You see, Uncle Dave'll be OK. He's, well he's Uncle Dave, ain't he? Nothin' bad ever happens to him".

Shirley cannot even get the words out now. She is just moving from side to side, her tears flowing hushed.

"Thanks, Doc. We'll wait, then".

Dean's utterly beaten. Nothing left to say. The news his wife is still alive is wonderful, but the bullet in the neck has put him back further than he ever thought possible. A thousand scenarios are going through his mind now. Coma, paralysis, wheelchair, brain damage, death. Slowly, he starts to whisper words to her. Words of despair, mixed with words of hope and love. He is walking up and down, each of them in their own private world now. He cries to heaven for help, to be met with just the stark, sterile white ceiling of the corridor, NHS standard. Something from within takes him back to the kids and they sit huddled together, bonded in their anguish.

He goes eventually for some more drinks and the four of them sit in silence, sipping the hot, sweet tea and coffee, so needed.

Once more, the doors open. This time, a doctor, still in his green theatre garb, together with a female doctor similarly clad walk towards the group. Shirley looks up and stands, walking towards them before they have even reached the desk.

"What? What is it, doctor? It must be my Dave. Oh, please let it be good news. Please?" She looks at the pair of them as if they were miracle workers, about to announce that some medical phenomenon has occurred and he's ready to go home.

"Mrs Hilton. Perhaps you would like to sit down with us? Over here? Yes, that would be the best place. Firstly, the good news is that your husband has responded during the operation to control his bleeding. He is still in theatre, but will be moved, like Mrs Bold, to the intensive care ward shortly. He received three bullet wounds, one to the thigh, which we believe was slowed down by the fact that it probably travelled through the door panel before entering. The second was lodged in his neck, rather similar to that of Mrs Bold, but not as close to the spinal column as we had at first suspected. I am delighted to say that we have managed to remove this one. What is giving us great cause for concern, is his head, where a third trajectory has actually travelled into the skull and exited, taking a piece of the bone with it. Substantial exit wound. We have sedated Mr Hilton and he will have to remain on his front for some time, until the results of tests come back. I am delighted to say that there does not appear to be any damage shown up by the brain scan. We're talking about a hair's breadth either way here, Mrs Hilton. Your husband, like Mrs Bold, is incredibly lucky. I have seen some gunshot wounds during my career in this hospital, but nothing like these. Quite which kind of gun they were using is not my job to determine, but no doubt the police will identify it sooner or later. On that note, I will bid you good night. It has been a very long day".

"Thank you so much, doctor. I thought he were gone". She leans over and gives him an impromptu hug, before realising that this is not quite the done thing. He doesn't seem to mind. Probably happens all the time.

"When can I see 'im? When can *we* see *them*? I so wanna see 'im".

"I'm afraid that for tonight, it won't be possible, as the intensive care staff like to get the patients to relax and be quiet. Their bodies have suffered some extraordinary traumas today, more than we will ever know. Let them rest. See them tomorrow, yah?"

"Alright, Doc. Thanks again".

As the two doctors recede into the distance, Dean and Shirley turn to each other and hug once more. The kids join them and for a moment, they almost look like they are the family.

After a few moments, they slowly make their way out to the car park.

"Leave your motor here, Shirl. Me and the kids'll take you home. Unless you want me to take you to Debra's?"

"I'm gonna let the kids stay there, Dean. I'm gonna call them now and just let them know their Dad's OK. I hope to God he is".

Dean gets into the driver's seat, Shirley into the passenger with Benissa and Troy in the back. They sit, just for a moment, then Dean begins to pull away. Just at that precise moment, Shirley lets it all out and bursts into loud sobbing. It's all become too much for her, the strength has gone for the day. Benissa leans forward, putting her arms around her aunt and holding her tight, as the car pulls out onto the A13.

The journey home is conducted pretty much in silence, though as they approach Canvey, Dean takes a detour to avoid the inevitable crime scene which is still crawling with Old Bill. They have set up a mobile incident room, overhead floodlights and a tent over the Porsche. He takes them well away from the town centre and towards the estate. As he drops her off at the darkened house, he is full of reflection. The lone figure walks down the gravel drive, past Dave's car and he watches her put the key in the lock, open the door and put the hall light on. Then, she's gone. Dave's wife. The electric gates close smoothly behind her.

It's not easy being a gangster's wife.

Chapter Twenty Two

Villa Therése, Torrevieja, Spain

"I don't give a shit what's happened, Don. The stupid bitch is going to be alright, isn't she? Great! Marvellous! *Maravioso*! Get him on a plane out here. Kidnap the bloody man if you need to. Señor Montoya is furious. I use that word carefully, as he never normally even raises his voice. He has placed considerable investment into this project and he is not going to stand by and watch it disappear. Call me back!" *Click.*

"I do not believe what I have heard. I just don't comprehend it, Padraig. What is going on? Who the hell are these people we have got ourselves involved with? This is not the way we work. Never, never, never. No sooner do we place our trust in them, they start some kind of stupid feud. What is this, the kindergarten? I expect Don to take some action here. He is *our* man in England, Padraig, let him do the work. I knew this would happen".

"Calm yourself, Marianna. This can all get sorted out. Let us hear what Don has to say when he rings back. There is no point in jumping to conclusions until we have the full story. Leave it to the men to resolve this".

"Well, it's the bloody men who have got us into it!" Her nostrils were flared, her skin flushed with rage. "I have spent years working with Señor Montoya to build up this relationship. It is only because of my family in the old country that we have this *connection. Dios mio*, I have even slept with the man for this business arrangement". Her eyes began to fill with tears and she wept like a child, her legs and arms close to her body, her grief total yet isolated. Withdrawing into herself. Padraig stared at her, not knowing what the hell to do with this control obsessed beauty.

"Padraig," she whimpered, "you know me, like no-one else. You know why I do this and you of all people know that I have no need for money. It is the *excitement* which I need but this kind of thing, no, a thousand times no!"

Slowly, the burly Irishman put his arm around her, holding her close as she poured out the anguish of years, stored up deep within.

"Don will deal with this. I have great faith in the man, so I do, and if he says he will sort it, then that is what will happen. Seamus will deal with anything that needs to happen out here and as for Paco, well, he has his own way of correcting problems. Each to their own, Marianna. The work you do for the organisation is crucial to its success. We all have our work to do. We cannot exist without each other, that is why we have always been so successful and why it will continue this way. Don is speaking to his adviser tomorrow and that will help us, so it will".

She is still in his arms, all her strength seems to have deserted her.

"Sometimes, it is very hard to see which way we are turning, Padraig", she whispered. "Señor Montoya is a very impatient man. He is also unpredictable. That is why his enemies fear him and why the authorities cannot catch him. No-one ever knows what he is going to do next. *I* do not know what he is going to do next. I do not want to lose the work of years with the cartel because of this stupidity in London".

"That will not happen, *princesa*".

She raised her head at his use of the word, a word he never normally uses, but it is the word of her father. Back in Venezuela, at the Embassy, she was always his little *princesa*, his little doll on whom he lavished luxuries and love until the assassin's bullet put paid to his short life. The oil revenues had made him rich beyond even his dreams, yet the wind of political change which had been blowing through the whole continent had resulted in an uprising which ended his life and that of many others. Her inheritance meant that she was a fabulously wealthy girl at the age of ten, protected and fawned upon for ever more. Her mother had descended into alcoholism, finally ending up in a Caracas asylum. At least *she* now served a purpose for Marianna's regular trips back to the old country.

"Forgive me, I just lost myself for a moment, Padraig. I am alright now. We must again attend to business". She was restored. Within minutes, the redness had gone from her eyes and she was herself once more. She had repaired to the ladies' room and the make-up was once again perfect.

"I need to restore the balance here, Padraig. I need Señor Montoya to regain his confidence in what has become a farce. A debacle".

"*Princesa*, I tink that maybe we're makin' this into something far bigger than it is, so we are. These people are potentially very good for us, that we know, and yes, the British market is large, but we don't have to make it the most important thing we have ever done. Or do we? Is there something that you are not telling me?"

"I have made it clear to the cartel, to the Señor himself, that we are going to increase our purchasing from them substantially. These are not promises I can make lightly".

"You *promised him*? You *guaranteed* to the cartel, to *him* of all people? Marianna, do you know what it means to me when someone says that? Jaysus, there are men buried up and down the Concession Road who have said that to me and failed. These are words with impact, *princesa*! Don will tell you the same thing. I cannot for one moment believe that he is going to just accept this if it goes tits up. We are going to need some feckin' cover story if it does. And I don't want to be the man to explain meself".

"So now you see my predicament, Padraig. Now it is clear for you, yes?"

"*Your* predicament? I tink it's *our* predicament now. If this goes wrong, who do you think he's gonna call? Ghostbusters? His people will be on the first plane out of Bogota and we'll end up in a feckin'war!"

"So we *must* get this *Dean* out here to explain himself and make some plans to put right what has so obviously gone wrong. I think that from what Don has told us, the problems are domestic, yes?"

"If he is correct, then it is a matter of pride over a minor management problem. One thing led to another, so it did. It happens in these dick-waving exercises. It often escalates when the issue is not correctly dealt with at the outset. The man in question was given some of the romper room treatment, but it was left *unresolved*. Instead of letting it lie, they then proceeded to shoot the prime mover of this rival firm outside his own pub, so they did. The next thing, was the feckin' unfortunate car-park incident".

"Yes, Padraig, your choice of words is…..appropriate. Are they both alive?"

"Don tells me that they are both in intensive care and there are serious problems".

"How tedious, darling. I suppose that this, *this Dean*, is going to be unfocused for a while…"

"I think that he will become focused when we tell him that a simple death squad will be despatched, destination him. That normally gets people back on track. I will not allow myself to carry the carn for this, so I won't".

"Then I think we should leave it at that. Don is *very persuasive* and I have no doubt that Señor Bold will be with us tomorrow. On that note, I would say good night to you".

"'Night, *princesa*. A pleasure, so it was".

As she leaves, Pilar's driver stands illuminated in the doorway of the Villa Therése. *Click.* An unmanned infra red night camera whirs into action across the valley. Padraig comes to the door, kisses her goodbye on both cheeks and she climbs into the blacked out Seat. The gates move noiselessly across.

*

"We've got movement at Victor Two. Bit late for him, isn't it?"

"Even terrorists are normally tucked up in bed with their slags by now, aren't they? This can't be business, surely?"

"I've told you, don't call me Shirley".

"That has to be the oldest joke in the world. What is the matter with you?"

"Well, you know the rules, you don't have to be mad to work here but it helps".

"I *never* know which way to take you, Rick. You're either very funny or a total wanker. The jury's still very much out".

"You certainly know how to give a boy confidence!"

"Fuck off, Rick. What's happening?"

"Camera's still running, so they haven't chucked the towel in. No, forget that, it's just switched off".

"If this turns out to be a stray cat, I am going to go fucking ballistic!"

"Even you must know that the new cameras don't pick up things as small as that".

"In that case, I am off to the bar, spend some of Weatherall's budget. You coming, clever clogs?"

"Go on then. Nothing better to do here. I'm leaving the monitor on, just in case. It will record if there's anything else, won't it?"

"Yep, just a row of dots, but we will get the full picture in the morning. The stories that car will tell….."

"Come on then, there's a glass of wine down there with my name written on it".

*

"Do you miss the old country, me darlin'? I've bin doin' a lot of thinkin' these past few days", he yells from the huge sitting room.

Therése O'Riordan comes in from her television room, dressing gown wrapped tightly around. Her face is impassive, quite expressionless, in fact. She walks slowly over to the sofa and sits down.

"I don't miss a thing, not one little thing. But you obviously do? What's on your mind, Padraig O'Riordan?"

"I know I'm not the oldest fella on the Costa Blanca, but jaysus, I'm startin' to feel like the man himself".

"Is it that bar o' yours? Yer spendin' long hours down there. As yer've asked me, I'll tell yous. Do you really need to be there all the time? You've Ronan down there and those other big lads. Why don't yer take a little break from it all, give yersel' a chance to unwind. Play some golf. Yer've always wanted ter play the golf, so yer have".

"I don't think I have it in me, Therése. It's like every mornin', I wake at five and I can't stop meself from puttin' on the working cap".

"It's not just that though, love. Yer spent all those years avoiding the British Army, very well too, Padraig, fair play to yous. Yer come over here, full of retirement and God knows what else and yer at it again. Fightin' the system. Is that all you know? Will it be like this till it's time for yer wake? Do we not have enough money? You're sure an easy man to find these days, if I say so meself. If I know where you are, how easy d'ya think it is for the British?"

"Arr, woman. That's all over now, since the Good Friday Agreement. The amnesty applies to anything that predates its signin', so it does. There'll be no more British kangaroo courts for this fella".

"That's not what I meant, Padraig, and you know it wasn't. Yer runnin' with some fast and furious people now, so you are. I'm not sayin' I don't like the money an' all that kind of thing, but where would I be without yous?"

"Woman, yer keep yersel' to yersel'."

"Is that an observation or an order, husband?"

The two of them face each other, quite close. He stands against the wall, all six foot four of brawn and no small brain. She sits birdlike, perched on the cream leather sofa, tiny, neat, *unsullied*. Her pale skin and bright red hair dramatic. He looks down at her, the one person on God's earth who can talk to him like this. Marianna's one thing, but this? This is reality. This is a small catholic church in Crossmaglen, June 1980, standing at the altar with one Therése Mary McAteer, spinster of this parish. Nineteen years old he was, thin as a rake then, lookin' like a bean pole! Seventeen, she was, that beautiful red hair all piled up on top, ringlets of it hanging down, framing her porcelain white skin. Her green eyes twinkling through the veil. At him. At me, he thought, the flashback now almost too painful to bear. What the hell have I done to this woman?

"Yer know which one it is, so yer do! Order? I'm terrified of you, so I am. Only person's ever tamed me, that you are".

For the first time in years, he sits down next to her on the sofa.

"Therése, girl, I need yer advice".

He takes her hand and holds it, looking down at the increasingly apparent veins threading their way under the milk white flesh. A *woman's* hand now, no longer that of the little girl from the eighties.

"I have a little problem yer might want to think over".

*

The hotel bar's slowly emptying now, just a few stragglers and a salesman making valiant but hopeless attempts to get off with the waitress. Bob and No spring to mind.

"You ever been, you know, *approached*? For money?"

Kim Evans is down the third glass of vino collapso now. A Marlboro Light dangles from her hand, the ash teetering dangerously towards Rick's exposed wine glass.

"Never had the pleasure, I am afraid. It does happen though, doesn't it? I've heard stories".

"You know there's rumours about that guy in Dover, don't you? You know, the one who crashed his car? The one that Weatherall was carping on about? Yeah, well, turns out that the girl in the car with him, his daughter, was at Roedean! The girl's school in Brighton. The fees there are over twenty grand a year! How the fuck was he affording that on a Grade Six salary? Seems he told people his wife came from money, but no-one believes it now. Apparently, at the funeral, she was there with her family and it looked like they didn't have a pot to piss in? There's rumours that they're gonna start an investigation, not only into that, but into his death. Something about the road and the car?"

"Where on earth do you get this kind of information from, oh great Kim?"

"Women's talk mostly. You know? Us girlies? Always talking, never working? Well, Mr Richard Whaddevveryernameis, I've got news for you. It's talking like that which gets things solved. Not standing in the bar waving your dicks around. *I've got this, it's bigger than yours* shit. We actually *get the job done!*"

"That smacks so much of Weatherall. Bloody feminist lesbian bollocks".

"That may well yet prove to be true, Ricky boy. I like the woman, I have to say. She *has* got balls and she's not afraid to ruffle feathers. Knows what she wants". The rough wine is really kicking in now and Kim's gone all slack. He's no better, downing the fifth San Mig and feeling the effect of no food, yet again.

"And she doesn't care how she gets it, is that what you are saying? I'm not so sure about that woman. Her rise during and after Metro made me think that there was a *lot* more to Janet Weatherall than you think at first. She's definitely got her own agenda and sometimes, I'm not sure what to think. When's the next team meeting?"

"What, our group or the whole team?"

"The big one".

"There's s'posed to be one before Christmas, then we're going to cool off and get cracking again in January".

"What the fuck's that all about? Crime stops for Christmas? Give a criminal a holiday? For fuck's sake!"

"You know the statistics as well as I do. They know we're busy at Christmas stopping all the booze runs. They're not going to run the risk of a random search discovering what they've just spent fortunes trying to hide. No. Mr O and his mates will be enjoying a bit of r&r the same as we will".

"Don't s'pose the Weatherall will pay for us to stay out here?"

"You know the answer to that. It's BMI Baby back to Cardiff and home. Reconvene at HQ in Jan before coming back".

"And she's really suspending operations over the period? You surprise me".

"I'm not inside her head, Rick. Just feel like I'm getting to know her a bit, s'all".

"Fancy another?" The bar looks like it's closing now, so he orders two more drinks each. So terribly British. Makes you proud, doesn't it?

"Do you think we're actually making any progress with Mr O? I mean, we've been back out here for ages now and nothing ever seems to happen". The San Mig bottle is almost permanently up to his mouth now, making his speech sound really weird.

"Maybe we'll know in the morning? Over breakfast?"

"If I didn't know you well enough, I'd say that was a come on".

"You should know by now. You can take the girl outta the Valleys….."

His face is a study. She is *actually coming on to him*. He looks across at her open blouse, just too many buttons undone. She's showing out. She's only up for it!

"You're certainly full of surprises tonight! Why don't we finish these?"

"Fuck that! I've got a bottle of Bacardi in my room. Let's get onto that and you can show me how you chat a girl up? Come on, last one back pours the drinks!"

She slaps his backside and drains the first of the glasses, taking the other with her.

*

"Would you be saying that you want out? Is that what this is all about?"

"When a man gets to an age when he starts *thinking*, then maybe it *is* time to move on".

"You're surely a man in a million, Padraig. There was me thinking that we were here for a while and now you're talkin' up and away. There's surely some of the gipsy in you, of that I am certain".

"I'm saying nothing of the sort, woman. Just thinking, that's all".

"Dangerous thing for a man to do; thinking!"

"If that was anyone else saying that…"

"Yer'd do what, husband? What would you do?"

They are back in the 'Cross now. August 1979. Sitting in a meadow, chewing grass, trying to avoid Mr McAteer and his sons. She's wearing a summer dress, he's got the regulation white shirt and black trousers on.

*

Rick and Kim are on her bed. The blouse is now undone, her bra's unhooked and he's licking and sucking at her tits. Through the half light, her pale hand is working hard on his erect cock. Their mouths are clamped together, feasting hungrily on each other, alcohol-fuelled lust in total control.

She pulls away.

"Have you got any cards in your room?" She looks down at his puzzled face.

"What the bloody hell do you want cards for? We're having sex?"

"Not yet, lover boy. Just need some cards, that's all".

"We're not going to play strip poker are we? I know poker's popular now but that would be ridiculous".

"I've just had a little idea. Don't spoil it".

He gets off the bed and tucks himself back in. Grabbing his jacket, he makes for the door.

"You are coming back, big boy?"

As he looks back, she's lain back on the pillow and opened her legs wide, her skirt is round her middle.

"What do you think?" he grins, frantically searching in the pocket for his room key.

He's back in a couple of minutes, tap-tapping at the door, having paused only to take two Viagra tablets. As she opens it, he is treated to her clothes being perfectly restored, her makeup back on,complete with thick lip gloss and a wicked expression playing around her face. Her hair is wild though, tousled and ruffled. Deliberately.

"Ready? Got the cards? Good boy!"

"Kim, what the hell are you up to?"

"Patience, boy, it all comes to he who waits!"

She pushes him down onto the bed with one finger. An extra light has been put on in the room, illuminating the bed.

"We'll play here. Know the rules?"

"If they're your rules, then I very much doubt it'"

"Simple. Each round is 'all in'. We get two cards, turn up the next five and whoever has the better hand gets to make the other player *do* something. Anything they want. Could be one item of clothing, could be drink a bottle from the mini bar or whatever. Let's see what you're made of, big boy!"

"What kind of tease are you? OK, we'll play the game. Deal the cards!"

*

Summers then were a hell of a lot simpler. Padraig would meet her at the back of the cemetery and they'd skive off to the meadow at the edge of the village. 1979 was a hot one. 'I don't like Mondays' by the Boomtown Rats was No 1. 'Still' by The Commodores spoke for every lover in the land. They'd lie there for hours, chewing grass, talking of the future, kissing, acting the giddy goat. God, she looked pretty. Her little cotton dress riding up, displaying her slim, sun-tanned thighs, freckly arms, her tousled red hair falling down over her bare shoulders. Innocent, yet enticing, ruby-red lips parted, smiling, laughing. Always laughing, she was. Knew nothing of where Padraig would go from time to time, 'with the boys'. Nothing, until Mountbatten was murdered at the end of August and the round-ups began.

They started in the 'Cross, then Jonesborough and finally Cullaville. Padraig and his brothers were all taken away by the

British, not to be seen again for two long years. During that time, the soldiers would come looking for more of the O'Riordans, until one day, they came looking for her. Someone had said something out of turn. The next thing, she was bundled into a Land Rover. They found her the next day, tied naked to a tree near the watchtower outside Jonesborough. A sign round her neck read, 'IRA Slag'. She had been gang-raped and tortured. When Padraig returned, he went straight to her and they were married the following month, at the height of the Bobby Sands thing. He knew what had happened, but said nothing. He wore a white frilly shirt, what with the New Romantics being all the rage. She wore a beautiful white dress, her shining red hair cut fashionably sharp, but people still talked about 'that day' behind their backs. Some said it was a marriage made in hell.

*

The whole game's kicking in now. He's down to his shirt and boxers and she's in her knickers and skirt. She's unhooked the bra again and is driving him mad. The cards have just turned against him again and now she's got him bending over, taking his boxers off and she's videoing the whole thing on her phone. The mini-bar's empty now and they're both hammered.

"Necks…round…all in. Whoever wins…chooses the rest of the night! Cccuuummmonnn, big boy!" She falls against the end of the bed, sliding down onto the floor. Her eyes are half closed, but she's still hanging on to the nearly empty bottle of Bacardi, now resting against her bare stomach. He draws the cards and lays them down in front of her. A two of spades for her, a jack of hearts for him. A two of diamonds for her, a five of clubs for him. Then the Flop. A four of hearts, an eight of hearts and a two of clubs. She's laughing now, an evil grin playing round her mouth. She starts to put on her bra.

"Bad luck, big boy. Looksshhhlike yer goin' without! Haha!"

The Turn. Ten of hearts. She looks up at him, curious to see his reaction, before returning to her blouse, half hidden under the bed.

The River. Ace of hearts.

"I think thaassme!" he slurs, drunken lust written all over his face.

"Howdidyoudotha'?" she slobbered, Bacardi spitting from her mouth.

"Jennullmansluck, darling. Getyerkitoff!"

He leans over to her and starts to unhook her bra. She looks up at him, angry but resigned to her fate. She's too pissed to care. This time, he's unzipped her skirt before she really realises what's going on.

"Whasssarrusshhh? We got loadsatime". He's stopped listening to her teases now. Despite the endless beer and rum, he's coming to life, just as she's losing her strength. He tears off her pants, ripping them in half. He unbuckles his belt and drops his boxers, leaving his shirt on, a sign of victory. Roughly, he plunges his hand between her legs and inserts two fingers deep into her, pushing them in and out. His mouth is over hers and he is tonguing her furiously. The drinking game and her perceived power over him has made her very wet, the outcome never planned. He pushes her back onto the middle of the bed and parts her thighs.

"You…you gotta wearacondommm! I'm not having it without". With that, he plunges straight into her, breaking into a strong, regular, deep rhythm. He pins her arms back against the bed, pumping firmly. She wriggles and writhes under him.

"No. NO, I said. For God's sake, Rick!"

"No more no from you, girl. It's time you were taught a lesson. I've heard more than enough from you, you fucking tease". He pushes harder and harder, right in up to the hilt, his thighs slapping against her fleshy arse.

"You BASTARD!" she screams.

"Don't waste your time, girl. There's no one else on this floor. Not very popular here in February. Save your energy".

He's got her by the hair now, roughly pulling it to one side, then the other so that he can bite her shoulders. She's fighting with all her might, yet she's getting wetter and wetter, the harder he fucks her. He wants true victory now, sensing he's getting close. Holding her down by the hair, he pulls out and immediately she pulls her thighs close together, her eyes spitting fire. He slaps her across the face, hard enough to make a mark and turns her over, face down. She is writhing like a snake.

"Right you little bitch". He forces one knee down between her wet thighs, then the other. Her rounded arse is sticking up in the air. He uses his free hand to prise open her cheeks and roughly sticks two fingers into her anus. Her arse and his cock are soaked in muskwish and he uses this to ease his way in. She squeals in pain as he takes her up there. His hands are now free and he holds her, pushes her down into the bed as he pumps her arse for all its worth.

"P...p...please don't", she sobs quietly as he drives himself deep inside, his Viagra enhanced cock tearing at her flesh. His hand twists her hair round and he tugs hard, making her head spring backwards towards him.

"What did you say? Please fuck me? Is that what you want, bitch?"

Her sobs have turned to whimpers, she is now totally subjugated. He feels himself getting closer, closer then he explodes deep up inside her, stream after stream of thick cum. His growls frighten her, she lies still, waiting for him to finish. Eventually, he is spent and collapses on top of her. He spots her camera phone at the side of the bed and reaches over. As he lifts himself out and off, he takes several close ups of her, then turns her over, continuing with several more.

When he is finished, he lies next to her, takes a couple more, then emails them to his phone, left lying two floors down in his jacket. The half light does not pick up her tears.

"See you in the morning. Don't forget, we've got work to do. Night". He gets himself dressed and throws the phone back on the bed, before slamming the door behind him.

When she wakes in the morning, she is still lying face down, in the foetal position, thumb safely in her mouth, the pillow stained heavily with her tears. As she crawls to the shower, it all starts to come back to her. She scrubs furiously, washing it all away.

Chapter Twenty Three

Canvey. Two days after.

Ali walked slowly into the intensive care waiting room. In that kind of respectful way that people do. From the desk, a short wide corridor led down between the six rooms. The first was empty, the second contained the comatose Gina, the third a road accident victim. Opposite him was another empty room, next to that was Dave, then a young girl who had been attacked and badly beaten. At school. Her family sat next to her comatose, broken little body, their lives totally destroyed. Dean sat on a chair next to Gina. The room was full of flowers, cards and tributes. On the other side, Benissa and her mate Becca sat silently, just looking, watching, waiting, dressed in green hospital gowns and masks. Shirley and the kids were in with Dave, same get-up. Both of them lay still, wired up to a myriad of machines and drips.

Ali stood still, looking through the glass pane which separated him from the Bold family. Eventually, Dean became aware of his presence and looked up to see Ali's beckoning finger. He had a face like a robber's dog and Dean knew he had to go out. He closes the door behind him, but the family are too grief-stricken to notice.

"Thanks for coming,Ali. Really good of you".

"I am very sorry for you. Er, and your children. This is a terrible thing. I have some flowers for Gina. Can I give them to you?"

"Just give 'em to the bird at the end. You alright, mate, you look like you've seen a ghost?"

"I have some news for you. I don't think you will like it, but there is something which must be done".

"What, mate? What the hell is it?"

"Word of this *incident* and er, certain other things that have happened recently have reached *the people* up in town. They're not very happy, not when it can impact on their business. There's a meet. We have to be there, Dean. To show respect, innit. There's no choice. I have had it from the family, my family that both sides are to be there at the table. He wants it sorted today. I know the way these things work. It's gonna cost us about twenty large. He'll ask for it, but we ain't got no choice, Dean. It's not the way they work".

"Both *sides*? 'Ow many of the other lot are there? What the hell's Dave been up to while I was away? Fuck me, Ali, it was only a coupla weeks ago he done all this. Has he started a fuckin' gang war and failed to let us in on the details?"

"I think you could say that one thing led to another, Dean. After Rainsford and the disrespect which was shown to you, as you know he went after Freddie the Fixer at his pub and, well, you know what happened there. Freddie's boys went to the Guv'nor and it looks like he's the one who called it on. I know it's going to be difficult but this has *got to be sorted*. There is literally no alternative. None where anyone gets to live, anyway. Do you want that for your kids, for your family?"

Ali deliberately looks across into the sterile room where Dave's still hooked up to drips and flickering machines, but no-one's returning his glance.

"Let's do it. This whole thing's got a bit out of hand anyway. I'll tell the kids something's come up. Give the flowers to the bird at the end, she'll sort 'em".

Ali looks away, away from Shirley and walks out.

*

"Are you tellin' me that we're goin' to a meet with Bold and his fuckin' cronies? Sit round a table and have fuckin' tea or something? What the fuck's that all about? I mean, I was fuckin' there the day we pulled Rainsford out of that skip *and* the day they done Freddie the Fixer. Fuck me, they don't want much, these people".

"You have to understand that there are *procedures*. Things which have to be obeyed, whether we like it or not. Without these rules in place, there would be anarchy. This doesn't happen very often. Just when it crosses over into their territory. Business *is* business, that's the way they see it and that's the way it *should* be seen".

"I ain't happy".

"I know that, but you see, once the meeting is over, things will be clearer. Shall we go?" The ageing Guv'nor gets to his feet, his slicked back silver hair shining in the glow of his open fire. As they turned out of the palatial driveway, through the village towards Ongar and the M11, his mind was cast back to the first time he had got into trouble for being a little hot-headed. It would be good experience for the boys. With a bit of luck, they'd be back in time for a spot of lunch at the Chequers in Matching Green. Moules marinières. That should do the trick. With a nice bottle of Sancerre.

*

Ali drove quickly but safely. His whole persona had changed from the normal kebab shop joviality approach. This was Ali the Coat at his finest. Just what they least expected, though as Dean's most loyal supporter, he knew when the time had come. The BMW's tinted windows gave nothing away to the outside world. The hour's drive passed as it does, *in these situations*. No small talk, bit of radio, then that gets turned off.

"You carryin'?"

"Yes, Dean. It's expected, but they'll take it from me when we get to the meet".

"Just nice to know you've got my interests at heart, do you know what I mean?" First and only time that Dean smiles today. They turn off the A13 just by the Silvertown flyover, up Lanrick Road and into the old industrial estate.

"This brings back a few memories of the 90s, don' it? Never thought we'd be back here. Not without the fuckin' church, anyway".

"Or the Extra-Terrestrial!"

Ali stops the car and waits. After a few moments, another car appears and flashes its lights twice at him. Ali returns the message, then the other car does it three times and drives away. Ali slips the Beamer back into drive and away they go. After a couple of twists and turns, they're outside a derelict old brick built warehouse. The shutter's up and a geezer's directing them in. Ali drives in and the shutter is pulled down the second he gets through. As he stops the car, the bloke walks over. He's holding a small Uzi which is pointed right at the window.

"Open the boot and the bonnet, please. Just need to check you haven't brought anyone else with you". Polite, direct. Helps if you've got an Uzi to back you up.

Ali obliges and then he and Dean follow another bloke, also tooled up. He takes them through a steel door, barely hanging on its hinges and into a large, dark warehouse unit. It's big enough to stage anything; football, bare knuckle boxing, dog fighting, anything really. They become aware that now they're in this cavernous space, second Uzi man is no longer there. The warehouse was cold and dark, save for the table which stood in its midst. A solitary light hung from the high ceiling. Seven chairs had been placed around it. One chair, until recently had remained empty, flanked by two seated figures.

Dean and Ali sat on the two vacant chairs, the Guv'nor and Ricky Razors on the others. Their heads were down, dwarfed by the sheer presence of the man who now sat down opposite. The warehouse was cold and damp, the noise of The Chairman's footsteps still echoing around its dank walls. In the shadows, several figures stood quite still, their weapons both obvious and visible, the deterrent quite clear to any lunatic who might try anything in the *presence*.

"No lies at the table. Gather round. I want *you* to speak first, then *you*. Then I will decide what is to happen. My decision is final. Before you leave, you will note that there is to be a collection. Twenty grand is required from each of you. For this small arbitration. My colleagues will come and collect it Friday. Don't give yourselves the indignity of not having it ready".

Deliberate seating plan. Very clever. It's the headmaster's study. The little toe-rags have been caught out and now it's time for the beak to decide. Normally, he'd let it go, but not this time. This time, it's gone too far.

"I have been briefed on what this is all about, and what both of you will never know is by whom. As far as I am concerned, the only good grass is the grass that grasses to me, understand? Good. Thank you, Mr Ali, Mr Storey for *making the arrangements*. You can start, Mr Bold. You seem to have brought this problem to the table".

"I don't think that's true. We star.."

"We are NOT here to argue. I will say one more thing. If you cannot manage your employees and what they do on returning from Europe, then don't blame someone else for the fallout. Do not interrupt me again. DO YOU UNDERSTAND?"

"Yes, understood. We dealt with Rainsford in the way we always deal with problems like him. We gave him a talkin' to and a bit of a slap. Next thing, he's telling every cunt we've gone soft. Fuckin' Freddie the Fixer starts spreadin' the fuckin' news all over the island and that's when we decided to do something about it. I was away on business, so Dave was in charge. He gets a little team together and they go over Freddie's pub. Well, they're pissed off so they give Freddie a few body shots, just to let 'im know what's what. I don't know what Dave really meant, 'cos e's in intensive care and e' ain't comin' out of that too quick, know what I mean? Now, my wife is in intensive care, my partner's in intensive care and I don't fuckin' know what's cummin next".

"Thank you. You see how easy it is to be honest when you want to? How easy it is to be *humble*? Ricky? Perhaps *you* would like to give us your version?"

"It's no *version* I can assure you. I only…"

"Now *you* are trying to influence proceedings. I am surprised at you of all people, I must say. Remember very well what I said to Mr Bold here".

"Rainsford worked for us. He took some work with, with *him* there and the next thing we heard was that he was dumped in a skip in Pitsea, smashed to fuck. Then out of the blue, Freddie gets it outside the boozer. I ain't havin' it. To add insult to injury, I hear *on the grapevine* that they were going to do Rainsford properly, this time at Tilbury Fort. Some kinda execution. Fuckin' liberty that is, what with him just out of hospital an' all!"

Dean's mind has just gone into overdrive with this news. He looks across at Ali, but he only has eyes for The Chairman. Wise man.

"I can understand that. Unfinished business, Mr Bold? Well, whatever it was, the business ends here. I will not tolerate any more of this behaviour by the lunatic fringe of your organisations. I know full well who is responsible for each of the measures taken. As I am sure, do you both".

His face is totally impassive, his eyes cold and motionless. There is such an atmosphere surrounding the table, you swear you could *touch* it. Despite the coldness of the empty warehouse, it feels like there's a furnace that's been burning for years. Both Dean and Ricky are sweating like stuck pigs. They know what might be coming.

The Chairman fixes Dean with a cold stare.

"How is your wife? Is she recovering?"

"We don't know yet. The bullet hasn't moved, but they still won't operate until she's more stable".

"Yes, yes. *Collateral damage*. May I assume that *Mrs* Bold was not the target? Am I also to draw the conclusion that Mr Hilton was not the target either? If not, it seems remarkable that he was driving *Mr* Bold's car *at the time of the measure*".

Dean's anger is barely contained at this point and he stirs in the chair. Immediately, a *click, click* shatters the silence. Just behind him, a Kalashnikov automatic rifle is cocked, ready. This guy is taking no prisoners. The *man in control* does not flicker. A bead of sweat travels slowly down Ricky's cheek and drips onto his blue Armani Jeans denim shirt, staining it. In the half-light, away from the table, it looks *just like blood*.

"No, we wasn't tryin' to hurt her. Really, we wasn't. It was a mistake".

"I do not wish to get involved in the whys and wherefores of these matters. As painful as it may be, and that is no concern of mine, you will leave here in your own vehicles having re-established normal business communications between yourselves, or you will leave via the furnace chimney next door. The fire is lit, just in case. The choice, *gentlemen*, is yours".

The moment. Not once have Dean and Ricky even *thought* of

looking at each other. The venom which is just waiting to spit forth from mouths, fists and guns lies ready. They are now about to perform an act which neither of them even would have dreamed of just hours before. The silence is total. The *man in control* does not flinch, not even a blink from him. He just stares, his hands lie crossed on the table, the 24 carat gold and diamond studded Cartier twinkling bright even in the dim glow of the forty watt bulb dangling like a dead man in a noose.

Slowly, very slowly, they turn to face each other for the first time. For this is the way that it is going to be done now. There is absolutely *no choice*. The thought processes work overtime. These are two powerful, proud, *wounded* men. Two *neutered men* now. Eunuchs lost in a miasma of superior power. One man in the room holds all the cards. This might sound strange to you. Why the hell doesn't someone kick off? For God's sake!

Because they are in the company of the man in control.

As their eyes meet, just for a second there is a kind of exchange. Some kind of interaction, maybe a reciprocal hurt is exposed. Then it is gone forever. Their eyes drop and hands are extended. The handshake is brief and barely tangible. It is done. Their seconds are seated just behind. They also exchange glances, but these are of a different kind. For Dean there is Ali. Ali the pragmatist, Ali the *realist*. For Ricky, there is Storey. Mr Storey. The Guv'nor. Retired. The wily old fox from the forest of Epping. He acts as second in exactly the way that The Coat has acted for Dean. They are the mediators, the cool heads when everyone else's burns hot with rage. Nothing else is meant by it. They exchange *the nod*. If you've never had the nod, then you won't know what it means. If you have, then you know *exactly* what it means. The work will begin after they have hopefully got out of this place with their heads still on and the right way round.

"Gentlemen. Can I deduce that we are making progress here? Can I also deduce that from this moment on, I can return to my home knowing that I am to hear nothing more of this? Nothing more which will cause me to take *measures?* For make no mistake. If anything further is brought before me concerning the pair of you, I will have no choice but to issue a termination. *That*, is both irrevocable and final. May we never speak of this again. Mr Bold, you and your party will leave first, then you, Mr Streatham, will leave with yours. Goodbye, gentlemen. Please leave your IOUs on the table. Before you *depart*".

With that, he stands and disappears into the gloom. The sound of a car staring up penetrates the darkness; in the far corner of the warehouse, a shutter is rolled up and he is gone. As Dean stands to leave, the Kalashnikovs have already vanished into thin air. Ali motions him to walk first, covering his back, yet at the same time knowing that there will be no further action. He places the package on the table. There isn't even anyone there to count it. Just not necessary. The car stands as they had left it. Climbing silently in, they do not even give backward glances as the others prepare to leave.

The Beamer roars into life and in seconds, they are out and onto Lanrick Road once more. They're just past Barking before Dean says anything.

"I swear, if anyfin' 'appens ter Gina, arm gonna fuckin' kill that cunt".

"I think we all know. That is why he asked you about her. He *never* asks such questions, Dean. He will never get involved beyond the arbitration. It is good business for him. Let us pray for her, Allah looks down on all, he will look after her now. I pray three times a day for her, Dean".

He's staring out of the window as they pass the multi-coloured flats and away onto the dual-carriageway.

"I need a fuckin' drink. Just find us a pub, mate".

*

"What did you make of that, Ricky? Your first and with luck, your last encounter with *real power*. I do not recommend further contact with him. It could be seriously bad for your health".

"If Bold leaves it out, I ain't startin' no fuckin' rows. That fuckin' geezer was well scary. I've had it with some cunts before, but he's something else".

"I think you had better call off whatever it was that you were planning. If they believe that they have not completed the task, they may decide to return and complete. That could, as you would say, really fuck matters up".

"You're fuckin' right, bruv. I'd forgotten about them".

"Not something to really forget, Ricky. And please don't call me 'bruv'. Reminds me of a place I no longer wish to revisit, even in my mind".

*

"Someone...is lying. Bold didn't know who the target was. The other fella didn't even know who'd done it. Stay close to this one. It's not finished. I can smell a third party in this."

"Right 'o, Mr Chairman. I'm on it."

The Chairman looked out of the blacked out car window, on his way back to Hertfordshire. Slowly, he dialled a number.

*

At the end of Upminster High Street, they sit in a small oak-beamed pub, fire blazing. Dean is doing his own version of the cave-man bit. He's gone all silent again and has just nipped into the gents for a toot. As the hooter kicks in, he starts to open up.

"D'ya know, this has fuckin' changed me, Ali. It's fuckin' scary, seein' the missus just lyin' there. Always thought I could do it all. Sort it, know what I mean? Sort the dustbins, sort me mum, sort the business an' all. I just don't know no more. Look at us, mate. We're sittin' in some posh boozer, middle of the day, drinkin' shorts. Fifty grand motor outside. Scratch comin' out of our fuckin' ears. Why do I feel like I've just been to the fuckin' headmaster's office? Right fuckin' slap down, that were. You think you're sorted, then he gets involved".

"Go to Gina, my friend. Don't get a downer on what's happened now, innit. Just leave it. Leave it where it is".

"Maybe yer right. Maybe I ain't got a FUCKIN' CLUE!" His voice is raised now. He smashes his fist down onto the antique table and kicks over a stool. The barman looks over and starts to make his way across to them.

"YOU CAN FUCK OFF AN' ALL, YER FUCKIN' POSH CUNT!" He gets up to lamp the geezer, but Ali's pulling him back. The old marching powder is kicking in hard and Dean's lost it. The veins are standing up on his neck and he's right back in the old ICF days. Stanleys at the ready. The whole pub's gone silent, but no-one dares even look in Dean's direction. Ali literally drags him out of the pub towards the car. He's still shouting and yelling abuse, but as he gets in, the shouting lessens and gradually evolves into quiet, then weeping and finally sobbing.

"What the fuck am I gonna do if she don't make it? I can't even think about it".

"I will take you straight to the hospital, my friend. Your place is with her now". Ali's soothing tones wash over Dean. He is a beaten man, destroyed by his partner's stupidity and his own hunger for success. From deep within comes a vestige of spirit. The old Dean is still in there somewhere, bloodied and down but not finished. Not yet. The remaining journey to the hospital is spent in total silence. His mind works from despair to overtime.

*

As Storey arrives back at the gated pile he calls home, he has in mind another of his little ideas.

"Get me a meet wiv that Ali, Rick. Seems like a decent bloke. Without the likes of him, things could have got a bit out of hand, what with the Kalashnikovs and that. Have a word".

Ricky Razors is still reeling from the experience of the morning. The drive back to Ongar was surreal in his mind. Things like that do *not happen.* Violence, death, knives, drugs, bank jobs, more drugs, brasses, charlie; fair enough. The list is endless, but it still never includes the Lanrick Road thing. He just sat there like some kid who's been caught with a spray can and an imagination.

Chapter Twenty Four

Ashendon Calvert Halse Solicitors, Liverpool

"The thing about a Customs investigation, Don, is this. If you don't put anything in at the beginning of the experiment, you'll get nothing out at the end. Do you honestly think they run operations as a result of good intelligence work? Do they *bollocks*! There are only two ways Customs *ever* catch anyone. One is that they stumble across something totally by chance, as in our friend at Dover and the other way is when somebody gets fucking greedy and grasses you up. It's as simple as that. It is science, not art. Good God, man, they have neither the wit nor the patience for it to be art".

"You see, I've bin givin' this some thought, James. That was quite some cock-up, that night. You've got one stupid fuckin' bastard who decides to go on the missin' list just at the crucial moment. OK, that's been sorted. There's plenty more of the bizzies will take the Queen's head when you wave it right, no fuckin' worries! You've then got the fact that it was *our wagon* which got stopped, out of the thirty on the fuckin' boat. *Then*, you've got the fact that they didn't find jack shit anyway. Put that in your fuckin' calculator and tell me what comes out!"

"Yes, I agree, Dover *was* an interesting equation. A conundrum, maybe. Our Birmingham office had an interesting case a while back. VAT, it was. It turned out no less than five different Customs investigations crashed together. Ended up in one trial in a kangaroo court in Northampton in front of the craziest judge on the circuit. Two of the boys in blue on the jury to boot! The paperwork was so complicated and you had five different regional offices running things. Can you imagine; five different operation names! They had some trouble trying to conceal the informants on *that* one. Which leads me to my most important point. None of the defendants in that case could believe it was their mates who had grassed them up. There are chaps in jail now who still believe their gangs were sound. Sometimes you can even show them the bloody evidence and they *still* won't believe it! The net result of that one is that there are three informants still working for Customs, still in the same business! Granted, one of them has had his house shot up twice, but if you go to a certain bar in central Birmingham this coming Friday night, you'll find said individual in there, buying champagne for anyone who crosses his path!"

"He wouldn't be buyin' nothin' if *I* had anythin' to do with it! The cunt'd be in a thousand fuckin' pieces!"

"Rightly so, Don, rightly so. Sadly, there are very few of your ilk left. Honour has been left behind, along with pounds and ounces".

"Are you tellin' me somethin' James? I mean, if you've heard somethin', then you'd better tell us".

"I have heard nothing, either substantiated or idle gossip. I recommend strongly that you re-evaluate your operation, however, in the light of recent Customs cases. Do you know that people are actually approaching them these days? *Actually going to them*! How easy are they making it? Look to your laurels, Don, it may not even be one of your organisation. Most likely, it will be a rival. Remember Caesar, Don, remember Julius Caesar. Sometimes they come for you in the night".

"I fuckin' hate it when you get all cryptic!"

"I am here to protect you, that's all. Stop you from doing anything *rash*. So tell me, what *are* you up to at the moment?" His face broke into a wry smile, the pencil he was twirling round his fingers now tapping up and down between upper and lower teeth.

"Spain's comin' on well. As you always say, when one door closes. Well, we thought one door had closed and instead, the fuckin' thing's cut a new one too. The bulk shipments are on, first lot's already on the way from Caracas. That's a new route. We've got a new customer down London way. Fuckin' cock on an' all. One of them chance meetings of yours".

"First rule of law. There is no such thing as a chance meeting. So how do you get round that one?"

"I've checked the fellas out and they're fuckin' sound. Proper old team from the East End. They've had a few internals lately, domestics you might say, but nothin' they can't handle. Turns out the firm they've had the row with had a bit of a misunderstandin'. Coupla' casualties. Best of fuckin' mates now".

"When you say casualties, are these Toxteth style casualties or Casualty style casualties?"

"Well, put it this way, nobody's dead. Yet."

"Hmm. I suppose that's something. Any interest from our friends?"

"There was a bit of a stewards when a fella got the back of his head shot off. They're puttin' the bastard back together at the mo. Ain't gonna hold nuthin' up. The other fella took three in the guts outside a pub. Nice funeral, apparently. Lotsa flowers, like. What kicked it off was just some fuckin' driver who took a few whacks in a warehouse. He's still eatin' his dinner through a straw, but he'll gerrova it!"

"Is that it, or was there any serious violence? Because from where I'm sitting, it sounds like a *bloody gang war*! What is it with you people? Why do you always have to sort things out like this?"

"It's just the way it is, James. It's the only language these people understand. As Lenny Maclean said, "Nothing a good right hander couldn't sort out"._

"My point exactly! *A good right hander*! From what you're saying, there are three people out there who are lucky to be alive, one stiff and God knows what else in the pipeline. *Is* there anything else in the pipeline? Please tell me they've put their guns away".

"Well, when the fella got the back of the head treatment, it seems his boss's wife took one as well".

"And is that going to be it, or are we going to lay claim to Britain's version of the St Valentine's Day Massacre?"

"I can't speak for a mad bunch of cockney bastards, but I've heard from our man that there ain't gonna be no more. They've all got too much to lose".

"So common sense may yet prevail, is that what you are telling me?"

"There ain't no alternative. Any more of this an' some serious people are gonna get involved. It's very bad for business".

"Better yet, Don, better yet. I don't wish to get involved in any more defence cases, especially those involving long sentences. Now that's bad for *my* business. Juicy frauds, yes. Keeping you people out of clink I can do without. Now concentrate on keeping this kind of thing out of the picture and check everyone's credentials. I am not telling you your business, Don, but sometimes a little consultancy goes a long way. Reach right into your organisation and while you are at it, look particularly at your new customers. New business always breeds new jealousies. Just as someone's about to make millions, someone else is having their nose pushed out. It's that one you have to worry about".

"That's why I like these cosy little chats we have, James. You always have your own angle on things. For a posh bastard, you'd have made a great blagger".

"And you don't see *me* as a blagger? Then you really are losing your touch, Don. I don't know about you, but I really could do with some lunch today. There's a new place opened down in Albert Dock. Does great fish".

"With chips?"

"For God's sake, I know we've managed to take the boy out of Toxteth, but just for one day, could we take Toxteth out of the boy?"

"Only jokin', James. I'm gettin' really used to this poncy food. O'Riordan's place serves top fuckin' scram".

"And how is Mr O these days? You haven't mentioned him".

"Things at that end are grace. The Fantastic Four are fuckin' brilliant to work with. I never thought I'd say that, but they are so fuckin' professional. The hassle starts when you get nearer the fuckin' sharp end. Mr O keeps *his* house in order. Proper".

"His reputation travels far and wide. He is very well respected".

"He's fuckin' worked at that. Never drops his guard".

"Shall we go? I feel in need of a glass of something cold".

"Lead on MacFuckinDuff! I'm gaggin' for a fuckin' drink!"

As they leave the office, James' leggy little PA stalks across the room to the photocopier, all mini skirt and heels, flashing her pert little arse as she bends over. He reckons he can put extra billing to most clients just for her.

Downstairs, James' chauffeur is waiting with the Bentley and within seconds, they are on the way to civilisation in the form of *Lobster!*, Liverpool's latest culinary extravaganza. On arrival, they are sandwiched between two tables, one containing two members of the Liverpool board, together with Rafa and a new potential signing from Seville and the other seating a well-known young TV personality whose entourage is more interested in getting to the Gents for a quick blow on the bugle. How times have changed.

"Isn't it time you came over to Spain to have a look at things? You know, give it all the once over?"

"Wrong country for me, old boy. Prefer France".

"Yeah, but this is business too, you know. You should sample a bit of the merchandise".

"I bet you say that to all the boys. Not for me, thank you. I prefer my Colombian rich roasted! On top of which, I don't think it would be very *professional* of me to be seen with you in Spain. Here is different. You are, when all is said and done, a client. The Law Society would look down on freebie trips to darkest Spain with known members of the criminal fraternity".

"Who said it was gonna be a freebie?"

*

"The message from the top is that it ends here, Dean. This is fuckin' well out of hand." Town's face is lined with anxiety, desperate for Dean's reply.

Thankfully, since the shootings, he's been off the hooter and his mind is as clear as it gets these days. On top of that, Town doesn't know about his little visit to Lanrick Road and if that message wasn't loud and clear, then he had totally failed to grasp the situation.

"Listen, Steve. I've done a lot of thinkin' since, well, you know. I think we kind of lost our way, hear what I'm sayin'? It's time we got back to basics, bit like old John Major?"

"Fuck me, bruv, don't bring that geezer into it. I know he was all for Essex man an' all that, but look what happened to him".

"Yeah, highly amusin'. We're a tight team, always been that way. Things got a bit out of hand. We're gonna get back to it now, get back to work. This business with her indoors. It's knocked me for six. Never thought I'd lose me head, but I ain't no good without her. She's me rock, mate".

"How is she today? Any improvement?"

"They still won't say. She ain't come out of the coma, but there's been some signs of activity in the brain. That's gotta be a fuckin' first, eh?" First smile there's been all day and it lightens the atmosphere a touch.

Town smiles, doesn't really want to laugh. That's really for Dean to do.

*

The restaurant is packed, though James and Don have a prime table by the window, across the way from Boardman and his crowd. A Chablis Grand Cru Les Clos 1995 arrives, complete with French sommelier. James tastes it, pronounces it to his liking and Don steams in. The bigger the glasses, the bigger the bill and these are huge. The golden nectar swirls around the glass as he savours the complex aromas. He's ordered a bottle of Chateau Ausone 1990 to go with the lamb they are going to order next. He always orders the wine, then orders the food to go with it. Proper way round.

"Promising start, James. That's what I like about you. Always full of good ideas. Got any more?"

"Ever thought about going direct to the cartels yourselves? I mean, the terrible two are all very well, but they are very expensive. There would be considerable savings".

"Er, I've often thought around that idea, but, always discounted it. You still need the right team, even if there are sometimes too many heads in the trough".

"Just enough, or too many?"

"The way I see it, we're just about right. The terrible two are making a lorra progress with the cartel and on top of that, we're gonna be movin' into bigger shipments, since our lovely lady on the inside got busy. Granted, she's a strange one, but the *princesa* guarantees her all day long and that's good enough for me".

"You have me intrigued by the *princesa*, Don, I cannot deny. I find her something of an enigma. What on earth she's doing with you lot is anybody's guess".

"A bit like you, then, James. Lie down with dogs?"

"Fifteen all, Don, fifteen all".

"I prefer one all. Don't understand tennis. Now give me a goal at the Kop end, that's a different kettle of fish".

"I might just have some interest from a couple of pals of mine, if you ever did think of going out on your own. Some, shall we say, institutional investors".

"Why wouldn't they invest now? With a fuckin' tried and tested system?"

"Too many heads for their liking. They like to know all the parties. Easier to understand. Despite what you might think, a lot of my friends are very simple people. Land, property, gold, diamonds. These things haven't let their families down in hundreds of years".

"So what do they want with a load of scallys like us?"

"The same thing as your *princesa*, I rather expect. Excitement! The thrill of the chase. Royal Ascot's nice for a day out, but it doesn't get the adrenalin flowing, Don, does it? Not like what you do. Oh, and the bottom line, of course. Profit *is* profit".

"Yeah, but to me, this is all I know. Same with Padraig and the rest of the boys. We'll creep into your fancy bars and places, but it takes a fuckin' long time to get Toxteth out of the boy. You said it yourself. At the end of the day, we're a load of fuckin' scumbags with Ferraris".

"You still send your kids to private schools, so you must believe in something".

"Of course, James, of course we do. We just don't do it the way you do. We have our own ways of resolvin' things, alright?"

"I think I am coming round to this Spanish trip. I must say I do like the sound of the *princesa*".

"She'd eat you for fuckin' breakfast!"

"I was rather hoping for something like that, dear boy. More wine?" He's got the public school boy face on now. The one he probably used to have when the local girls' boarding school used to turn up for the Friday night disco. You'd swear the bastard's bow tie is moving. There is nothing more focused than James when he gets a sniff of gash.

"You ain't gonna last five minutes in Spain with that fuckin' lot. You'll have to go into trainin'!"

"Sounds marvellous! Suddenly, I think I am going to do it. Live for once! It will be a proper adventure".

Beevers is looking at him now. Staring intently.

"You're fuckin' mad, you. You call me reckless an' impulsive, an' here's you changin' your mind mid-mouthful!"

"Perhaps I'm learning from the master? You know I find you fascinating, Don. If I were a psychiatrist, you'd be my favourite patient".

"What the hell am I supposed to make of that, you cheeky cunt?"

"Language, dear boy. Language!"

"Listen, James, I'm not bein' funny, but do you really think this is a good idea? I mean, what if things go wrong? These are some very serious people, you know. She may well be the *princesa* I talk about, but she *knows people*. One fuckin' false move, mate, and things could go very sadly wrong".

"Aah! The perfidious princess!"

"The what?"

"Perfidious. Look it up in the dictionary, Don. Remember it, whenever you meet someone new. Maybe even someone you've known for a long time".

"She's still got some very heavy connections.

"And you don't have *connections*? For God's sake, Don, I've been around you for long enough to know what risks are".

"But these are *real risks*. You've never had nothin' to fear from me. You don't really know what goes on, only what I choose to tell you. You might just find things out first hand. You might not like them".

"It's too late, Don, I've made up my mind. I'm your legal adviser and I want to come with you. See exactly what you're up to. Good sport! More wine?"

He's got that kind of Bunteresque face on. A kind of Bunter/Toad mix. You could just imagine him in a few years time, overweight, or at least more overweight than he is now, still wearing the paisley bowtie, sweating at every turn, podgy fingers stuffing nifties down lap dancers' thongs. Hotel bedroom, some poor little slag stuck underneath him, having the very life squashed out of her by this whale-like parasite. I think you've got the picture.

"Yeah. I'll have another glass. As many as yer like, James. I ain't got nothin' ter do this afters. I'm going down to London tomorrow. Get things sorted. Got fuck all to do now, till tonight's little appointment at Anfield".

"Some things never change, eh Don".

"Priorities, mate, priorities. A man's got to have a sense of priorities!"

Chapter Twenty Five

Canvey

The house is quiet, the only sound is Dean blundering around the kitchen, trying to be quiet and making a right bollocks of it. Benissa comes in, all bleary eyed, holding a huge pink teddy bear.

"Dad, what are you doin'? It's soddin' four o' clock. Duh? Go back to bed. We're gonna see Mum this morning?"

"Err, I...I...gotta go to Spain, princess".

"What, now? *Right* now? Are you mad? Yer can't just go an' leave us, what with mum in the hospital and that".

"I gotta go, babes, it's business".

"*It's business*. It's always business with you. Ain't you ever gonna turn off just for a minute? It's bleedin' business that got us in this mess in the first place".

Her pleading look is lost on her father, his mind already far away.

"Look, princess, I'll be back tomorrow, early doors. We'll go and see your mum then, yeah? I ain't joking, I really have to go and do this. I got no choice, babes".

Her head drops, the early morning fighting spirit already gone back to bed. He gives her an empty squeeze, then he's gone too, out to the waiting taxi.

As the front door slams, she whispers, "Bye, dad". Wiping away the latest of so many tears, she wanders aimlessly around the vast kitchen before pattering back up the curved staircase to bed.

*

The morning sun begins to warm the sea-front terrace of Doolans; the boys are already washing down the pavement and Dean's taxi is entering Torrevieja town as we speak, straight from the airport at Murcia. He sits nervously in the back, his mind going over and over the planned way he's going to get out of this. He and Town have talked it over. Padraig is going to be the problem. Beevers will do his usual thing and see which way the cookie crumbles before he jumps in with the coup de grace. As for anyone else, he's going to play it by ear. A hundred scenarios, a thousand solutions. He hopes. The car draws up outside, to be greeted by Ronan's icy stare. He walks over to the door, opens it and ostentatiously pays the driver before Dean can even retrieve his money clip.

"You'll be wantin' to follow me, Mister". Total change from the last time they met. A proper dose of South Armagh. He about turns and walks in. At this ungodly hour, across the *Plaza*, a delivery van sits parked, its darkened windows hiding motion cameras from view. Officer Andy Meacher's still camera clicks away until the pair disappear.

Inside, the place is deserted, save for the cleaner mopping away in the corner of the back bar.

"Up here".

They climb the stairs up onto what is still a very cold roof terrace. The tables are bare, the wooden decking still wet from last night's shower of rain. Ronan motions him to sit down and then he disappears, before the sight of Padraig O'Riordan comes into view from behind the stairwell.

"Dean. We've some talkin' to do. RONAN!"

He appears back up from inside the well, his face a mask of harshness.

"Will ya get this fella some coffee. He might need it".

Ronan once again disappears down the stairs and away.

Padraig takes his seat. He is, as always, dressed in the trademark white shirt and black trousers. This time, no mobiles, no wallet, no keys, bag or accounts book. Just the man himself. His expression cold yet focused.

"Don's been tellin' me of your wee problems, so he has. Would you like to fill me in on the details? You see, I don't think I've quite got the picture yet and I'm not a man who likes to be kept in the dark. Are you with me?"

"Yes, yes Padraig, with you all the way".

"Yer see, I'm not a vindictive man. I like to think I'm a fair man, so I do, but when it comes to business, Dean, especially when it comes to my money, well, it gets a little serious. I don't know what you do all day over there in London, but when a man plays games with my money, I like to keep tabs on him, so I do. Am I clear?"

Dean swallows rather hard, but this is, after all the second dressing down he's had in days and he's getting just a bit used to it.

"Good. I am fully informed as to what has gone on, Dean. Fully. I may look like a thick Paddy man from the old country, but I do have my contacts over there with you. One thing I will tell you is this. I have had what could be termed, 'domestic difficulties' within an organisation before. Sometimes, these things go undetected, until it is too late. Fortunately for you, it became simple to uncover what was going on in front of your very eyes in the form of this stupid and oafish man Rainsford. How is he in himself, these days? Don't answer that. You'll get your turn, so you will. Where you went wrong, Dean and this is the crux of the matter, is that you left unfinished business. You cannot do that in our line of work. You cannot teach people a lesson. They either catch themselves on, or they don't. Now, take you and me. I know all about you. You know feckin' nothing about me. Which gives me something of an advantage, does it not? Don't answer that. Before me is a man I know who did not finish what he had started. A man who did not control his soldiers until it was too late. You have my sympathies, Dean, so you do. How is your wife?"

"We've got our fingers crossed. Her and me partner, we're hopin' they're both gonna make it. She's still in a coma, but the brain scan's good".

"We will pray for her this Sunday at mass. I will get Therése to light a candle for her in the church, so I will. And the fella, your partner. He was the one who put the hit on this Freddie the Fixer, am I right? Anyway, the main thing is, we have to move on, Dean. I have to know. Are you a man who will make the same mistake again? You were given a big chance by your friend Mr Hall. We have been aware of him for some time now. Then he brings you. Gives you a good report. You come to see me, then we start to talk. I like you, Dean. I don't say that about many of the eejits who come into this fine establishment. For reasons known only to the man upstairs and meself, I am going to tell you something now. Your reaction to it will play a big part in my decision as to what to do with you. Twenty years ago, I was an impulsive young man. Much younger than you are now. I was involved with some very heavy people and working well for them. Making money for them too. Helping the cause, you might say. The trouble was, that I decided to get into a little private enterprise of me own. Stole a little time here, a little time there and soon, I had a thriving operation spread all over the Six Counties. From Dundalk to Derry and all points in between, I was the king of the weed. Worked with some of the best men in Dublin, so I did. Used the name of the boys to give meself a bit of clout, so I did. And when you did that, people used to sit up and they'd listen. Terrified they were. Wasn't a man stood in shoe leather who wouldn't listen when he heard those three little letters. As often happens with a man, a young man who finds himself in such a position, his head's for the turnin' and he becomes greedy. Not happy with a nice big cake, he wants the feckin' cream too. It wasn't long before news of me empire reached the powers that be and I was summoned to a meeting in Newry. There was just one thing that saved me. Two of the local command wanted it done there and then. Straight down Concession Road and in a ditch, just like they did with the bad boys from Dublin. Bullet in the back of the head. Bang. End of, as you say in London. But I was lucky, because one very powerful man from Belfast, he was lookin' at the idea of using the profits from the weed to fund the semtex. They'd always used the money from the fruit machines, the smokes and the whisky to fund such things, but never the puff. It was a little like the families in New York in the 1950s. Some wanted to get into the game, some didn't. Anyway, I was given a compromise. Get out that night and never come back or take me chances. I left the man me contacts and that was that. Now, Dean, as I said to you before, I'm not a stupid man. What would you have done?"

"I'd have fuckin' legged it, Padraig".

"You would have run, then?"

"Too right, mate. Me and the missus, we'd 'ave been in the motor and whoosh! Fuckin' wouldna' seen us no more".

"What was the line in that fillum? 'He chose wisely'. D'ya know the fillum, Dean?"

"Not into films. More Gina's thing, know what I'm sayin'?"

"'Twas the third fillum in the Indiana Jones trilogy. Sean Connery and Harrison Ford. Wonderful scene where he picks up the cup and it's the right one. A simple cup, the cup of a carpenter. The rest of the silly feckers have turned to dust. A simple cup, a simple choice. That's what you just made, Dean".

"I'm bleedin'glad, but what? What did I say?"

"You would have collected your wife. The woman who keeps yer goin', fella. We're nothing without them, Dean, nothing at all. Take my Thérése, for example. There is nothing I would not do for that woman. She's everything to me. I take her advice, run every blasted thing past her before decidin'. She said, 'ask the fella the question. You'll know the answer before he says it anyway'".

"Why don't she ever come 'ere? Your missus. I mean, my Gina, she don't come near the office. Wouldn't want her there. Wouldn't be right".

"She does, Dean, she does, but 'tis a very rare occasion. I never put pressure on her, she never puts pressure on me. That makes a marriage last. You've enough pressure as it is. When you get home, you need to get the pressure off, not add to it. I don't hold with any of that feminism. No feckin' way. There's no room for it in a proper marriage. Respect. *That's* what you need in a marriage, Dean. Respect and love. Anything else is a bonus, so it is".

This is absolutely the last thing that Dean expected. He sits quietly, contemplating what has been said. His arsehole is still going in and out like a starfish on sulphate, but as the morning sun begins to warm the terrace, he feels the life returning to his empty world.

*

At that precise moment, Gina wakes up in hospital, blinks and screams. There is no-one there. She cannot move. The sensation of terror begins to grow. Down the corridor, a monitor blinks and a warning bleep is emitted from under the screen. By the time the nurse enters Gina's room, her face is contorted with fear.

*

"Lead from the front, Dean. If you want to run your boys right, lead by example. We're all bad lads here, no-one's sayin' otherwise. When we're together, I'll have *no lies at the table*".

Dean shudders at the use of these words, the second time in as many weeks. He suddenly feels very, very small.

"They tell me you've become quite a user. Would a man be right in thinking that?"

"What do you mean, Padraig?"

"The charlie, Dean, the powder. *Mucha coca, valle*? You should stay off it. Affects a man's judgment, so it does".

"The shootin's given me a right knockback. I ain't touched the stuff in days, honest I ain't. This has given me a right reality check, I can tell you".

"Now, I've got to have a meeting about all this. The decision is mine and I've already made it. Do you understand what's happened here today?"

"All day long, Mister O'Riordan. Yes, I have".

"We've much to do, Dean. I want you to stay here 'till tomorrow, then you may go back to your family. You'll be with me. In the meantime, Ronan will drive you up to your house, so you can check on things. You'll take another coffee before you go. You look like you need one, so you do".

Padraig gets up from the table and walks to the stairwell, leaving Dean to his thoughts. He sits there, terrified yet relieved. He feels like a weight's gone off his shoulders, yet at the same time, fears the worst. There is a menace to Padraig that even Dean has never before experienced and his native sixth sense tells him to beware. If only he knew from which direction. Is it the calm before the storm?

Divide and rule, Padraig smiled to himself as he walked down the stairs and into the bar.

"Get yer man another coffee there, Ronan. He looks like he needs one. Less is more, cousin, less is definitely more. Once he's had it, take him to his house". He walks away and out into the sunny Plaza Colon, standing stock still for just a moment before wandering over to examine the fast maturing bougainvillea overhanging the white-washed wall. Tenderly, he picks at the dead flowers and removes them before returning to the warmth of Doolans.

Across the square, Meacher is still in the van.

"I think we've company, Ronan. How long's that van going to be deliverin' over there?"

"Declan here spotted that too", he said without looking up, gesturing towards a newly scrubbed freckly lad fresh from Monaghan.

"Good lad, Declan. Good lad. Ronan, make sure our guest leaves via the back door. We won't be wantin' anyone across the square getting too excited now, so we won't. It's Plan B now".

Padraig walked up the stairs to the first floor, to a small window which overlooked the vast square. He picked up a small pair of strong binoculars and trained them on the delivery van. He traversed up and down its side several times before putting them down again and returning to the bar.

"Ronan, would you make some coffee and send it over to yer man in the van? Poor bastard's been busy observing all morning, so he has. It must be hell in there".

"How do you know for sure, Uncle?"

"Have you ever seen a delivery van with small glass windows in the sides. Small *darkened* windows in the sides! Not very professional, if I say so meself!"

*

"I don't bloody believe it! He's only sent some bloody coffee to the van. What the hell am I going to do?" Gibbs is on the phone to his team leader whose tone, understandably, expresses despair at this unforeseen development.

"Well you can't flaming well stay there, can you? What's he going to do next, put on a fucking show for you? Get out of there, NOW!"

*

As the van pulled away, Padraig smiled, then quickly, his expression turned to one of concern.

"Ronan! I thought we'd seen the last of that lot? We don't even know who they are, but a pound says that it's the British. Just doesn't seem like a local operation to me".

"We ain't seen them in months. I thought we'd been let off the hook too. I've got the registration for yous".

"That's grand. I'll get it checked out with Pilar, see if it's one of theirs. If not, then we *know* who we're dealing with. And Ronan, how long is it since we had this place swept?"

"It was before Christmas, Uncle".

"We're getting' sloppy, so we are. Get it done again. Use that fella Felix recommended. He sounds like the dag's ballacks!"

"Right you are. In the meantime, do you still want me to take our friend upstairs home?"

"Not now, if they've got someone on the villa, it'll just bring the whole thing on top. Take him the back way, but take him down town, maybe to the *Internacional*. The fella there opens early for the staff and if you take him in the back way. I'll call Paco to pick him up from there and we'll rendezvous later. Take the coast road, not the motorway, up past the back of the airport and along the beach. The scenic route, so it is".

Ronan returns once more to find Dean looking out to sea over the wall.

"You'll not be thinkin' about jumpin' now are yous?" Ronan's normal jovial expression has returned now. Dean spins round and smiles.

"You surprised me there, Ronan. I was fuckin' miles away".

"You will be in a minute, Mr Bold. There's been a slight change of plan, due to operational difficulties! We had some unwanted company and we think it's best if you're not in the vicinity of this place for a while. We'll be off to Alicante and we'll see Mr O later. I think you know Paco from the last time?"

"Oh, yes, mate, I know Paco alright. We're not going back to that bleedin' club again are we?" As the words leave Dean's mouth, he knows exactly where they are going.

"Better put me Ray Bans on, then! Don't want no-one recognisin' me!"

He follows Ronan down the narrow stairs and out into the back yard. They climb into a white Seat and Dean goes straight into in the back, lying flat across the seats. Usual thing.

"Keep your head down, Mr Bold. There's some crafty people about these days". He revs up the Seat and they're away, round the back of the restaurant and onto the strip. Couple of quick turns and back doubles and they're away up towards Orihuela and Alicante. Ronan's making good progress, but that won't make any difference to the newly fitted tracker which sits just underneath the offside rear wheel arch. Two miles behind, Emily Loader and Andy Meacher sit in the front seat of a specially fitted right hand drive Vauxhall Vectra. In place of the satnav, there is a map showing the precise location of the white Seat up ahead.

"This is a right result. I don't know who they've got in that car, but after this morning's fiasco with the van, something's got to give. Where the hell is he going at this time of the morning anyway?"

"Wherever it is, he wants to be there double quick. I just hope he doesn't get caught by the Guardia! That'll really bugger things up".

"Surely lightening can't strike twice in one day?"

"Have you heard the rumours about Kim?"

"I heard she and Rick had fallen out over some obs timings?"

"Bit more than that. She left her phone on the desk in the office and when it rang, I picked it up and there was a photo of her and Rick in bed on it".

"What? And you just *happened to find it* did you? You sneaky cow, looking at a colleague's phone like that".

"Weatherall told me to do it. Apparently, they've been watching her for a while. Reckon she could compromise the operation?"

"That's outrageous, Em. Kim's a really good officer".

"Good enough to go to bed with a colleague?"

"For God's sake. It wouldn't be the first time. What are you, some kind of prude or something?"

"Just trying to protect the integrity of the operation, that's all".

"*Just trying to protect…* blahdee blahdee blah! You wanker! Get a fuckin' life. You're turning into one of Weatherall's fuckin' lesbian robots".

"Where the hell did that come from? Take that back, this minute. I'm not standing for that. Not now. Not ever".

"Sorry, Em. Just got a bit carried away. You do see my point though. If you can't have any privacy, whats the point?"

"I don't think it's really on having sexy pictures on a service phone, do you?"

"I guess not. So there's nothing wrong with sexy pictures then?" He grinned at her, sticking his tongue out lasciviously.

"What is it with you? Too much sun? Down boy…this instant!"

The journey continued in a more restrained fashion, changing only when they hit the backstreets of Alicante port and lost the Seat completely, having it return to the screens moments later as they reached a main avenue. Turning into Avenida Loring they spotted the Seat disgorging its human cargo in the form of Dean Bold outside the *Club Internacional*. The camera began to do its work as they drove past and then he was gone, deep into the darkened club.

"What do we do now? Should we hang around here, or head back? Trouble is that now the Seat's gone, we don't really know what we're looking for".

"I'm for staying on this side of the street and seeing who pitches up. Just drive down to the end and turn round. We'll park there and pretend we're tourists".

The car moves ever so slowly along the *Avenida*, acquiring just a little attention from impatient locals, turns round at the roundabout and crawls back up, parking twenty metres beyond the club's main entrance. The avenue is crowded with morning shoppers milling to and fro and the car draws up totally unnoticed. Inside the club, Dean is met by the manager who escorts him to the rear.

"*Queres algo a tomar, señor?*"

"Whassat, mate?"

"To drink, sir, what would you like to drink? Some coffee? Perhaps a little brandy? It is the time".

"Blindin', yeah, brandy. I could do with one after that!"

As the manager disappears, Dean takes a wander around the empty club. There is a starkness to nightclubs during the day. If you've never been in one, it's like a kind of film set. Black walls, tawdry, cheap stained furniture, beer and winesticky floor, a thousand nights of cigarette butts, sweaty leather, chromium plated poles on the stage still marked with the previous night's action, tiny booths filled with God knows what. With the house lights up, clubs are garish and dirty, foul smelling and worn. Take yourself back to the buzz of Paco and Sandwich with the girls. Same place, another time, just like life. Only thing that's different is the day and the time. As he wanders the dance floor, Padraig is on the mobile back at Doolans.

"Yeah, we've got company, so we have. Don't know what we're gonna do this time. We've got to have this meeting today. It calls for something of a diversion, I think. A piece of South Armagh comes to the Costa Blanca. Yeah. Bold's gone to Alicante with Ronan, but he's coming back here, so he is. Leave it to me. It's time to have some fun at the expense of Her Majesty's feckin' Customs and Excise. I'll call yous". *Click.*

So, there you have it. *That's* what you can do with unlimited funds and a good sense of humour.

The manager came out again from the kitchen, armed with coffee and a new bottle of Carlos Primero.

"My name is also Carlos. Like the brandy. Carlos Silva. I am very pleased to know you".

"Dean Bold, mate. Likewise".

"You will stay here with me and then someone will come for you. I think there is some kind of problem. Please do not tell me. I just want to help, that is all".

"Blindin' service, this".

"Señor Reyes, he is a very generous man. He tells me to look after you, I look after you. He tells me to kill you, I kill you!" He lets rip with a gale of laughter and hits Dean so hard on the back that he spits out the coffee all over the table. More laughter from Carlos and it looks like things are turning out OK. Dean's relief at what happened, or didn't happen earlier has made him keener than ever to hit the brandy hard and he does so. Carlos watches him, amused.

"You must come to my club sometime, Dean!"

I've been here before, mate. You just don't recognise me!

"I think maybe you come with Señor Paco and Señor Reyes?" he continues. Señor Paco. Everyone, but everyone calls him that. From Alicante to Valencia and all points in between. He's a bit like Big John down Covent Garden Market. Now you'd think there might just be more than one 'Big John', but no. Just try asking for 'Big John' the next time you're over there around four a.m. They'll know who you mean. Some people are just larger than life. *It's the way it is.*

Now Felix, he's another kettle of fish. Señor Reyes. Alberto Felix Reyes. Sandwich. He's one name to some and all names to others. Just depends on the scenery. The girls all know him as Sandwich. *Bocadillo.* They know that if he's only with one girl, then there is a little vacancy on the other arm, and later on, when the money shows up, he'll be looking for some nice little *honeypot* to give it to. Two dollops of honey to go with his bacon.

The phone rings once more. It's Padraig again. He asks for Dean to be put on.

"Yeah. Yeah, blindin'. What a blindin' geezer. Thanks for sortin' this. What's that? Yeah. OK. I'll be waitin'. Yeah, back door. Yeah, I'll tell him". *Click.*

"He says you've got to go out the front, look up and down the street, come back in and take one of your boys, wearing my coat up the coast to Beni. Yeah, Benidorm. Make sure he keeps 'is head down".

"What will happen to you?"

"They're sendin' someone to the back door an' he'll take me from 'ere. You take your time going up the coast. When you get to Beni, leave the coat in the car and the pair of you just go into a bar. Make sure they see you, yeah?"

"I think the coat is your idea, yes?"

"How did you guess that?"

"I think you like the wind-up!"

"We better get on with it, then. Chop,chop."

Dean drains the brandy, necks down the last of the thick, black coffee and hands his long leather coat to Carlos. Slowly and deliberately, he walks from the darkened club and out into the bright winter sunshine, looking this way and that. He cannot see the car, but makes like he's checking the whole street out. He comes back in, by which time, the barman is dressed in Dean's coat.

"Look after it, bruv", he laughs, knowing that it will never be seen again. They leave via the front door and Dean slips out the back into an anonymous white Seat taxi. Once more, he lies down across the seats and waits to be driven away. Out in the street, the plan looks like it's worked and as Carlos' Blue 300SL draws away, a British registered hatchback follows suit, pulling into traffic two cars behind.

In Torrevieja, Padraig's plans are going into action. Up at the Villa

Therése, car after car after car is arriving at the gate. Out step around twenty ladies from the Torrevieja Irish Catholic Women's Group, hats on, dressed up to the nines for one of Therése O'Riordan's impromptu charity mornings. Miss them and die. Literally. The camera across the way is running hot, clicking on and off faster than an X-rated peep show flap. With each car, the warning light goes off down in town and it's already come to the attention of London control. They decide to take another car up to see what's happening, and when it arrives, they just cannot believe the news. First the car going into Alicante and now this. Next, Declan the barman leaves Doolans via the front door and takes a walk across the square to get some cigarettes from the newspaper shop. As he walks back, he darts down an alley and onto a small Vespa parked next to Doolans' dustbins. A swift kick and the moped zooms out of the alley and into the Plaza, haring off up the street and into the Avenida. The control centre at the Hotel Europa's going mad now, there's phones going off, lights flashing and a report coming in from Alicante to say that the man from the Seat is now travelling up the coast towards Benidorm and Calpe, with Meacher and Loader in hot pursuit. At this precise moment, the pad on the lawns of the Hotel Esmeralda receives a visit from a small, but perfectly formed helicopter, complete with Felix Reyes at the controls, where he is joined by Marianna Benitez da Sancha and a heavily disguised Pilar Estravados-Lopez, complete with fur coat and Chanel sunglasses. The assigned observer comes running out of the hotel, having been watching the coffee lounge for the whole morning, just taking his eyes off them for a moment as one of Padraig's famous 'South Armagh' moments takes place, in the form of a huge Irish labourer spilling twenty Euro notes all over the foyer. The ensuing pandemonium ensures that the girls have made a safe getaway. They smile down at the hapless pursuer through the cockpit bubble, before Felix expertly turns the 'copter away and out to sea. The coup de grace is issued by Padraig himself as he walks nonchalantly down from the terrace, across the strip and onto the white sandy beach. Jésus the Jet-Ski is looking bored as he fires up the midnight blue Sea-Doo . The big man strolls towards him, handing him his shoes, walking straight into the shimmering Mediterranean and climbing onto the spitting beauty, trademark black trousers and white shirt flapping in the midday breeze. He opens up the throttle and pulls away, leaving the one remaining member of the team standing gobsmacked on the beach, a resigned looking Señor Jet-Ski explaining dejectedly that all his other machines are *kaput*.

*

Just at *this* moment, Declan has started up the boat in the marina. The observation car is pulling out, having been ordered by the control centre to withdraw back to Doolans, via the Villa Therése. It arrives in the narrow lane in perfect time to be boxed in by a 1960s Mark 10 Jaguar containing a very large and very grand lady wearing an enormous hat, who is not amused to have her arrival eclipsed by this interruption. As the remaining ladies from the Torrevieja Irish Catholic Women's Group come to see what the fuss is about, Rick Gibbs' mobile rings. It is the control centre, wondering where he is and what is going on. The language is unrepeatable. Well, almost.

"What the *fuck* are you doing trapped in a lane? It's all kicking off down here in town. They're up to something, we've been spotted and now they're just taking the fuckin' piss! Meacher and Loader have chased up the coast towards Benidorm, they're following this morning's arrival. Looks like they're the only ones who are actually *doing* anything! Get out of the fuckin' lane and get back to the Europa. Fucking now!"

Mark 10 Jag woman is standing in the road having an animated conversation with her hostess, who has now come out of the house, down the driveway and into the road. She is totally clued up as to what is going down and out of the corner of her eye, spots Gibbs going ballistic in the sweaty little car.

"Don't look now, Mary, but there's a man in the car behind yous and I don't think he'll be wanting any of me coffee the morning!"

*

Ronan has the boat's diesel engines idling some four hundred metres off the beach now, the Jet-Ski is loaded on the back and the helicopter has already deposited its cargo on the tip of La Manga del Mar Menor, ready to be picked up in a few minutes by the careful Ronan. Padraig is below with a very surprised and slightly wet Dean.

"Yous'll be meetin' the others soon. Very soon".

A surge of raw power travels through the boat's infrastructure and Dean feels it rise up almost out of the water. Already, the white horses are forming in its wake and soon they are away and at the tip of La Manga, collecting the valuable cargo before disappearing from shore view. There is an atmosphere of sheer excitement, the adrenaline pumping overtime through their bodies. Marianna is visibly elated, flushed with the apparent ease of their getaway. Now they are all assembled in the huge cabin, eyeing each other like dogs in a park. It's intro time and Padraig makes a point of starting with the errant Dean. Present at the meeting are Dean, Padraig, Ronan-though only really as a trusted spectator, Marianna, Paco, the heavily disguised Pilar and Beevers.

"He'll not be the prodigal son returning, but he's explained himself to me, so he has". Dean sits just to Padraig's left, Ronan to his right. The boat is stopped now, crystal blue water lapping gently against its gleaming hull. The others eye him with a mixture of suspicion and curiosity. Padraig is not given to this kind of behaviour.

"The opportunities in London are growing by the day. There is a new kind of punter in the marketplace now. There's over a million regular users in the UK now, so there are. *One million*! That is one feckin' big payday for whoever wants to seize the day and it is time that we were those people. Marianna, you are certain now that we have the supply? No more problems with Mr Montoya?"

"The old fox will never show his hand, Padraig, but I am satisfied that he is prepared to continue with our plans. As you know, I am due to visit Venezuela again in ten days, during which time we will have many meetings. There are things to discuss, but most importantly, by then, we will know what to expect in the way of business from *this man*". She fixes Dean with a hard stare, but there is warmth creeping through. He is an unknown to her. She is intrigued. She is also highly aroused, fidgety, fingers playing with her glossy mane, eyelashes flickering.

"Don, you two will meet in Liverpool".

"Okay, mate. The warehouse situation in Bootle is sorted. It's used as a bond, not a wet bond, but T1 goods, that sort of thing. Lot of gear from the Middle East. Trucks in and out all the time. Scallys all onside, know what's good for them".

"Dean, you will exchange numbers with Mr Beevers here. I don't even need to tell you to be discreet".

"We're usin' the cover of the Liverpool v Hammers game. Town and I are goin'. Travellin' up on the official train from Euston. Leave the rest to us, Mr O. If the church is watchin', they ain't gonna be there!"

"Marianna, how soon before you and your lovely colleague are ready with the deep sea contract?"

"As you know, tomorrow we have a rather unexpected visit from a strange quarter, in the form of *Miss* Weatherall from British Customs. Whatever she is doing, it is some kind of covert operation. Not even my contacts at the British FLO knew about it and believe me, if they know, *I* know!"

"And how much does *she* know? Pilar, you must find out!" Beevers natural suspicion of authority spits through gritted teeth.

"She is a very ambitious woman, not afraid to break some eggs, of that I am sure. I believe that she is running a well-funded and high-level operation. My contact wasn't really able to reveal much to me, but it is what she didn't say that should be of concern to us. What I don't believe, however, is that her visit to us is properly sanctioned. Her ambition is getting the better of her and I believe that we could take advantage of that. She has certainly no suspicions about our set-up, though I believe that she is probably behind the surveillance which has been annoying us for some time now".

"Is this bit of work on top, or what? I don't like the fuckin' sound of this one bit!" Beevers stared her out. "It sounds to me like the fuckin' doors'll be comin' in right soon".

"I don't think so, Don. I will tell you why. Number One. They don't know where this is coming from. Number Two. The British *never* ask for help if they don't need it. You know how secretive they are. She may have a big jigsaw to play with here, but many of the parts, they are missing. I think we will give her some nice pieces to play with. Her problem is that she will not realise they are from another puzzle!"

*

As Benissa and her brother arrive at the intensive care reception desk, they are met by a smiling ward sister. Even Troy's embarrassment at being hauled out of class, in his school uniform by his inappropriately dressed sister seems to wane as she escorts them to their mother's observation window. Despite her heavily bandaged face, her eyes say it all.

"Can we go in, Miss? Can we?"

"Is she gonna be OK?"

"Just for a minute?"

"Of course you can. Before we do though, I have to tell you this. Your Mum is a very poorly lady. It's going to be quite a while before she is allowed out of this room. When is your Dad coming in next? Is it tonight?"

An uncomfortable silence began to envelop both Benissa and Troy. Their heads down, their eyes averted.

Finally, Benissa looks up, "He's away. Away on business. Urgent stuff. He'll be back tomorrow".

"Well, Benissa, I think it would be nice if it came from you that your Mum's awake. Why don't you ring your Dad when you leave here? Better not use your mobile in here. The Staff Sister goes mental!"

"Yeah, OK. Troy, you can ring him. You ain't spoken to Dad this week".

"That is because he's never there". Eyes still fixed on the highly polished floor. Troy's embarrassment is restored.

*

"Ma'am. I think you may want to take this call. It's Watchtower Three".

Weatherall grabbed the handset from the outstretched arm of her Observations Assistant.

"Yes, Janet Weatherall. Who is this? Ah, Rick. What do you have for me? WHAT? You *lost them*? You fucking incompetent. How can you lose them? There? There of all places? I mean, where can they go? What did they do? Disappear into thin fucking air? Right. You are to return to Echo Two and……" Her voice trailed away as the full extent of the debacle began to unfold in her mind. *Observations compromised. Camera van no longer usable. Coffee brought out from Doolans. Jet-Ski.* She put the still live 'phone down on the desk and stared out of the window. In the background, Rick Gibbs' voice was faintly discernible over the noise from the adjacent operations room, but she had long since switched him off. If looks could kill……………. With Rick still talking on the 'phone, she picked up her briefcase and stormed out of the office, down the stairs, into her car and away. She had plans to make for tomorrow.

*

"For now, I suggest it's business as usual. Today should have taught us some lessons, so it should. We can expect some increased traffic at the restaurant. Probably going to need some activity which leads nowhere. Few false trails, like. I've invested too much in this for it to fall flat on its airse at the first feckin' fence. The sooner we get the deep sea operation up an' runnin', the better. Talkin' of which, how's Plan B doin'?"

He raises his head to look directly at Paco.

"That is really for Señor Reyes to bring us up to date, but as far as I know, we are very close to having everything ready. The *Compagnia* is in financial trouble and they have no choice but to co-operate. This way, they get a re-financing package which allows them to trade their precious commodity and we have what *we* need!"

O'Riordan's face lights up. "This really appeals to me, so it does. It appeals to what you call the *rebel* in us all, Paco. I would give a lot to see that working! And to have Her Majesty's finest doing the donkey work……..it's enough to give a man the horn, so it is. 'Tis a great shame we have to start before that's all in place".

"If we do not, Señor Padraig, then we lose the will of the cartel. Without their support……."

"I know…I know. Just a little flight of fancy, so it was. Where's your sense of humour, girl?" He winks lasciviously at Pilar, before his expression returns to its usual impassive state.

"Then we return? There is much to do". Paco is already on his feet and motioning Ronan to begin the return journey.

Dean's silence is deliberate. He barely conceals his delight at the way the meeting has gone, yet he knows that to show out in front of this select gathering would be an act which would come back to haunt him. Very soon.

No more slip-ups. He knows it.

Chapter Twenty Six

Aeropuerto El Altet Alicante

Passing through passport control always gave Janet Weatherall just that little frisson of power. No-one, but no-one was going to stop *her*. The fury of yesterday and its accompanying loss of composure was gone. Adjusting tortoiseshell sunglasses up into her short cropped hair she strode through throngs of tourists grouped in the crowded luggage hall towards the exit. Hundreds of budget airline passengers fighting to be first in the queue for hired cars downstairs further blocked her way before she was eventually able to break free, her black trouser suit seeming somewhat out of place amongst the shiny tracksuits and mini skirts of the Brits; Hermés scarf setting her even further apart from fellow travellers.

The glass doors opened automatically as, amongst the first, she walked out into the public area, scanning the sea of faces for an all-important taxi board. After a short while, she saw her name, albeit spelt nothing like the original.

She walked towards it, smiling a very forced and artificial smile. The smile of deceit. As she neared the placard holding man, she thrust her hand in his general direction, shouting,

"Janet Weatherall. Her Majesty's Revenue and Customs. I am delighted to meet you".

"*Encantado, Señora*. Juan Cordero. Taxi driver. At your service".

Her face was a study. All the bravado gone in a second, to be replaced by snorting fury. A taxi driver?

"Well you can carry my bag then". She just carried on walking, the now dutiful Juan following on behind, somewhat perplexed at her change in attitude.

The journey into Alicante port was silent, punctuated only by the *Click, Click* of Weatherall's mobile as she became increasingly frustrated by the lack of signal and coverage, which was further compounded by the constant ringing of Juan's phone.

Eventually, after the bemused taxi driver's rather skilful route into the bustling port had taken them round the ring road three times, they arrived outside the headquarters of the *Aduana Nacional*.

"*Muchas graçias*, that will be twenty-five Euro, please". By then, Weatherall's face was contorted into some kind of mask, having endured the pleasure of Juan's lack of air-conditioning. Not that it wasn't there, you understand. It just wasn't switched on. '*Kaputt*', as Juan-Bautista Hernandes-Cordero liked to say. When there was nothing wrong with it, that is.

She marched into reception like a blue-stocking mother arriving late to collect her child from the Hampstead Montessori. All long skirt and ten to two walk. Scary? I should co-co.

"Hello! My name is *Janet Weatherall* and *I* am here to see Pilar Estravados, *please*!" You don't mess with *that* tone of voice.

"Jess. Good afterrrnooon, Señora Weatherall. We have been expecting joo. Did joo have a gooood flight todayee?"

"The flight is of no concern. I am hot and tired. Is *Señora Estravados* here?"

"But of course, Señora. She is waiting for joo in thee boardroom. You are our very *h*onoured guest today!" She beams one of those big smiles, which takes Weatherall completely by surprise.

"But first, please to sign here and take the badge. It is for the security. Could I see joo passport please?" Hissing like a snake.

This is just too much, but what can she do? After a swift rummage in her handbag, it's out and on the counter.

"Thank you. Now please go to thee third floor. I am very sorry, but thee lift is broken today. Thee stairs are over there".

"Right, fine. Okay then. But can I *please* leave my bag here at least?"

"Jess. Of course. We will have to send it to be scanned, but joo will have it when you leave. Is this OK for joo?"

"Yes. Yes. It's fine. Now please can I go?"

"Jess. Thee stairs are over there. Thank you and please have a nice day". Metaphorical smoke billowed from her ears as she attempted the three flights to Pilar's office.

Eventually, she arrived at another reception desk, somewhat lower than that downstairs, but manned nevertheless by an equally charming girl. I guess it's time for the barriers to come down a little. A bit like an endurance test. It gets better the further you go on.

"Gooood afterrrnoooon. Are joo Mrs Weatherall?"

"It's *Ms*! *Ms* Weatherall, please!"

"Whatver joo want, *Mzzz* Weatherall. La Señora Estravados-Lopez is just coming now for joo. Please take a seat". She pointed to an uncomfortable but chic looking sofa across from the desk, flanked by some rather exotic looking plants. Just as she sat down, a door opened at the end of the corridor and out stepped a very glamorous if slightly windswept Pilar, lipstick not on quite straight, almost imperceptible to the naked eye, well, the naked *male* eye, that is. Weatherall looked her up and down, before they shook hands and moved to the large open office at the end.

"I have booked the boardroom for us first. I thought we could have a small meeting there and if you like, I can show you around the building. Show you what we do over here, how we do things. That sort of stuff".

Pilar's command of the vernacular shocks Weatherall. "You speak excellent English, Señora Estravados. Where did you learn it?"

"You are so kind. But please, call me Pilar. When all is said and done, we are now colleagues together, no? I learned your beautiful language in London, before coming to work for the bureau. I had an English boyfriend. When I was au-pair? I lived in London and Windsor. Such a nice town. I worked too. In a restaurant there. Very nice. Perhaps you know Windsor?" Making up for lost time, she realised the Weatherall ice was starting to melt.

"I am afraid that you have the advantage of me. I don't know it".

"But do you know Spain, Señora Weatherall? Or are you here to find out a little more about us?"

"Please, you must call me Janet. I am here to discuss some delicate matters with you, Pilar. Matters which could affect both our countries!"

Beneath the desk where Pilar is sitting, tiny LEDs danced magically with the rise and fall of the two women's voices.

"I am fascinated. I must say fascinated at the way you have approached us. It is most unusual for someone as high ranking as yourself to come here at such short notice and not via the normal channels and protocols. However, I am intrigued by the way you have done this and maybe in the future, we can be of assistance to you. If, of course, that is what you want".

"I had rather hoped that it would be a little sooner than the future, Pilar. I had hope that you would be able to assist us right now! You see, we are currently involved in the surveillance and monitoring of certain individuals based in Europe. They are people in whom we have maintained an interest for some time and there is one particular person who resides within your jurisdiction right here in Alicante province. In Torrevieja to be precise. I do not know if your department have made you aware, but there has been a low-key UK operation running over there for some time now".

"Drugs or money laundering?"

"For now, we believe that it is solely drugs on your patch. It is our belief that the laundering is taking place elsewhere. We have been watching a bar called Doolans".

Not a flicker.

"Ah, yes, my headquarters in Madrid has made me aware of this operation. In fact, I have met Señor Stubbins. A very nice man. He came to see the four officers you have working here, no?"

So far so good, Janet. She doesn't know about the other twelve.

"Are you yourselves aware of Mr O'Riordan? I mean, has he come up on your radar at all?"

"We are naturally interested in all matters which occur in our region, Janet. However, at the moment, we are very interested in matters here at the *Aeropuerto*. Our intelligence suggests that a major gang is trying to establish permanent cargo routes into Spain via El Altet. You will appreciate that over the past few years, we have experienced an unprecedented growth in foreign nationals moving to the Costas. They have brought their lives with them, including the darker side. We have the Chinese, the Russians, the Albanians and our old friends the Latinos from South America. All living right under the nose here. They too wish to establish business and they have much money with which to bribe the officials. *That*, Janet, is what we have to face here. Only last week, we made arrests in Calpe and confiscated over three million Euros in cash, four hundred and seventy DVD recorders and a large quantity of heroin. All from the Chinese. All from restaurant connections. And all the time they are here, they make much money but bring us much problems. This year, we have had our first Chinese on Chinese murder. There will be many more as they fight for turf rights. All the time this is going on, the Russians build more and more blocks of flats, hotels, marinas. Oh, yes, of course it looks very fine on the postcards, but is anyone going to do anything about the corruption? I don't think so".

"Wow! That was quite a history lesson".

"History, no, Janet. Current affairs, yes. We are living in the present here. Be in no doubt of that. If you are here tonight, I take you to dinner. You will see for yourself".

"I look forward to that. But what I really look forward to is some results on the Torrevieja front. We are certain that O'Riordan has been supplying the UK for some time now, using mainly his old Irish connections".

"Certain, Janet? That is a very strong word! Your sources must be very good".

"They are. We are trying to ascertain, following some recent intelligence in London, exactly how he is getting his trucks loaded and from where the goods are coming. It is our belief that the cocaine is coming here, maybe via one of the traditional routes, but the quality is very high. It is that which has us rather perplexed at Custom House, I have to admit. It is very different from the usual cut once, cut many times fare which normally hits our streets. Have you been experiencing such seizures here?"

"As you know, cocaine is not such a popular drug in Spain, with the exception of the Costa del Sol. However, that may well change with the influx from Russia. I understand it is the drug of choice now in Moscow and St Petersburg. Until recently, we are mainly concerned with heroin and marijuana".

"But surely you must be interested in being prepared for the worst?"

"Of course, but like you, we are very restricted as to resources. We just don't have the manpower to cover all the angles. However, it *is* possible that your problem is emanating from activities at El Altet. We have many more direct flights now and on top of that, the hourly arrivals from Madrid bring new issues. We have a big problem with immigration from South America. They don't just stop in Madrid any more. They know about the Costas and the work which we have here in construction. There are also the pickpockets, the gangs".

"But these are not all problems for Customs? Surely you have your other enforcement agencies?"

"Naturally, but over here, we like to work alongside each other, in harmony, rather than secretly. We do not have a culture of secrecy the same as you do in England", Pilar smiled.

Weatherall visibly bristled at this thinly veiled reproach.

"Hmm. Anyway, I have brought one recent report for you to look at. Perhaps that could wait until later?"

"I would like that. For now, let me show you around, I think perhaps you would like to meet my colleagues who are involved with the airport operation?"

"If you think that is a good idea, then let's do it!" Weatherall is already on her feet, sensible shoes ready for action. Pilar gave the receptionist an effusive '*¡Hasta!*', then led Weatherall down the stairs to the car park and her Seat Ibiza.

"It is just a short drive from here to our operations office in the port. We will talk with the team leader who is co-ordinating operations with our colleagues in Bogotá. We have good intelligence over there, but sometimes, the intelligence, it dries up.

Then we find our operatives with their heads and hands removed, floating in the river, no? Then we start again. It is an amazing thing, the risks people will take, don't you think, Janet. The risks for such a small reward".

"I think life is rather cheap over there, isn't it?"

"Life is always cheap in that world. And however cheap it becomes, there is always someone for whom the price is right. Greed is a terrible thing. It makes people do very stupid things. Shall we go to the port?"

"I am in your hands, Pilar. Totally in your hands".

*

Leaving the office by the rear entrance, they walked across the deserted railway sidings and between the port's shadowy buildings, unseen eyes watching, waiting. After all, who watches the watchers? A mile away in the town, a mobile phone rang.

"We have her in sight now. You are quite correct, she has someone with her. She looks like an English. Yes. Terrible clothes. I think that she is doing the job very well. The English is very serious. She is being led away from the area. Do not be alarmed. It seems that our lady is a professional. The *princesa* was right! OK." *Click.*

*

"So, this is where we co-ordinate our sea based operations, Janet. Historically, like you we are a maritime nation, so all importations are controlled and headed up by the *Aduanas Marítimo* even if they are to do with the airport. Our main operations centres are here and at Cadiz, Barcelona, that kind of thing. We see that the future of drug trafficking will take two forms, one in bulk by sea and the higher value stuff to come in by air. Control of the airports is crucial to both their success and ours. Whoever has control there, wins the game. It is as simple as that. I think that you have many, shall we say, *difficulties* at London Airport, no?"

Again, Janet Weatherall bristled with hurt, then let it pass. Her enthusiasm for information took precedence, besides which she was thrilled at last to be part of some real international cooperation.

"Our island status makes us very attractive to drug importers. That and the dramatic increase in cocaine use in the UK over the past ten years. We estimate over two million active users! That is five billion pounds per year profit for the cartels".

"Can you imagine the tax revenues on that, were it to be legalised by our politicians?" Pilar again smiled, this time with curiosity attached.

"That could never be. We would simply never allow it. We have always had a policy of prevention in the UK. Detection and prevention. Sentencing for trafficking in the UK is getting higher and higher. They are getting thirty years now".

"Yet still every year there are more and more prepared to take those risks, just like our friends in Bogotá, no?"

"We are committed to this, whatever the result. We must send out a strong message, the strongest possible to these people. They must know that we mean business!"

She became aware that they had been surreptitiously joined by a heavily moustached and rounded man, standing almost to attention.

"Hmm. Janet, please may I introduce you to my colleague in the Air Department, Señor Fernando Toro. Ms Weatherall is on a visit here from London, as I explained to you".

"¡Encantado, Señora! Please, come to my office. It is more comfortable there, no?"

Toro's serious expression did not drop until they were safely ensconced behind closed doors.

"Fernando, I would like you to explain an outline of what we have discovered concerning the arrivals of cocaine from South America, please. Ms Weatherall, er Janet, has come to find out what we can help her with regarding the onward shipment from Spain to the UK".

"Very good! Please, some coffee. Juanita will serve you. Now, to business. We have discovered from our sources in Colombia that new air routes are being opened up in preference to the traditional sea channels which your Royal Navy, in conjunction with our fast boats from the *Islas Canarias* have become very good at disrupting. It is true that when they get one through, the profit for them is huge, but they cannot afford too many hundred million dollar seizures. Already there are rumours of murders relating to these seizures. Informants, betrayals, tip-offs. The cartels are starting to fight each other, which is very good for us, no?" For the first time, he broke into a smile. The tape recorder in Pilar's handbag missed only this.

"Yes, it is true that the Royal Navy is playing a big part in the seizure of drugs" replied Weatherall. "What we do not get from those successes, is to find out where it was going in the UK. There are powerful principals behind these deals, people we would love to put out of business for a very long time. For ever, if we could". Her fingers are drumming impatiently on the arms of her chair.

"Yes, this is true, but these operations take a lot of time and resources. Has your government changed its mind about the allocation of such monies to you?" interjected Pilar, anxious to unnerve the abrupt Janet.

"Let us say that there has been a recent change of heart". A self-satisfied smugness surrounded Weatherall now.

"So you enjoy the full support of your Prime Minister. That is good!" replied Pilar, comforted by the gentle vibration of the tiny tape recorder against her elegant stockinged calf. "If only we could have the same support from Madrid, eh Nando?"

The corpulent Customs man nodded and with furrowed brow turned to Janet,

"Is it your intention to propose a joint venture with our airport discoveries embedded within it, Señora Weatherall?"

"Janet, please. We are all friends here".

"Janet. OK. Well, Janet, you see if you have the kind of resources which you say you have, then we may be in a position to request of our authorities the same. Do you think this possible, chief?" he raised his considerable eyebrows towards Pilar.

If looks could kill.

"This is indeed an ideal world you speak of, Nando. Of course we would welcome this, but I feel that our two governments are still some way off *this* level of co-operation, don't you think, Janet?"

"Indeed, indeed. That is probably true, though my aims throughout these kind of negotiations are always to foster stronger and better communication between *all* the detection and prosecuting authorities in the EEC. We are, after all, part of one big happy family, are we not?"

"Yes, but that works better for some than for others. Your own Customs & Excise have not been known to be overly helpful with reciprocal requests, no? I think you call it the 'one way traffic?"

Yet again, Weatherall smarted from the sting of Pilar's latest barb.

"Hmm. Traditionally, we, as an importing nation, we have been the ones requesting help from Europe, not the other way around. We are still putting systems in place for such mutual understanding and co-operation!"

"Anyway, that is not what we are here to talk about, no? You want to know what we have on some individuals, I have no doubt".

"You are correct in that, Pilar, certainly. Our intelligence tells us that there is a large scale smuggling gang operating in this area and that they are intending to continue, indeed step up their activities. The report I mentioned to you earlier is here. Perhaps you would both like to see it?"

Pilar and Fernando's surprise at this approach is self-evident.

"I think we should not be disturbed. Nando, please see to it that no-one comes in".

"Of course. No-one".

He drew the blinds across the large window facing the communal area and guided them to a round table situated at the far end of his office.

"Is this comfortable for you? I hope so".

Weatherall removed the folder from her capacious handbag and spreaded out the report on the desk, together with some photographs and observation logs.

"I consider this to be at present a highly covert operation. We are still unsure of where it will lead, but one thing we are certain of is that the main players are serious and well-financed. Here is the chemist's analysis of what has been turning up on the streets in London and Birmingham. I think you will be surprised".

She hands out sheets to each of them, with graphs and detailed chemical formulae.

"The cocaine is 92% proof, what they call 'Mother of Pearl', in the trade. We have not seen this kind of powder in London for years, maybe never. It is highly unusual to find any kind of uncut Class 'A' in any case, but to find this is, well, it is unprecedented. We were very fortunate to intercept this package. It came to us from an informant and if you look closely at the photograph, you will see that it still carries the stamp of the cartel which produced it. You see, this is some find!"

"Of that you are surely right. An informant, you say? And he just gave you a whole kilo like that? You have some strong informants, that I can say".

"He is, we believe, a disaffected member of a gang who has been cut out of his traditional markets. It is the first time he has come to us. The curious factor to this is that we do not believe the importers of this particular shipment to be an old established gang. Quite the opposite, in fact. This carries all the hallmarks of newness. Our network of informants has come up with nothing. Nothing at all!"

"And what do you know of this new gang? How much has your 'new informant told you'? Is there anything that we can do here?" Pilar's curiosity almost got the better of her at that moment and it took all her training and powers of self-control to keep her mind in check.

"He is being very cautious so far. We do not wish to push him into going to ground, or worse, giving his position away to his bosses.

Oh, no. For now, he is just Zulu 21. We have him under observation by a separate team to that which is under my direct control, so as not to breach any security issues which may exist on our side".

"What is your time scale on this operation in Spain, Janet? I think you said that you had four officers operating here under the Mutual Assistance Directive? I know from our records that they have been here for some time……over three months, I think?"

"Yes. Yes, that's correct. The four officers in question have been based in Alicante and Torrevieja since August, since the first piece of intelligence pointed to a road based importation centre in this region".

"Three months! That is indeed a long time for an observation of this kind. We would like that kind of financial support, eh Nando?"

Pilar's obvious enjoyment of Janet's explanations and general discomfort had her manoeuvring around in the leather chair. In doing this, she became aware of the English woman staring for just one nanosecond too long at the glossy sheen of her newly crossed legs bathed in the autumn sunlight. *Oh, really! What do we have here?* Now, she's having a ball!

Fernando's face was beset with concentration as he attempted to size up Weatherall's purpose. His reasons different from those of Pilar.

"That kind of operation can only be sanctioned by Madrid these days. They promise us autonomy, but we get nothing else. Empty promises. Even the budgets are controlled from *there*". His anger was barely concealed.

"The airport initiative we have now will start to yield results very quickly. They do not expect this in Spain, these drug cartels. Up till now, they see us as quite friendly. A *soft option*, I think you call it?" She writhed, cat-like in against the leather, all the time watching for Weatherall's reaction. Her *weakness*. Hidden from view, she could feel the growing moistness between her legs.

"I like what you're saying, Pilar. We have to fight them using their own methods. Yet we must never lose sight of the facts that in order to achieve results, we still have to get past the bloody court system. Everything is put there to frustrate and to hamper the good work that we do. For every decent judge on our side, there are more with their bloody lily-livered approaches to the law. It is proving harder and harder to find a judge in the UK who will laugh a good defence out of court. They *do* exist, but they too are monitored closely. Do you know that there are even groups of criminals in the UK who profile judges? Check them out to see if they are *suitable*? How many more of our methods are they going to steal, mm?" She permitted herself a wry smile at this, which did not go unnoticed by the wilful Pilar.

"It is good to hear such a refreshing, no nonsense attitude from a senior British Customs officer. Of course, under Franco....."

"Whoa! Don't get me wrong. I am not advocating *that* kind of regime. I just want to be able to fight on a level playing field with these gangs. It is simply not good enough to run an investigative operation like this, only to have it thrown out on some ludicrous technical point by a judge simply having a legal wank!"

"I was going to say that under Franco, we had a swift and strict legal system. These investigations both in Spain and I am sure in the UK take years to come to court. The judicial system becomes weary of such matters, no?"

"We are not granted the resources to speed up matters. We become victims of our own success. When we *do* get a result in the courts, government will make political capital out of it in the press and then cut our finances in the following chancellor's budget! We cannot win". Weatherall was on a roll, sensing a soul mate.

"Let me change the subject, if I may. The Costas have long been known as havens for criminal gangs, especially those from the UK. How active do you consider your partner law enforcement agencies in Spain to be? How successful?"

"Well, Janet, let me tell you this. Since the 1980s, we have had a lot of success in investigating the links between Spanish organised crime and those gangs from abroad who seek refuge in our beautiful country. I think the days of such high profile British gangsters as Ronnie Knight, Charlie Kray and John Bindon are over. The new ones have become more sophisticated. Blended in,

I think you say. They own businesses now and are harder to prosecute. We don't get as many London gang murders as we used to. That is now the prerogative of the Chinese. They are our newest problem. And the Albanians, of course. They move quickly. First it is the immigrant workers, then they open a café and before you know where you are, the clubs and brothels are full of their women and then there is an epidemic of violence which follows. All this in just a few years. Even the Colombians are awestruck! These gangs learn quickly from each other. Methods, communications. They have their different ways of enforcement. We used to have the occasional shooting back then. Now it is ritual murders, decapitations, mutilations. I think even you would be surprised by what the *Policia* must deal with. And now Europe wants to disband the *Guardia Civil*! Are they mad? Just because it was started under the *Generalissimo*, they say it is paramilitary and there is no room for that in the Europe of Bruselas and Strasbourg. Perhaps you and me, Janet, we are like the dinosaurs, no?" Pilar leans forward engagingly, pouring more coffee, her blouse revealing just a glimpse of smooth, tanned breasts.

Weatherall's dry swallow indicates the effect she is having and she senses the increasing devilish wetness between her own slim thighs.

"I think that tonight we go out and I show you some of our beautiful city, no. I am sure that you are tired after your flight?"

"That would be enchanting, I am sure. I will leave my report for you. Perhaps we could discuss it further over dinner. My treat!"

"I would not hear of it, Janet. You are our guest here and guests do not pay in Spain! I have everything under control. I will arrange for you to go to your hotel, then we meet later. Conchita, please telephone downstairs for one of the field staff to take our colleague from England to town. Next time, Janet, you should allow us to book a hotel for you. We have special relationships!"

Inwardly, she beamed as the atmosphere thawed and her train of thought moved forward to the evening.

As Weatherall bade goodbye to Nando and Juanita, Pilar fixed her back with a focused stare, permitting herself a wry smile only when she was finally alone.

Click.

"The English woman has gone. Until tonight. I think that she suspects something, but she is still in the dark for now. My suspicion is that there may be an informant in the UK. She is not revealing much, but maybe tonight will tell us more. If only I had your *skill*, I am sure that she would reveal the secrets of the Crown Jewels! Don't worry, by the end of tonight, we will surely know more than we know now! *Hasta, cariño*".

Chapter Twenty Seven

Custom House Team Leaders' Progress Meeting

"I am going to hand you over to Kim now to give us an update of what is happening with your team. I trust you had a good flight this morning and are ready to bring us all up to speed? Kim! Are you with us?"

Janet Weatherall stood four square at centre stage, flushed with perceived success from the secret trip to Spain and her meeting with Pilar Estravados-Lopez, fixing her audience with laser-beam eyes.

It was as if Kim Evans was in a world of her own. She rose slowly to her feet, but it was a sullen and embittered field officer who took to the stage, report clasped closely to her chest. She was facing *him* professionally for the first time since the *game went wrong..*

"Thank you, ma'am. The updated position in Spain is this. As you are aware, the operation was partially compromised as a result of the discovery by at least one of the targets of the van stationed outside Doolans. They led us, I think it is fair to say, a merry dance and we do not have full knowledge of what went on during the little boat trip. However, we *did* make some positive IDs and those are now being followed up. As we speak, operations have been extended to Liverpool. The net is widening, however the net will shortly be closing. In more detail, we have the following".

A video screen dropped down to reveal digital still images of Padraig (Zulu 1), Sandwich (Zulu 5), Marianna (Zulu 14) , Don Beevers (Zulu 15) and Dean (Zulu 13). Their pictures are evenly spaced, as if to emphasise the individual importance of each. They are grainy, distant exposures, the result of remote cameras and hurriedly snapped moments.

"Of particular interest to us is this man. Now Zulu 15". She pointed to Beevers and the photo which seems to have been taken at El Altet airport.

"He was the only one we were able to track from the boat trip, with the exception of O'Riordan, of course. We traced him back to the airport, where he boarded a flight for Manchester. He was travelling under the name of Richard Major, though so far we have been unable to authenticate the passport. It was a genuine UK issue, though, so we may be dealing with a man of that name. He was tracked to an address in Liverpool and that has now been added to our obs. Can I pass you to Joe just for a moment for this as he is now handling the Liverpool development?"

She sat down, obviously fighting to keep a lid on her emotions. The rumour mill had already begun to turn.

"Thank you, Kim. So far, we have Zulu 15 at a large firm of solicitors in the docks area of the town, driving various high value motor vehicles, spending time in the company of several KTUs and in particular, two known duty diverters. All that in the space of just a few days, so he already looks promising. The Local Office has him on CCT and he *is* known to us. However, there is nothing to suggest from his behaviour so far that he is in the process of arranging to receive a large shipment from Spain. I believe that there are others so far unknown who are in place for that purpose. However, it may still be Liverpool or it may be somewhere else".

Weatherall jumped to her feet.

"I will just interject for a moment here. Thank you, Joe. This operation is growing by the day. I have requested further support and man hours and we should have an answer this morning. I *am* confident. Be on your guard, people, be vigilant and most of all, be aware. One little thing, the slightest detail could be just what we need to complete the picture. Back to you, Kim"

Evans was already back on her feet, desperate to get this over with.

"Second one, the woman, Zulu 14, may only be there as eye candy, but for now, she will be included in our planning. She has not been seen before but judging by her appearance, we believe that she is either a Spanish national, or possibly Croatian. She may be the money laundering connection. For now, her photo is all we have. I have passed it on to our liaison contact within the *Aduana Nacional* in Madrid. Once they have checked her, if there is anything on the radar, we will be the first to know. Yes, Emily?"

"I wasn't aware that we were working with our Spanish counterparts at such a close level. Are these the original contacts of Graham's?"

"Er, yes, the contact came from Graham's files. He had been working for some time with their people. Since the likes of Ronnie Knight and John Bindon, relations with the Spanish have moved on somewhat. Anything else at this point? Good. As far as we are aware, O'Riordan has never involved a woman in his business dealings so the eye-candy theory is the most likely. Something of a dinosaur is our Mr O. Having said that, the world of international drug trafficking has thus far been strictly male dominated. However, we have no record of her arriving on the boat at all. Did she just appear out of thin air? That is a mystery which we would love to know the answer".

"How can we be sure that this *boat trip* was actually anything to do with our investigation?" Emily's eyes scanned Kim's face for any kind of reaction. Her antennae most definitely up.

"Well, apart from the extraordinary lengths which O'Riordan went to in order to put us off the scent, we know that he has been aware of limited covert surveillance for some time. A man with his background? He expects it. As you are all aware from Graham's files, a number of officers have attempted to crack the thus far impenetrable Doolans to no avail, so we decided after considerable deliberation to mount a mobile unit across the road. You know what they thought of that, though I understand the food and drink were of the finest quality. Haha! It seems that despite his bog-Irish connections, Mr O'Riordan has some style".

Considerable bum-shifting and murmuring at this highly un-PC comment of Kim Evans's. Others laugh conspiratorially with her. A divided group, then, just for a moment.

"In addition to that, this has all the hallmarks of a classic 'meet'. It looks like they've got all their ducks in a row and all they need is the final go-ahead from the boss and it's show time. Zulu 13 is an interesting one".

She taps Dean's photo with the pointer.

"So far, we have been unable to identify this gentleman. He wears a lot of gold jewellery and seems to be very much a part of the 'handshakes all round' set. They *must* know him well. For now, despite the fact we have nothing so far from CCTV at the airport, we are making the assumption that he *is* a UK or Irish national. The body language which was picked up on the cameras would suggest this. Have we been able to check all the local airports, Rick?"

"Er, we're awaiting news on that one, I am afraid, Kim. I've had nothing back from Spanish Immigration".

"Don't be afraid. Just get me the bloody reports. This should have been done long ago. What the hell are you doing when I am not there, just sitting on your fat arse?"

At this point, everyone looks at their favourite part of the wall and there is an embarrassed hush. The whisperings begin again.

"Anyway, for now, we have circulated his image to all departments and we are running it through Scotland Yard to see if they have anything for us. I am expecting at least something from SOCA and Interpol. I can't believe this one hasn't come up on the radar before. Any questions so far?"

"Don't you think that now the van surveillance has been rumbled, that they will either go to ground or try something else?" A question from one of the Dover team relaxed the tense atmosphere just for a moment. A pensive looking Rick Gibbs beat out a tattoo on his teeth with a rubber tipped pencil.

"I mean, I don't want to be negative, but don't you think we could be wasting our time from now on?"

"If we took that attitude, then we might as well give up and go home now. We must keep this op alive. We owe it to Graham if to nobody else. Would you agree, boss?"

"Well said, Kim. Graham worked tirelessly on this and even on the day he died, he was about to be promoted to head up the Spanish liaison office for this and all future co-operations. We *do* owe him such a lot". Her smile says it all. She looks around the room for affirmation. She gets it.

"Ten minutes break, people".

As they got up to go, the groups of two and three formed as usual, into sections and departments.

Fuck me, the Evans is coming on a bit strong today and *What's her problem?* seemed to be the order of the day as they wandered off sparking up Marlboro Lights by the dozen.

"Boss, I need a word. I've been wanting to talk to you for a while but it hasn't been possible. I think I may have to file a report about one of the team". Kim's round about approach hid her true devastation at what took place that dark and torrid night at the hotel in Torrevieja. As she left the room with Weatherall, the wagging tongues went into overdrive. The moment they were alone in the corridor, Kim Evans turned to Weatherall, but before she could speak;

"Are we talking discipline or worse? Actually, before you go any further, is this going to be the time or the place, or can we leave it till another time? Maybe later?" Weatherall's face suddenly turned to stone, as she picked her mobile up from the table and hurried to her office.

Kim, now isolated in the middle of the deserted corridor, felt tears begin to fall, her make-up streaking . Finally, she walked away, dejected, alone. As she neared the end of the seemingly infinite corridor, sorrow gave way to anger. A mounting anger which she could not contain.

The meeting room still contained the non-smokers. Conversation on the balcony reminiscent of spitting cobras with Rick Gibbs conspicuous by his absence.

"What the hell was that all about?"

"I know. Where did that come from? She's not normally like that".

"Huh! Women. Wrong time of the bloody month more like. See, the trouble with you obs lot is that when the pressure's on, you just ain't up to it! Simple!" Meacher stood back to wait for the retaliation.

"Well, clever clogs; you should know. You work out there with her. All getting a bit claustrophobic is it? Or is there something else you're not letting on? There *is* isn't there? There fuckin' well *is*? Wrong time of the month my arse!"

Like a pack of wolves sensing a kill, they surrounded Andy

Meacher, baying for blood.

"Nothing I know about. Honest".

When they realised that nothing in the way of gossip was going to come from Meacher's normally babbling brook of a mouth, they gradually made their way back to the desks and the Weatherall eye. Before resumption of the morning's meeting, a young and ambitious officer from Dover sidled up to the boss and requested an 'after hours' meeting. One on one. The normally icy cool boss's curiosity was back on full alert and she agrees.

"Okay, okay. Back on your heads, please! We now move to the informant position, the seizure at Dover and the kilo of 92% sitting downstairs in the vaults. Our handler cannot brief the meeting today as he actually has a meet with said CI. Unavoidable. So far, this gentleman has been 100%. As he is new to us, we are still treating his information with a large pinch of salt. Having said that, we don't get given this kind of quality on a daily basis, so let's not look a gift horse, okay, people? We believe that he has some valuable new information today, possibly to do with a major shipment. We do not know when or where. This could be it!"

*

Click. "Look, I'm tellin' ya. I ain't meetin' in no pub, fuckin' *capiche*? It's the building site in Stratford or it ain't nowhere. What *is* it with you people? Are you tryin' to bring the whole fuckin' shebang on top or what? No, fuck off. We do it my way, or we ain't fuckin' doin' it at all. Half-ten. By the creek. The Wates site."

*

Unnoticed amongst the comings and goings at the Lower Thames Street office security barrier, a pony-tailed and dishevelled backpacker made his way up the incline, into Sugar Quay and up towards the Tower Gateway Docklands Railway station. He stopped to buy a 'Big Issue' from the guy with the dog just outside the main entrance, then climbed the steps and onto a waiting West Ferry train. Once seated, he adjusted the tiny microphone hidden under the folds of his grimy leather jacket and stared out of the window at the changing skyline.

*

Ray Harper's two identical mobiles sat on the pale blue formica-topped table in front of him, just far enough away, between the tomato shaped sauce bottle and the sugar. Next to the chipped ashtray. His mug of tea was nearly cold, his mind fixated on the end of the road, barely visible through the Superkings' haze. He sat one table back from the window in Vera's Café. *Come on! COME ON!* His fingers tapped out a monotonous rhythm. Eventually, a figure turned the corner and loped along the road towards the site office opposite. *At fuckin' last!*

*

Candyfloss whispered into the lapel of his jacket. *Time now 10.48am. Walking along Gribley Street towards Olympic Village Site No 17 Wates Construction Entrance 4. Contact not currently in view. Awaiting call.* He slowed down to a snail's pace, pausing to light a roll-up, before moving on to the mud-caked entrance. From across the street, strewn with broken cobbles, a large figure bent low against the biting wind, dressed in a luminous yellow jacket walked towards him.

*

"We ain't goin' in there! With Vera's fuckin' connections? She'll suss you in under a minute. Fuckin' moody hair, moody jacket! No, mate, you're comin' with me. Onto the site. Get yourself a titfer an' follow me". They walk in past the security guard who doesn't even look up from his worn copy of Nuts. Harper removes two safety helmets from the warmth of the hut and they step out into the 2012 Olympic Village mud.

"There's an 'ut next to the tower crane. It'll be empty for half an hour. That'll be enough for you. Oh….sorry about your daisies! Haha!" The handler walks on behind, his boots already caked in dark mud and soon they are in the warmth of the small metal hut. Harper turns to his contact,

"Right. Before we get onto anythin' else, when am I gettin' the fuckin' gear back?" Harper's up close and personal, his spittle sticking to the undercover officer's beard.

"Er, there's been a bit of a hiccup on that. They…they're still testing it…"

"Testin' it? What the fuck is there to test? You know it's what it is. Listen, matey, if that gear ain't back in Metro's Silvertown unit by the end of the week, all nice and cushti, I am fuckin' fucked. An' if I am fuckin' fucked then you, my friend, are *proper fucked*! I fuckin' knew this would happen. Fuckin' knew it. You cunt. You told me two weeks. TWO FUCKIN' WEEKS! You've had the gear four now. What the fuck is goin' on, twat? I tell you what! Fuck this. Fuck your meetin'. Fuck any more fuckin' info 'till I get me gear back. You twatting, fucking cunt. Take me for a mug?" Harper punches him hard in the chest so that he falls back against the metal shelving on the wall, sending everything crashing to the floor.

"Call me when you've got somethin' to tell me. Cunt!"

He storms out of the shed, then goes back in, removes the handler's hard hat, hits him across the side of the head with it, then walks out again.

*

Click.

"Control? Put me through to Watchtower ops. Tell them it's Candyfloss. Yes, it *is* urgent!"

*

A remote bleeper lights up on the desk, its insistent red LED demanding attention. As Weatherall outlines the next steps in the operation, her deputy signals for Kim to leave the room and answer its call.

*

Once the codewords have been exchanged between Candyfloss and control, Kim listens to his report of the morning's debacle in Stratford, before replying,

"I hear you, make no mistake, but I don't think we've finished with it yet. You'll just have to go back to him and tell him to bear with us. It's just not acceptable, making demands like that. Just tell him! These things take time. Look, I don't know. I'm not bloody forensics. Look, I'll pass your message on. I have to go. We're in a meeting. Later". *Click.*

*

Candyfloss returned through the site unnoticed, before making his way towards Stratford Underground station and his train back. Using his designated mobile, he called Harper again and again, but each time, it was just the recorded message. As he walked onto the Central Line platform and looked up at the departures board, he could see a North Woolwich train on the low-level line in the distance. Stopping at Silvertown, the digital indicator said. Changing his mind, he hurried back down the steps and onto the eastbound Richmond line platform, just as the two coach train pulled in.

*

"Ray, your brother's been on the blower for you. Your old mum's not well. Says you got to get over the flat and take her down the hospital. Said he's been tryin' your mobile all mornin'".

Harper turned right round and walked out of the shutter door, past the thousands of palletised cases of wine and onto the loading dock. He jumped the four feet down onto the tarmac and round the corner to the car park without a word. As he drove away towards the Canning Town flats, a lone figure walked along North Woolwich Road, across the disused tramway and into the Metro Bond yard.

*

Click.

"Mick, it's Ray. What' up with mum? Yeah. I'm on me way now. Where was I? Had to pop out. No. Nothin' important. See you later. I'll give your love to mum, yeah? Cheers. *Click.*

*

The bearded figure stood patiently outside the bond office, as dockets and collection notes were passed in and out, drivers stood talking and smoking and the 'phone rang constantly. Eventually, after about five minutes, his suspended animation was shattered by a "Yes, mate?"

"Is Ray about? Ray Harper?"

"Who can I say wants him? He don't normally come down 'ere".

"It's...its's Jim. Jim Glover. Only need a quick word".

"I'll see if 'e's about. Hold on".

The bond foreman makes a big thing of checking the extension number on the wall, then picks up a grimy telephone handset and punches out the digits.

"Sandra? It's Vernon. Is Ray there? Some geezer down 'ere wants 'im. What did you say your name was, mate?"

"Glover. Jim Glover".

"Did you get that? No. Glover, not bruvver! Dozy mare. What? Okay, love. Tata, darlin'".

"You've just missed 'im. She says try his mobile. Right, who's next?"

Candyfloss is already history and he turns away and walks back down towards the station, already dialling again. This time, he gets through.

"Ray. Look, don't hang up. I know you're pissed off, but this is not the time to start. Just give me a break, yeah? Where are you? Look, there's no need to be like that. Give me two minutes, yeah? I guarantee I'll get the stuff to you by the end of the week. Don't worry. The whole operation could be compromised if the stuff isn't there. I know that. We all do. I'm going back there now to sort it out. If I have to bring it back myself from forensics, then I will, but you *will* have it back. I just need to have that piece of information from you. We *need* to know what the next step is. If we don't get it now, we could lose the whole advantage we've built up. Which *you've* built up. Think about it, Ray. You'll have helped us crack a huge gang operation. Can you imagine how many brownie points that's going to give you. It's carte blanche, Ray. In two years, you could have made enough to retire. We're not going to be looking too close at whatever you get up to, you know that. For God's sake, you of all people know how everyone at Metro got looked after. Play the fucking game, Ray. You know it makes sense. Stay with us. Just give it some thought and get back to me later. I won't hassle you today. But just think. Okay, mate. Laters, yeah". *Click.*

*

"What did the hippie want?"

"What hippie?"

"That geezer, the one with the ponytail and beard. He come in with no motor. Don't get many of them".

"Wanted to speak to Ray".

"'He didn't look like one of Ray's mates".

"Well, 'e weren't local".

"'Ere, pass us them release notes. We got the fuckin' Wine Vault boys turnin' up in 'arf hour".

*

"We're getting very close now".

Weatherall was right out on a limb. Winging it like crazy.

"I have been informed that our contact will provide us with dates and times of the next shipment. From the start, this has been an intelligence led operation and I am very proud of the way that you have conducted yourselves. It has not been an easy time for the service, but we have stuck to the task, people. Done it by the book. That is the way I wanted it done at Metro back in the dark days of the 1990s and now that they are listening to me at the top, we have a bright and successful future ahead. Give yourselves an *interim* pat on the back". She looked around the meeting room at the assembled faces, stopping and engaging with each one as she went. Dedicated. *Committed.*

Kim Evans looked up at her and blinked. Just momentarily. *By the book? Who the fuck does she think she's kidding?*

As the applause died down, Weatherall leaned across to her deputy and whispered,

"Get Candyfloss to come in straight away. I need to know exactly where we are with the informant. We cannot afford any banana skins now".

She returned to her brood, smiling now. Basking.

*

Click.

"It's Simon. Yes, mate, long time no speak. Listen, can you do me a little favour? I might be in the market for some of your finest. Yeah. Nice little deal. You get me a bit of bail on a kee, say around 50% pure and I'll have you a kee back within a week or so. No, mate, my stuff is the bollocks. 92% Pure Mother of Pearl. Guaranteed. You could cut it three, even four times. Got to give me the bail, though. Can't do it any other way. Yes, of course I know what *guarantee* means. No worries, mate. Need it Thursday. Laters!"

Candyfloss placed his *other mobile* back into the leather jacket inside pocket and smiled to himself. Result! Back on track and in business. The remainder of his journey back to Tower Gateway was spent in a better demeanour.

*

Dean sat at his wife's bedside. Save for the whirring machines and monitors, the room was quiet. Low, soft lighting gave it an eerie feel. It was as if there was no-one else in the hospital. He spoke in a low, monotonal voice, re-assuring her, trying to *break through.* As he uttered these words of comfort, mixed with stories of what the kids were up to, how the salon was doing, tales of West Ham woe and why they should never have bought the Argentineans, his mind wandered away, towards his business, his *other life*. He looked around, then back to his comatose wife.

"Am I out of me depth, babes?" He held her hand tightly, looking for any kind of sign that she was improving. The bandages still covered her damaged face. It would be a while before the true extent of her injuries would be exposed to the waiting world.

"It's too late, anyway. There's nothing I can do now. The wheels are rollin'. It's only when I come 'ere to talk to you that it all comes clear. Know what I mean, Gina babes? If you was listenin' now, I don' even know what you'd say. Probably 'ave a go at me. Somethin' like, 'You ain't the man I married, Dean Bold. It don't sound like you at all. Pull your bleedin' self together an' lets have a bottle of bubbly!' I'd give anythin' for that bottle with you now, girl. I'd give it all up for you. Just come back to me. Whatever you do, don't go. Not yet. Not till we've had the bleedin' presents for the Silver Wedding!" He starts to laugh, but quickly, the laughter turns to tears. He rests his head against her legs and sobs himself to sleep. A sleep of nightmares.

*

"What time you off, bruv? I'm fuckin' dyin' for a pint".

"Finish at two. Be in the Custom House at five past. Get us a Stella in. Just got to do these delivery notes for the mornin'".

"I'll join you an' all, then". Ray Harper's voice boomed out across the vast warehouse.

"Fuck me, where'd you spring from? I fought you'd gone down the hospital".

"I did. The old girl's alright now. Just needed to get her settled. She's in her favourite ward. Even knows the bleedin' sister by name. Besides, me brother Mick's goin' over later. Reckons he's doing the rounds tonight. One of his mates' missus is in intensive, so he's in there after".

"Oi! You comin' or what? Leave them dockets for Stormin' Norman. Lazy cunt don't do no work anyway."

*

To: Janet.Weatherall@hmrc.gov.uk

From: Field Team

Date: 17*th* January 2007

Subject: Informant Handling (Top Secret-Your Eyes Only)

Janet

I think I've pulled this one out from the fire. Have persuaded Brighton Rock to play ball this week. Will need to have the powder back by close of play next Friday. Certain.

Regards

Jim

*

"Some geezer come lookin' for you this mornin' Ray. That Sandra in the office said you was just gone. Jim something. What was 'is name, bruv?"

"Glover. You're fuckin' memory's gone to pot. Silly old cunt. Glover. Jim Glover, that was 'is name. Looked like a bleedin' hippie, 'e did. Mate of yours?"

Ray Harper's composure was gone and back in a split second. Just after he nearly shat himself, that is.

"Jim? Yeah. He said he might pop in".

"Fuckin' strange place to pop in, bruv. Bit off the beaten track".

"He likes a walk, does Jim".

"He must do. Owe him, do you?"

"Fuck me, what's with the Spanish inquisition?"

"Just askin', that's all. Don't want you comin' to any harm, like".

"Won't 'appen. Same again? Here's a score. Get them in. I'm goin' for a Jack Bash".

As Harper disappeared from view towards the Gents, his two colleagues looked at each other.

"Likes a walk? Is he having a giraffe, or what?"

"One of us is goin' to have to let Mick know. He told us to look after Ray".

"Yeah, look after him. Not spy on the cunt".

"I'm just sayin', that's all".

Chapter Twenty Eight

Oficina Aduanas Nacional, Alicante

"Before we go on, I would remind you that everything which is discussed in this room stays in this room. Am I clear?" Nando's steely glare made it perfectly clear to his audience that he meant business. His two colleagues nodded in agreement.

"As we suspected, the British have their limited operations running here. The woman Weatherall seems to be working on a semi-undercover basis. But she is a senior officer, no? The question we must ask ourselves is this; do we give them a carte blanche to work incognito, do we offer them further help, or do we just let them get on with it? It is most irregular".

Pilar's absence from the office caused by her monthly reporting visit to the Head of Customs in Madrid had got the rumour mill working overtime. Fernando Toro sat square onto his desk, master of all he surveyed with Pilar away. Opposite him, two department heads from the container port and the airport of El Altet. Señor Manuel Guzman and Señora Juanita Ribero-Castellano.

"I think there are not many *options* available to us. My department is already totally overstretched. We are spending more and more time trying to detect weapons, bomb making equipment and such things. The *priorities*, as Madrid calls them. If she asks for help, then we must say no. I have enough trouble saying that word to my own people. She must come further down the list of priorities for *us*!"

Manuel Guzman sat back in his chair, eyeing Toro's reaction carefully. Before he could answer, Juanita Castellano seized her opportunity to speak,

"I think that perhaps my position is different. Since intelligence has made the airports of Spain a number one urgency in the fight against terrorism and drugs, we have actually had our resources and budgets increased. You will forgive my scepticism, but when this is not any more the flavour of the month, we will be back to the Finance Ministry with our begging bowl like the rest of you!"

"Yes, Juanita, but for now………..YOU are the flavour of the month!"

Nando's clumsy praise and barely hidden jealousy relaxed the meeting just for a brief moment.

"What do you think she really wants? Her visit…..? What was the real purpose of her visit? In twenty years of working in this office, I have never before heard of an approach like this. What do YOU think, Manuel?"

"She is ambitious, I think, from what you have said. If she comes here not even in an official capacity, yet she walks in here like she owns the place, then I think she must feel very confident of her position. My feeling is that the British Customs & Excise are very *keen* to achieve whatever it is they are trying to achieve. I do not think that this time they are too concerned about protocol and international law".

"So nothing new, then?" Nando laughed out loud at his sideswipe, his colleagues reluctantly joining in.

"It is true that their reputation goes before them, but this? A top official from London, coming to a regional office in Spain, *without a real appointment*? It is most unprecedented".

"So I come back to what we said before, my friends. What is it that she wants?"

"Number One. She wants to take all the praise for whatever she is doing. Number Two. She must have some clear evidence of the link between this region and London. We know from what she told us that it is drugs. What I believe is that she has something new. Something they have not seen before".

"Is it crystal meth, then? That is new. We made our first seizures of that recently". Juanita's face was flushed with success.

"I do not think you should praise yourself too much for that. It was only a small quantity and besides, the scum who are involved in that business can make it themselves here. It was probably a sample, maybe for the laboratories here to test. You can rest assured that whatever plans they have for us here in Spain with that dangerous concoction, it is already here and in place. No, my friends. I think this is something far more sinister. And something far more dangerous. If she is unwilling, *or unable* to make an official approach, then she must believe that her presence here could be compromised if it were revealed to the gangs she may be investigating in England. There have been many rumours since the death of the FIOD officers in Rotterdam. If gangs are prepared to murder our colleagues from Holland in broad daylight, then this thing has got a whole lot bigger".

Click. Nando's mobile sprang into action on the desk.

"*Si? Diga me!* Yes, Pilar". He indicated the blindingly obvious to his two colleagues and they obligingly left the office for a moment. He listened to the earpiece for some time before interjecting.

"Yes, of course I will do that for you. No, do not worry, I will not alert our Liaison Office at the London Embassy. Of course. When will you return? Three days. Very well. I will arrange everything for you. *Hasta!*"

Nando stared through the Venetian blinds which separated him from the rest of the departmental office and his two chattering colleagues standing by the coffee machine. *What was Pilar up to?* After a few seconds, he beckoned the others back in.

"We will have to go on this one alone for now, my friends. I have been informed that Señora Estravados will be detained in Madrid for a little time. She has asked that you, Juanita, continue to maintain the profile of our undercover officers at the airport, paying particular attention to the cargo section. She has just come out of a mutual co-operation meeting with our friends from Colombia. They believe that cocaine shipments are to be stepped up and that we were right in our belief that they are going to target regional airports from now on, bypassing Barajas and the obvious problems they experience there. I think that we might see some action shortly!"

*

Pilar smiled at her lunch date. An engaging and intriguing smile to the eyes of any casual observer. But not to the exquisitely coutured Marianna da Sancha sitting cat-like opposite. The long and luxurious table-cloths of Ristorante Antonio in Madrid's financial district hid a multitude of sins and lunchtime indiscretions.

This table was no exception. For this was what they both lived for. Away from prying eyes and jealous male attention. Marianna's hundred euro stockinged calf brushed delicately against that of her friend. The momentary friction caused a brief spark of electricity between them. Hearts raced, yet their courting ritual continued unabated.

"So, everything is taken care of". Next to the silver ice bucket, dripping seductively onto pristine white cotton beneath, her jewelled Dior mobile phone lay silent, its purpose completed for the day. "Now we can party!"

"I must keep my work phone switched on though. I do not wish to have my office discover where I *really* am!" Pilar's husky voice purred across the table to her exquisite co-conspirator, exciting and teasing.

"How tedious it all is. But sadly necessary and oh so exciting, when the work is complete, darling! Tell me about this *English bitch* from Her Majesty's Customs & Excise. What is she like? Is she *corruptible*?"

"I think, Marianna, that everyone is corruptible. It is only ever a question of the price. Sexually, she is putty in our hands, but she is on a mission. Despite her being obviously attracted to me, she would not deviate from her course".

"Mmmm! How delicious. I bet *I* could corrupt her!"

"I think, *angel*, that you could corrupt the *Papa* in the Vatican himself! *Salud!*"

Glistening crystal glasses brimming with Krug champagne were touched together briefly as the courtship ritual continued. Marianna's power was manifesting itself physically on both of them, the sexual tension becoming more apparent as the minutes ticked by. Bowls of tiny marinated elvers gave way to fresh lobster and oysters, the Krug to a bottle of Le Montrachet 1990. Marianna slipped her hand underneath the long silk Chanel skirt, over the deep lace of her stocking tops and against her swollen, wet labia. Ensuring that she had Pilar's undivided attention, (she always did!), she brought a taloned finger up to her lips and let the end run over and against her barely visible tongue, closing her eyes in ecstasy as the musky aroma took its toll. Pilar could feel herself becoming unbearably stimulated and she twisted her legs under the table again and again. Her heart pumped, raced as she sought to contain her arousal.

"This wine, it is like nectar, no?" Marianna smiled again as she permitted the oily liquid to slide effortlessly down. "Tell me, before we go to my hotel, for that *is* where we are going, is it not..............?" She watched as Pilar swallowed again and again. "What do you *feel* about the new people from England?"

"I...I...my feeling is that they could be very useful, if a little gauche".

"Yes, deliciously so, don't you agree? Dean seems a little fond of the *marching powder* whereas his friend, Steve could have the potential to join my 'little bit of rough' club. Once the shipment is completed, I think that perhaps they should come to Ceuta and spend a little time in the *house of pleasure*! I never feel that I know a man until I have seen him there. I don't think you have seen the video playback of the two gentlemen, my friends, from Alicante, have you? It is *delicious*, darling. The new cameras I had installed worked perfectly. I had no idea the close ups would be *quite* as detailed as you said. The wonders of modern science! My girls work so professionally. Dirty little bitches! They get paid for what they love. The wealthy one, Felix? I know now why they call him *Señor Bocadillo*! That is some *chorizo* I can tell you! I will have to discover what the English boys have. Oh, I am sorry, darling. Do I upset you?"

Marianna delights at her friend's discomfort, but knows just how far to take her.

"It is time for the check, no? I need to feel your skilful tongue on me, *angel*!"

She calls for the bill to come and soon, her driver is outside, the long wheelbase Jaguar is warm and the leather soft against their stockinged thighs.

"To the hotel". Her wrapover silk skirt falls open to reveal deep lace stocking tops and just the tiniest glimpse of smooth white skin.

"There is the most wonderful hot tub in the suite. Just right for the afternoon, no?"

Pilar is in ecstasy.

*

As his two colleagues departed from the meeting, Nando sat ponderous for some while. His mind worked overtime at the various permutations which had surfaced during the preceding two hours. What would Pilar do? He picked up his official mobile and began to dial.

*

Click. "*Si? Estravados.* Nando! How nice to hear from you. Yes, the meetings are going well. *Very well*! You have been thinking about what? Yes, naturally. Yes, I would put two of the Investigation Bureau onto it straight away. If there *is* something happening under our noses, then I wish to know all about it. No. Don't worry about taking someone off another case. Just tell them that I have authorised this as a temporary measure. Prepare the necessary paperwork and sign it on my behalf. Yes, Nando, it *is* OK! Now I have to go. I have another meeting this afternoon which will go on for quite a long time. My mobile will be on voicemail and they have been instructed not to disturb us! I will call you when I am finished. *Hasta,* Nando!"

Marianna's skirt rode up as the journey neared its end, her driver negotiating his way skilfully around the narrow streets of the Spanish capital. Just as it was about to expose her salon waxed mound, the car came to a stop and the uniformed chauffeur was at the door in seconds. Pilar's heart was ready to burst at what was about to transpire.

*

Click.

"Señor Toro? I have an urgent call for you. It is the Embassy in London".

"Put them through, *immediately*!"

Nando rose to shut his office door and grabbed the handset in one movement.

"*Si? Diga me.* First Attaché! How nice to hear from you. Yes, they have put you through to me because Señora Estravados, she is in Madrid. Of course. I am in charge here". Nando listened intently to the news from London.

"OK. I will get a message to her to call you straight away. She will be very interested to learn of your news. This is indeed a major breakthrough! Thank you, First Attaché. *Adios.*"

Barely had the light gone out on the handset, than Toro picked up his mobile and dialled his boss.

*

Pilar's mobile sat flashing unnoticed on the low mahogany table, ringtone switched to silent. Its owner lay between her lover's legs, lustrous black hair falling carelessly over open thighs as her expert tongue lapped at Marianna's musky wet lips. The half-light of dusk crept through the window and over their entwined bodies; low, soft moaning the only sound in the vaulted presidential suite. Pilar kissed and loved her flame, alternating tenderness with an animal passion which manifested itself in raised scratched welts. Her French manicure contrasted with Marianna's dark red impossibly long talons which dug deep into her naked shoulders as her quarry neared climax. Musky aromas filled the whole bedchamber as both women passed into ecstasy, Marianna's orgasm exploding over Pilar's sensual mouth. As the climax neared its completion, she opened her eyes to watch her lover's tongue perform its final task, lapping and loving every last drop of ejaculate from her swollen labia. The warm pool of liquid which had now formed on the crisp, white cotton sheet felt comforting against her exposed thighs. She motioned Pilar to lay on top of her, gaping cunt against her mouth, a favour to return. She came in seconds, expanding and contracting alternately with each lash of Marianna's tongue. Finally they came to rest, exhausted, in each other's arms. Gentle kisses ensued, then sleep.

The mobile flashed again and again, unnoticed.

*

"Conchita! I would like you to ring the Central Office *Aduanas*

Naçionales and find out how long Señora Estravados' meeting will last. Discreetly, please. She is very busy today".

The group secretary turned on her stiletto heels and marched back to her desk. This was far too big to leave until later. Toro sat quiet, not for the first time today. He could barely contain his excitement from the rest of the department but this was crucial to the successful outcome of what he had just learnt. A gentle knock on the door brought him out of his trance.

"Señora Estravados' meetings finished this morning, Señor Toro. They say you can get her on her mobile if you like. She will not be in the office again until tomorrow morning at 8.00am. Is there anything else? Do you have her mobile number?"

"Of course I have, you stupid girl! Yes, that's all!"

Conchita's departure went unnoticed. He was already moving the day on, intrigued and confused. Once again, he dialled the now familiar digits. Nothing. Voicemail. Pilar's husky tones reaching out to him with………nothing. It was getting close to home time. His mind was going into overtime. *Overdrive.* Where was she? What was she doing? Was she working with Weatherall? The possible permutations tortured Toro's mind. As he lurched from one scenario to another, he did not notice the lights dim in the main office. He did not notice the arrival of the contract cleaners as they wearily removed their coats and settled down to work. He did not even notice the girl empty his bin, so deep and far away were his thoughts. Eventually, a loud noise from outside disturbed him. The refuse collectors with their cheery yells. Slowly he rose to his feet, put on his coat and hat and made his way to the exit. By the time he left the building, the car park was deserted, its only working light illuminating his grimy Seat León. As he climbed in, its interior light illuminated his face for one brief moment, just enough to augment the grainy digital image caught from a car parked on the opposite side of the tarmac lot. This was duly logged and recorded. As Toro drew away, a discreet distance was maintained, then mobile surveillance commenced at seven-ten pm.

*

Pilar lay in the arms of her lover, fast asleep. Under the warm cover, Marianna lay with her eyes wide open. Her mind was racing ahead. The next trip to Venezuela would prove crucial to the future success of the venture. The darkened room lay silent as she made her plans, the only noise the evening traffic eight floors below, an occasional car horn shattering the Madrid dusk. Every time her thoughts visited Caracas, she would find herself going back to her teenage years, to the time before her father's death. To when things were different. To when there was a kind of innocence no longer part of her world. She sat on her favourite horse, black riding jacket and black Spanish brimmed riding hat. Bolt upright. Proud and haughty. Fifteen years old, her black stallion aching to gallop. She would let him go, eventually, then they would ride for miles across wide open countryside. She had not a care in the world.

But then.

Then it all changed.

It all changed the day she went out alone. It had begun to rain, but her inexperienced horse knew nothing of fear. He had approached a wide ditch with the usual gusto, yet this time, the rain had formed pools of water just at the point where he would make his leap. The sky was black and through the driving storm, visibility was down to almost nothing. He slipped and as he landed on the other side, his front legs gave way and she was catapulted over his head and onto the ground. Out cold.

When she came to, she was lying awkwardly. The stallion could not get up. One of his front legs was damaged and he would walk no more. In the distance, she could hear voices. She called out and soon, some gauchos arrived over the brow of a small hillock. Soon, her joy turned to fear. They surrounded her, laughed at her, mocking her fine clothes and porcelain complexion. *What do we have here? A little rich bitch. That is what we have here!* One of them looked at the horse, then calmly took out a *pistola* and shot it. They then turned their attention to her. After some jokes and rough stuff, they held her down, tore off her riding breeches and panties. Then, one by one, they raped her. Time and time again, until they were done. Eventually, they left her in the ditch, lying against the dead stallion. She did not even know what they were doing, such was her innocence then. When finally she made her way to a nearby village and back to the safety of the *residencia* in

Caracas, her father broke down. In the following months, he had heart attack after heart attack until one day, it was too much. In that short time, she had lost everything. It took two years before she spoke about what had happened to her, then one day, it all spilled out at her finishing school. How they had used her like a toy, then thrown her back into the ditch like discarded food wrappings. She befriended a girl there, in her last year. A girl who showed her friendship, then tenderness, then one night under a harvest moon, love. Love of the gentlest kind, soft kisses and caresses, slow, innocent love. When they were through, they had lain under the bright moon till dawn, tight in each other's arms. When eventually, they drifted apart, Marianna was whole again, but now she was a different Marianna. It was as if she had had her whole separated permanently into pieces. There was sex, warmth, emotion, communication. All there, yet never again would they come together naturally. They would come together *when she was ready*. She could switch her emotions off and on when it suited her. Faith and love were gone. Forever. In their place a woman with immense power. A woman whose morals had been stolen along with her modesty. A woman without fear yet with a brutal iciness which could chill a firestorm.

Chapter Twenty Nine

Canvey. The Bold House

"Come over, babes. You ain't been out since Dave went into hospital. I know you don't wanna go out out, so come over here. Benissa's goin' with her mates to Southend for the night. Troy's over the neighbours again, so Aunty Debra's all on her lonesome. There's a bottle or two of wine 'ere with your name on".

"I dunno, girl. It's not like I'm being disloyal though, just comin' to you, is it? D'ya think Dave'd mind?"

"He ain't likely to know, is he? Not in his state. Oh, babes, I didn't mean that, honest I didn't. Just want you to have a night off, that's all".

"I know that, Debs. Go on then, I'll be over. Our Leanna can babysit, lazy little cow".

"It's not like you to say things like that about the kids, girl?"

"I dunno what's come over me since this all started? It's like I'm havin' to be the man, the woman and everything, Debs. Don't even know who I am no more".

"Best you get yourself over here now and we get that bottle open".

"Think you might be right. See you in a min. Bye".

If only you knew, girl, if only you know what your old man is really like. Was really like, probably. *He* won't be doing much shagging around for a while. Debra went about the kitchen getting it ready. The wine chilled, Domino's menu's on the table and she'd got a 'little something for later' in her handbag. Her heart's in the right place, Debra, but everything else is too and this girl really needs a night off from the man hunting.

Half an hour later, and the door bell rang. Opening it, she was amazed to see Shirley *with make up*! She actually looked half-decent; heels, black leather trousers and a white silk top. She'd even lost some weight!

"Hello, darlin'! Come in, you look fantastic. Goin' somewhere nice?" They hug. Debra really is the original tart with a heart, the proverbial good time that's been had by all.

"I got some really nice wine out of Dean's cupboard. Here you go, nice big glass. Cheers, babes! He's away 'till tomorrow. In Holland or somewhere. Didn't really take much notice, to be honest. So we got the house to ourselves. Just how I like it". She giggles that very girl giggle that seems to work every time with most guys. That and the boobs she's now sporting, courtesy of the trip to the clinic in Cyprus. Shirley looks down at her magnificent mounds.

"How're you gettin' on with them, Debs?"

"They are sooooo cool! Even people who don't know me just come up now, want to talk to me. You have no idea how much of a talkin' point they are".

"Two points, Debs! Never realised how big your nips are, neither!"

"Shirley Hilton! What *has* got into you?" The wine was flowing freely by now and Shirley was into her second glass already, having necked down the first without it even touching the sides.

"Well, you said come out, so I'm comin' out! What we 'avin to eat, then. Let's get that over with before we get down to a proper girly chat".

"This is a first, Shirl, I have to say. You've blown me away".

"I didn't always look like a bleedin' housewife. I know you think I'm obsessed with me kids, but they're all I've got, really. That and the big daft lump in the hospital. Yeah, that's my Dave. He wouldn't be nothin' without Dean, I know that". More wine. The pizzas arrived, courtesy of a frightened young lad on a moped. Or at least he was frightened by the time the lovely and very drunk Debra had given him the once over, asking him if he'd take payment in kind. His change lay scattered all over the gravel drive. They ate.

"He wouldn't be nothin' without you, you mean. He loves you, you know that. Evryone says Dean this and Dean that, but you look at it, girl. What would he be without the likes of Dave, Ron and Kev. Not to mention the Turkish geezer. He scares me, he does. I think he's gay or something. I've tried everythin' with him".

"Yeah, well you've tried everythin' with every man in bleedin' Canvey, you dirty mare!" They both shriek with laughter at Shirley's observation, sloshing wine all over the kitchen table.

"Even grabbed 'is cock one night. Know what happened? Nothin!"

"You're right, he is a bit weird. I mean, I know what goes on, I ain't stupid or nuffin', but I've never understood where he sort of fits in. The other boys is like, well mates from football an' the estate an' that. Fuck knows where 'e come from. I heard he was from Peckham somewhere. All them Cypriots is down there".

Debra's dividing up the pizza slices and pouring yet more wine, having opened another bottle. She's at that point in the evening, the water shed, or in her case, the wine shed.

"Shirl?"

"Yes, girl?

"You ever been done up the arse?"

"What, you mean by Dave? Had it up the arse with Dave? Is that what you're sayin'?"

"Yeah. It don't have to have been with him, though. What about when you was at school?"

"Your havin' a laugh! Them boys back then wouldn't 'ave done nothin' like that. You was lucky if they lasted more than a couple of thrusts! Aaaarrggghhh!" She collapsed in fits of laughter.

"Blimey, Shirl. You're a bit of a dark horse! I never knew you was like that at school? You was worse than me!"

"There was a lot before Dave, darlin'. He, the daft old fool that he is, saved me really. There's always been just a grain of sand in him that I thought was a rock to cling to. Turned out he was the one who needed a rock instead. So I become it".

"He'd changed a bit an' all, ain't he? When did 'e go all flash?"

"Well, I ain't certain, but I think he's bin havin' some of Dean's charlie. It's like he'd gone all, well, distant, you know. He hadn't come near me in ages. I swear, if we get through this, I'm gonna try a lot harder for him. I've spent too much time on the kids and not enough on him. It's just 'cos I had such a shit time as a kid, I wanted to give mine what I never had. There's nothin' wrong with that is there, Debs?"

"Nothin' at all, girl. I've always been too far the other way. Too cock happy an' no real man to love. It's funny, ain't it? You're talkin' bout lookin' after your man more and I'm wishin' I had kids. Right bleedin' pair we are!"

The phone rang. Dean.

"What's that? Yeah, everythin's fine. Shirley's 'ere. Yeah. We're avin' a pizza. Benissa's out with that Jimmy Jag's boy. Whassisname? Yeah, 'im. Troy's round the neighbours, as usual. We're goin' in again tomorrow to see them. Yeah. Gina's still showin' good signs, Dean. They're operatin' on Dave again an' all. Alright, love, we'll see you tomorrow night. Take care. Alright. *Ciao*". *Click.*

"Is he alright? He ain't half away a lot, these days".

"He's got a lot on his mind, ain't he? He's got no Dave doin' his runnin' around".

"Yeah. Do you know, I still don't know what the hell he was doin' in the bleedin' car with Gina. It's like we've all forgotten about that bit. Swept it under the carpet, like".

The wine was taking its toll and Debra started to cry. Big, hot tears flowed down her face. No matter how hard she tried to be the hard Debra, the together Debra, it wouldn't work.

"I can't fuckin' keep this up no more. It's all too much, too close to me. I can't lie no more".

"What is it? What's the matter, love?"

"Well. It's them, innit".

"What? Whaddya mean, *them*? Who are you talkin' about?

"Them! Them in the bleedin' hospital, bleedin' beds opposite each other. I know she's me bleedin' skinny an' all, but I ain't coverin' up for her one more day".

"What? For God's sake, Debra, what're you sayin'?"

"Gina. And your Dave".

"Yeah? What?"

"Well, it's obvious, ain't it?"

"They're... they've been...'avin an affair". She buries her head in her hands once more and sobs, cries more than she's done in years. It's all coming out now, the failed affairs, the abortions, the unrequited love. The disaster that is her life. Shirley's expression goes from questioning to incredulous.

"No. NO! You're wrong. Wrong! How can you say such a thing? Dave? And Gina? She's his best mate's wife, for God's sake. No, Debra, I ain't havin' it".

"It's too late for that, girl. It's beenn goin' on for months. Dean ain't bin near her neither. Just like you an' Dave. She told me, Shirl. Told me everythin'. Where they meet, what they do. The dirty slag".

There was fire in Shirley's eyes, but suddenly, the realisation that her life was a sham hit her like a train crash. The room was silent for what seemed like ages. Debra had her face totally covered by her hands, tears spewing out, all the pent up emotion flooding forth. Shirley's incredulity turned to anger, then rage, then stony cold.

"How long have you known about this? Who else knows? I bet every bastard knows, don't they. They always say it's the one who's been cheated on is the bleedin' last to know. Who, Debra, who knows about this?"

"It's just me, girl. Honest! I swear. Who could I tell about this? She told me in confidence one day an' I've kept it to myself ever since. I've hated myself for it an' all. I know I'm a slapper, Shirl, always have been, probably always will be. But what she's done, it ain't right. Not to you, or to Dean or to Dave. She's bleedin' led him on, I know she has. She's got a way with men. Thing with her is that she can keep 'em. Not like yours truly, fuck me an' forget 'me. They always come back for more with her, it's like she's got some kind of *smell* they can't resist".

"How long, Deb? How long's this been goin' on behind my back?"

"I dunno, girl. Think it started at one of them parties round at their house. You know, the Saturday ones after the Chinese. After Dean's finished givin' it the big 'un. I dunno where you was, where you could be found. Maybe you went home to the kids or somethin'. Dean was in the fuckin' bedroom, tootin' his fuckin' Uncle Charles. I think it was just a snog at first, then, well you know, one thing led to another".

"No, Deb. I don't know. I thought me an' 'im was good together. I ain't stupid, an' I know what those boys get up to when they're away, but there's no way I thought he'd shit on 'is own doorstep like that. An' it's not shittin' one fuckin' time, it's fuckin' twice! His oldest mate and his bleedin' wife an' all! And the pair of 'em are lyin' in that fuckin' hospital, on drips, an' we're out here feelin' sorry for them. If they hadn't been havin' this affair, they'd 'ave never even been there anyway. I'm dreadin' the Old Bill comin' round again. I was good at getting' rid of them before, but I ain't so sure now. We're still goin' with the mistaken identity bollocks, but they ain't swallowin' nothin' for now".

"What you gonna do, Shirl?"

"Do, girl? Do? I ain't gotta a fuckin' Scooby doo at the moment. I'm sittin' 'ere in her house, at her table, drinking out of her glasses. Me ole man's lyin' there, opposite her. Dunno what's 'appenin with this bleedin' operation tomorrow. He could live, he could die. The way I feel at the mo, I couldn't give a shit what happens. How am I gonna look 'im in the face after this, that's if he's got a face when the surgeon's finished with him". She laughed, well more of a cackle. She didn't know whether to laugh or cry now. Her emotions lay all over the place, in tatters and Debra came round the table to hug her. The two of them rock to and fro in tearful silence.

Silently, Benissa moved away from the kitchen door and crept up the stairs to bed. Her date didn't go well. She'd been standing outside, listening, for a very, very long time. As she entered her bedroom, the tears began to flow, like never before. And she has cried so much.

Chapter Thirty

Custom House, London

"I want Emily back from Spain to organise the UK knocks. She is a people person and knows how to get things done. I like her style. We need her recalled. The teams will have the BrickBugs in place shortly and that will reduce the need for round the clock obs. I am anticipating in excess of twenty addresses countrywide so we are talking a total of around one hundred officers. She can sort out the LVOs and liaise with the knock team leaders."

Janet Weatherall is pacing up and down the thick carpeted office, tapping a pen against the open palm of her left hand. Her new deputy, Duncan Deegan sits opposite her desk.

"Yeah. Like Emily. She's good, isn't she? Good operator. Gets things done. Smart cookie. Go far. Not using Kim Evans for this one, then?"

"Er, no. Not this time. I don't really feel she's quite ready. Needs to spend more time in the field".

Janet's recent private conversations with Kim had elicited little from the goings on in Spain, but she was far from convinced. Her 'trouble antennae' had been well and truly up for some time, ever since the, *May I have a private word* conversation.

"Emily it is, then!"

"I am glad you share my opinions, Dunc. How are you getting on with Mr Gill? No problem areas you have identified?"

"He is turning into a very good organiser. In fact, I am considering recommending him to lead one of the post knock interview teams. He has a very engaging manner and gets right to the point in such a way that could even be described as disarming. Don't know whether it's an ethnic issue or not, but these Sikhs certainly have something about them".

"And you don't see his family connections ever getting in the way of objectivity?"

"Not at all. He's an extremely polished young man.........an asset to the service. Besides which, now is hardly the time to be questioning his loyalties or otherwise".

"That's good to hear, Dunc, I must say. Fine. OK. Put him on the London team. The arrest packs are due to be drawn up once we've had the green light from King's Beam House. I loathe having to put everything through them, but without that, the whole operation will turn to rat shit. Do you know, I have never really considered it before, but have we ever looked into the idea that the mole is in there? Because mole there most certainly is. You mark my words. There were a few examples back in 2002 when key suspects went missing just prior to a knock in Birmingham. Happened twice, as a matter of fact. Both times, the suspect flew out of the country the day before. Kind of makes you think, eh Dunc?"

"You sure you're not seeing conspiracies behind every door, ma'am?"

"Cheeky sod! No I am *not*! I maintain a healthy suspicion of all that goes on around me. You know that's what makes a good officer. This whole organisation thrives on suspicion. Question it and question it again. That is what we should be doing".

"How many arrest packs are we talking about, by the way?"

"The FLO and our teams in Spain are anticipating around twenty. We've more or less got to cover everyone of interest at the bar, we have anyone who is involved in loading the lorries and the warehousemen too, wherever and whoever they might be. I think it's going to be more like twenty. Then we have the Essex boys. Depending on how reliable our informant is, certainly another ten or so there, plus we will have to interview everyone at the offices. As you well know, it's surprising who turns up post knock. We might even be bagging ourselves a bigger fish than we thought. There are some serious operators around at this level. I am proposing a post knock increase in obs in both Essex and Spain. It's a shame that we haven't been able to turn anything up in Croatia so far, but I have a hunch that they will uncover something sooner or later. Intelligence tells us that O'Riordan and his little coterie have been making regular trips there and I would wager anything you like that they haven't just been going for the sun. I just wish that Metro Bond wasn't involved, but at least we know the guilty parties are confined to one or two this time".

"And the charges?"

"Well, the plan is to bring Emily back tomorrow. She will go to Dover first when she gets back to Gatwick, then return here for a debrief. With luck, we'll have had something back from the solicitors' office and will have some idea of where the legal eagles stand. Naturally, there is the coverall conspiracy charge to get the ball rolling, importation for those actually involved. We'll have backup money laundering charges to flush some of the squealers out, especially if we throw in the 'funding terrorism' phrase. It's amazing what some of them will confess to if you dangle the chance of Guantanamo Bay in their faces! The major players are staring twenty-fives right down the barrel if the quantities are what we are led to believe. The rest of them, anything between four and fourteen. Not exactly home for Christmas. Any bloody Christmas!"

"And we're entirely happy with the timings of the operation, ma'am? Not a chance of letting the first one run up the flagpole and seeing who salutes?"

"Not a chance. Not with this quantity. Can you imagine the press if it leaked out we had let major quantities of cocaine enter the country under our very noses?"

"Nice one, ma'am. The News of the World wouldn't have come up with anything better than that!"

"Very amusing. I know where you're coming from, Duncan, but it is far too great a risk. Anyway, we stop this now, we get a result and we move on. I still believe that we could be looking at more arrests further down the line. Our informant's information has so far been first class. Let us hope that he has not let us down on the amounts".

"Ah! The disaffected one. What would we do without him and his ilk?"

"Greed, Duncan. Pure greed. It's what drives the criminal mind. They just won't share with each other. One becomes marginalised and the next minute, bingo. He turns. Happens so often".

"I take it your handling of him has been done by the book?"

"Naturally, Duncan. We cannot afford any more Metro Bond debacles".

"Was he there during the 90s?"

"He was, but he never came up on our radar. Quite clever, I have to say, what they have done. One thing's for sure, they won't be using that one again. Not after we've finished with them!"

"We're going to meet some resistance on remands in custody, don't you think, ma'am?"

"Naturally. These people can afford the best lawyers in the land. We are going to have to demonstrate substantial assets abroad, strong risk of absconding from bail and more. Usual thing. As long as we find the usual weapons that are associated with drugs, the problems will largely go away. They frighten the life out of most magistrates, even the bleeding heart liberals".

"What do we have in place for the day?"

"I will know nearer the time, but we have some choice allegations ready, just in case we do meet stiff resistance from the magistrates' benches. Terrorism, gun running and money laundering are the buzzwords at the moment. Turn up a few terror connections and bob's your uncle. I am sure there'll be some of them in there somewhere. I am rather hoping that the Croatia end will reveal at least *something* soon. I am surprised in a way that nothing has come at all from over there. Just the merest hint of Al Qaeda links and the whole lot of them will be toast in the current climate. How things have changed, eh, Dunc?"

"Yep, you're not wrong. Talking of which, anything from the crowd over at Five?"

"Diddly squat for now. They've been monitoring traffic through Bristol as normal, with our American friends as team leader, but we don't really seem to have had the help which was originally promised. In fact, what this whole shebang lacks is a USA connection. If we had that, then the dollars would have come rolling in. Shame our Mr O'Riordan doesn't have connections in Boston".

"I am sure he has. We just haven't found them yet. All his sort have family over there. Same crowd who used to rattle the collecting tins, eh?"

"Dunc, I want you to look into things a bit more closely in Armagh. Call Newry, speak to Diarmuid O'Hagan. He's a good man and he had a lot of contacts in the fuel laundering brigade. I am sure that at least some of Padraig O'Riordan's acolytes have been recruited from there. We could gain a lot of kudos if we could link him to some of that. There's a hell of a lot of our colleagues whose careers have faltered over failed ops in the world of red diesel. I *know* that O'Riordan's at the top of this particular tree. I can feel it in my bones. He has all the right credentials and let's face it; who in their right mind is going to fuck with him?"

"I'll get straight onto it. I…"

"Make sure you don't speak to anyone other than Diarmuid. The Newry office has leaked like a sieve since initial internal investigations identified a certain officer and his connections with paramilitary organisations".

"Very well, ma'am. Point taken. By the way, it seems that our Zulus in Liverpool have been increasing their activities. The reports are on your desk. It seems that they too have friends in high places".

"That is always true when you get to this level. Money talks and this kind of money screams and shouts. My campaign to increase field officers' salaries continue to fall on deaf ears, but until our staff salaries are paid commensurate with their tasks, this kind of thing can only increase. We have been recruiting some fine individuals from the old red bricks recently, but far too many of them are being tempted away with salaries five and ten times what the service can offer them".

"Let's assume that this operation is a success. So far, we have achieved miracles in a short time, ma'am. What are the plans for the future? I mean, until now, we have not had anything like the kind of resources that this operation has had thrown at it. Does this imply that we could have our own department for major drug intelligence led investigations, or will it all just go back into the woodwork like before?"

"Are you angling for a promotion, Duncan?"

"You are a true cynic, ma'am. Perhaps that is why you are where you are. No, that is not the main purpose of my question. I would like to know whether we are on the threshold of something new. Something the others and I can really get our teeth into".

"One step at a time, I think. Let's get this one under our belts before we start to make plans for the future".

"What about the informant? Any chance of using him again?"

"I think you know as well as I do that it will depend largely on whether we have to use the cocaine from Metro as evidence. You know my views about everything to do with that place, but if it comes to it, we may have to bite the bullet".

"Trouble is, ma'am, that judges have long memories".

"Yes, when they want to! I have every intention of putting pressure on King's Beam House to make sure this is tried in a friendly court. I want results, Duncan. This time, *I mean business!*"

She banged the mahogany desk hard with her fist, causing pens to go flying and paper to flutter down to the floor. Her eyes were shining bright with tension and excitement. A timid looking assistant poked her head around the large oak door but thought better of it and fled. Duncan Deegan looked up from his leather bound chair and regarded his boss for just one moment. *A woman on a mission*. Driven by God knows what kind of demons.

Chapter Thirty One

Ceuta. Castle of Monte Hacho

Marianna sat alone in the Café Moustafa. At a small table, in the window, overlooking the port and beyond. In front of her, a thin and delicate porcelain cup filled with steaming sweet unbelievably strong coffee. At the seat opposite, another cup. Untouched. The seat not even pulled out. Her open Chanel handbag contained small but highly powerful binoculars, ready for the moment that the container ship crossed the headland and up the rugged Spanish coast towards the Costa Blanca. For the moment, heavily tinted Dior sunglasses hid her appearance from any prying eyes, her uncharacteristically subtle dress code for the day making her seem just like another mainland tourist come to admire the views across towards mainland Spain. A black silk trouser suit and Hermés scarf completed the barrier she wished to place between herself and the rest of the world. Removing a gold cigarette case from her Chanel clutch, she selected a Balkan Sobranie, admired it, then lit it with a diamond encrusted Dunhill lighter, allowing the smoke to plume skywards before re-training her gaze on the horizon. Gradually, as if being drawn into view by a slow motion camera, a vast container ship, black, Panamanian registered, appeared in the distance. *The host*, she smiled deliciously, training the binoculars carefully on its upper deck. As she scanned the containers one by one, she began to play a game, wondering which one indeed was playing cocoon to the valuable, *invaluable* cargo. Señor Montoya would be pleased to see this, she thought. She let her thoughts drift back to the 'old country' as she sometimes called it. She checked her gold Cartier, its diamond jewelled bangle shining bright in the sun's reflection. Eleven thirty a.m. Six-thirty in Caracas. They would be rising now. Horses being brushed down and prepared by enthusiastic young grooms, kitchen staff preparing the breakfast ritual, chauffeur polishing the fleet of limousines always ready at the Don's pleasure. Soon, she would return, back where she felt truly at home.

The ship was fully in view now. Soon, it would turn north east, past the sandy surfing beaches and hotels of Catalan Bay on Gibraltar and steam steadily towards Alicante and its container port. She played another of her little mind games. She called it 'The Chain'. She was again in South America, but this time in the Colombian *coca* fields beyond the melting pot of Medellin, away from the knife-edge world of AK47s and Uzis. With the families whose whole lives depended on the crop coming in, their precious plants whose progeny would spawn kilo packets of white powdered gold dust. In the laboratories and factories where specialists would manufacture and test this product for which the western world seemed to have an inexhaustible desire. At the dockside as kilo after kilo was loaded carefully on, before making its laborious journey across the Atlantic Ocean to the open arms and nostrils of London, Paris and Berlin. She began to experience growing arousal as her mathematical brain began to calculate. One million users in the UK alone. Just one gram a day each would bring see €14,000,000,000 pass through the *Platja Blanca* organisation. *Fourteen billion Euros.* Enough to start an empire.

Enough to start a war.

Marianna's role within the group had long since passed into folklore. No-one ever really knows how criminal organisations evolve, or even start in the first place. They just kind of happen. Over a period of time. She thought of Señor Montoya, with his collection of Velazquez, Goya and Picasso. The Salvador Dali bought from the Spanish Ambassador for 'a favour'. His business interests in land, property, wine and construction. His ranch with its Japanese gardens, lakes and golf course. His exquisite dinner parties for the great and the good. His charity work.

Untouchable.

Is he really untouchable? she pondered, lighting another Balkan Sobranie, her beautiful talons pincer-like around the brightly coloured cheroot. *Or is it simply a question of expediency?* She regarded her surroundings, the bustling little café, its proprietor a million miles from Señor Montoya. Yet was he really so different? As he made coffee, poured brandy and raki for his growing band of mainly Moroccan clients, she considered *his* life, just for a moment, then she was back with the chain. Señor Montoya, Marianna (she loved it that *she* was the only contact with him. The power was such an aphrodisiac!), O'Riordan, Felix and Paco, Hall, Beevers and now Bold. She thought of where the tiny packets of white powder would *terminate*, the clubs and bars of London, bright and full of life. Electrifying.

For the first time, she had control of pure *coca*. Now, *she* had the power. No longer would her organisation have to kow tow to other dealers and importers. Because of her deal with Señor Montoya and the cartel, they had the financial muscle at last. She looked out of the grimy window once more, but this time it was not to observe the now distant cargo vessel, but to envisage her plans for the enclave. This remote outpost of once great colonial Spain. The derision with which her fancy friends had constantly treated her would be no more. It was big enough. Enough to become the Dubai and Las Vegas of the new Spain. The powerful Spain. The Spain of the future.

They called her 'Queen of Ceuta' behind her back. Now she could make it happen. There would be a new international airport, hotels, casinos, nightclubs, five star restaurants, marinas, million euro villas. Everything for the wealthy of Europe and beyond. She had been quietly buying up waterfront land for years. Scrubland which no-one wanted. Everything was perfect; the climate, the location, *the timing*. Under the protection of Spain, this would be the place they would come to. Already, the investors were pulling out of Dubai. Nervous, wary of extremist Islam on the march. She would see to it that Arab Africa would be kept at bay. Let the British keep Gibraltar, then we can keep this little gold-mine. Except that this was far more than that. This was *real power*. Her one and only chance to actually run a small country.

Moustafa placed a fresh coffee in front of her, before returning to the conviviality of his counter. She never even saw him. It was the discomfort caused by her now intense arousal which brought reality back. She looked down at her elegant crossed thighs and was grateful for her choice of black silk trousers. As she surreptitiously uncrossed and re-crossed her slim legs, she could feel the muskwish oozing from between her hot thighs.

This time, she drank the coffee hot, feeling its stimulating effects course quickly through her body. Before leaving, she made one short call on a pay and go mobile 'phone. As she left the bar, her chauffeur, who had been waiting across the square, started the engine and opened the rear door for her. Her heels clattered across the cobble stones. She stood tall, before climbing elegantly in.

"Take me to the old town, to the house. I need to relax".

As the Mercedes wound its way through tiny streets, she was interrupted by the sounds of life through the open window; stolen conversations, laughing children and the clatter of domestic chores carried out with stoical resignation.

Soon, my people, she thought. Soon you will not even recognise this place. Then, they were outside the tiny roof-gardened house. She dismissed her driver for the day and went in, removing her clothes as she walked up the narrow stairs and into the candle-lit den. Strong, spicy aromas of hash and incense greeted her arrival and she lay down on a large, soft, silk covered scatter cushion and selected a prepared bong. Her talons worked their way down between her legs to play and soon she was lost in a world of beautiful drug induced sensuality.

Chapter Thirty Two

Alicante Port 5.45am

Paco sat at the counter of the dockside bar, the powerful aroma of thick black coffee emanating from a tiny cup towards his bowed head. Totally professional. An already well-thumbed bar copy of 'El Mundo' lay in front of him on the dirty marble top, but he paid little more than lip service to it. His fellow loungers sat huddled in groups, turning round at every new interloper bringing with him the icy chill from Alicante's winter morning wind. Brandy. Coffee and brandy was their only solace. The TV stood over them in the corner, silent. Too early even for the breakfast show from Madrid. Outside, night's icy blanket lay comfortably undisturbed over the silent harbour.

Click. Barely audible, followed by a vibration felt only by him. Removing the mobile from his left pocket, he stared at the screen, taking in the details displayed. Just as he was about to press the button and bring the 'phone to his ear, the other pocket went off and the dilemma of which one to answer first hit him fair and square. Sandwich on one, Padraig on the other. He elected for his fellow countryman.

"Si. I am waiting for the nod. Yes, he's just down in the shed now. She is here. We just wait for the dockside services to swing into action and everything is fine. The old man has everything under control. *Ciao!*"

Padraig had already rung back before Paco could even begin to return his unanswered call.

"Good morning, my friend. All is well, I hope? Good. I am going to call you in around a half an hour. Then I will have a time for the bride to be collected. I think she is looking beautiful, no? Yes, I hope so too. *Ciao!*"

Paco's activities went completely unnoticed and he returned to the now cooling coffee, draining it, before calling the barman over for a refill.

Five hundred yards down the quayside, the old man sat alone in his threadbare armchair in a dilapidated hut, poring over a ship's manifest, his half-glasses still besmirched with the grime and rain of his last venture into the wintry gloom. Slowly and methodically, his pen ticked off reference numbers against the *Aduana's* official bills of lading. When he was at an end, he looked up at the calendar, shook his head and picked up a telephone receiver, barked staccato instructions into it, then replaced it in the dirty black cradle. He paused to roll a cigarette, then opened the wooden door to let in the outside. Removing a mobile from inside his blue *trabajo* overalls, he dialed the number which would start everything off. The sound of rain pouring onto silent railway tracks outside the hut was almost deafening, thanks to the long since broken downpipe, now lying forgotten against the shed's outer wall. He maintained his composure however and felt his phone connect to Paco.

"*Ola, chico!* The lady is awake and having her breakfast. Then she will take her bath, get dressed and soon she will be ready, I think in three hours or so. Her taxi is booked, yes? *Bueno!*"

Paco's watchful vigil recommenced, whilst forty miles down the coast, a delivery vehicle swung into action. A crudely hand-painted Ford Transit van with the logo 'Tony's English Produce' written on the side emerged from a lean-to at the back of a small supermarket in Orihuela, already open for business. As it turned onto the main road and past the doors, there were already a number of underdressed British looking pensioners queuing for pasties, pies and chutney. That sort of thing. Tony was doing a bomb.

Except Tony was now on his way up the *autopista*. Direction Alicante.

*

Slowly, very slowly, the crane began its work. As it moved slowly along the rain-shiny rails, what passes for dawn began to show itself across the harbour, lighting up the containers stacked high on the ship. Orange clad dockside navvies toiled at long familiar tasks, their voices calling from one side of the quay to the other. One by one, the rusting 40` metal container boxes are moved from the storm lashed deck to the wharf, stacked one on top of the other. Priorities allocated by uniformed foremen below, the crackle of walkie-talkies indicating the fate of each container. The old man walked slowly from the relative comfort of his hut and makes his way towards the crane control office, pausing only to re-ignite his stub of a cigarette for the fifth time, grimy lacerated fingers immune to the Zippo lighter's stinging heat. Once inside, a short but telling conversation, followed by the discreet passing of a small packet to the controller and he was gone, this time to the café. The yellow-jacketed crane driver was given further instructions and his eyes moved up and down a numbered container manifest sheet until he rested on what he was looking for. From a vantage point high above the dockside, he scanned the container ship's emptying deck for corresponding reference numbers. Slowly and methodically, his eyes traversed the rain spattered boxes.

It was not there.

Tony's transit entered the Port of Alicante boundary via the south gate. He showed his contractor's pass, exchanged a few words with the security guard, hiding from the rain in his smoky hut, and edged forward ready for the barrier to be raised so he could continue his journey. Parking up, he too joined the growing numbers in the crowded quayside café, sitting alone underneath the TV set, awaiting instructions. The old man was there too, sipping at a glass of early morning brandy, puffing on a filterless cigarette proffered to him by another of the card playing throng at a neighbouring table. Paco sat patiently at the counter, closely examining the football pages of 'El Mundo'.

The crane controller stared nervously through the diesel film and rain towards the remaining few containers, before finally allowing himself a smile. He issued an instruction by walkie-talkie and the container was selected, hooked up and swung swiftly across the railway tracks and onto the ground, doors facing away from the quayside. Removing a mobile phone from inside his sou-wester, he dialed a number, waited for it to connect to the ringing tone, then snapped it shut again.

Click. That was all the old man heard. His facial expression did not alter one jot. He drained the brandy and walked up to counter, stubbing out the remains of his cigarette in a large chipped ashtray before once again heading out into the storm. Out of the corner of his eye, Paco witnessed this and pressed the send button on an unregistered pay-as-you-go mobile. Within seconds, a small vibration in Tony's breast pocket caused him to drain his coffee. He left a few coins on the formica topped table and threaded his way between the card schools and brandy swilling, chattering dock workers, made his way back to the transit and removed the 'phone.

Dockside Hut 3

He glanced up, looked along the wharf from his location in the van park and in the distance, worked out which hut was referred to in this brief text message. He turned the ignition key and the Ford diesel engine clattered into life. He inched his way along the uneven road surface between the containers stacked five high until a boiler suited figure emerged from the rainy gloom.

"*¿Donde es la cabina tres, por favor?*" he asked of the man.

"*Diez metros, detrás de aquí*". He pointed towards a parking place, indicating the hut's location. Tony eased into the narrow space and approached from the rear. Huddled figures struggled to and fro against the biting winter wind, each concerned with his own private battle, unconcerned. He entered the hut without knocking and handed his papers to the outwardly nonchalant old man, whose seemingly careless scanning hid meticulous attention to detail. He was given a numbered ticket, countersigned on the reverse in the old man's scrawl. Another sou-wester'd docker entered the hut and was given a small plastic envelope containing a seal and metal identification disc. Tony was motioned out together with him. Ten yards from the hut, a blue container, numbered MX8686 stands waiting. Swiftly, the man extracted a pair of cutters from under his waterproof coat, cut the metal wire seal and raised the handle. Gradually, he eased open the rusty door, shone his torch over the container's load, pausing on each illuminated box, until finally settling on eight polystyrene cartons stacked against the side.

"*Bueno. Tu coche. Ahora.*"

Tony returned to the Ford and reversed up to the open container. Before he came to a complete halt, he heared the rear doors snap open and the sound of the first box striking the van floor. One by one, they were placed inside, the doors were closed and the *bang, bang* of the loader's open hand on the transit's roof indicated that it was time to go. As he pulled away, the container had already been closed up and an identical wire was being wound through the metal eyelets and its identification seal affixed. Slowly, ever so slowly, he eased his way between the high stacks of forty-footers before turning onto the quay and away. His next stop was across the other side of the harbour. The fish market. Gangs of men and women shouted the odds to each other as the catch was allocated. Tony drew up outside his regular supplier's unit and climbed out of his cab to shake the man by the hand. Whilst they exchanged words at the rear of the van, boxes of trawler fresh-frozen cod, mackerel, hake and haddock were loaded on top of the polystyrene cartons and soon, the van was full of the aroma of freshly caught fish. Pleasantries swapped, Tony said his goodbyes and made his way around the harbour wall, past the sailing club and back into the port. He joined the queue of leaving early morning vehicles, their loading completed. Ahead, the *Control Policia* barrier was raised and lowered every few seconds. The rain was coming down sideways now, sheets of water lashing the side of the blue and white shed. Eventually, it was Tony's turn and he wound down the driver's window, papers at the ready. The official barely acknowledged him, before raising the barrier and finally, he was away. He wound the window back up, pressed the cigarette lighter in and turned on the radio. He slowed momentarily to spark up a Marlboro, bending down to retrieve the now red hot lighter, before again speeding up ready to enter the steady stream of traffic heading south along the coast road. Just as Tony was about to take his turn at the now green traffic lights, a yellow jacketed *Aduana Naçional* officer emerged from his car and raises his hand, signalling for Tony to pull over. On the opposite side of the road, a small white Seat van was parked outside a tobacconists, its occupant obscured from view by the lowered sun visor. He was already pressing digits on a swiftly employed mobile 'phone as Tony wound down his window once more, this time to speak to the Customs official.

"*Buenas Dias, señor.¿ Habla español?* Do you speak Spanish?"

"Er...yes...no...not very much".

"Which is it, *señor*, yes or no?"

"Er...no...no".

"Very well. This is a routine stop. We are conducting a survey of early morning users of the port. Can you tell me what you have been doing here today, please?"

Tony swallowed hard.

"Of course. I've bin' collectin' me fish from the *Mercado Pescadores*. It's all the imported stuff. For the English".

"Do you use the port regularly for this activity?"

"Every week, mate. Regular as clockwork".

The official leaned a little closer, trying to shield his face from the driving rain. The aroma of fish was beginning to waft from behind the driver's seat, which became increasingly apparent to the officer's nostrils. He looked through the rear window at the back of the cab at the boxes stacked roof high and returned to face Tony.

"Those boxes? You cannot see out of the rear. Are you overloaded?"

Tony sat square in his seat, trying not to look too closely into the officer's eyes. Across the road, an animated conversation was taking place on mobile phones from within the Seat.

"I don't think so, mate. This fish don't really weigh that much, an' I got the extra wheels".

Momentarily, the officer looked along the side of the Ford, before returning to his conversation.

"Thank you, sir. That will be all, but make sure you can see through the rear window. We would not like to discover you later, involved in an accident. *¡Adios!*"

He walked back to the sanctuary of his official car and climbs in. Tony drew up the window once more and pulled relieved onto the main road south towards Orihuela. Inside the white Seat, conversation on the mobile ceased and it pulled unnoticed into a slow moving queue of traffic heading past the Algiers ferry terminal, headlights torch-like, piercing the morning gloom. There were just five cars between it and the transit. Tony drove on, eventually reaching the entrance to the *Peaje* toll booth and the motorway towards Murcia and Torrevieja. The white Seat was just one car behind now.

*

A man nodded to the seated Paco, planted firmly at a corner table in the dockside café, paying scant regard to the now blaring TV above. He felt the Nokia's gentle vibration. Before he could answer it, the man was gone, out into the morning mist.

"*Si. Diga me.* Yes, now the lady has left. I think she will be there in time for lunch, no? Certainly she is on time". *Click.*

*

"Ronan! Get your arse over to Orihuela. The lady's on her way. Just unpack it an' stash it". Padraig sat at the bar, the previous night's takings' sheets laid out in front of him. His unconcerned and matter-of-fact manner hiding a nervousness consistent with the unfamiliarity of the job. As Ronan took the van keys from a key rack behind the counter, his gaze returned to the columns of alcohol and food receipts. He didn't look up again when his nephew called out from the back kitchen, announcing his departure. The relief showed on his face. He was once again alone with his thoughts. Jumping into the unmarked van, the boy drove quickly away. As the alleyway at the rear of Doolans was left behind, a navy blue Peugeot 307's engine ignited and its driver eased carefully into traffic three cars back. He turned the corner towards the main square and picked up his mobile from the passenger seat, maintaining a constant state of alertness. Drawing to a halt at the lights, he rapidly entered four sets of digits into the tiny screen before hitting the send button. Some sixty miles away, Paco's unregistered mobile buzzed into life, his face broke into a smile and he noted down the Spanish car registration numbers. A short call to his friend in the Policia Local yielded the information he needed and within five minutes, Ronan was fully appraised of the situation. He doubled back towards the square and drew to a halt outside an English bar called 'East Enders'. The shutters were partly down, the door was open and there was trade of some sort going on, in the form of two rain-coated Brits drinking milky coffee under a rain-soaked awning. A small dog sat obediently at their feet, its fur hanging pathetically sodden, its expression one of total resignation.

Ronan jumped out of his warm cab, leaving the driver's door open and walked into the bar, carrying a delivery note. On the right side of the street, the 307 pulled into a parking space and its occupants waited. And waited. Eventually, the passenger got out onto the pavement and sidled across the wide tree-lined street, walking up and down past 'East Enders'. Save for the aproned barman, the place was deserted.

Behind the bar, lies a parking bay where once, a motorbike lay standing. The only evidence thereof, a large oily padlock and chain. Three miles down the main national road to Orihuela, a still smiling Irishman made a steady hundred kilometres an hour, weaving the Kawasaki in and out of the morning traffic queues.

Click. "We've lost him. Yes, I know. I know. He gave us the slip. No question of it. Pre-planned. I'm not even going to go there. He's gone somewhere and wherever that is, you can be sure he didn't want us as company. You know the manager will have a cover story. We're on our way back to Doolans."

As the barman cleared away the empty cups, a discreet glance across the street told him what he needed to know. Calmly, he walked up to the van, removed the keys, slammed the door and returned to the familiarity of his work.

Ronan eased the roaring bike into the suburbs of Orihuela, along the strip with its garish furniture stores, hot-tub outlets and out-of-town restaurants, eventually turning off into a side street bordered by broken down warehouses and rusting cars. At the end, he slowed to a walking pace mounting what was left of the pavement, before riding between two corrugated iron sheds and parking up at the rear. He entered, having unlocked and removed a padlock, sat on a discarded crate and waited. After several minutes, the silence was broken by the increasing volume of a diesel engine clattering its way up the street. After a short while, it stopped, then nothing. Ronan walked across the darkened shed and peered through a crack in the front window slats, being careful not to disturb the intricate cobwebs now festooning his way. Tony sat in the transit's cab, tapping digits into a mobile 'phone. From this vantage point, Ronan cast his eyes up and down the deserted street, painstakingly pausing at each building, scrutinising for any discrepancy. Nothing. Tony put down the mobile and looked up across the street, first to one side, then the other. He was twenty metres away from Ronan. His mobile lit up. The incoming text issued instructions. He started the engine, pulled up to the end of the street and turned left along what is left of a goat track and round the back of the shed. By the time he parked, Ronan was standing outside. A quick handshake and the van reversed up to the rear doors of the shed and the unloading began. Within ten minutes, the fish had been replaced in the back, the boxes hidden under a pile of planks inside the unlit shed and Tony was on his way to Torrevieja via the motorway. Ronan returned straight to Doolans and was logged as he entered, bold as brass, via the front entrance.

Chapter Thirty Three

easyJet Flight EZY9989. Somewhere over the Pyrenees. 6.30am.

"Hello again!"

Dean began to come to from his early morning slumber. It's that slavering, slobbering, drool down the collar sleep you do when you're on a very early flight. Your eyes are stinging, you've had way too little sleep and you really want to be home in bed. As the swimming, watery sensation cleared from his eyes, his vision became one of an orange clad lovely called Samantha. A smiling, caring, *wouldyoulikesomecoffee?* Sam.

"Weren't you with us last week, Sir?"

"Y…yeah. Yeah, I was. I remember ya'. Kept me in vodkas. Bet I was a pain, weren't I?"

"Of course not, Sir. Can I get you something? A drink perhaps or a sandwich?"

"Just some OJ, darlin'. Bit early for the old coffee".

As she moved down the aisle, three rows behind, a leather jacketed man permitted himself a wry smile and returned to his newspaper.

*

Jalon Valley, northern Costa Blanca, Spain.

The early morning sun was already finding its way through tiny cracks in the old wooden finca's door. While two boiler-suited locals kept watch, small metal containers were being filled with stamped packets of the finest cocaine. In the corner, an arc welding kit was being fired up, ready to seal the containers airtight and watertight. Up on the hill, high above the Jalon valley, a lone man stood watch, hidden behind a large olive tree, his binoculars occasionally catching the light, a rifle stood casually upright against the gnarled bark. The men worked quickly and quietly, anxious to get their job done and away. Outside on the road, a *'Se Vende'* sign indicated the likely fate of the four hundred year old ruin. A *click* of a well worn mobile, followed by the briefest of conversations indicated that the operation was about to come to a close. The men held thick woollen blankets up against the window whilst the welder worked his magic, then the arrival of a van making its way up the dirt track announced that it was time to move. The gunman's binoculars moved from finca to van and back to finca, watching for the slightest irregularity, the merest indication that something was wrong. It did not come. The dirty white Ford Transit reversed up to the barn-like door at the rear of the old house. Two sets of doors opened in unison, the goods were transferred and within seconds, it was travelling back down the dusty track and onto the road back towards the N232. Four men dressed in agricultural clothes walked away and up the track towards the tree line. Shortly after that, a wisp of smoke began to emerge from the roof of the finca followed by licking flames which gradually engulfed the whole building. The roof fell in within minutes and after that, nothing was left, save the four walls. The gunman packed away his tools and made his way over the hill.

*

Custom House, Lower Thames Street, London 7.00am

The mood was quiet yet there was an understated excitement pervading the large meeting room. Low rumbling conversation throbbed like a sub-woofer left on overnight. Audible but unintelligible.

"Okay, people. Let me call this meeting to order. Is everyone here? Everyone who should be, that is!" Nervous laughter.

"Good. Excellent. First things first. Coffee will be served in a moment for those of you who are still mentally in bed. For those of you who are still in the land of nod, LISTEN!" More nervous laughter, this time at the expense of those who were nursing pre-meeting last night piss-up hangovers. A rejuvenated and buoyant Kim Evans took the floor.

"Okay. Janet sends her best to you all. We're getting very close now and she is as we speak co-ordinating final liaison with the FLOs and foreign jurisdiction representatives. Number One. Surveillance. I have here a report from the O'Riordan house. As you will know, we fired a 'BrickBug' at the place last week and it has already yielded much. The one at the bar has given us even more, but we are still short of the actual truck and timing information. We are monitoring all locations 24/7 now and I am confident that something is going to give in the next couple of days. Guys, we are getting very close on this one now. Patience is not a virtue of mine, but if we hang on just that little bit longer, it's going to pay off, in spades.

Number Two. We have a positive ID on the man previously known as 'Mr Bling'. His name is Dean Bold, he is from Canvey Island in Essex and his house and office have been added to the lists. He is also now under 24/7 Obs. This news is hot off the press, people. *Very hot!* Thanks to the new computer system, I have been able to liaise with Maidstone and Dover IMPEX and it appears that Mr Bold is well known to them as a suspect swerver. He has connections to haulage and, shock horror, Metro Bond. However, we do not, at this stage, believe that the old debacle will come back to haunt us as it has so often done in the past. I am awaiting final clearance from IMPEX that we can go ahead and knock him as part of Watchtower II. We now know that he has sent two trucks to the Alicante region of Spain in the last week and we believe that it is these trucks which will be used to transport Class A drugs back to the UK. It seems that it is quite likely there *is* an airport connection to the drugs' origin. That has yet to be confirmed but for now, our aim is to stop the drugs from getting onto the UK market and to apprehend those responsible for that. This is the beginning of what could be one of our biggest ever operations. We have the opportunity to strike a blow against what could be a major importing gang. Now, subject to ongoing obs in Spain, from the moment the trucks are loaded and on their way, we have a minimum of two and a half days to get teams in place for knocks countrywide. The FLO in Madrid is working closely with Interpol, the Spanish police and Customs in the Alicante province. Trackers are in place on both the trucks, courtesy of the Dover team on their outbound journey and we have monitors in place at the Perpignan border crossing and at strategic points en route. There will be teams of obs vehicles to maintain 24 hour surveillance. I have worked closely with IMPEX to ensure there are no repeats of the 1999 fiascos, where vehicles were left unobserved and incomplete logs were maintained. We cannot, and I mean *cannot* afford any more cock ups like that. We live or die by this one, people. I am afraid that it is going to be the Yellow

Brick Road or the Road to Hell. Which one you choose is partly down to your own instinct and training. Let's make this a good one! Emily!"

As she sat down, spontaneous applause began to echo around the room, bringing forth a glow of pride. Eye contact was made across the tables, a sense of expectation hung heavy.

Emily Loader rose to her feet and took the floor.

"Thank you, Kim. We will *not* let you down. OK. Since I came back from Spain, we have had one piece of news this morning which does not exactly fill us with joy. It seems that Zulu 3, Ronan O'Riordan left Doolans yesterday morning using the delivery van and made a deliberate and pre-planned switch to an unknown vehicle, sited probably at the rear. As a result, we were not able to ascertain where he was going or who, if anyone, he was meeting. The obs team maintain that they must have been spotted, as the manner of O'Riordan's escape would lead us to believe that this was one of possibly several diversionary tactics they have in place. As a precautionary measure, we have allocated the last known location where he was spotted to mobile surveillance. The decision has been taken that this is to remain a 'follow and discover operation' for now. We have the trucks on satellite tracking. The moment they arrive in the area, if, that is, our intelligence is correct and the two vehicles in question are to be our 'couriers' back to the UK, then mobile will move in and observe the switch and load. Any questions?"

A hand goes up at the back.

"Er, from where we're sitting, it looks like the operation could have been compromised already. I mean, if they're already mounting counter-surveillance manoeuvres......"

"I hear you. Certainly this was one of those, but as you are well aware from previous operations of this kind, these people regularly mount this type of activity. It helps to keep them on their toes. It also gives them an enormous sense of well-being. They think they are getting one over on us and they always believe that ultimately, everything's gonna be alright. Expect more of it, is all I will say at this stage. What they almost certainly *don't know* is that we are following the trucks from a distance and that they will lead us right into the lion's den. They can introduce any kind of tactics such as this. It won't stop their inability to undo what we have discovered. That brings us to an update on Brighton Rock. We're well over the hump with him now. His handler is here, so I'll pass you over."

Emily sits down next to Kim, folds her arms and waits.

"Thanks. It looks like we've got Brighton Rock back on track now. There was a potentially sticky moment over the return of the Class A, but that seems to have been overcome, partly by the intervention of a more relaxed policy from above and partly by some good field work".

"Yeah, and partly due to a fucking good bit of luck," whispered Meacher from somewhere near the back.

"The goods recovered from Metro Bond have been tested and have been shown to be 92% pure cocaine. Even the cartel's own original stamp is featured on the outside. If this is the quality that we are dealing with here, then this could well be the first seizure of its kind on mainland Britain. Brighton Rock is in place, though we do not believe that Metro or any of its directors are involved. We strongly believe that it has been used simply for storage. Right under our noses, you might say". Laughter echoes around the room.

"Thanks. Another great piece of work, under what I must say has been formidable pressure from the word go. I'll hand you back to Emily to wind things up".

"Thank you, Kim. Thank you to all of you. This has been a first class operation form start to finish. It looks like we've got all our ducks in a row now, people. All we need is the final go-ahead from upstairs and it's show time!"

As Emily sits down to rapturous applause, the murmurings begin.

"Where have we heard that before?" whispered Andy Meacher. "She must have actually been listening to what the Welsh slapper said. What's with the Em and Kim show all of a sudden? Something we don't know? And another thing; why the fuck do they all talk in clichés all the time? Is it something to do with promotions? It's like they lose touch with reality once they get through the glass ceiling."

"I'm not convinced by all this at all. There's too many egos in this room. They'll do more than lose touch with reality. They've already lost touch with this case. *Learning from our mistakes*, my arse. Does anyone ever learn *anything* in here?"

Chapter Thirty Four

As the 737 touched down at Stansted, tyres smoking a familiar trail through the dark Essex evening, Dean was already fidgeting, ready to get up and out of his front row seat as soon as the plane came to a halt. The successes of the previous twenty-four hours' meetings with Padraig were at uppermost in his mind yet now he thought only of his daughter, waiting just beyond the barrier in the arrivals hall to greet him.

As the cabin lights came on, he was up, grabbing a small leather Versace holdall from the overhead locker and away, shuttle bound, leading the charge for the air bridge. Straight through, passport in hand, he spotted her in the throng, dressed in a pale pink corset and leather trousers. She rushed round the gaggle of waiting families and into his arms.

"Oh, Dad, I'm so glad you're back. Me an' Troy, we've missed ya so much".

"I've missed you too, babes, but I've only been away a day! How's your Mum?"

Her head is down, staring at the floor.

"Still the same".

"We'll go an' see her tomorrow, yeah?"

"Yeah". Whatever.

"Brought you some stuff from the shops an' all!"

She squeezed him tight, not wanting to let him go. He put his arm around her shoulder and they walked towards the car park.

"Bought you a couple of nice bits from the duty free, girl. We'll wait till we get home, yeah?" She didn't even answer this comment, she just hugged him even tighter, staying this close until they reach the Z8.

"Do you want to drive?" she said, almost pressing the keys into his free hand. He took them and chucked the bag into the sports car's little boot.

They were back in Canvey in under the hour to find the house lit up like a Christmas tree.

"I told Troy to put the lights on, make you feel at home. It's been really weird without you this time, Dad. Dunno why, the house didn't feel right. Like it wasn't ours. I love you, Dad". Yet another hug. Dean's puzzlement began to grow.

"You alright, babes?"

"Yeah, fine". She walked over to the fridge and opening it, handed him a Stella.

"Right. Great. Shall we have a pizza?"

That's it. She just burst into tears, big loud sobs and ran into his arms.

"It's alright, babes. Don't you worry about a thing. There, there, you just let it all out. Your mum's gonna get better. She'll make it, she's made of strong stuff, your mum".

"It…it's…not that. It's…HER. She…she's the bleedin' problem. She should never have been in that bleedin' car". Her face was pressed hard against his chest, huge tears staining his shirt.

"Course she shouldn't, baby. It was all a big mistake".

"No it weren't. You don't know what I know. Oh, Dad, last night was horrible".

"What? What's happened? Has someone hurt ya?"

"Only in 'ere, Dad". She placed her hand over her heart, tears still flowing freely down her cheeks.

"It's Shirley and Debra. You know they was here last night? I went out with Sean and we had a row, Dad. He's nice but I weren't in the mood, so I come home, like. Shirley's car was in the drive, so I parked in the road, under the tree. They can't 'ave heard me, else they wouldn't have been talkin' like that".

"Like what, babes? What the 'ell was they sayin'?"

"They was talkin' about Mum an' Uncle Dave. In your car".

"Yeah? What of it?"

"It weren't no accident, Dad. Debra told Auntie Shirley that mum… an' 'im, they was…they was 'avin an affair".

Before she finished the sentence, his head had dropped. Like he *knew*. The terrible secret which not only now haunted his daughter, but was brought to the surface in the cruellest of ways to haunt him. The sub-conscious became the conscious, the thought never again to be buried amongst doubt and self-delusion.

"No, babes. No. You must have mis-'eard 'em. Not that, no, please". The tears began to flow once more, the terrible realisation that Pandora's Box was open, never again to be sealed. Benissa moved close to her father and held him tight as the agony rose to the surface.

"Why, babes? What the 'ell for? She's got everythin' 'ere".

"It was awful, Dad. I came back in an' they was in the kitchen. They was both pissed and talkin' about Mum and him. Turns out it's been goin' on for months. I just dunno what to think no more. I mean, she's our mum, for God's sake. How could she do this to us?"

Benissa's constant questions went unanswered. Dean sat quite still, unaware of his withdrawal into himself. The upbeat feelings of yesterday which he had wanted to bring back with him long gone, to be replaced by gloom and despondency. After a while, he raised his head and looked at her.

"When? When did it start? I wanna know".

"They said it was at one of your parties. You know, the ones after Mr Chan's".

"What, the Saturday ones when the bleedin' house is full of strangers? Fuck me, girl. How stupid have I been? Right under me nose. Me wife and me best mate. That is bang out of order". He got up out of his chair and went over to the sink, picking up a carving knife and examining it. He turned round. His daughter's expression one of absolute terror.

"Dad? Don't do anythin' mad, please? I can't lose you as well.

We've 'ad enough in this family already".

He came to his senses momentarily and put the knife back on the draining board. He looked down at the pine kitchen table, at a magazine. Essex Life. *Essex fuckin' death more like.* He picked it up and underneath lay the evidence of last night's pizza party. It hid a messy stain that was lying there. Quickly, he put it back, before Benissa saw the deep red tomato paste, splattered against the pale wood. Silence descended on the room. They sat opposite each other for what seemed like ages, before she spoke again.

"What you gonna do about Mum? She's getting' better, Dad, really she is. I know she loves you. She's always tellin' me how much".

"Enough to do it with me best mate? I ain' havin it, girl. Just ain't wearin' this. Is that how much she loves me, the slag?"

She came to him once more, throwing her arms around his neck.

"Please Dad, please don't call Mum that. She's not a slag. She's worked really hard for this family, just like you. We can work something out, I know we can. I know you're upset, Dad, really I do, but we need to talk this through. We 'ave to. It's not just me an' you. There's Troy an' all. He really needs her at the moment. Since she's been gone, he's out of his 'ead with worry. He don't speak much, just goes in that room playing with his Playstation 3 and that computer he's always plugged into. It's like livin' with a robot".

"I have to talk to 'er. Before I decide what I'm gonna do. Me head's all over the place. I need a drink. Get us a vodka, princess".

She walked zombie-like to the freezer and removed a new bottle of Smirnoff Black and placed it in front of him.

"Can I have one an' all, Dad? I don't think you should drink alone".

"Help yourself, love. Might as well. Think I might go out after this".

"No Dad. Please don't go out. You don't know what might 'appen. What if someone upsets ya? Some melt of a geezer who don't mean no 'arm, just gets in your way, like? Mood you're in, you'd probably kill him. Then where would we all be? In the bleedin' court room watchin' you go down the steps? I ain't havin' that Dad.

I've nearly lost me Mum. I ain't losin' the both of you in less than a month. Stay with me, Dad. We can 'ave a nice drink 'ere. Just the two of us. We ain't talked like, for ages".

"This is fuckin' out of order. I can't get 'em out of me 'ead. Just keep tryin' to imagine why".

"Dad? I have to ask you this. I mean, it's not like I'm your little girl no more…"

"Benissa, love, one thing you'll 'ave to understand is that you will always be my little girl. Even when you've got kids of your own. That don't change".

He was up on his feet by now, going for the car keys. She lunged for them too and for a brief moment, they struggled to gain the upper hand. She looked up at him, their eyes met and the tears returned. First from her, then as he realised the effect his anger was having, from him.

"I'm beggin' you, Dad, if you go now, I dunno what I'm gonna do. Please, *please*, don't go an' do something stupid".

He held her close once more. *Click, click.* His mobile lit up on the table. Town.

"I gotta take this, babes".

He pulled away from her and flipped open the handset.

"Yes, mate. Yeah. No worries. Listen. I'm a bit tied up at the mo, yeah? Do we 'ave to? Alright, mate. Yeah, I'll see you there in an hour. Get the Coat to come an' all. No, I'll be there. Yeah. Loads to tell ya. Cushti. See ya". *Click.*

He put the phone in his pocket and turned to see an empty kitchen.

"Benissa? Where are you, princess? *Benissa!*"

He ran out of the kitchen, into the living room and the conservatory. Then all over the house, shouting, screaming his daughter's name. But *he* was alone. *He* ran into the pool room and over in the corner of the rippled water, there is a shape face down. *He* stopped dead in his tracks, as if it's all come on top in one short passage of time. *He* was scared now, frightened to move, terrified to stay.

"NO! No, not that". *He* broke into a run, skidding and skating across the slippery tiles. As *he* reached the other end, his mind was filled with confusion. Gina's prized full length silver fox fur lay lining down in the deep end, the word *slag* spray painted in pillar box red across the shoulders. *He* looked around at the ornate room, the roman pillars holding up what is left of his world. *He* picked the coat out of the water and lay it across two sun beds, then walked out, straight to the front door, the car and away. A thousand thoughts raced through his mind, yet they all brought him back to one conclusion. All roads lead to *revenge*.

The Range Rover screeched away from Canvey, down the A13 towards London.

*

New bottles and packets littered Shirley Hilton's dressing table. Her face close up to the mirror as the make-up was trowelled on. She'd had her hair done and the crash diet she'd been strictly adhering to since Dave had the back of his head blown off was finally starting to work. She'd shoe-horned herself into a corset top and she was even wearing heels.

"Mummy?"

She turned round to face Carla, her elder daughter who was framed by the open bedroom door.

"Hello, little angel. Shouldn't you be tucked up now? Where's that Lorna? I thought you was playing Sims?"

"She's putting Kiera to bed. She's being naughty".

"Who is, love? Lorna or Kiera?"

"Oh, Mummy, you are silly. You look really different. You look really pretty".

"Thank you, angel! Mummy's going out".

"Will there be other Mummies there?"

"Yes, darling, there probably will. It's a place for all the Mummies who go out".

"Why are you going out? Why, Mummy, why? Is it because Daddy's not here?"

*

Dean's torn up the '13 towards Barking and his destination, the 'T-Bone Steak House' in Longbridge Road. A couple of lines snorted, double quick time and the old Range was flying. Mobiles were ringing and the hi-fi was kicking out some heavy beats. No more of the old stuff, this is strictly Basement Jaxx. The sub was making the whole chassis vibrate and he was zooming. Benissa, Gina and everything else ending in 'A' was out of his mind, including Spain.

Click. "Yes, mate. Yeah, about ten minutes. Stick yours in Park Road, round the back. What time's Ali getting' there? Yeah. Tell him an' all, then". *Click.*

*

With her daughter's words still cutting deep, Shirley too was on her way, trying very hard not to look back as Lorna the babysitter slammed the solid oak front door. She was making her way to 'The' in Chelmsford, it's Thursday night and time to let the hair down. She's meeting Paula there, who had also asked Debra along. This was going to be very, very dangerous. Three tons of silicone, Debra style, plus one scorned woman who hasn't had any for months and you could imagine what was on the menu.

*

"For fuck's sake! They've only got a fuckin' Greek Night on".

The three of them are stood in the middle of Longbridge Road, staring at the door. The bouzouki music was loud enough to drown out the street and the party was well in full swing. They were just about to go, when the manager spotted them through the window. His face lit up and that was it. No chance of escape. He was out the door and all round Dean before he could get on his heels.

"Great to see you, innit! What you doin' round this neck of thee woods, innit? Ali! You still livin' in my Uncle house, you dirty Turk!" He and Ali the Coat embraced like long lost brothers.

"It's my house! You live in Grandma house in Paphos, I live in your house in Kyrenia. Simple. Fair exchange is no robbery! It's barter, innit!" They were almost dragged into the restaurant, where the music was deafening. A full band sat in the corner, well amped up. In the middle of the floor, a very pretty young girl was belly-dancing for the assembled Barkingites. She was dressed in the full regalia, her long eyelashes tempting the men to throw money, their wives' faces a cross between encouragement for the girl and daggers for the men's backs!

"Come through, come through, please!" he shouted to them. "We have special table for you, right here". He cleared away some place settings and sat them down. It was perfectly obvious that this had been booked for someone else.

"What you drink, innit?" he asked, all the while calling for two bottles of champagne to be brought. They arrived as if by magic, double quick, and that's it. He'd got them. The barman shouted something in his general direction but the bouzouki player won hands down and the words were lost somewhere between mouth and ear. He pointed at the table, but to no avail.

"We'll 'ave champagne, then". The music came to a crescendo, the girl shaking her assets for all they're worth and the crowd's gone wild. Bells and tambourine perfectly in rhythm and she was right in front of a table of guys out on a stag night, her belly ring just inches from the groom's face. Bejewelled feet stamped faster and faster, everyone was clapping and when seemed as if the band could play no faster, a loud shriek emanated from her mouth, the playing stopped and the lights went out. Dead silence. Just one half second later, a spotlight illuminated the middle of the floor and there she stood, stock still, her arms raised, her legs wide apart. The crowd broke into spontaneous clapping and cheering, wolf-whistling and foot stamping. She went off with rapturous applause ringing in her ears. The background music took over and the diners gradually return to the tzatziki, taramasalata and dolmades.

"Is fuckin' good, innit?" the manager smiled and poured more champagne.

"Theo, can you make sure we're left alone. We gotta bit of business to sort".

"It's OK. I make sure. I send you over some snacks, OK?"

He wandered over to the bar and had what passed for a quiet word with the heavily perspiring young waiter.

"Dean, bruv, you alright? You look like you've lost a bar an' found a score".

"Yeah, yeah. Just tired".

"You need somethin' to pick you up?"

"Well, it just so fuckin' 'appens that I do".

Town slipped him the necessary and he's away.

"What the *fuck* is his problem? I know he's got the missus in the hospital, but she's on the fuckin' mend, ain't she? I had word that everything is cushti in Spain, all ready to go".

"I don't know, Stephen. He seems to have become very distant, like he's either hiding something, or he's worried. It's not like him at all. It's almost like he's *lost something*. He hasn't stopped looking around since we got here. What the hell is that all about?"

"Well I don't think he's gonna bubble up what's transpiring to us".

Within a couple of minutes, he was back from the gents looking altogether more bright eyed.

"Right, let's talk. The trip was fuckin' blindin'. I tell you, they may be quiet when you first meet 'em, but once the business is sorted, they go right into one. We're on for the move. It's called on. Ron's got his best drivers on it, the smudge is being arranged this week. Even we won't know where it is till everything's safely through".

Suddenly, the sounds of breaking crockery shattered the quieter music of the sound system and it's all kicked off. The difference was that the manager and the owner were up on their feet in the middle of the floor, they've got a stack of plates each and they're smashing them, one after the other on the floor, to the sound of clapping and cheering from everyone, especially the stag party.

One does it, they all do it and next thing, there's about twenty people up on their feet, smashing for Barking.

"What about the scratch?"

"I've given them a bit up front, just to show willing. Beevers is coming down to pick up the balance once we've got it home and in the slaughter."

"When are we seein' him, Dean?"

"We're goin' up day after tomorrow. I said we'd go to his house, seein' as normally, he comes to ours."

"Fuck me, I get nose bleeds if I go north of Watford."

"Ali, can you sort the rest of the situation with your people? When we call it on, I don't want any delays or nothing."

"They're all sweet. You've no idea how excited they get when there's a sniff of ninety-two percent Mother of Pearl. This is a right first".

The realisation of their fast-track careers through the hierarchy is not lost. Sometimes, in life, opportunities come your way. You can choose to take them or you can choose to leave them. Failing that, there is the third way, which is also the most commonplace, and that is the one where even if the opportunity came right up to you and smacked you in the gob wearing one of Kev's KDs, you would totally miss it as it passed through your bleeding gums and out of the back of your head at one hundred miles per hour. Look back for just one moment to the time when Town came back from Spain for the first time. Just a couple of months ago. He's turned them from quietly making a good half a bar a year each, to the big top; flashing lights, dancing girls, trumpet blaring premier league of the criminal fraternity. The big time. They're going to make five bar from this one. One hundred and fifty kilos of the very finest Columbian Marching Powder. To the tune of Dean Bold's fiddle. Playing to a waiting world. Back of the net.

"What about the ongoing, Dean? This is nice, but you know the way my people work. Give them a taste of something and they want it all day long. It'll be, 'OK, that's this week sorted, what about next?' I just know it will".

"Marianna assures me that they can keep things goin'. The problem they had, whatever it was, is gone now. That bird from the church over there is fuckin' sound, I tell you. Never thought I'd hear meself sayin' it, but she is fuckin' proper".

"I still ain't comfortable with 'er, bruv. I know they all say she's the business over there, but it's just habit, I reckon. I never thought I'd say it, but even Padraig's judgment seems to have taken its eyes off the ball".

"Yeah, but that's just you, ain't it? We have to trust these people now. They ain't gonna fuck with a hundred an' fifty keys of hooter, are they? Well, are they?"

"I'm just sayin', that's all, Dean".

"Well, don't, Town, don't at all. You're bein' very quiet, Ali? Cat got your tongue? Get it? Ali…Cat. Blindin'. I ought to be on the radio with that type of stuff!"

Thankfully, the snacks arrive. The full Mezes. Snacks, my arse. There's everything from king prawns to tiny slivers of fillet steak, fish, garlic potato, stuffed vine leaves, humous, pitta bread, baby lamb chops with coriander, twenty-seven kinds of olives, greek salad, haloumi cheese, goats' cheese, filo wrapped parcels of cheese… you name it.

"Theo, you said snacks, not the complete meze!"

"I don't want you Turks saying that we don't feed you, innit!" He flashes his gold tooth at them, winking like a naughty boy.

"This is all Turkish food anyway, you bubble! You stole it all from us!"

Theo laughs and pours more champagne, calling up two more bottles from the now totally overworked barman.

*

'The' is packed to the rafters with the over thirty crowd. Fake boobs, fake tans, fake sunglasses, fake you name it. Fake. The place is buzzing and Shirley, Debra and Paula are standing at the bar, glammed up to the eyeballs. They're on the cocktails, being chatted up by a load of solicitors out on a jolly. Debra and Paula are just overflowing in the tit department and the increasingly hammered boys can't believe their eyes.

*

"The trailer's bein' sorted with the compartment down there now. They reckon it's the safest smudge they can do. Reckon no-one will ever find it".

"I fuckin' well hope so".

"Now who's the bleedin' misery?"

Four guys come in just at that point. The band's giving it very loud and you can't hear yourself think, never mind work out a multi-million pound drug deal. However, the boys are up to the challenge and it is the perfect cover. Four big lads they are and they come straight over to the bar, shouting that they booked a table. The barman's trying to check with the manager, who is busy making sure that our boys have everything they need and he means everything. Eventually, the four new lads, fresh from the pub and well pissed have had enough and go over to Theo, who by now is serving two couples out for a bit of a knees up. He's pouring wine and generally doing the right thing. One of the four taps him on the shoulder and you can tell straight away that the tone isn't exactly friendly. Theo looks at him and taps his watch, all the time looking over at the barman and shaking his head. Matey is far from happy and starts asking him *what the fuck has happened* with his table. Eventually, Theo explains to him that it's been given away due to the fact that they were two hours late and didn't ring. This really hasn't gone down well with the ringleader who by now is getting a little hot under the collar. He starts poking Theo in the chest. This really doesn't go down too well with our man and he politely requests that the man desists from his actions. This, in turn, fails to have much of an impact and the poking becomes prodding. A subtle but nevertheless discernible difference. Now our lads are playing Carry on Smuggling to the best of their abilities but haven't failed to clock said altercation. Dean, having kept himself well fuelled by the old Colombian Military Two-Snort decides that the bashing being received by the Bold left ear must cease forthwith and joins in on behalf of Theo, who, up to this point had been handling things rather well. But,

Dean's got to put his five eggs in, so here we go.

The first punch lands fair and square on the ringleader. Right on the side of the head. He crashes down against the side of the bar and slumps to the floor. One of the blokes takes a swing at Dean, who ducks out of it just in time, before another one of them smashes an elbow right into his nose. Not a good plan. He can feel the claret welling up and as the first of it begins to decorate the front of his shirt, Ali's picked up a giant pepper mill and brought it down fair and square, right on top of one geezer's head. The music's so loud that most of the diners haven't even noticed what's occurring. Theo's got one of them half-way over the counter, holding him down with his head buried almost completely in an enormous floral display which is now looking like it's seen better days. He's shouting in the bloke's ear to call off his boys and to *get the fuck out of here!* Dean's turned into a one man war machine; the combination of cocaine, champagne and desire to crack their heads open makes for a dangerous cocktail. He's got one bloke wedged in a corner, next to the bar and is wading in with his fists, first the left, then the right, alternating until the left can do no more work. He's concentrating on what's left of his nose, working it nicely into an unrecognisable pulp, before grabbing his hair and smashing his head repeatedly against the stucco'd wall. Ali spots the blood spattered white wash and pulls Dean away just in time to avoid a manslaughter charge. It's all over in less than two minutes; Theo's lads from the kitchen drag the remaining bloodied lumps from the restaurant, out the back way and into the alley behind, where they ceremoniously pour freezing cold water all over them

*

The girls are well away now; most of the solicitors have drifted off save for one rather persistent bloke who's really got the hots for Shirley. Debra and Paula are certainly the focal point at the table they've now repaired to and they're playing 'guess the bra size' with five blokes who are on a sales conference at the University. They've already given them chapter and verse on the operations and what it feels like to have, well, massive tits. The solicitor is persistent and he and Shirley are matching each other drink for drink, the champagne working its magic for all to see. All except Debra and Paula, that is. They are too far gone for anything. Slowly, ever so slowly, Shirley feels herself becoming aroused.

The guy's a player and she's loving it. He's saying all the right things, the music's just right and for the first time in a very, very long time, she's starting to feel a real woman again. And so is he. He's done the hand touching, the body language and the leaning forward and now, his hand is stroking her stockinged thigh. He's spotted the suspender clip, she's made sure of it and now they both know. Her head's on one side, she's playing with her hair and looking out from under her false eyelashes. Hooked.

*

"Dean, bruv, we've got to go. Get away before the old Bill turn up. Someone's bound to have called 'em. For fuck's sake, come *on*!"

Ali and Town are holding him either side, ushering him out the back way. All you need is some wise one with a camera phone and they're on top. Theo's already got the thing back on track. There are beers being handed out, the belly dancer's getting ready for another wiggle and the bar staff are clearing up the mess.

Out the back, the alley's clear now, the geezers have legged it.

"Get the motor round here, Ali. I'll take him home in his, you get off to where you have to be. We'll sort the fuckin' fall out tomorrow".

Dean's still raving and storming but slowly, the *coca* rage subsides.

Chapter Thirty Five

Torrevieja Marina, Spain

"I cannot believe I'm breakin' the habit of a lifetime. I must be feckin' mad".

At precisely 3.00am, the low throb of marine diesel engines started up, followed by a slight rocking of the boat as Paco rejoined after casting off.

"I am sorry to do this, but you must understand it is not a decision that any of us can take alone".

"You're right. Deep down, I know you are, but it still doesn't stop making me nervous. I just don't do things like this, so I don't. It's too close to kick-off. This is exactly the time we should be a million feckin' miles from each other. Not having meetings!"

"This is as safe as it gets. Marianna will meet us in San Antonio."

"And how do we know that she's not on top? Answer me that, if yer will".

"The *princesa* is always careful, Padraig. She will have made many detours to get to The Island. For her, it is like a game. But it is a game that she must win. Every time. Not for her the chance of losing. That is why you do not see her at the tables, unless she *knows* the outcome. She is like a block of ice, when she wants to be".

Padraig eased a gleaming white hired Sunseeker out of its marina lair and onto open sea. Radar and GPS would ensure safe passage across the Mediterranean channel between mainland familiarity and intriguing Ibiza. The dashboard lights glimmered and twinkled as he rotated the wheel a fraction to the left, direction north-north-east.

"We'll take her up to the Peñon d'Ifach, round the rock to the north-west and then veer east. Takes us away from Alicante and Benidorm harbourmasters' control and before we're picked up at Denia. We'll go through the Calpe fishing fleet and away. The timing is perfect. At least I get to drive a boat this way!"

Paco looked across at his skipper. Companionable silence ensued, as the Sunseeker's sleek lines cut majestically through the calm moonlit sea.

*

Marianna's scheduled flight from Madrid to Palma de Mallorca sat ready on the tarmac at Barajas, final checks being undertaken by the two man Iberia crew. Her ever-present chauffeur retrieved small, hot black espresso coffees from the one open café in the VIP lounge of Madrid airport's main domestic terminal, eerie night time echoes created by its new vaulted ceiling serving to remind the few waiting passengers of their intrusion. Suddenly, the tannoy crackled into action and the first flight of the day was called to Gate 27. As less seasoned travellers made their way quickly from uncomfortable public seating to the now open gate, Marianna sat elegantly leafing through Vogue in a sumptuous new leather armchair, her slim legs coiled snake-like beneath, strappy Manolo Blahnik stilettos momentarily discarded on the thick carpet. Eventually, as the announcements became more and more urgent outside, she glanced up at the blinking monitor above the exit door and announced it was time for their departure. She uncoiled her fabulous legs and slipped her Dior stockinged feet into the sumptuous leather heels.

"Take my arm, you. We must, above all, keep up appearances".

Every inch the rich bitch as they walked across the polished floor to the departure gate. So flagged up and obvious that save for the admiring or jealous glances of her few fellow passengers, she was forgotten in seconds.

*

At the break of day, the Sunseeker was already making good progress, twenty eight knots of sheer elegance slicing through crisp blue Mediterranean waters on its way towards the Balaerics. The half-way mark had long since passed as Marianna's Iberia 737 passed through the clouds overhead on its short journey to Majorca.

"She'll be takin' a flight from the heliport, so she will. It'll be time for breakfast when we get to the San Antonio marina. Do we have any kind of agreement on this so far? I have a feeling I think I know what she's going to say and I don't think I'm really against it. It's got to be said, though."

"I am glad, Padraig, that you see things like that now. This trip, it is true, is something we would like not to make, but with two hundred million at risk, I think we must do it, no?" Paco's grin said it all. The thrill hadn't left him. Not at all. His boyish zest for life belied what smouldered beneath.

"The *princesa*, she moves around like a thief in the night. Always, she is on the move. For me, she is an anachronism, like one of those 1950s movie stars the women in the children's home would watch. For her, everything is beneath the surface, everyone there to serve, but she is still the most fantastic woman I have ever met. *She* is the reason I do nothing with my girl. I cannot explain it, Padraig, but she is the one thing that has power over me. It is like she *owns* me. Perhaps she owns a little piece of us all, no?"

"Maybe she's the one for you, eh, Paco? She is the girl of yer dreams! Have you never made a play for her?"

"You are an insane man! Me and her? Never. She would destroy me. She loves me, like she loves all the men, but she would destroy me and then she would watch me destroy myself. She is like the serpent, the scorpion. She would ensnare me like *that*! Also, I would never be enough man for her. She is always wanting the sex but never can she be satisfied. *Never* I tell you!"

"So you're tellin' me that she's under your skin and you can do nothing? Is that what you're sayin' to me?"

"You are right, Padraig. There is nothing that I can do".

"Jaysus, you're in a right mess, so you are. What's brought this on?"

"This last few months, I have spent more time with her than in the previous five years. I see her, I *watch* her. I watch the way she moves from me to you to the cartel to her powerful friends in Madrid. For her, the transition is effortless. I swear to you, that woman could be Prime Minister of Spain, she could even find a way to be Queen if she wanted. She frightens me."

"You? Frightened by a frail woman? You could snap her in half if you wanted to, so you could."

"*If* I could! And that is the problem. None of us really knows how powerful she is. Look at her. She can call on favours we could only dream about. And, Padraig, why would I want to try and destroy her?"

"Bite the hand that feeds yous? You would be feckin' mad. She's a politician for sure. She keeps all of us at a distance, never really permits too much contact. But when it goes operational, where is she? Back in that feckin' hideaway of hers in Africa, that's where. I admire that woman. But as for you, forget these ideas. She is never going to take you to Madrid. Not for you, meeting Juan Carlos!"

*

Marianna smiled deliciously to herself, the juicy strands of warm semen still adhering closely to the tops of her stockings, coating her exquisite thighs. Her companion sat at her side, admiring the view from the tiny window on the port side of the Bell helicopter as it swept over the bay and into San Antonio heliport.

"We will take a taxi into the harbour. You will return when I send you the message. You will get money from the pilot. Enjoy yourself, whatever you choose to do!"

He nodded before returning his gaze in the direction of the yachts bobbing up and down on the white fringed sea surrounding Ibiza. Soon, they would be down. She clicked on her brand new mobile, transmitted a pre-arranged text message, then climbed elegantly out of the helicopter and into a waiting Mercedes. Within minutes, she told the driver to stop the car and her companion climbed out. The reply was received and by the time the car entered the marina yacht club car park, Paco was in plain view, sitting outside underneath a white umbrella, Ray-Ban Wayfarers hiding nothing from her. He jumped to his feet and was at the rear door before the driver had fully brought the car to a stop.

"*Señora,* would you step this way please. Your guests are waiting for you."

He made a play to settle the taxi fare, then escorted the immaculately coutured Marianna through the club house and onto a carpeted jetty in the direction of the gleaming Sunseeker.

*

Canning Town, East London

"This is definitely the last time I meet you. It's too risky now. I ain't diggin' meself out for no-one."

"We'll make it quick, Ray. I promise you. I know you weren't happy with me coming to see you at the warehouse, but I had no choice. I needed to reassure you that everything was OK. We're not unsympathetic to your situation, you know?"

"*Unsympathetic?* I should fuckin' 'ope not. If it weren't for me, you wouldn' even 'ave this gear".

"Well, you'll have it back in your safe hands by the weekend. I have given you my word. It cost me a lot of favours in the big house, but you know that they're always going to give in when a man of your calibre is involved!" Candyfloss looked carefully at Ray's reaction. Perfect! His chest was puffed out like a pouter pigeon.

"Yeah. Well. Just don't take the piss, that's all. You want everythin' double quick but you ain't so fuckin' smart when you have to give it back. You could've brought the whole thing on top. You know it."

"Yeah, yeah. Anyway, what's this you're going to tell me?"

"Well, you know there's two drivers. *Two* trucks an' all. All I know is that they're pickin' up in Spain, southern Costa Blanca's all I know. Then they're pickin' up groupage in Barcelona, Biarritz and Bordeaux. What I don't know is where they're *actually* pickin' up the gear."

"Leave that to Customs, Ray. We've got obs on the yards and as long as your mate doesn't get too clever with his outgoing run, we'll be following. Can't tell you any more. Besides, I don't really think you want to know." Candyfloss grinned cheekily at Ray Harper. The man's need to know had just run out.

*

The low throb of the Sunseeker's twin diesels provided a subtle vibration to the hull as Padraig eases her out of the marina and round the headland. He anchored fifty metres out to sea from a small sandy beach as Paco eased the cork out of a perfectly chilled bottle of Krug Grande Cuvee.

"*Princesa*, I would like to welcome you on board the Mariposa. We thought it was better not to use one of our own boats."

Handing her a slim crystal glass, he toasted her, along with Padraig who had now come astern from the skipper's cabin area.

"Thank you, boys. You are most kind! I think to business, no?"

They nodded as she sat back in the plush leather seat to examine them one by one. Her encounter vigilance, she called it.

"The news from the cartel is this. They are very pleased about the shipment. Very pleased indeed. Since the collapse of the Madeira connection and the subsequent losses sustained, there has been an understandable *regrouping* in Medellin and beyond. Many positions had to be *re-filled*! I am sure I don't have to paint a picture for you, gentlemen, yes?"

Paco felt an increasing dryness in his throat and gulped at his glass of Krug.

"Now that we have this new route, they wish to ensure that it is preserved. I am to believe that the merchandise is safe? Good. Good. Señor Montoya will be satisfied with that. And you, Paco, you have the other goods ready, as I requested? Excellent. As I understand it, no final decision has been taken until after today's meeting. That is what they want and that is what I have promised them. How is Señor Bold?"

"He is ready with everything at his end. Since the meetings in Doolans, he and Don Beevers have been working together on a modus operandi for the UK. Beevers was not so happy at first. He thinks that his position is in danger, but we have explained to him that he is going to be a very rich man soon. Now he is quiet!"

"Padraig, all is OK with you? I think that the surveillance has not been too much of an inconvenience?"

"Nice choice of words, so it is. No, we've been right on top of it since you last came to grace these shores."

"OK. The cartel has great faith in what you are doing. Your activities have not gone, shall we say, unnoticed. However, what I am about to say may shock you. Señor Montoya does not believe that the current planned shipments should go ahead as we originally intended. He wants to use this as a kind of 'dry-run'. Everything is in place, it is true, but there is also a lot on unwanted attention from British and Spanish Customs. We know from Pilar that the operations from Madrid are now focused totally on the airports. They are combining terrorist and anti-drug measures. It is basically a cost-saving exercise. The politicians are happy that they have a department which is starting to get results and the treasury is happy that it is not costing too much. Since we pulled our troops out from Iraq after the Atocha railway station bombings, Spain is not seen as a primary target for Al Qaeda, but it does not mean that they want to be seen as a soft option for the terrorists to smuggle in their bombs and guns via this country. So, I feel, gentlemen, that once we have got rid of this British Customs woman and her team of insects, we will be able to work efficiently at last. Unhindered!"

"Bravo, *princesa*. But what are we going to tell the others? That they are not going to make any money? That they are probably going to be arrested? That we are playing some kind of game with them? These are not the kind of people who will just shrug their shoulders and walk away".

Padraig just sat there, listening.

"In the long term, this is the best solution. The best for everyone. If we do let the shipment go as normal and we lose the two hundred kilos, I do not think I want to be the one to try and negotiate with the cartel. I do not think I have enough credit with Señor Montoya for that. Not even the pope himself could get away with it!"

"So are you saying that we should not tell them? There are going to be arrests, if the British are as close to this as we think they are. We are certain that they don't know we have the goods now, but they seem to have had plenty surveillance on the bar and around Torrevieja. Do not forget the day on the boat!"

Padraig smiled at Paco's recollection of his jet-ski day. Time to speak.

"Maybe I've had some kind of experience of this. Sadly, there are two expressions which spring to mind, so they do. One is *collateral damage*, the other is *expedient*. They are words which the British Army used to use frequently during the 1970s and 1980s. The Provos and the UVF were not slow to take this up and soon, if you read a communiqué, you didn't even know from which side it came, so you didn't. What you have to remember is that under British law, there is such a crime as 'Conspiracy to Commit the Impossible'. Look it up some time. If we do substitute the right stuff with some white stuff, I am not sure we're still not committing a crime anyway."

"*Dios mio*, Padraig, you have lost me now. How can you commit the impossible? It is impossible to do that!"

"Tell me more", purred Marianna, lighting a long and elegant cigarette and spraying herself liberally with Chanel.

"They will argue that if they have what looks like a crime in front of them, that there is some kind of crime being committed. It is probably a good question for that fat lawyer Beevers hangs around with in Liverpool. Maybe I'll give him a call, so I will. Make the bastard earn his corn. Imagine this. A group of people get together and decide that they are going to destroy the earth. They plan to destabilise the moon from its orbit and bring it crashing into the Pacific Ocean, thereby creating the world's biggest tidal wave, killing everyone and knocking the planet off balance. Now we know that's impossible, but it's still a conspiracy and anyone mad enough to believe that it *could* be possible is barking mad and should be locked up for their own safety as well as ours. Think about it!"

Marianna felt the oncoming re-arousal growing between her sticky thighs. She was finding the whole business ever such a little delicious.

"Do you realise that this way, we could get rid of the problems which are thrown up by any arrests? They will have to show their hand, we will know what *they know* and we will be able to fill in the gaps left by the ones who are in jail. By the time they are released, everything will have moved on. I do not believe that the

British authorities will be able to hold them for long, once the cocaine is found to be icing sugar! Sure, they will have an uncomfortable time in prison, but I think that it will be good for them. They will see the error of their ways. They will know that the cartel does not appreciate problems. *That* is a powerful lesson indeed!"

"Are you saying that the cartel is ordering this? Do we really have any say in the matter?"

"What I am saying, boys, is that if or as I suspect *when* things go wrong, I may not be there to defend you! *That* is what you must consider when you make your decision. As you can see, we are three and I? Well, I am just a woman!"

"Bravo once more, *princesa*! You speak and we respond. It is the nicest way I have had a gun put against my head in a very long time. You do it well. Do you have a gun with you, or is that in my mind also?"

"Haha! Paco, you amuse me so. Of course I do not have a gun. I leave that kind of thing to you boys. You love your guns. I love.....other things!" She waved her hand in the air as if to dismiss him, but there was a smile too. A smile of fondness. The one chink in her armour. Appeared, smiled, gone in a flash.

"Well, Marianna, that was the most brilliant way to get a vote passed I have ever seen, so it was! As the man whose bar has been under almost total surveillance for the past six months, I applaud you for savin' me skin. I have a feelin' I'll be one of your men in jail, but that won't be the first time an' sure as eggs are eggs, it won't be the last. Thérése'll be feckin' brutal, so she will, but I can live with that! I hear they serve wine in Spanish jails now. Would I be right in that?"

"Only at the weekend, Padraig. For the rest of the week, it is *cerveza*!" Paco's grin stretched from the boat around the bay to San Antonio.

"Boys, boys. I do not understand your humour about this. Do I have agreement?"

The two men nodded with a mixture of resigned acceptance and guilty decision. Kismet.

*

<u>Canning Town, East London</u>

"How are you going to get the gear back in?"

"Listen, you do your fuckin' job an' I'll do mine, alright? Just make sure you get the gear back to me double fuckin' quick. I ain't jokin'. If they find it's gone missin', there'll be the biggest stewards since the fuckin' false start at Aintree. And the fuckin' outcome'll end up as dog meat an' all. Don't cunt me off."

"You have my word, Ray. It'll be back as agreed."

"*You have my word, Ray*..........how many times have I heard that?"

"Look, it's crucial to the success of the operation. You know that, we all do. There is no way on God's earth I am going to allow this whole thing to get fucked up over one measly kilo of coke. Besides, we're going to need it for the court case."

*

"I'd better get me toothbrush packed then. You too, Paco. There's no way you're not getting your collar felt. The *princesa* here will go off into the night now. I can't think for one minute that Her Britannic Majesty's Customs & Excise are going to plot up in her little corner of Africa! Don't you worry 'bout a thing, me darlin'. We'll be seein' yous sooner or later. I just wish I could see their faces when they find out what's really in the trucks."

"*Lo siento*. I don't like to think of you boys in the prison. It is so uncivilised in there."

"And you would know, would you?"

"I have a very vivid imagination, Padraig. And I am serious, this time. You are, what is it that you say in English, taking one for the team?"

"It had better be a short one."

"Come, come, darling, you know that it will be for no more than a few days. You are in Spain for one. The boys in England will not have such a good time, I think. But they will get through. I know it."

"Well, that's grand then. If it's all settled and Bejaysus it sounds like we're organising some kind of charity event, it's about feckin' time we went back and got on with things. We've some icing sugar to load. I've been out sweating over a hot fraud for long enough to know that the final touches are the most important part. Marianna, as always, the pleasure has been all yours!"

Padraig jumped to his feet and offered her his arm in a gesture of mock servility. Paco looked sullen and careworn but did not show this to the *princesa*. Instead, he too walked out onto the rear deck and onto the jetty. The car sat waiting on the other side of the yacht club entrance and the ever present chauffeur stood by the rear door, having just discarded a Marlboro Light. They watched as she climbed in, effortlessly, then returned to the boat, via the yacht club bar and two very large Carlos Primeros.

Chapter Thirty Six

Canvey

"You can fuckin' drive, mate. I ain't in the mood". Dean's hired M5 sat clean and proud out on the road, champing at the bit to do battle with the M1, direction Liverpool. The guy from P1 has been and gone.

"Didn't fancy the Bentley then, bruv?"

"What, take a Benters to Liverpool? Are you fuckin' mad? They'd have the fuckin' wheels off before we'd even stopped. Don't even know if Mansell would insure us for goin' up there neither!"

"It ain't all like that up there, bruv".

"Was the last time I looked. We went up there in the eighties with the boys. Fuckin' place looked like a war zone".

"It's all different now, bruv. They've even got a marina".

"What, a Morris Marina? Fuck me, they went out with the ark".

"Daft cunt".

He pulled away, the M5 desperate to get to grips with the journey. Bit of Eminem on the iPod link, blaring out over the speakers. The A13 gave way to the M25, the Marshall to The Streets. Troy's would miss his music today. As they hit the M11, the sound of The Zutons took over, as if welcoming them in a Scouserley direction.

"Was they really okay with everythin'? When you was over there?"

"You could've knocked me over with a feather, mate. I was expectin' fuckin' murders, but the Irish fella went all philosophical on me. Started talkin' about chances and don't start what you can't finish. All that bollocks. But d'ya know what? It all made fuckin' sense. Reckon I must be getting' old. It was like he was sayin' everythin' what I've been thinkin' for ages. He's quite a fuckin' geezer, your mate. Right dark horse an' all. Fessed up some real personal background facts. He was a fuckin' boy back in the eighties, just like us".

"*Just* like us? I don't think so, Dean. I don't remember lyin' in trenches an' shootin' at army checkpoints, unless there was something I missed?"

"You would've missed anyway. You couldn't hit a cow's arse with a banjo".

"Fuck off, bollocks. So we're gonna get a proper friendly welcome from the Mickey Mouser then? We ain't walkin' into no minefield?"

"Padraig will have been onto him double quick. After that business the other day, they're fuckin' gaggin' to get this show on the road".

"Well, speakin' personally, I am more than happy with that!"

"Don't you find dealin' with these top guys is a fuckin' change from the usual suspects? I mean, if that had been a couple of years ago, we'd have had fuckin' murders over all this. Instead, we get coffee and brandy and a chat. Well fuckin' civilised".

"Just depends on the day, bruv. When this lot decide you ain't needed no more, it's fuckin' curtains faster than you could snort a line. An' they *do* finish what they've started".

"Yeah, I wanted to talk to you about that. Me an' the Coat had a bit of a strange one the other day. He come into the hospital an' took us to one side, said we had to go an' meet the Family".

"What? *The* Family? Fuck me, bruv. You never brought that to my attention till now? Who did you see?"

"How the fuck do I know? They're not exactly known for puttin' their monickers on the Six o'clock News! The Coat takes me down Lanrick Road. That fuckin' took me right back, I can tell ya. Next thing, we're in this abandoned warehouse an' it's gone all 1960s black and white fuckin' Michael Caine movie. You know, *Get Carter*, that was the one. Matey's sittin' behind the table, this light's swingin', just like the beginning of Callan and then he starts. 'No lies at the table, gentlemen'. He fuckin' meant it an' all. There's Ricky Razors and old Storey from Epping. The Guv'nor, they call 'im. I have to shake hands with the cunt an' I don't reckon I'd have got out without that".

"Fuck me. I'd call that surreal".

"And you wouldn't be jokin'. Only thing that weren't surreal was the four geezers standin' around the wall with automatics trained on the little team round the swingin' lamp. That, was fuckin' real".

By then, they were really flying along. Town was keeping it to around ninety, just to give them a fighting chance of avoiding Northamptonshire's finest. The Beamer was effortlessly eating up the northbound miles, slowing only for the idiots who hadn't quite grasped the techniques of British motorway driving. The mobile rang to interrupt Dean's account of the potential brown strides day of last week and it was Beevers.

Click. "Alrigh? Where are yous? Where? Where the fuck's tha'?"

Eventually, they got their location across to him and that's that. *Click.*

He sat in his favourite cafe on the Stanley Road. Almost within spitting distance of his beloved Anfield. The motor sat on a double yellow line. There was hassle from the Bizzies all over the area, but no-one, no-ONE went anywhere near the gleaming 500SL which sat defiantly outside Sheila's Breakfast Bar. He went in there every day. A kind of habit. Just like all the other habits which ruled his life. This was no ordinary scouser, no ordinary man.

Outside, a red Vauxhall Vectra and a blue Peugeot drove to and fro, taking it in turns to keep watch on both the Merc and the cafe. Occupants spoke with forked tongue and they were *not natives*. Not friendly. Not at all.

"Zulus 9, 17 and 18 still in café. X-Ray 7 still in position on double yellows outside the Stanley Road cafe. Out".

Don, Jeff and Barry sat chewing the fat, literally in Jeff's case. Best fry-up this side of the Mersey, or so it said on the door. A boyhood ritual which had never changed.

The M5 was well on its way, the story resuming as they hit the M6 toll road.

"Fuckin' cheek. Paying to avoid Birmingham. They should fuckin' pay us to avoid it. Cunts. Anyway, later, after the pub thing, we're up Green Lanes, in some café. They're playin' all that Turkish bollocks on the radio, there's poker in the corner and some geezer dealin' on the blower. The Coat introduces me to some geezer who turns out to be 'is uncle. Got connections down the Old Kent with all the usuals. Turns out they all go back to Cyprus. The Old Coat's a dark 'orse. Sometimes wonder what the fuck he's doin' with us, but I ain't complainin'. Gives us a kind of cosmopolitan flavour. Whaddya reckon? Bloke reckons he will always help us out. Seems to think he owes us somethin'. Couldn't make any sense of it. Don't mean nothin' to me, but some of these foreign cunts don't make no sense half the time, anyway".

"So what was the point of the meeting?"

"Fuckin' search me, mate. Next thing, all this food starts appearin'. Fuckin' cheese things, lamb, taramafuckinsalata, vine leaves, you name it; it's on the table. The Coat's just sittin' there. You know, like e' does. Never eats, just sits and watches you. When does that cunt eat, do you get me? Right in the middle of all this, the uncle starts tellin' me how much Ali thinks of us, you know, you an' me an' Ron an' that. Like *we're* his family. How many families does he need?"

"Well, you know how important family is to those people".

"Fuckin' shame it never rubs off, ain't it?"

"What do you mean, mate?"

"You'll find out soon enough". With that, Dean turns up the music and sits back in the leather seat, arms folded, eyes closed. It's a sign.

*

"I fuckin' hate cockneys. Fuckin' jellied eels. What the fuck is that all about? They're no better than Pakis and Mancs. Why the fuck are we doin' business with them?"

"Because *I* say we are, that's why. I don't fuckin' pay you to think, do I, alright? We're all expandin' now. There's a new spirit of co-operation".

"Co-operation, my arse".

"Look, Jeff, don't go all provincial on me now".

"Fuck! Where did you learn words like that?"

"That'll be his mate, Billy Bunter. The fuckin' fat brief! Him an' his fuckin' posh mates. Don't you fuckin' forget where you came from, Don Beevers!"

"You'll never fuckin' let me will you Barry, you fuckin' twat. An' while we're on the subject, how's the warehouse in Bootle? Your Irish mates all sorted?"

"Sound as a fuckin' pound. The place next door is taken for six months. Deliveries will go in there. Everythin' then goes into the old air raid shelter, under the path and into our place".

"An' the owner of the bond?"

He's havin' what you might call an extended holiday, on account of the envelope he got last week. He won't be back before we need him".

"An' the cash. What about the cash, Jeff?"

"Sorted, Don, sorted".

"Are we lettin' these cockney bastards move the cash an' all? Fuckin' hell. They'll be up here doin' the deals next".

"Spain want them to do it. First one's a test. If it goes OK, we'll be doin' more. We're part of a bigger team now, Jeff".

"Bigger team, more chance of gettin' fuckin' grassed. You know what happened to our mate".

"He was too high profile. Takes more than a fuckin' shell suit to keep your head down up 'ere!"

"I'm just sayin', that's all".

"It needs sayin', Jeff. Just not all the time!"

*

"So are you tellin' me you're just gonna stand for it? That's that?" Dean was driving now as they pulled off the flyover from the M62 and up the dual carriageway towards Anfield and Stanley Road., which made one passenger in the car somewhat uncomfortable.

"Look at this fuckin' place. It's like somethin' from back in the seventies".

"Naa, bruv. It's all changed now. You should see what they've done down the docks. Penthouses, apartments, flash bars. Bleedin' birds everywhere. Scouse birds know how to have a good time". Town winked at Dean, but his mind was on the road. They turned left at the lights towards Bootle and soon they were on Stanley Road.

"Get Don on the blower. Find out where this fuckin' place is".

Click. "We're here. Where are you? Dean, have a butcher's for his motor, he says. Reckons you'll know which one it is. Yeah, we're lookin' for it. Yeah, on the road you told us. We fuckin' are! Yeah. Alright, we can see you!" *Click.*

"I'm stickin' it behind his. Last time I came up here, I stuck it in a side street and when I come back, the fuckin' thing was on bricks!"

All parked up, they walked into the café and it was handshakes all round. Just like a crowd of dogs in the park. Cockney dogs and Scouse dogs.

"Dean".

"Don. You know Town, don't you?"

"Yeah, sound. This is Jeff. Barry".

"Allo".

"Sheila, can we have some more tea? Get these lads what they want. D'ya want black puddin'? Give 'em some black puddin', Sheel".

A careworn, lined woman wandered over and took their orders. No black pudding. Beevers fixes the Londoners with an icy stare.

"Everythin's sorted 'ere, Dean. The lads weren't happy you're doin' the cashin' up, but we're goin' with the big fella's wishes. How soon are we gettin' our bit?"

"It's due in next week. Two days turn round and it'll be in your slaughter the next day. Cushti. Regular, bonded haulage, no less. Take it straight in. The man with the van'll be up to divvy up the scratch when you're ready. Route's all sorted. It'll be back in Spain before the weekend". Dean sat back to eye up the response.

"Hang on, hang on. We have to give a bit of bail up 'ere you know. It'll have to be the week after".

Town Hall leaned across the desk towards Don,

"Does Padraig agree with all this?"

"'Course he does. You don't think we'd get that past him, do ya, if he didn't agree?" Barry started laughing. "Besides, once we get goin', we ain't gonna be worryin' about a bit of scratch. These lads up 'ere know what the fuckin' score is. We shoot first an' ask questions later. You got your bit of hassle sorted now?"

"That cunt from the caravan site? No worries. All sorted. We was always mates really, wasn't we, Dean?"

Dean sat quietly, just listening. *Always mates.*

*

Gina sat upright in bed, propped up by pillows and surrounded by flowers. And her mates. And her daughter. Debra paid great attention to her acrylic nails while the rest of them are drank some of the champagne which Dean had sent in upon hearing the news that she had recovered consciousness.

"Mum's havin her bandages off next week, with a bit of luck, that is".

"Oh, Bee, that is great news. She'll be able to see what a lovely job I'm doin'!"

"Aunty, what's the latest on Uncle Dave? Don't s'pose you want some shampoo?"

Shirley stood just a fraction away from the others, having stuck her head round the door from visiting Dave.
"I'll surprise you, darlin'. I will have some. Give us a nice glass full, there's a good girl".

Shirley took the glass and got half way down before coming up for air. The rest of the girls didn't even notice. Benissa didn't miss a thing.

*

Shirley walked confidently along the pristine hospital corridor towards her husband's private room, stopping to look through the glass window at his bandaged head. A wry smile played around her red lips.

*

Just as Debra put the finishing touches to Gina's French manicure (with jewels), Shirley returned from across the gleaming corridor.

"You got'ny more of that champagne, Bee?"

"Blimey, Aunty, what's got inter you? Good news? Won the Lott'ry?"

"Just fancied it".

"Come on, there's another bottle in the fridge. Might as well 'ave that. Dad's payin'!"

Benissa popped the cork and began to pour out the golden bubbles. Just as Gina's monitor went berserk.

*

"An' the next thing, Dean, the fat cunt said he wants to come out to Spain! I think it's the *princesa* what's done it. Kind of appeals to his curiosity. He's never happy till he puts people in boxes, okay?" Don ordered yet more tea and lit a cigarette. "So long as e' don't end up puttin' us in fuckin' boxes. I ain't much for that!" Dean laughed nervously.

"James is OK. Besides, we know enough about him to bury the cunt if we needed to. It works well. He needs us an' we need him. Only time you ever 'ave to worry is when one of us don't need the other!" Don's boys nodded in agreement.

"Hey, whose mobile's goin' off. I said no mobiles here!" Don's face changed in an instant from geniality to anger.

"It's OK, Don", whispers Town as Dean picks a Motorola Pebl from his pocket and answers. "He needs that phone for his daughter. It's in case there's any news from the hospital".

Dean's face went from happy to hear his daughter to contorted and then devastated. He walked outside the café and onto the narrow pavement outside.

Zulu 1 outside 96 Stanley Road. Zulu 1! This is interesting.

"Well how bad is it? What does the doctor say? Look, babes, I'm comin' back. In Liverpool. No, don't worry, I'm on me way. We're all done 'ere anyway. We're just on to the fuckin' war stories now. Town can drive".

He rushed back into the café and relayed the news. Quick goodbyes and they're away, in the motor and off back to the M62.

Dean's anger turned to rage as the car turns onto the motorway slip heading for Manchester and London.

"This is too much, mate. Too fuckin' much. What the hell was she doin' in the Porsche anyway? What the hell was she doin' with him, that's what I want to know?

*

"Shit…shit…*shit*! What the fuck am I goin' to do now, Sean? Me mum's had a relapse and Dad's on the way back down South. He don't sound too happy, neither. I've only gone an' bleedin' told 'im what I heard me Aunties talkin' about. Yeah, that's right. *That!* He fuckin' knows, Sean. If he gets in here in the mood he's in, he'll fuckin' kill Uncle Dave, I know he will. You ain't seen him when he gets mad. It's like this red mist comes down and there's just no stoppin' him. Me mum told me some stories about when they was young. He never done nothin' to her, but the things he used to do at football an' that was legendary. He ain't changed. No-one ever does. Sure, he looks like he's calmed down, but it only takes one thing an' I reckon this is it. Sean, what the fuck are we goin' to do? Can you come over? Yeah? Okay, I'll see you in reception". *Click.*

Benissa returned to the observation window outside her mother's room and just pressed herself as close to the glass as possible. Everyone had been ushered out and now there were just doctors and nurses galore in there. She's been pumped her full of diamorphine and even the de-fibrillator was in there, ready charged and waiting to be called on if needed. Debra, Tammy from the salon and Shirley were just sitting there, the colour long since drained from their faces.

"Is...is she going to be OK, Bee?" Shirley's demeanour had changed from one of slightly drunk to very sober in seconds. She looked guilty. What the hell had she got to feel guilty about?

"I dunno, Aunty. Me Dad's on his way".

"Oh, that's good, then".

"No it ain't. He's in a foul mood. I ain't heard him like this in ages. He's ravin' mad. I wouldn't get in his way, if I was you".

"I don't think I've got anything to fear from your Dad, darlin'."

"No, Aunty, *you* ain't…"

"What d'ya mean, girl? Is he after someone?"

Shirley and Benissa looked deep into each other's eyes.

"I…I…gotta go. I'm meetin' someone. See ya…"

With that, she turned tail and ran towards the exit, leaving Shirley, Tammy and Debra looking terrified.

"Is she OK, Shirl?"

"I don't know, darlin'."

Debra reached out for Shirley's hand and the three of them sat there in the corridor. The silence was terrifying.

*

Dean's mood changed rapidly from outwardly enraged to seethingly quiet. Town just drove. Stays stumm. The M5 ate up the miles. They were doing well over the ton down the M6 toll, then it's the A14. Two hours after leaving Scouse land and they were on the M11.

"I'll pull his fuckin' tubes out, the lying cunt. I've brought him on from fuck all. Fuck all, that cunt had. He'd be stackin' cuntin' shelves in Sainsbury's if it weren't for me. What the *fuck* is 'e doin' with my missus? Sniffin' about like some fuckin' hound. Turn my fuckin' back, an' this is what fuckin' transpires. How long before we get there now?"

"About an hour, mate".

"You carryin'?"

"Well, the usual, but we ain't got no shooters. Just the bat and a coupla' blades."

"The blades'll do. I wanna watch the cunt bleed. See the look on 'is mug when I go to work".

"Mate, I don't wanna take a liberty, but don't you think you're bein' a bit hasty?"

"*Hasty*? How much fuckin' evidence do I fuckin' need? I ain't standin' for it. Bit of fuckin' loyalty, that's what I need right now. No, I ain't 'avin it. I'll deal with her later. I ain't decided what's comin' to 'er yet. Bee sounded right fuckin' upset. I ain't comin' between her an' her mum for now. No, bruv. It's his fuckin' turn now. Get what's comin' to him. We don't need the cunt. He don't do nothin' anyway. Never was anythin' more than a fuckin' gofer. Fuckin' expensive one an' all. One less fuckin' mouth to feed. Last thing he's gonna taste is a hospital pillow when I stick it in his cheatin' gob".

*

"Look, me Dad's on 'is way. I spoke to Uncle Steve when he were in the carzie at the services. He's fuckin' lost the plot. I know what me mum and Dave done was wrong but it ain't gonna be nothin' compared with what me Dad'll do. I ain't losin' him on no murder charge".

"So what you tellin' me for? What can I do?"

"Well you can start by tellin' your old man. He knows Dave's brother Vern, don't he? Tell him if he don't do somethin', the next thing he's gonna do is arrange a funeral. Do it, Sean. *Now*!"

The boy shook with fear as he speed dialed Jimmy. Two calls later and the Hiltons were up to speed.

"We're gonna have to stop me Dad gettin' in. If they can get Uncle Dave out before he gets 'ere, I reckon I could stop him. It's gonna have to be the women what sort this. I know me Dad. He ain't gonna go through me. I got to do this, Sean. If the Hiltons can get Uncle Dave out, me and Aunty Debra's gonna' have to do the rest".

"Why don't you wait outside? We can talk on the mobiles, check they're comin' an' that".

"Yeah. The next problem we're gonna have is Aunty Shirley. What the bleedin' 'ell are we gonna do about her?"

*

Vern Hilton drove like a bat out of hell towards Basildon Hospital. Shouting into a mobile the whole time.

"Get hold of matey, the one with the minibus. Get him to meet us down by the market, next to the pub. Yeah, *in the fuckin' car* park! Tell him he can have a monkey if he gets this sorted. Just tell the cunt anythin'. We're gonna have to get me brother out of the back of there double quick and away. Go and drag that cunt Patel out of bed if you have to. If we had more time, we could nick an ambulance but that ain't gonna happen. This ain't the fuckin' movies. He'll have to go in the back of the fuckin' Shogun an' like it. Patel'll have somethin' to make him sleep. We'll take him over Maldon. To the barge. It'll have to do for now. Double quick, mate. This ain't no rehearsal".

*

Click.

"Look, Bee, I've done all I can. I ain't gonna stand in your Dad's way, am I? He'll top me an' all".

Sean stood facing his girl, shaking with fear but doing alright. She paced up and down, just like her old man.

"This is a bleedin' nightmare. Look, just wait 'ere for a mo. I'm gonna go an' check on me mum and Aunty Debra".

She rushed in, running past the casualty department. *At least they were close to that if it all kicked off.* Not even funny.

The three of them, Debra, Shirley and Tammy stood there, staring, useless, like rabbits caught in a truck's headlights as the life support team worked frantically on Gina. Dean and Town were just minutes away now. Converging, along with Vern Hilton and ex-Doctor Ram Patel. Vern screeched to a halt outside A&E, just along from the crowded emergency entrance. On the blower to Patel, just a minute behind him.

"I don't care what the fuck you have to do, just get him out. Get it right, Ram. Don't fuck up. You know where he is." *Click.*

Vern slipped in, unrecognised by the waiting Sean. Straight along the corridor towards Intensive Care. The further away from A&E he got, the quieter it became. He slowed down, to a walking pace. Just inside an open door, there was a white coat. Just hanging there.

Patel's in, having gone totally into Doctor mode. Like riding a bike. A word with the receptionist, effortless queue jumping. A minute later and he'd got a temporary pass. Two minutes later and he'd acquired a clip board and a house doctor's garb, courtesy of the unattended locker room down the hall. Spotting Vern twenty yards further along, he called out. The big fella span round to see Doctor Ram Patel, ready for his rounds.

"Vernon, that coat does *not* suit you. Better you take this".

He handed Hilton a green orderly's overall.

"Look the part. You'll look a lot more convincing when you wheel him out of here. *We* don't do that sort of thing!" Patel grinned for the last time, then they were away, marching purposefully along the corridor, all the time, Patel whispered to him, telling him what to do. There was no-one at reception and the women didn't even see the two uniformed figures enter Dave's room. Except for Benissa.

"Aunty? Why don't you take Aunty Shirley and Tammy for a coffee? You all look like you need one. I'll stay here and watch over mum. Go on!"

She ushered them away. The moment they disappeared round the corner, she was away, striding back towards the main exit, already on the phone.

"Where are you, Dad? I'm here at the hospital, of course. Where did you think I'd be? How long? Five minutes? Okay. See you then." *Click.*

As she emerged into the icy cold night, she saw Sean standing against a supporting pillar.

"They're here, then."

"Who's here, Bee? Oh no, not your Dad?"

"Dave's brother's here. Just saw him. We've gotta keep me Dad out here as long as we can. I'm gonna tell him they're in with mum. Tell him Intensive Care's out of bounds".

"'He ain't gonna listen to that, is he?"

"Course he ain't, but it'll buy us a bit of time. Vern had some kind of Doctor geezer with him."

"How long d'ya think he'll be? Five…ten minutes? I know you're his little girl, but if he's in the mood you say he's in, we could be proper fucked."

"Not as much as Uncle Dave if he gets hold of him. I swear to you, Sean, he'll fuckin' kill him, tubes or no tubes. You ain't seen him when he gets the red mist. He ain't never had nothin' like this happen before. He's always relied on me Mum. Sure he's let her have her salon and that, but no shenanigans. He ain't the sort of bloke who pokes up with that. It's only gonna end one way. We just got to make sure he don't do it here."

Patel had pulled the curtains closed on the inside of Dave's room and was working feverishly with his drips and tubes, attaching them to hooks at the back of his bed.

"Put the monitor under the bed on that ledge, please. Just pray that he doesn't wake up until we're outside. I don't think we have very long. I don't have a good feeling about this."

Outside, the hired M5 screeched to a halt, tyres smoking. Dean removed a rounders bat from beneath the seat and hid it under his leather jacket. Behind the windscreen, Town pleaded with him not to overdo it, to keep calm, but it had no effect. Benissa had lost two valuable minutes because she didn't recognise the hired car. She watched her father legging it across the car park towards her and stood right in front of the main entrance.

"Dad, DAD, *DAAAD!*" she screamed at the top of her voice, bursting into simultaneous tears. She threw her arms around his neck and held him as tightly as she could. It put him off balance just for a moment. She hung on for grim death.

Patel had got Dave unhooked by then and the blinking monitor was hidden underneath Dave's hospital green sheets, pulled down over both sides of his bed. As they left, Vern switched off the room's main lights and opened the main access doors from the corridor out into the main reception. Once they were out of the Intensive Care suite, Patel shouted orders to him as he wheeled Dave towards the lift.

"What's 'appenin'? Is your mother okay?"

"Yes…yes Dad, she's with the consultants now. There's nothin' you can do, nothin' any of us can do. We just got to wait. Why don't you come an' have a hot drink with me. Aunty Debra's here. She's in the coffee bar. Aunty Shirley's here an' all."

And it was all going so well.

Dean's face passed into contorted rage in a split second. Pushing Benissa away, he began to run towards the entrance. She cried out after him but this time, it had no effect.

As the lift doors opened, Patel motioned Vern to push the bed in frontways. They both got in and the former doctor pushed the basement button.

"It might just buy us a little extra time. They will not think to go down first".

Dean ran full speed down the long brightly lit corridor towards the lifts and Fourth Floor Intensive Care. He pushed the buttons frantically then saw the staircase. Benissa, Town and Sean were just a few paces behind him, trying desperately to keep up. They were no match for his coke-fuelled rage and he reached the top a full thirty seconds before them. He tore though reception, through the double doors and was met with two scenarios. To the right, his wife's room, now brightly lit, the team working intently on Gina. To the left, a darkened, curtained off room. For a moment, he was calm, something had just kicked in which stopped him bursting in to either of them. He was rooted to the spot.

The lift door opened in the basement.

"Give me the keys. Quickly, the keys to your vehicle. I can bring it right up. We can load him in here, there is less chance that we will be seen. I think that if anyone sees us upstairs, then they will tell this madman what they saw. I don't think he is the kind of man who takes no for an answer, no?" Patel took the keys from Vern and ran back to the stairwell. "Look after him!"

And what the fuck am I gonna do. Vern stood over Dave's sedated body, transfixed by the slow-pumping drips and tubes.

"DAD!" Benissa was level with her father as he suddenly sprang into action and kicked open the double doors to Dave's room. It was in total darkness, the gloom permeated only by the remaining monitor, its heart-rate flatlining ominously across the screen.

"Where's the fuckin' lights?" He turned around and moved towards the door, locating the switches with his probing bony fingers. As the lights flickered on, his eyes blinked, trying desperately to adjust to the increased luminosity. He span around, removing the wooden bat and strode towards the middle of the room.

Patel was into the minibus and heading away from the rear entrance. He drove swiftly around the hospital's east wing towards the underground car park, flashing his temporary pass at the barely interested security guard who obediently raised the barrier. The minibus passed beneath the concrete lintel with barely inches to spare and headed towards the lifts. Its headlights silhouetted the waiting Vern and he screamed to a halt, the rear doors close to the unwieldy hospital bed.

"Where the fuck is that cunt! Where is he?" Dean rushed out of the room and into the reception area. The desk was momentarily unmanned. Benissa rushed after her father and managed to catch hold of his jacket.

"Dad, please, just wait a minute. I dunno where Uncle Dave is, but ain't you here to see Mum? She's in there, fightin' for her life. Please, Dad, don't do somethin' you're gonna regret."

"Where is the cunt? He should be in there. Where's fuckin' Shirley? She knows somethin'. Where is that bitch?"

"I'll get her, Dad. I will, honest. Just don't go mad or anythin' till I get back. Sean, stay 'ere with me Dad."

"No fuckin' way." Sean's off the other way, shitting it. "I ain't stayin' with him."

Benissa ran off in the direction of the café as her father started banging on the door of his wife's room. A nurse turned around and saw him, motioning him to stay away, then realised that it was, indeed, Gina's husband. With a rounders bat.

She opened the door and stared directly into his eyes.

"Mr Bold. What do…"

"What, where, where is he? Hilton, where the fuck is he?"

"Calm yourself, Mr Bold. What do you mean, where is he? He's in the room diagonally opposite, of course."

"No he ain't. Don't piss me about. He's gone. He ain't in there. There is a *fuckin' gap where his bed was*, darlin'. A stark realisation crept across the nurse's face as she saw the drawn curtains.

"Why…why are they closed? They should be open at all times." She almost pushed Dean out of the way as she entered the room.

"Oh, my God!" Running from the room, she hit an alarm button on the wall.

"Where is everybody? Where's the policeman?"

"He ain't been here for weeks, love. They lost interest in this case long ago. Now would you mind finding out where Mr Fuckin' Dave Hilton has gone. Cos' from where I'm standin', it looks like you've mislaid one of your intensive care patients."

The sight of Gina's comatose body calmed Dean for a moment as he turned around before concealing the bat and heading off towards reception and the lifts.

"Why couldn't they have got some of these seats out? It would have made the job so much easier!" Patel and Vern lifted Dave's monitor and drips off the wheeled bed, then half lifted and half dragged his sedated heavy body in through the back doors.

"You are going to have to drive as carefully as you can without attracting attention, Mr Hilton." Patel lay on the floor of the van, removed a hypodermic syringe from his pocket and attached it to one of the many lines inserted into Dave's right hand. Slowly, the van pulled away around columns of parked consultants' Boxsters and Mercedes SLKs towards the exit. Once the syringe was emptied, Patel put all his weight against Dave's body as the van began to mount the ramp and called out to Vern to drive as slowly as he can.

Dean rushed out into the freezing night and got straight on his mobile.

"Ali, I'm at the hospital. There's been a right fuckin' cock up here. Gina's had a relapse and fuckin' Hilton's gone on the missing list. I need you to find out what the fuck is goin' on. Some cunt knows what it is an' it ain't the bleedin' Bill what's lifted him. Yeah! Lifted him. You heard. Even the fuckin' bed's gone."

A white minibus swept around the corner and out onto the A13 sliproad, as Dean turned to walk back into the main reception.

Chapter Thirty Seven

Canvey 7.30am

Click. "Town, I am fuckin' knackered. I ain't drivin' again today. Fuckin' place. Who the fuck do them cunts think they are? You better come an' pick me up. I ain't doin' no more drivin' period. Pick us up in twenty". *Click.*

Click. "Ron. Where are you? Good. Meet me an' Town at the warehouse. Yeah. Essex. Bring Ali an' all. Half hour". *Click.*

He sat and stared at the marble topped kitchen table, his reflection just visible in the low light emanating from the worktop spotlights. The betrayal had hit him like a train crash, the silence of the empty house magnifying his already black mood. He thumped the table until his knuckles began to bleed, his eyes burning with hatred. Hatred for *that cunt*. He was back in Vange again, round by the garages, rusty bikes, old cans. He was fourteen again, Dave was there, his brother Vern, Jimmy. Standing. Smoking. There was a bird at the end of the street. Nice. Flowery top, Oxford Bags, platform shoes. Little blondie. It began to rain, so the bird made for the bus shelter. It just about did the job, on account of the fact that there wasn't a pane of glass left in the fuckin' thing. She sat on the bench, looking over. Smiling. Dave and Jimmy looked at Dean. Looked at her. Back at him. *Go on, you daft cunt. She wants you.* They pushed and shoved him. He walked over, with all the dignity that he could muster, cool like, his leather jacket and tank top lookin' the business. *Alright? Sort of. Whatchoo doin'? Nothin'- they your mates? Yeah. You're Dean Bold, ain't ya? Yeah. You wanna go wiv me? Yeah, OK. There's a garage wiv no lock on it... we'll have to be quick. What? NOW? 'Course now, silly. Gotta live for the moment, ain'tcha, Dean Bold? Er, yeah....right. Come on then? I gotta be over me Gran's in Pitsea for tea.*

The moment. In a lock-up garage, over some musty old furniture. The little blondie had her trousers down in seconds, he'd come in little more than that. Barely got it in before he'd shot his load. Dead rat on the floor, in the corner. *Blimey, you're a virgin, ain'tcha, Dean Bold? Well you ain't no more, izzya? Come over me house later, round eight an' I'll let you have me again. Forty six Chatham House. Fourth floor. Me mum's at bingo then and me sister's down the pub. See ya.* There was a bit of a cum stain on the brown nylon Oxfords, but she headed off down the broken pavement without a care in the world. Quickly, he did himself up and left the stinking lock-up. Out into the dirty rain. He turned round. Casual, like. The others had gone, except for Dave. *Didya do 'er? Didya? What's 'er name? DEAN! Who is she? Name? I dunno, do I? Fuckin' hell? What IS her name!* And that was it. They walked home. Into the warm. Simple as that. They used to share everything.

The reflection was clearer by then. On account of Dean's tears. Droplets of the past lay on the squeaky clean surface. His anger had become sadness, now anger again. He went out the back, into the shed at the back of the pool house. Rummaged under a tarpaulin. The trusty old sawn-off. That would do. Wrapped in an oilcloth. *Click. That's the stuff.* Silently, he replaced it in the soft sheath and returned to the house. Waited for Town. The new friend will take him there.

*

Click. "Ali, this is the one. Fuckin' Dave had better have proper legged it this time. Soapy cunt. Dean wants us at the warehouse now. There's gonna be a right fuckin' stewards". *Click.*

Thankfully uneventful journeys took them to the back of Essex Transport, to a small table, chairs. When Ron and Ali arrived, Dean and Town Hall were already there. Dean was drumming on the metal table top with his wedding ring finger, the sound echoing around the warehouse like a call to arms. To battle.

"Thank you, gentlemen". It all went quiet. No-one wanted to start talking.

"For those of you who don't know what transpired last night, I will take a second to bring you up to FUCKING SPEED!" He smashed his fist onto the table so hard that a huge dent appeared right in the middle. Ron's car keys jumped up in the air and crashed down onto the concrete floor.

"That CUNT, Hilton, got away from the hospital. Someone, and I don't know who yet, grassed me up. Someone tipped the cunt off. How the fuck did his brother get to hear of it? He was seen there. What are we? What, for fuck's sake? A fuckin' radio station? Are we havin' hourly bulletins? Are we puttin' round some kind of

Court fuckin' Circular? *This evening, Mr Dean Bold will kidnap his cheatin' fuckin' cunt of a mate from Basildon Hospital, take him to Tilbury Fort and top the cunt!* I am gonna get to the fuckin' bottom of this and when I find which cunt has been talkin', he's gonna get the same treatment as that fuckin' lousy Hilton. I am gonna personally tear 'is fuckin' tongue out and stick it up his arse! Ron! What the fuck is goin' on?"

"I ain' heard nothin' yet, mate. Me an' Ali'll get straight on it this mornin'".

"Me an' Ali! Me an' fuckin' Ali! Why wasn't you 'on it' last fuckin' night? I don't fuckin' pay you to sort things after the event, do I? Do I? No. I fuckin' don't. You two, never fuckin' let me down. Well you've fuckin' let me down this time. First fuckin' load's on its way and we've got this now. What're the fuckin' cartel goin' to say about this then? More teethin' troubles, Mr Bold? Never fuckin' mind? I don't think so. I am not about to get fuckin' washed up in the Estuary with me cock n' balls in me gob just 'cos you lot fucked up. Who knows about this?"

"Just us an' the Hiltons, Dean. There was no Old Bill at the hospital last night when they took Dave out. Shift change or summin'. All they got now is a missin' person. Since Gina's relapse, that is".

"Yeah. Well leave her out of it for now. She ain't goin' nowhere".

Their heads were down. No-one wanted to go there just at the moment.

"So let me get this right. Vern Hilton turns up at Intensive an' just waltzes out of the gaff with Dave all wired up to drips an' that? Do I have the scenario correct?"

"There was someone else with him. Some mate or somethin'."

"Some mate………. Well, do you fink we could find out which fuckin' mate it was who so kindly spirited the cunt away? I've had just about enough of this. *We* are supposed to be the ones who know what the fuckin' score is round here. Not some mysterious fuckin' mate of that useless cunt Vern. Outwitted by a fuckin' nightclub bouncer. That's gonna do our cred a right fuckin' good turn! If we don't fuckin' sharpen up, we might as well all jump off fuckin' Tower Bridge right now. Where does this cunt Vern live?"

"Already checked that, Dean". Ali's on this now; taken over. "If there was anyone there last night, they've already legged it. Place is all closed up. The mate lives over Burnham way. We're gonna check that next".

"Town. You an' me are goin' over the hospital now. Things must've calmed down a bit now. Play all concerned about Dave. Offer our help. We've got to find out what state the cunt must be in. We're gonna have to contain this. Before it gets out".

The relief was palpable by then. You could almost smell it, touch it. Sensible mode had just landed and gone through passport control.

"Ron. Ali. Just find him. Don't care what it takes. Just fuckin' find the cunt. Keep in touch".

With that, he was up and away. Town glanced at the other two. No words needed. As the metal door clanged shut behind them, Ron turned to Ali,

"Thank fuck for that. He's back in Top Cat mode now. All we need now is Officer fuckin' Dibble an' we've cracked it". Ron's face was a study, but Ali wasn't smiling yet.

"If we don't find Dave, *inshallah,* this is going to get a lot worse. What I don't understand is how this happened".

"Maybe, but is it better to find him, or better to *not find him*? I am not sure which is the best in all our interests. We have already had some narrow escapes. If this goes Pete Tong, you can add the cozzers to the growing list of people interested in our extended family".

"But Ron, if we don't get some news for him and he goes into one again, we may not be so lucky. If he gets to Dave first............?"

"We need to find Dave anyway. Look, it ain't fuckin' disloyal if we do find him. He ain't goin' far or doin' much, state he's in. they'll have him holed up in some gaff. Won't be far away, neither. Vern's no player. They're probably usin' some mate's gaff. He's gonna need medical attention an' all. He won't last long in that state. How the fuck did they get him out of the hospital?"

"That's not the problem now, Ron. This is going to require some careful thought. Seeing as you and me is the only ones capable of that at the moment, I suggest we put our heads together, look at the *bigger picture*! Something the guvnor isn't going to be able to see this side of the summer. We'll find him first, *then* we'll work out what to do next. Dean needs to focus on the work in hand. We're on the threshold of the biggest job we've ever pulled, innit."

"The way I see it is this. If they've got Dave plotted up somewhere okayish an' he *has* got medical attention, then he's gonna recover. He's over the worst anyways, Ali. Main thing is that he's got the steel plate on and it's taken. They were a lucky pair of cunts, I'll give 'em that. Reckon Gina took the worst of it, to be honest. Least she's still in good hands".

"You don't think he'll do something about her, do you?"

"Him? No way. She may have fucked him about, but at the end of the day, she's still the mother of his dustbins, an' that ain't gonna change."

*

Maldon's watery sunrise cast a pastel hue through the rusting canal barge's east facing porthole. Ex-Doctor Patel checked Dave Hilton's blood pressure and heart rate for the umpteenth time that night, before administering a new drip to the line protruding from his patient's bruised and blackened hand. He turned to see Vern standing in the doorway.

"I have to be honest with you, Mr Hilton. Your brother is not a well man, as you know. His heart rate and blood pressure are erratic to say the least. Soon, he is going to need more attention than I can give him. He has recovered well, it is true, but he requires more than medicines. This is going to take time."

"But you must have some people you know. People who can get him sorted."

"Everything is possible, but it requires money. You must know that."

"Listen, bruv, we got money. We might not look like we 'ave, but we ain't short of a few quid. I want the best for him. He's been the fuckin' mainstay of this family for fuckin' years an' I ain't standin' by to watch him croak for the sake of a bit of scratch."

"I will make some enquiries for you. The first thing we are going to need is some more heating. The cold helped to keep him alive last night, but now he is stable, we require warmth. Is this place safe?"

"Safe? Course. No-one knows about this place. Definitely not the fuckin' Bolds, anyway. Dave didn't know about it. That means Shirley don't neither."

"Good. The last thing he needs now is to have to be moved again."

Chapter Thirty Eight

Southern Costa Blanca, Spain

"Just pull the fuckin' slats out!"

"What?"

"The slats. The fuckin' slats, you cunt. Pull the slats out, then we put the boxes in right at the back. Weld 'em in. They'll never find 'em there. There's just enough room to put the gear in. Just pull 'em out an' stack 'em in the corner."

In the half light of *Garage Hidalgo*, two trucks, curtains tied back to reveal their flat wooden beds, empty for now, were being systematically prepared. Two boiler suited gentlemen, recently discharged from Her Majesty's Prison Ford, full sentence, no parole, discharge grants only, were working up a sweat. Carefully, they slid twenty ten kilo lead-lined boxes along the narrow ledge behind the rear bumper bars, along the slat trays and butted them up tight against the metal wall nearest the cab. A precision cut thin metal strip was then pushed flat against the rearmost boxes, the oxy-acetylene welding torch ignited and carefully, the seal was completed.

"Put some dirt an' dust on the back of that fuckin' strip when it's cooled. Then spray it wi' water. It'll have rusted proper within a couple of days".

Outside, it was still dark, the moon casting an eerie luminescence over the warehouse. Across the square from the war memorial, a blacked out Seat stood partially hidden by the bare almond trees. Occasionally, a plume of smoke rose from a narrow crack left by the barely open nearside window.

Inside, the job was completed, the curtain slats carefully replaced tight against the metal strip. Perfect fit.

*

"I still have a bad feeling about this, Therése, so I do".

"I don't know why you're doin' it. Padraig O'Riordan. You're an enigma, of that there can be no doubt. A real enigma".

"I can feel something in me waters that's not right. I've a cover story arranged, just in case. It's one we've had well rehearsed for a long time now. The Moroccan one. It's why we often let them come and use the place in the hills. Kind of covers our arse, if you know what I mean, darlin'!"

"Cover stories. Moroccans. You *know* something's not right. Why don't you call it off? We could take a holiday somewhere. Till it all dies down. You'd know then if it was on top or not".

"Nice idea, woman, but it's not going to happen. No. we stay and we see what happens. We've all the angles covered anyway. It's just first night nerves, so it is. It was always the same back in Cullaville. Before we went out on an operation. Jitters".

"Sweet Jaysus, Paddy, I hope you're right".

*

"I'm gonna need a fuckin' drink when we've done 'ere. Fuckin' back-breaking. It's worse than bein' on the gardens in Ford".

"You are having a giraffe. Worse than bein' inside? You've gotta fuckin' short memory, you mug". The larger of the two stood against the light cluster and sparked up a Golden Virginia roll-up. Old habits die hard. The two gleaming new trucks stood hesitant, like kings of the road. Sleeping giants holding back for the starting signal, prepared to deliver their pristine white cargo to a waiting world.

"Would you rather be drivin' then?"

"Do you ever stop moanin'? You was just the same when we was diggin' over the beds in them polytunnels. Never five bleedin' minutes between complaints. Miserable old cunt, you was. Still are! And no, I would *not* rather be drivin'. What, go back to London when we can stay here? Least we don't have the bleedin' old Bill breathin' down our necks round this manor".

"Fair play. He's been good since we got out". The short one continued to stack the wooden planks against the metal sheeting of the warehouse wall whilst the larger one puffed away on what was now a dog end. "You know they say everyone goes fuckin' stir crazy over 'ere though, dontcha? See, it's OK when you first get 'ere. All bleedin' sun an' sangria. Mistake we made was to come straight 'ere after getting' released. We should've stayed round Barking for a bit, *then* come over. See, we don't know the bleedin' difference no more. Maybe we could've got jobs on the Olympic site. Who knows?"

"Yeah, an' pigs might fuckin' fly. Who the fuck is goin' to give us a job with proper dough? You've got half of eastern Europe knockin' on the door, happy to work for a fiver an hour, passports an' papers all cushti, or you've got us, fresh from bleedin' prison, record as long as your arm an' wantin' a decent wage. Not much of a fuckin' contest, is it?"

*

Padraig sat reflectively at the kitchen table. He was at *the point*. He looked up at Therése, quietly getting on with making porridge and tea. *Do I, or don't I*. The occasional domestic noises emanating from the Aga range and the kettle just made it worse for him. *Reminded him*.

Companionable silence.

It was something they'd always been good at. Right from the word go. They both needed it and both recognised the need in the other. *It was like they knew*. Telepathic. That was it. Telepathic, they were with each other. *The thing is, Therése, are you being telepathic now?* He fought with his conscience. He knew it was going to be alright, or at least he thought he did. But did she? Did she really believe him? Twenty years they'd gone without trouble, but she could sense something. *For God's sake, the woman's been through everything with me*. He felt the pressure rising in his veins. He wanted to swallow, but there was nothing *to swallow*. He stretched his neck to try and find something in his throat to alleviate the dryness.

"Darlin', will you hurry up with that tea. A man could choke of thirst here, so he could".

She turned around and just smiled. Dark, rich Irish tea was poured into china cups, the strong aroma immediately rising to meet Padraig's senses. He poured in the milk, added some sugar and drank a huge draught straight down. Once quenched, he looked up again at his wife's still attractive form, her silk dressing gown barely concealing womanly curves. He was dying to tell her. To warn her? No. Not that. He wanted to let her in on it, let her know that it really was going to be alright but he couldn't. He just couldn't do it. It went right against the grain. The code.

It's going to be alright. Was it? Was it ever going to be alright? He was brought back from his trance.

"Is it ever going to be alright, my darlin'?"

"What are you sayin'? Are you wantin' out of here, is that what it is, woman?"

"Jaysus, Padraig O'Riordan, will you listen to yerself. How long have we been livin' like this? You've given me a grand life since those days back then. A woman could want for nothin' with you, but I see you, Padraig. I see you alright. You'll not be keepin' anythin' from me. If you choose not to tell me, then that's your bed. I'll not be tryin' to wheedle it out of yous. I know better than that, so I do".

*

Custom House, Lower Thames Street, London

"Duncan, can you let me have the final knock and arrest pack sheets, please?"

"They're already on the way up, ma'am".

"And the maps? What about the association maps?"

"On the interactive white boards in the ops room. Would you care to come and see what we have done? The whole place looks rather James Bond!"

Janet Weatherall basked momentarily in the whole ambience of the place. At last! Something's actually bloody *happening*! As Duncan Deegan walked out of the room, feeling for some reason that he needed to show her the way to her own operations room, she paused. We're on, she thought. This is finally it. The culmination not simply of six months work, but of far more than that. This was her destiny and she was not about to let *anything* get in *her way*. Having collected her thoughts, she was on her feet and away down the long wood-panelled corridor, the sound of her heels echoing long after she had turned the corner.

*

"When's the gear arrivin' then?"

"Don't ask me, mate. I ain't privy to that kind of info. Once we got this ready, an' I mean ready, we just gotta get the gaff locked up and we're away out the back. Matey's gonna give us a call, then we'll come back an' sort the weldin', put the slats back and bob's yer uncle. Home and hosed. Be in the bar in no time. Sorted".

"How much d'ya reckon's gonna be in there? It's gotta be Charlie, ain't it? I mean, from down 'ere, it can't be nothin' else".

"Don't even fuckin' go there. You must be fuckin' mental, even thinkin' fings like vatt. Turn over Stevie 'All? And Jimmy? Do you want to keep your gonads intact?"

"I'm just sayin', that's all. Judgin' by the amount of room what's in there, you could get a bleedin' ton of the stuff and no-one'd know. How much is a ton worth?"

"More than you can count on your fat fingers, you daft cunt. Just forget these things an' get the last bit done".

"While you stand there, yeah?"

"Well you ain't gonna keep a dog an' bark yourself, are you?"

By the time the larger one had skinned up, they were away and out the back, locking the sheet aluminium door carefully. By then, it was dawn and the sun crept slowly up into a cloud streaked sky, sending a garnet red light across the dusty scrubland at the back of *Garage Hidalgo*. Across the square, at the front, the Seat pulled away, to be replaced by a dark green Fiat Punto some two minutes later.

*

"If I told you it really was goin' to be alright, would you believe me, woman?"

"Padraig, if you told me the moon was made of cheese, I'd believe you. Don't you think it's a little late for belief or doubt? I just know that you're up to something beyond what you normally get yourself involved in. If you tell me that it's all goin' to be OK, then that's grand".

"So why are you keepin' on? You like pickin' at a thread, so you do. Pullin' it to see what happens. You've never been like this before".

"And nor have you, husband. So that'll be the pair of us deceiving!"

Therése sat down next to him, poured fresh tea and stared into his eyes, smiling all the while. But it was a hollow smile. *Her* Irish eyes were not smiling.

"I'm goin' to the restaurant now. I'm late as it is. I'll tell you one thing, Therése, 'fore I go. *All is not what it seems*". He stood up, rising to his full height, chest out proud like a pouter pigeon, before bending down to kiss his seated wife's dark red hair.

As she returned his kiss, this time full on his lips, he said,

"You still do it for me, you gorgeous woman. Don't you be goin' anywhere far from here!"

With that, he turned away, grabbed the keys to the 4x4 and walked out into the watery winter sun.

Across the valley, a mobile video camera began to whir into action the moment Padraig appeared, the night shift's final task before changing over. As the car left via the bougainvillea lined narrow lane and down towards the town, he clicked on his mobile and began the final arrangements.

*

"As you can see, ma'am, in line with the arrest packs, originals for which have all been signed by the solicitors' office and sent to the respective arrest teams, we have positioned the main conspirators according to rank and hierarchy. Team One will knock and arrest O'Riordan and his wife and should there be any other inhabitants of the household, the accompanying and liaison officers from the Guardia Civil and the Policia Local will have additional powers of arrest. This knock team will be in direct contact with Team Four in South Armagh. We are anticipating several house guests at the O'Riordan property there. We are certainly envisaging a large amount of false ID. These people are experts at slipping through the net. They have done it before and we cannot possibly allow suspects to flee the nest. We have a little surprise lined up for the Irish end! Team One will also apprehend staff at Doolans, notably Ronan O'Riordan, the nephew, his management and the accountant. At worst, we will disrupt his business sufficiently to cause him a severe cash flow problem! In conjunction with our Spanish counterparts, Team One will also arrest Spanish nationals Zulu 6, Federico Alvarez and Zulu 29, José Hidalgo, the garage owner. The remaining arrests in Torrevieja and Alicante will be undertaken by the Spanish authorities. Team Two, Essex, will cover Zulus 9, 11, 13, 15, 19 and 20".

"I would like to stop you there, Duncan. A particularly apposite moment, I feel. Zulu 19 is the brother of Informant No 1, Brighton Rock. Mr *Michael* Harper has been, unlike his brother Ray, a thorn in the side of the law for far too long. I have consulted with our counterparts at Scotland Yard and, indeed, Interpol and we share the view that this is an opportunity to arrest and most likely charge brother Mick at long last. He has been suspected of involvement in protection rackets, drug dealing and vehicle ringing, along with Mr Clapton. I would imagine that when *we* have finished with them, the boys in blue may well want a word".

Blinking lights across the room indicated contacts reporting in with final information and updated observation bulletins.

"Are we planning anything for Raymond Harper, ma'am. You know, so as not to arouse suspicion?"

"Quite the opposite. The view upstairs is that if we were to bring him in, he is sufficiently far away from everyone else that it could even draw suspicion onto him. It could be a double-edged sword. Candyfloss is in daily contact with him and he has been assured to just continue as normal. He will report to work at Metro Bond as usual and just pretend he knows nothing. For a while, he is going to be the last thing on the gang's minds. Before they can start the stewards' enquiry, they will have to be able to get hold of each other. Initially, Bold, Hilton – if we can find him and Hall will be brought here to the interviewing suites. The rest of them will go to police stations across Essex and the 'E' postal districts. Remands will be done in several magistrates' courts. I want to charge as soon as we have sufficient. Bold's connections with the trucks is enough for him. Add the obs and his frequent trips to Spain and I think that'll be more than sufficient. We will arrest Shirley, Hilton's wife. I am hopeful that it may flush him out of whichever rat hole he is currently hiding in. He is Bold's right hand man and it is inconceivable that he is not involved in some way. Team Three is Liverpool. There are to be four arrests there. SOCA's report into the activities of Ashendon, Calvert and Halse Solicitors shows major suspicion of large scale money laundering through their client account for Liverpool based drug gangs. That and Mr Calvert's long standing association with the man we now know as Don Beevers should have our friendly neighbourhood Bunter of the Bailey shaking in his Guccis! How I would love to be there to witness *that* one! Team Four is at Dover and will arrest the drivers. I want obs vehicles stationed up on the cliffs too. They're bound to have a watcher up there and it would be a boon to the whole long term future of this operation if we could get *his* mobiles before they can be destroyed. I know that we still don't have the full picture here but the solicitors' office tell me that they can make enough of this stick. We have the picture, we just need to paint in the cast and the job is over to the legal eagles".

*

Click.

"Paco, what time are your lads getting the gear up to the meeting point? Good. I want them away first thing in the morning. You know why. Have you decided who's going to trail the loads up to the border? Grand. Two cars? OK. *Click.*

*

Further down the road, a mobile tracking van picked up the steady beep emitted by the two tiny transmitters situated under each trailer. *Garage Hidalgo* was silent and in total darkness.

"Emily, how long do you reckon?"

"How long do I reckon what?"

"Before someone comes to pick up the trucks. What the hell did you think I meant?"

Emily Loader returned to her computer screen, mindful of the need to remain vigilant at all times. Her desire to succeed eclipsed that of her partner and she wanted more than anything else to do a good job on this.

"Do you know how long these tracker batteries last?"

"Haven't a Scooby. Weeks probably. They do plant them in containers from the Far East and such like, so I guess it must be weeks. This is so boring".

"Yeah, and can you imagine how important this is to the whole operation? These trucks almost certainly are going to be used to take whatever quantity they've got lined up. *Two trucks*!"

"Do you reckon one of them might be a decoy?"

Emily regarded her fresh-faced young replacement partner with more than a little disdain, but then relented. At least he showed some interest in what was going on. Rick Gibbs' recall to London under what seemed like a growing rain cloud had caused wildfire gossip to spread through the team and she was quite relieved to keep small talk to the job and not to speculation as to what may or may not have gone on.

"Hard to tell. These people are not exactly new to the game. It's all going to be down to Dover at the end of the day. I expect they'll pull them both in and see what happens. The warrants will allow us to hold them as long as we need anyway. Certainly long enough to be able to take the bastard things apart, piece by piece if necessary!"

"Don't you feel like you're just...I mean, *we're* just tiny cogs in a big machine. I mean to say...well, we're just like mushrooms, really. You know, you an' me, we sit here in this van, watching, waiting and everything else is going on miles away. Do you think they're armed?"

"Wow, you sure ask some questions, don't you?"

"Just want to know. I am keen to learn".

"Let me ask you this. If you feel like a mushroom, imagine how they feel back in the ops room in Thames House. All they see is computer screens. Day in...day out. Phones ring, emails come in. but they don't actually *do* anything, do they? That's why all the excitement is at this end. The grass *isn't* greener, I can assure you. In fact, you're pretty lucky getting out here on this job so soon. Daddy know someone upstairs, does he?"

"I wish. No, just did well in my adaptability assessment, I suppose. It's funny, but no-one else seems to know anything about this operation. It's like it *doesn't exist*. They even made me sign some kind of extra paper, you know, like a kind of Official Secrets Act with knobs on?"

"Well, it's not very secret if you're telling me, is it?"

"Yeah, but, well, I mean Emily, you're part of the team, aren't you. You obviously know all about it".

"First tip for you about the service. Never assume anyone knows anything. Never trust anyone outside your own field of ops. There are a lot of empire builders in Customs, politicians, gong chasers. All kinds, really. Me? I'm a team player. Always have been. Hockey team at school. Never could really understand individuals, mavericks. That's why I joined the Service. This is the biggest, most powerful team you'll ever come across".

*

Click.

Text.

Click.

"Looks like we're in business, lad. Show's over, I'm afraid. It's on for tonight. No more lap dancing for you this trip. Better get back to the hotel and get some bloody kip. We've got to break the back of this bloody journey home tonight, at least as far as the border."

Henry and Darren Fenton sat at a roadside bar, San Miguels and burgers piled up in front of them.

Chapter Thirty Nine

Orihuela, Spain. February 11th 2007 11.30pm

"It's bloody child's play. They come out 'ere. They bring t'shitty furniture. They stay for a while. Then they miss t'weather or owt in England. So they sell their shitty 'ouses and take thay shitty furniture *back* to England. The fookin' furniture isn't even worth the two thousand euro' it costs to take it back. Fuck 'me. Stupid twats. If they want to pay me to take t'shitty furniture to and from England every few months, what am I going to do? Eh? What the *fuck* am I supposed to do?"

Henry Fenton. Owner driver. In the corner, leaning up against the wall and rolling a cigarette........Darren Fenton. Son and heir. Comes with en-suite Sheffield Police ASBO.

Inside the furniture repository, sofas and beds lay stacked up against walls and against each other. Some going to villas and apartments on the Costa Blanca, some going back to housing estates in Hemel Hempstead and Burnley. Going home. Tried it once and didn't like it.

Four boiler-suited locals languidly loaded up the two British registered artics with tea chests and began the jigsaw puzzle task of trying to fit as many reproduction dining tables and chairs in as possible. In contrast with Henry's diatribe, they said little.

"And when they get home, back to t'fuckin' council house, within a couple of months, the daft bastards wanna come back!"

"For fuck's sake, give it a fuckin' rest, will you. You're doin' my head in, you daft old cunt!"

Henry muttered something under his breath, but no-one was listening.

At the side of the warehouse, a light shone from within a small office. Two figures poured over documents and papers, occasionally looking up at a computer screen. As one of them sat down to type, the other emerged into the cavernous depot.

"Señor Fenton! Yes, Señor Fenton senior. A word, please".

All Henry's bullshit and bravado went in a flash as Paco walked over to him, carrying a goods manifest.

"Here are the addresses. There is one just north of Barcelona, on the road to the border and one in France. Barcelona's booze……..two pallets. They'll be your first drop. Into Metro Bond at Barking. The French pick up is in Bayonne. Just one pallet of wine. That's going to Ilford. Duty paid. The REDS papers are here. You'll get the rest of your instructions on this".

Underneath the papers was a buff padded envelope. Paco gestured for Fenton to hold out his hands and a mobile phone dropped out. Basic Nokia.

"Usual rules, Señor Fenton. *Our rules.* They are very simple. You do not use the 'phone. You do not make calls, you do not answer unexpected calls. You do not give the number to anyone. You do not use the text message service. You do not use the contacts list. The phone is new and unregistered. It is French. It will not work until you cross the border at Perpignan. Until then you have the Spanish phone which you will destroy and discard as you have been shown. There are three numbers recorded in there under the names 'Green', 'Amber' and 'Red'. The 'Amber' number will call you in Calais. You are to answer it and take instructions. If all is well, the 'Green' number will call as you drive up the hill above Dover onto the A20. You will await instructions, only from the 'Green' number. If *at any time* you receive either a call or a message from the 'Red' number, the job is to be aborted immediately. You will halt at the next truckstop or motorway services. You will lock the vehicles and leave them. You will then wait for further instructions. Do you understand me fully, Señor Fenton? And I mean *fully*".

"Yes…er, yes. Fully. Totally".

"You will not deviate from the route shown on the maps. These have already been placed in your cabs. There will be several cars joining and leaving you during the journey. Do not look for them. Do not attempt to make any judgments. It is *they* who are there to make sure you do not have any unwelcome attention from the authorities or indeed anyone else who might take an interest in your loads. You have a great responsibility. It is no lesser or greater than anyone else. Do not forget that. These measures are for your own protection as much as for everyone else. Good luck, Señor Fenton".

As Paco returned to the *oficina*, Fenton could feel a dryness in his throat which almost caused him to gag. His heart was racing. Shaking hands fumbled for a duty-free Superking before he walked over to his son.

"We're on. Looks like we'll be out of 'ere soon. An' that won't be soon enough. That bloke scares the fookin' shit outta me".

"Yeah, whatever. I just wanna get on t'fuckin road, me. I'm sick of these fuckin' Spanish. How long are they gonna take to load t'fuckin' things anyhow?"

From within the *oficina* Paco and Ronan observe the father and son.

"I hate usin' new people, so I do. Every time, me heart's in me mouth, so it is".

"Yes, my friend, but they are very highly recommended. The appearances, they can lie, no?"

"It's just caution, so it is. Runs in the blood".

"In mine too, my friend. When you come from backgrounds like ours, the feelings are always the same. No trust, no faith. Anyway, our monitoring teams are ready. I do not anticipate any problems with the journey. I understand that these drivers have worked with Mr Dean's man for many times. Our contact in France will report anything unusual when they go to collect the wine from Bayonne. It will be just the son's unit which will collect that. The father will have the liqueurs from Barcelona. We will see how they handle that. Every last detail is made for them. I have never seen your boss take so much care over things. He is, it is true, a very meticulous man, but this time, *Dios mio,* he is the perfectionist".

A loud crash, followed by swearing in guttural Valenciana interrupted them and Paco rushed out. A dressing table lay smashed to pieces on the ground and one of the boiler suits hopped around holding his foot, while the other laughed hysterically.

"Guys, please, a little decorum, yes?"

It was enough. Paco is just not the sort of bloke you fuck with. Henry and Darren returned to their work and in a short time, it was finished. The bravado on hold. At least until they're on the road. Which they were very shortly. Paco gave them the paperwork for the trip.

"Usual deal for you *gentlemen*. Here is the payment for now. When you arrive at the destination, everything else will be paid. I remind you once more, do not deviate from the route, do not take any unexpected turns or make any unexpected stops. Remember, there are vehicles accompanying you all the way to England. You will not know who they are. It is not your job to look out for the Customs. It is the job of the spotter vehicles. That is what they are paid for. You are paid to drive. You do it very well, I am told."

"Thanks, pal. Don't worry, us won't let you down."

"No. Indeed."

The briefest of handshakes and Paco returned to the office. An old man emerged from the gloom, pulled the shutters apart and two times thirty eight tons of Scania truck eased out into the Mediterranean night.

Twenty miles away, two computer screens lit up like Christmas trees.

"Tell London. Looks like we're on the move".

Mobiles, emails and telephones clicked into action as the two trucks made their way in convoy through the dimly lit back streets of Orihuela towards the A7 and the north.

Paco left via the rear door of the warehouse, carefully checking that everything had been removed, then climbed into the anonymous Seat. From under a blanket on the back seat, a low voice called to him.

"Paco, has everything been done at *Garage Hidalgo*?"

"Everything. Even if the place has been under surveillance, they will find nothing. As for the rest of it, I assume the babies are safely sleeping?"

"All is taken care of. We do not need to worry about that for now."

"My friend. You know that the decision to do this was not taken by me. It was agreed by the *princesa* and the Irishman. I was not in favour of it, but now I think it is the only way. Are you comfortable with this?"

"Paco, for me, it is a simple choice. This way, we will find out where we have the problems. This is a very long term project, something which will make you a very rich man and something which will make me a very...I don't know what. Do you know I just don't really know why I do this any more? Perhaps it is because I can or maybe because every time I do it, I put up one finger to Madrid and those smug, self-satisfied *conchas* who sit there telling us what we can do. Yes, perhaps that is it. Simple really. You want the money, I want the *power*. We both *need* it."

"But you, you will not go to jail, I think. The Irishman is convinced that we will have some problems with this. The *princesa* the same. It is not a matter for us to simply walk away. It will take time for the British customs to discover that the product is not what they think it is. We know that they have made a big operation here. Pilar has told us so. They will be very unhappy that they have not got what they want. And there are many questions which need answers. How did they find us? Do *we* have a problem?"

"That I do not believe. What we have are some internal difficulties which could be eliminated by whatever may happen. That is what appeals to me."

"You are starting to sound like the *princesa* yourself. You sound like a cold Latino."

"Nonsense. How can you say that?"

The car moved along the coast towards Alicante and the comfort of the *Internacional*. To the last supper.

Chapter Forty

Basildon Hospital 5.30am

"Mr Bold. Mr Bold. *Mr Bold!* It's time to wake up".

The whirring machines in intensive care were the only audible sound in the softly-lit room, save for the soothing tones of the staff sister. Dean stirred, then shook himself awake.

"Hello darlin'. We oughta' stop meetin' like this! How's my favourite nurse?"

"Just grand, Mr Bold. And how is the lovely lady today?"

Gina sleeps soundly next to them.

"She's on the mend. I know it".

"She's a fighter, to be sure".

There was an urgency in the room. A desire to believe.

*

High above Dover, once again the watcher waited, the bone hard winter ground offering him little comfort. His eyes do not waver from the thousands of lights shining on the Eastern Docks below. The 'Pride of Calais' had just opened its doors and forty trucks began to emerge from its cavernous vehicle decks, their lights shining ghostlike through the morning mist. As he trained his binoculars onto the Ro-Ro lanes, the first of them began to pass through and onto Channel View Road. Two red curtain-sided thirty-eight tonners eased onto the rain spattered tarmac and took their turn to edge forward.

*

In Torrevieja, Padraig O'Riordan was already awake, sat at his kitchen table, well into the first imported Irish tea of the day. The basher phones were far away; well hidden, just the one facing him on the table, fired up and ready to go. Brand new, pay-as-you-go. Spanish, unregistered. Similar phones lay awaiting the signal in Liverpool, London, Essex and Ceuta. To be used once and then destroyed. All links severed. Just waiting for the word.

*

The 'knock' teams were in place, over fifty of them spread far and wide from South Armagh to Torrevieja, via Liverpool, London, Essex and Alicante. The dedicated high-tech operations room at Lower Thames Street buzzed with traffic, both telephonic and email. Computer terminals and video screens blinked constantly. It had been a long night for the teams of officers and they were desperate for the go signal. Team leaders were rang in, anxious to get the nod. The text messages to go sat ready on the server. Just needing the word from Duncan Deegan and over two hundred and fifty officers of Her Majesty's Revenue and Customs would swing into action.

*

"Would you like me to get you some breakfast before Mrs Bold wakes up? Build you up a bit. You've hardly eaten anything since you came in!"

"Na. S'awright, love. You get on. I'll stick around 'ere. Wait till she's compost mentis, know what I'm sayin'?"

Staff Nurse Flynn laughed at his unintentional malapropism and left them to it. Dean turned to Gina and held her hand, stroking her until she stirred. Slowly, her eyes flickered open and she smiled. One small tear began to fall down her heavily bruised face. She hoped it was OK.

*

Duncan Deegan stood on a raised platform in the operations control room, Custom House, Lower Thames Street. Ringmaster and Lord of all he surveyed. There were guards on the doors and anyone not directly connected to today's knock forbidden entry. He had several mobile phones sitting on the kidney shaped desk in front of him. The atmosphere was tense and there was an eerie silence. He stared intently at just one phone. The one which would kick off the whole operation and start a chain reaction which would cross borders and affect lives forever.

*

Bassy, powerful throbbing from the Scania's huge turbo engine helped to reassure its driver, one Harry Fenton. The fug of diesel fumes hung thick in the morning mist, the columns of trucks snaking around the dockside area, gradually coming to order, then lining up obediently in one snake-like procession. Just one more in front, the familiar Willi Betz yellow curtain sider inching its way forward to the Customs booth, then it would be Harry's turn. His fingers tapped an involuntary tattoo on the enormous steering wheel. In the door mounted mirror, he could see his son Darren in the truck behind. Slowly, the Dutch registered lorry ahead pulled away and he is almost level with the sou-wester'd officer.

*

The watcher pulled out a shiny new basher from his Barbour top pocket. The number was already dialled onto the keypad. Just needed the final push and he'd be through with the good news. It was getting a little lighter; on the far distant horizon, a watery sun is began to show its face. He could feel his heart pounding as Harry Fenton eased out the Scania clutch and drew to a complete stop.

*

Click.

*

In the nanosecond it took for the text message to pass from Dover Officer Gordon Hunt's standard issue mobile, nearly two hundred and fifty people across Europe and beyond sat and waited, not knowing what was about to transpire. It was just like one of those 'minute's silence moments'. Everyone respectful, everyone on the edge of their seats, yet secretly, everyone wanting it over with, yet it was the emotion no-one ever admitted to.

Just before the receiving *click* and bleep, Duncan Deegan was, for the briefest moment in time, the only person outside Dover who knew what was going on. In the red-alert gloom, the muted glow of the operations' computers its only relief, the mobile came to life, casting an uplit illumination of his face, eerie, ghostlike.

"Go".

The operators hit 'Enter' buttons and within a second or two, the fifty knock teams got their go-ahead. In less than one minute precisely, matchwood was made of front doors from Cullaville to Canvey. Accompanied by the Guardia Civil, the *armed* Guardia Civil, that is, officers of Her Majesty's Revenue and Customs stood outside the O'Riordan residence in Torrevieja. Smiles all round.

*

The watcher enjoyed a luxury not accorded anyone else. He lay flat on the frosty ground, watching helpless as the two red Essex trucks are surrounded, the drivers pulled out from the security of their cabs, then escorted into the Customs shed. He had already sent his message to what was, just seconds ago, a waiting world. One which would not now be answering him for a very long time. As panic set in, he started to try and call his controller in London. Then stopped.

Chill.

He put down the mobile, then re-trained the binoculars as the rear of 'Essex Two' disappeared behind the vertical plastic door strips of the search and detain shed. Methodically, he removed the back of the phone, took out the battery and hurled it over the edge of the cliff. The sim card next. Out from its holster and then broken into six pieces. Two were flicked meticulously over the edge, the remaining four buried separately as he walked carefully back towards the waiting Land Rover, pausing to scan the road for any unexpected and unwanted attention. There was none.

*

The Bold's front door hung splintered off its hinges as the knock team began its painstaking search of the Canvey house. The children stood silent in the vast cold kitchen, heads bowed.

"If he's not here, *Miss* Bold", hissed the team leader, "then where the hell is he? Where? He must be here. We *know* he is".

"Well he ain't 'ere. Look outside. Is 'is motor on the drive? No. Bit of a clue, ain't it? You can tear the bleedin' house to bits. Still won't find 'im. Troy, d'ya wanna bit of breakfast? I'll make it while these muppets mess up the gaff". She looked pointedly at the two officers standing unwelcome in the hallway.

"Okay. Please". All Troy's bravado and teenage lairiness had deserted him. Big sis firmly in charge.

"Are you just gonna stand there? Why don't you go an' rip up some floorboards or somethin'?" She turned on her heels and stalked into the walk in pantry. Troy sat at the kitchen table, head in hands, tears began to fall onto the marble top. She waited a few seconds before peering out from behind the door. They had gone. Quickly, she removed her phone from the dressing gown pocket and started to text her father.

*

As Padraig O'Riordan walked slowly down to the gate to see what the commotion was, he already suspected what he was going to find. No mysteries. Back in the house, the new basher, minus sim card was already working its way around the washing machine. Back at the gate, the card was currently travelling down his oesophagus and into the stomach.

"Mr O'Riordan? Mr Padraig O'Riordan? I am Andrew Meacher, Officer of Her Majesty's Revenue and Customs. I have a warrant here for your arrest. Would you be kind enough to open the gate please? We wouldn't want to cause any unnecessary damage, now would we?"

Once he had fully taken in the situation; the *Guardia* with their drawn pistols, the British and Spanish Customs officers with their drawn smiles, Padraig reached across to the wall and pressed a hidden switch. Slowly, the gates pulled back and the eager throng pushed forward and up the driveway. As he was cautioned, the burly Irishman permitted himself just one smile, before being led away. One *knowing* smile.

*

The distant sound of waking Irish dairy cattle gradually gave way to the once familiar throb of twin rotor blades. Times two. And sleep gave way to the waking state; that 'half world' where dreams and reality co-exist uneasily. Where the mind plays tricks. However, just a few moments later and Kelly's trained mind was fully *in the waking state*. His trousers and boots were on and he hurtled down the stairs. What light there was, coming through tightly closed curtains was suddenly extinguished by the partial eclipse caused by the landing Chinooks. Soldiers poured from the already open hatches and within seconds, the O'Riordan farmhouse doors and windows came in, glass flying, wood splintering.

"IDENTIFY YOURSELF! IS THERE ANYONE ELSE IN THE HOUSE? I REPEAT, IS THERE ANYONE ELSE IN THE HOUSE!"

Just a few bursts of staccato Glaswegian Protestant and Kelly was transported right back to the 1970s and the streets of Belfast. Stones, bottles, petrol bombs. The stench of death. Screaming soldiers began to fill the house, kicking in doors and knocking down tables. The sight of raised and cocked machine guns had him lying flat on the floor as the Newry Customs officers read him his caution and slipped on the bracelets. He knew that they would find Martin Keenan soon enough. His mind was already visualising the spot on the police station wall that he would stare at for the next however many hours. Days. Weeks. Who gives a fuck?

Outside, the whole village was cordoned off. Two hundred soldiers, RUC and Gardai Siochana congratulated themselves at the success of the morning's operation. As Kelly and Keenan were bundled into the Chinooks, the quiet man spoke for the one and only time.

"Bit over the top, so it was……..".

*

Benissa waited frantically for the text message acknowledgement from her father's mobile. *Please, Dad. Pick up. PICK UP!* A voice called her.

"Miss Bold? Do you have a key for this door? We don't really want to have to break it down, now do we?"

"Hang on. I'll have a butchers". She stares at the 'phone. *Come on. COME ON! For fuck's sake!*

Someone had come into the kitchen.

"Miss Bold. I really have to insist you tell me where your father is.

We urgently need to speak to him. Er, to eliminate him from our enquiries. If you don't tell me immediately, I am afraid that you are going to be arrested too".

"Bollocks to that, mister. You ain't arrestin' me or no-one. Not in this house".

Benissa returns defiantly to pouring milk on Troy's Cheerios. With that, the officer was called out into the cavernous hallway and a whispered conversation transpired.

*

Padraig was led away and the search team began its thorough hunt. Likewise at Beevers' Albert Dock penthouse in Liverpool, Town Hall's place in Abridge, the Hiltons, Frank's seafront home in Holland, Jimmy Jag's, Mick's and Ron's. Debra and even the manager of the Waterfront Restaurant are arrested. All at precisely 5.55am.

*

Dean rested his head in his wife's lap and felt his eyes gradually close, the night finally having got the better of him. Gina put everything into raising her hand from the bed and placing it against his cheek, stroking his unshaven face. She looked down at him, before lowering her head back onto the soft pillow. What she saw reflected in the glass, outside the observation window filled her with terror. She was panic stricken and tried to speak, but the only audible sound was a kind of choking. Dean was fast asleep. She tried to rouse him, but it was to no avail. Her hand would move no more. His mobile sat at the side of the bed, silent, switched off. Hospital regulations. *Click.* As the door opened, his head rose from the bed. Too late. Tears began to flow freely down her face.

"Mr Bold? Mr Dean Bold?"

THE END

Characters

There are a lot of characters in Greed, in more ways than one. If you need help with any of them, here they are.

1) **Benissa Bold**. Born 1987. Daughter of Dean and Gina Bold (née Higgins). Daddy's little girl, she works at the tan stand in Canvey and is rather overweight. Puts it about a lot and is best friends with Dave and Shirley's daughter Chantal. They are a deadly duo at the Yates in Basildon, an updated version of their mothers' haunt all those years ago. Benissa secretly looks down on her but is really jealous of her friend's size 8 figure. If she tried, she could do better.

2) **Dean Bold**. Born 1966. Haulier. Lives with Gina, his wife, Benissa (pronounced Beneeeesaaaah) and Troy. They live in Canvey Island, having escaped their origins some years before when the haulage business took off. In partnership with Dave Hilton, boyhood friend and co-conspirator. Nasty increasing cocaine habit, struggles to get it up and can't really keep Gina-G very happy.

3) **Troy Bold**. Born 1991. Younger brother of Benissa. Bright lad and a bit of a snob, looking down on his Mum and Dad's approach to life. Privately educated as opposed to his rather 'chav-like' sister. Has something of the old man in him when it matters.

4) **Dave Hilton**. Born 1966. Haulier. Married to Shirley. Having affair with Gina-G. Old mate of Dean's from school, when they attended. Saved him a few times during the ICF days.

5) **Shirley Hilton**. Born 1968. Devoted wife and mother, especially mother. Has a lot of headaches.

6) **Gina (G-String) Bold**, (née Higgins). Born 1969. Married to Dean, who she met at a disco in Basildon in 1984. (Officially. Maybe it was at a bus stop). One sister, Debra.

Gina is sex mad and manages to keep this from Dean as he prefers the 'leedle white powder'.

7) ***Debra (Dildo) Higgins***. Born 1971. Sister of Gina. Married 1987. Divorced 1990. All round good time girl and local bike. Still good looking but very hardened. Piggy-backs on Dean and Gina's success and is a constant thorn in the side of Dean and his aspirations. The slapper gene is alive and well in Debra, though secretly, her sister would prefer to keep it just to Dean. She would do anything to become the next Mrs Dean, but thinks he's fucking up with all the Charlie he takes.

8) ***Jimmy 'Jag' Clapton, aka 'Stanley'***. Born 1964. Vange. Mate of Dean's from Hammers' days. Member of the ICF in the 1980s, before doing an eight stretch following the undercover police operation to expose football hooligans. Now a car dealer, haulier and owner of a limo hire company on the A13 at Pitsea. Made his money helping with protection rackets in the East End and minding/debt collecting and a bitta Charlie. Tight as the proverbial duck's arse. Also still partial to a little of the Colombian marching powder. Divorced. One son, Sean, who he is trying to get in with Dean.

9) ***Padraig (Paddy) O'Riordan***. Born 1961. Cullaville, South Armagh. Lives in Dublin and Torrevieja, Spain. Spent a little time in the IRA during the 1980s, but was thrown out for involvement in drugs. Moved to Spain, where he had made contacts in the drinks and cigs game. Met up with some London gangsters and began to really get going. Graduated onto cocaine and is now a major player in the UK and Ireland, serving the new rich of Dublin as well as London. Owns a bar in Torrevieja called Doolans. Full of villains and wannabe gangsters. Has a small stud farm back in Ireland and always in trouble with the CAB. Always uses other hauliers. A very bad guy, and when Dean and more importantly Dave start to get greedy, he makes plans to finish them off by dobbing them in to Customs.

10) ***Seamus Kelly a.k.a. 'The Closer'***. Born 1965. Jonesborough, South Armagh. Works with Padraig and

they go back to the old IRA days in 'Bandit Country'. Works as an enforcer and strong arm man for him. Maintains interests in Spain, Portugal and Croatia, where he also looks after new property for Padraig. Has a photographic memory and never forgets a face.

11) **Martin Keenan**. Driver, helper, sometime 'babysitter' for O'Riordan. Totally trusted. Arrested along with Kelly at the O'Riordan farmhouse in South Armagh.

12) **Ronan O'Riordan**. Born 1971. Crossmaglen, South Armagh. Nephew of Padraig and manager of Doolan's Irish Restaurant. Local organiser for his cousin and trouble-shooter in the port of Alicante.

13) **Ali 'The Coat' Halil**. Born 1963. Paphos, Cyprus. Long time friend of Dean. Never takes coat off. Runs a chain of kebab shops and has a small hotel in Kyrenia which is run by his family. Very shrewd and intelligent. Worked from the age of seven as the breadwinner of his family. Came to England after the 1974 invasion of Cyprus complete with his Mum and half the contents of a Greek bank. AKA Ali Hali.

14) **Mick 'The Teeth' Harper**. Born 1967. Vange, Essex. At home. Warehouse manager. Brother to Ray who works at LCB. A real street fighter, he works with Dean and adores:

15) **Karen Harper (née Bull)**. Mrs Mick. Born 1972. Southend on Sea, Essex. A real 'Shrimper' is Karen. Southend and praaard of it! She's got that real hard look about her but loves her Mick to bits.

16) **Ron 'One Language' Langridge. Lingo**. Born 1958. Basildon, Essex. Dean and Dave's transport manager and trouble-shooter. Quiet hard-nut. Done time for attempted murder. Knows Stevie 'Town' Hall from a spell in The 'Ville. His wife has cancer but he is very private and keeps himself to himself. Dean's paranoia almost gets him killed when he convinces himself that Lingo's gone over to the other side. This starts to bring him to his senses but it's too

late.

17) **Steven 'Town' Hall**. Born 1972. Ilford, Essex. Drug dealer, smallish but wants to get bigger. Keeps Dean in the 'white stuff'. Meets O'Riordan in Spain when on holiday with his bird at Dean's villa and tells Dean about him. They meet when Dean and the family go on a trip to the villa.

18) **Emily Loader**. Born 1970. Peterborough. Customs Officer. Observations in Spain on O'Riordan. Seconded from IMPEX London.

19) **Duncan Deegan**. Born 1959. Senior Customs officer. UK deputy to Pearson, drafted in after Graham Stubbins' demise.

20) **Jatinder Singh Gill**. Born 1976. A member of a prominent Sikh business family, his entry into the service was perceived by both his community and Customs as a surprising one. Rising through the ranks from Local VAT Officer into the NIS, based at Lower Thames Street, he has outshone most of his original fellow intake.

21) **Andy Meacher**. Born 1972. Milton Keynes. Customs Officer. Observations in Spain on O'Riordan. Seconded from IMPEX London.

22) **Kim Evans**. Born 1974. Pontypridd. Customs Officer. Observations in Spain on O'Riordan. Seconded from IMPEX London. Gets anally raped by fellow officer Gibbs after a bit of 'prick-teasing' goes wrong.

23) **Joe Gibbs**. Born 1976. Canterbury. Customs Officer. Observations in Spain on O'Riordan. Seconded from IMPEX London.

24) **Graham Stubbins**. Born 1960. Rotherham, West Yorks. Case Officer, Operation Jehovah. (Named after the magazine of the witnesses, Jehovah after the watch towers were removed from Armagh, thereby reducing the effectiveness of observations on the O'Riordan place).

25) **Emma Pearson**. Born 1956. Senior Customs Officer based at Lower Thames Street. Lesbian. Department head for Operation Watchtower II. Heavily involved in London City Bond.

26) **Shotgun Kev**. Kevin Blackwell. Born 1963. Hoxton, London N1. Car-dealer friend of Dean's. In and out of jail for armed robberies he runs the car lot down the road from the unit in Thurrock. 'Deals' with Dean's problems be they automotive or personal. The 'Gun' is a man of few words. 'I'm not much for all that talkin'. Now give me a balaclava and a sawn off and I'm right at home....'

27) **Dawn Murphy**. Born 1984. Kildare. Only daughter of Niall Murphy, racehorse owner and 'legitimate businessman'. Stunning, leggy redhead Irish beauty. Mainstay of the office at Bold Transport. Not quite as stupid as everyone thinks.

28) **Freddy 'The Fixer' Bassett**. Born 1966. Deal. Kent. Operates in Canterbury and Rainham. Haulier. Rival to Dean, previously no history between them. Dies in a pub shooting.

29) **Federico Alvarez. A.k.a. Paco**. Street boy turned cocaine dealer. Partner of Sandwich. Drinks with Ronan O'Riordan.

30) **Sandwich a.k.a. Alberto Felix Reyes**. Born 1970. Toledo. Independently wealthy playboy partner of Paco. Nicknamed because of his predilection for having two girlfriends. Cocaine dealer, property dealer, friend of Padraig O'Riordan.

31) **Marianna Benitez-da Sancha**. Born 1972. Madrid. Daughter of a Spanish diplomat, she is the power behind the drug cartel connection from Bogota to Ceuta. She is extremely beautiful in the haughty, horse riding, hat wearing aquiline nosed variety. A true aristocrat. She is utterly ruthless and has killed before. Power turns her on and she has personal connections with the families in

Medellin. Journalist.

32) **Pilar Estravados-Lopez**. Born Valencia. 1965. Spanish Customs Chief. Friend of Marianna Benitez da-Sancha. Invited on the boat by her to discuss plans to bring in a whole shipload of coca to Alicante.

33) **Ray Harper**. Brother of Mick the Teeth. The inside man at Metro Bond.

34) **Ricky 'Razors' Streatham**. Rival gang boss to Dean.

Made in the USA
Charleston, SC
24 November 2015